MORE PRAISE FOR O...
BOOK IN THE CHLO...

"Propulsive and superbly written, this first entry in a dynamite new series from accomplished author Kathleen Ernst seamlessly melds the 1980s and the 19th century. Character-driven, with mystery aplenty, *Old World Murder* is a sensational read. Think Sue Grafton meets Earlene Fowler, with a dash of Elizabeth Peters."—Julia Spencer-Fleming, Anthony and Agatha Award-winning author of *I Shall Not Want* and *One Was A Soldier*

"A wonderfully woven tale that winds in and out of modern and historical Wisconsin with plenty of mysteries, both past and present. In curator Chloe Ellefson, Ernst has created a captivating character with humor, grit, and a tangled history of her own that needs unraveling. Enchanting!"—Sandi Ault, author of the WILD Mystery Series and recipient of the Mary Higgins Clark Award

"*Old World Murder* is strongest in its charming local color and genuine love for Wisconsin's rolling hills, pastures, and woodlands … a delightful distraction for an evening or two."—NYJournalOfBooks.com

"Clever plot twists and credible characters make this a far-from-humdrum cozy."—*Publishers Weekly*

"This series debut by an author of children's mysteries rolls out nicely for readers who like a cozy with a dab of antique lore. Jeanne M. Dams fans will like the ethnic background."—*Library Journal*

"Information on how to conduct historical research, background on Norwegian culture, and details about running an outdoor museum frame the engaging story of a woman devastated by a failed romantic relationship whose sleuthing helps her heal."—*Booklist*

"[A] museum masterpiece."—RosebudBookReviews.com

"A real find … 5 stars."—OnceUponARomance.net

The
Heirloom
Murders

A CHLOE ELLEFSON MYSTERY

The Heirloom Murders

KATHLEEN ERNST

MIDNIGHT INK
WOODBURY, MINNESOTA

FIRST EDITION
First Printing, 2011

Book design and format by Donna Burch
Cover design by Kevin R. Brown
Cover Scythe illustration © Charlie Griak
Editing by Connie Hill

Midnight Ink, an imprint of Llewellyn Worldwide Ltd.

Library of Congress Cataloging-in-Publication Data

Ernst, Kathleen, 1959–
  The heirloom murders : a Chloe Ellefson mystery / by Kathleen Ernst. —1st ed.
    p.   cm.
  ISBN 978-0-7387-2758-5
1. Women museum curators—Fiction. 2. Murder—Investigation—Fiction.
3. Heirlooms—Fiction. 4. Wisconsin—Fiction. I. Title.
  PS3605.R77H45 2011
  813'.6—dc22   2011015965

Midnight Ink
Llewellyn Worldwide Ltd.
2143 Wooddale Drive
Woodbury, MN 55125-2989
www.midnightinkbooks.com

Printed in the United States of America

AUTHOR'S NOTE

Old World Wisconsin is a real place. I had the pleasure and privilege of working there for twelve years, starting in 1982. However, this book is a work of fiction. All characters, including Chloe Ellefson, were born in my imagination. I freely fabricated events to serve the story.

The Eagle Historical Society does exist (and today operates a museum). The Swiss Historical Village Museum in New Glarus is also a real place, and includes a small cheese factory. (The Imobersteg Farmstead Cheese Factory, restored at The National Historic Cheesemaking Center in Monroe, Wisconsin, also provided inspiration.) Seed Savers Exchange, which was founded in 1975, is located near Decorah, Iowa. My characters' interactions with these sites and organizations are completely fictional.

To learn more about these fascinating places, and to plan your own tours, visit their websites:

http://oldworldwisconsin.wisconsinhistory.org/
http://eaglehistoricalsociety.org/
http://www.swisshistoricalvillage.org/index.html
http://www.nationalhistoriccheesemakingcenter.org/
http://www.seedsavers.org/

ONE

"The guy tried using a *pistol?*" Roelke McKenna asked, as he opened his locker door. It was almost eight in the morning. He was coming on-shift; Skeet Deardorff was going off. Roelke always arrived at the Eagle police station early enough to catch up on news.

"Yeah. Oh, man." Skeet was laughing so hard he could hardly speak. The phone rang, and he waited until Marie answered it before gasping in a lower voice, "He couldn't loosen the lug nut with a wrench, so he figured a shot or two would—"

Marie's hand sliced the air so fiercely that Skeet stopped talking. She swiveled her chair to face the officers. Roelke's nerves snapped to full alert.

In the sudden silence she said, "Ma'am, I'm sorry, I've got some static on the line. Can you repeat what you just said?" Then she pressed the speaker-phone button.

A woman's voice: "—said, I'm about to kill myself."

Jesus. Roelke snatched a daily report form and pen from a nearby desk and scrawled, WHERE? Before he could even thrust it at Marie she was asking, "Where are you, ma'am?"

"I'll tell you in a moment," the caller said.

Skeet fumbled for his duty belt. Roelke grabbed a radio.

"Please, ma'am, let's talk about this," Marie said. "I might be able to help. Can you tell me your name?"

"My name is Bonnie. But—"

"I'm Marie. Can you tell me a little about whatever is bothering you?"

"I appreciate what you're trying to do," Bonnie said. "Really. But there's nothing to discuss."

Roelke reached for the car keys. The hook was empty. Where were the damn keys?

"I'm only calling because I want the police to get here first." Bonnie sounded young-ish. Twenty-five, maybe? Thirty? "I'm in a public place. I don't want kids to find me."

Roelke rifled the counter below the key hook. Papers sank to the floor with a languid rocking motion. Skeet snapped his fingers, then held up the keys. Roelke snatched them.

"I'm driving a Cadillac Cimarron," Bonnie said. "You'll find my wallet on top of the left front tire. I removed my credit cards, but left my ID. My keys will be in the right pocket of my jacket."

Roelke felt the seconds ticking by with frenzied impatience. He stared at Marie, willing her to find a way to stop this. Marie spread her hands in a helpless gesture, but said, "Please, Bonnie, just tell me where you are."

"I have a plastic garbage bag with me. I'll be as tidy as possible."

Roelke closed his eyes. He could feel Skeet quivering in the doorway beside him.

"Bonnie, *please* give us the chance to help you." Marie was clutching a pen so hard that her knuckles were white. "If you just wait until one of our officers can get there—"

"Please tell the officer that I'm sorry." An audible breath in, out. "I'll be three hundred paces up the White Oak Trail—"

Roelke and Skeet bolted outside. Roelke slid behind the wheel of the squad car and was almost out of the parking lot before Skeet got his door closed.

The White Oak Trail was a short loop in the Kettle Moraine State Forest. Twelve minutes tops, Roelke thought. "Call it in," he told Skeet. Marie would do it if she could, but there was still a chance that Marie would be able to keep Bonnie on the phone. To keep Bonnie talking. To keep Bonnie alive.

Skeet radioed for backup: Waukesha County, Department of Natural Resources, Eagle Fire and Rescue. Roelke switched on the flashers. He shot through a stop sign, then veered around a pickup that was too slow to yield.

"Hit the siren!" Skeet urged, as they left the village behind. He sat with feet and arms braced.

"No." Roelke's hands tightened on the wheel as they flew around a curve on Highway 59. "Maybe she's having second thoughts. If she hears us coming, she might pull the trigger."

"She didn't sound like she might have second thoughts."

"There's always a chance. Hold on." Roelke braked hard and turned onto a side road. The small parking area that marked the White Oak Trailhead was ahead on the right. Gravel flew as he swerved into the lot.

A white Cimarron sat in the shade of a huge old oak tree. No one was in sight. "Tell the EMTs to stage around the bend," Roelke said, as he pulled in beside the car. Maybe there was still time. Maybe—maybe—maybe.

He jumped from the squad—leaving the door open, still worried about noise—and hit the trail at a run. Twenty steps … ninety seven … one hundred thirty-two …

At one hundred and eighty-six he rounded a bend and stopped abruptly. "God *damn* it."

The body lay on the trail beside an old stump and a clump of ferns. Sunlight sifting through the canopy dappled the garbage bag that partly shrouded the woman's head and shoulders. Jean-clad legs, feet in yellow high-heeled leather sandals with thin straps, extended from the bag. The woman's left hand was visible too, resting against the earth, palm-down. Her wedding band glittered with tiny diamonds.

The top of the garbage bag was not intact. Shreds of brown plastic and gray matter splattered the dirt and dead leaves nearby.

Roelke crouched on the right side of the body and carefully pulled aside what was left of the bag. He instinctively reached to check her pulse, but there was nothing left beneath her jaw to touch. In almost any circumstance he would begin CPR, but in this case… "God damn it!" he exploded again. A 9 mm Smith and Wesson had fallen from Bonnie's hand, and lay near her throat.

Skeet emerged from the trees and skidded to a halt. He stared for a long moment, then leaned over, hands on knees, panting. Roelke didn't know if the other man was struggling with heat or exertion or nausea.

Roelke was struggling with searing rage. "I could have helped you," he muttered. "If you'd just given me a chance, I could have helped you!"

———

Within half an hour Roelke had carefully photographed the scene, tucked the handgun and shell casing into evidence bags, and established a perimeter. The medical examiner, a pudgy man with dispassionate eyes, arrived and did his own assessment of the body and its surroundings. Then he and Roelke watched two EMTs secure the body in a Stokes Basket for transport to the parking lot. Bonnie had positioned the gun under her chin, damaging the airway and eliminating any chance of keeping the physical body resuscitated long enough to harvest organs for donation.

Marge Bandacek, a Waukesha County deputy, sidled closer. "You want me to call in our evidence team?"

Roelke shook his head. "No need."

"We've got better equipment—"

"No *need*," Roelke repeated. As first on the scene, he'd taken command. He'd examined the area carefully, collected everything there was to collect, documented everything there was to document.

Marge opened her mouth, as if about to argue. Roelke fixed her with a stare. Although he'd bundled his anger deep inside, it hadn't diminished. This was state forest land, but the DNR responders weren't second-guessing him. He was in no mood to take any crap from Marge Bandacek.

Marge hitched up her belt as the EMTs began their march back to the ambulance. "If you say so."

Roelke waited until the parade had disappeared, and took one last look around. The police tape looked obscene in this peaceful place of greens and browns. He pounded one fist against his leg, and turned away.

Back at the parking lot, Skeet was handling the scene log. "Have you searched the car?" Roelke asked.

"Not yet," Skeet said. "Traffic control, including a couple of reporters."

"Piranhas," Roelke muttered. He didn't hate the press. He did hate reporters who thought it was OK to, in this case, broadcast a shot of Bonnie's car before the cops had a chance to reach the family. "I'll ask Bandacek to handle them."

After siccing Marge on the press, Roelke searched the Caddy. "Simon and Bonnie Sabatola," he read from the vehicle registration. The form listed a Town of Eagle address.

What he did not find was Bonnie Sabatola's wallet. "That's odd."

"What?" Skeet asked.

"She said she'd leave her wallet on top of the left front tire. It isn't there. It's not in the car, either."

Skeet leaned against the oak tree, folding his arms. "The woman was about to blow her brains out. I don't suppose she was thinking clearly."

"Clearly enough that she didn't want anyone but us to find her." Roelke turned away and scanned the gravel near the car. Nothing. He moved out in widening circles, moving the tall grasses bordering the lot with his foot. Still nothing. Finally he spotted an unnatural patch of brown along the trail, almost invisible against the leaf litter. "Got it."

"Hers?" Skeet called. He hadn't bothered to move from the shade.

Roelke flipped the wallet open. The coin pocket and bill slot were empty. Three of the four little credit card-sized sleeves were empty, too. The fourth held a Wisconsin driver's license. Roelke stared at Bonnie Sabatola's picture. Her face was thin and elegant; her chestnut hair obviously styled with care. Her expression seemed to hold something more than the blind stare he usually found in drivers' license pictures. Birth date, July 21, 1954. She had killed herself one week after her twenty-eighth birthday.

Bonnie Sabatola had been the same age he was.

Why did you *do* this? he asked her silently. What made you lose all hope?

The ME waddled from the woods. "That her license?"

"Yeah." Roelke handed it over.

The other man scrutinized it for a moment, then handed it back. "No doubt on the ID. Approximate time of death is consistent with the call she made to your office. I'll go through the motions, but the cause of death was obviously a self-inflicted gunshot wound."

The DNR ranger on the scene stopped a Chevy that had slowed to turn into the lot, and spoke through the window to the driver. Skeet straightened, dusting off his trousers. "Listen, do you mind if I catch a ride back to the station? I can still make class on time. You'll handle this, right?"

Handle it: the death notification, the paperwork. "I'll handle it," Roelke said. "But something isn't right."

"The wallet? Listen, she just tossed it on her way down the trail. It doesn't mean anything." Skeet waved a hand in a vague gesture of dismissal.

"The steps were off, too."

Skeet sighed. "What?" He had ginger hair, and a pale complexion that betrayed his impatience.

"The steps," Roelke repeated. "She said she'd be three hundred paces up the trail. I found her at one hundred and eighty-six."

"So what? You were running. No way her strides were as long as yours. I'll see you tomorrow." Skeet headed toward the ME's sedan. "Hey, Sid! Give me a ride?"

Roelke watched them go. Skeet was a family man who still found time to take college classes in Waukesha. That might well put him on top when the next full-time, permanent job opened up. The police department in Eagle, Wisconsin, was tiny. Roelke was committed to the department, and to the village he had come to care so much about. But opportunities for advancement were few and far between.

Then he stared back at the driver's license in his hand, at Bonnie Sabatola's enigmatic face, and his ambitions and worries disappeared. He looked again at the Cimarron, the clearing, the trailhead. Bonnie must have stood right there, by the little shed that housed the toilets, where a pay phone had been installed on the exterior wall. She'd already walked away from her car, and was halfway to the trailhead. So why had she told Marie that she'd leave her wallet on the tire?

TWO

"Good Lord." Chloe Ellefson's jaw dropped with dismay as she climbed the final steps and emerged into the attic. "Geez, Dellyn! When you asked for my help you didn't mention we'd need a backhoe."

Her friend winced. "Don't abandon me now. I'm begging you." Dellyn Burke wiped sweat from her forehead. The attic was broiler-hot.

Chloe pulled a string dangling from a light fixture, and was immediately sorry. The bulb's sickly yellow glow only accentuated the bewildering assortment of *stuff*: a butter churn, three dressmakers' dummies, chairs upholstered in chintz and horsehair, several trunks, a cradle ... and boxes. Hundreds of boxes, pushed low under the eaves and piled high beneath the crest of the ceiling.

Dellyn clutched her elbows, crossing her arms across her chest. She was shorter than Chloe, and younger too—late twenties, probably, to Chloe's thirty-two. She wore paint-spotted jeans and a faded T-shirt that might once have been blue. Her hair was pulled into a simple ponytail. She was lovely in a straightforward way; a woman who didn't waste energy on what didn't matter, like make-up. But her expression was strained.

"In the interest of full disclosure," Dellyn said finally, "I should tell you that you haven't seen half of it. There's twice this much stuff in the barn. And my dad's study is crammed, too."

"Collection obsession," Chloe said bleakly, then immediately wished she hadn't. "I'm sorry. I shouldn't have said that." Dellyn's parents had died suddenly, in a car crash, only a few months earlier.

Dellyn touched a child's rocking horse, setting it in motion. "It's OK. But most of these aren't family heirlooms. My parents helped found the Eagle Historical Society—oh, probably twenty years ago. They were only collecting stuff until the society can afford a building of its own."

"That was a good goal," Chloe said charitably.

Dellyn nudged the rocking horse with her toe, keeping it moving. "Both of my parents grew up in Eagle. They did more to preserve and protect this village's history and heritage than anyone. Once they began talking about starting a little museum ... well, people started giving them stuff. My folks didn't know how to say no to anyone. Things obviously, um, got out of hand."

"Well, I can understand that. I got a call at work yesterday from someone who said that she had a lot of valuable antiques she was *sure* Old World Wisconsin would want, but if I didn't come take them that afternoon, she was putting them out for the garbage collector."

Dellyn shook her head. "I wouldn't want your job. I'm much happier collecting seeds. They're small."

"Small sounds good," Chloe agreed wistfully. "And to think I took the curator of collections job because I thought working with artifacts would be easier than working in education." She'd only been employed at the huge outdoor ethnic museum on the outskirts of Eagle for about two months, but she'd quickly learned that collections work had its own share of problems.

Dellyn shoved her hands in her pockets. "I shouldn't have asked for your help."

"It's OK," Chloe said quickly. She'd been glad to give up her lunch hour when Dellyn had asked. It felt good to be needed. Besides, Dellyn was nice. Chloe had been in short supply of friends lately.

"I just don't know what to *do* with all this!" Dellyn's voice rose. "I have no idea what's valuable and what isn't."

"There's monetary value, and there's historical value," Chloe said. "But first, who actually owns this stuff? Did your parents legally transfer it to the Eagle Historical Society?"

"No. That was the plan for ... one day."

"That's good." Chloe lifted the flap on the closet box. Flow-blue china, packed in straw. She tucked the flap back into place. "You're free to cull."

"I definitely want to save whatever might be of value to Eagle." Dellyn leaned against a dresser, smudging a fur of dust. "But ..."

"But?"

"I'm pretty tight on cash right now." Dellyn began swiping dust from furniture. "I'm an artist, for God's sake. It took everything I had just to move back here from Seattle."

"Ah."

"My parents left me the house and its contents, but they didn't have any real savings. My sister and her husband paid for the funeral. If there are even a few things I could sell with a clear conscience—things that have no meaning for Eagle's history, I mean—it would help. A lot."

Chloe could relate. Her own job at Old World Wisconsin was a permanent one, with benefits and a reasonable salary. But although Dellyn was head gardener at the historic site, she was an LTE—a Limited Term Employee with the state. Low salary, no benefits, no security.

"You never know," Chloe said, striving for a cheery tone. "People find treasures in their attics all the time."

"Maybe I'll find the Eagle Diamond."

"… Beg pardon?"

Dellyn waved a hand. "I forget you're not local. About a century ago, some guy digging a well in town found this huge diamond."

"No way. Don't diamonds come from Africa?"

"Not this one," Dellyn insisted. "It's a true story. My dad was collecting information for a book, and this woman I know just published an article about it."

"So, where is this diamond?"

"It disappeared. It was stolen, but nobody really knows where it ended up." Dellyn smiled ruefully. "You figure my dad might have gotten his hands on it, and socked it away?"

"Probably not. Let's just settle for something antique collectors are hungry for. An ambrotype of Abe Lincoln. A signed first edition of *The Jungle Book*. Betsy Ross's girlhood sampler. Something to give you a little pocket change." Chloe scanned the attic again. "Did your parents keep records? Knowing provenance—where an item came from, how it was used—will make a big difference in deciding what to keep."

"I think so. It's probably all down in the study."

Chloe slapped her palms against her thighs. "Well, let's see if we can find the records. Once we do, we'll just start sorting."

"*Thank* you." Dellyn's shoulders slumped with relief. "I didn't even know where to begin. I want to show you the barn later, too. There's a lot of agricultural stuff out there. Some of it might work nicely for the Garden Fair at Old World."

Chloe regarded her. "Don't take this wrong, but what on earth compelled you to propose a new special event? You've only been on staff for what, a month more than me? I'm still learning people's names."

"I just thought it would be a nice idea to showcase the historic site's heirloom vegetables and flowers." Dellyn's tone was both defensive and apologetic. "I want to help visitors understand how much diversity we've lost. And how important fairs were to nineteenth-century families."

"Oh, it's a great idea," Chloe assured her. "It's just ambitious for someone who already has more work than she can handle."

"I've got some great volunteers to help. One in particular—Harriet Van Dyne—have you met her? And the interpreters are excited ..." Dellyn cocked her head. "I think a car just pulled into the driveway."

Chloe followed Dellyn down the stairs gratefully. By the time they'd descended to the ground floor, the temperature had dropped by at least twenty degrees. Chloe lifted her long blonde hair and held it massed on top of her head, wishing she'd been smart enough to pin it up that morning. Maybe Dellyn had some iced tea or lemonade in the fridge—

"Oh God." Dellyn froze in front of the screen door.

"What?" Something prickled nervously over Chloe's skin. "Dellyn, what's wrong?"

Dellyn didn't answer. Chloe peered over her friend's shoulder and saw a police car in the driveway. Officer Roelke McKenna was walking up the sidewalk, followed by a second man she didn't recognize. A man wearing a clerical collar.

"Oh God," Dellyn whispered again.

Roelke's eyes widened when he saw Chloe, but he masked his surprise quickly and focused on Dellyn. "Miss Dellyn Burke?" he asked.

Dellyn grabbed Chloe's hand. "Yes."

"I'm Officer McKenna, and this is Reverend Otis. May we come in?"

Dellyn didn't move. Chloe gently pulled her backward so Roelke could open the door. The four of them stood in the narrow hall. The walls were lined with old family photos, making the space feel even more crowded.

"You are Bonnie Sabatola's sister?" Roelke asked. Dellyn nodded, her eyes wide.

This is going to be bad, Chloe thought. Bad, bad, bad.

THREE
1876

"Let's go," Charles Wood said brusquely. "The day's getting away." He grabbed his pickax.

You're welcome, Albrecht Bachmeier thought. Sure, neighbors helped neighbors. And Charles was paying him, a bit. But was a word of thanks too much to ask? Digging a well on a hot day was harsh work. The two men had dug through almost ten feet of loose gravel the day before, and here Albrecht was again, neglecting his own chores, giving Charles a hand.

Charles began climbing down the shaft. Albrecht glanced toward the house. Clarissa Wood was turning sod with a shovel for a vegetable garden behind the small log house. Her dress was already dark with sweat. Her sweet face was hidden beneath her sunbonnet. She used one foot to force her shovel blade into the earth. It took obvious effort to toss the slice of sod aside.

Albrecht felt his fingers tighten on the shovel in his hands, aching—actually aching—to turn his back on Charles and help Clarissa instead. She was a thin thing, game for work, but not strong. It would probably be easier for Charles to dig a well alone than for Clarissa to dig her garden.

"You coming?" Charles called.

"*Ja*," Albrecht barked back. Taking one last look, he grabbed the rope and started backing into the pit.

FOUR

EIGHT HOURS AFTER LEAVING Dellyn Burke's house Roelke hesitated, his hand on the phone in his apartment. Should he call Chloe? Yes, he should.

No, he should not.

"Damn it," he muttered, and dialed the familiar number. There was a time, after he'd met Chloe in June, when he would have simply driven to her house, wanting to see for himself that she was OK. No way could he do that now. Not with Alpine Boy in the picture.

While the phone rang, Roelke stepped to the window of his tiny apartment. It was early evening. After the shock of seeing Chloe standing beside Dellyn Burke that afternoon, Roelke had done what he needed to do at the house, and back at the station. Now he was off-duty. A pleasant twilight was slowly descending on the village of Palmyra, where he lived. It would be a good time to walk to his cousin Libby's house, see her kids, play T-ball, grill brats, and try to forget about Bonnie Sabatola and Dellyn Burke. But first—

"Hello?"

She sounded a little breathless. Had she run from outside? Or was Alpine Boy—

"Hello?" Chloe said again. She sounded more impatient than breathless, now.

"It's me. Can I come by?"

"Sure."

Roelke felt a tight place in his chest unwind a notch. "See you in a few," he said, and hung up before she could change her mind.

Chloe lived in an old farmhouse in the next county, a pleasant fifteen-minute drive through the Kettle Moraine State Forest. Roelke found her sitting on her front porch, a glass of what he was pretty sure was diet soda and rum in her hand.

"Hey," Chloe said, and raised the glass. "You want anything?"

"I want to make sure you're OK." Was that too personal? Avoiding her gaze, Roelke latched on to something else. "Why do you have a piece of moldy wood on your porch rail?"

She gave him an exasperated look. "It's not mold, it's lichen. I brought it home because it's beautiful."

"O-kay." He settled into the empty lawn chair beside her. Maybe he should clarify his first remark. "I want to make sure you're OK after what happened this afternoon."

Chloe sipped, staring out over the hayfield across the street. She was still too thin. The angular planes of her face were accentuated because she'd pinned her braided hair in a twist behind her head. Roelke couldn't imagine a more beautiful woman.

"I'm alright," she said finally, looking back at him. "Just sad for Dellyn. And Bonnie too, of course."

"Did you know Bonnie?"

"No." She blew out a long, slow breath. "After you left, Dellyn kept saying, 'I'm all alone now.' It's horrible! After her parents …"

"Yeah." Roelke sighed. "Did she say anything about why her sister might have done such a thing?" He'd asked a few perfunctory questions while at the house, but hadn't wanted to press.

"She has no idea. She'd been living in Seattle, and only came back after her parents died. Dellyn's a painter and a gardener. Bonnie was an executive's wife. I guess they didn't have much in common anymore." Chloe lifted one slender hand in a gesture of futility. "But Dellyn was already feeling guilty for not spending more time with her parents before they died. Now she's thinking the same thing about Bonnie."

Roelke pulled an index card from his pocket, and wrote *artist/ gardener, executive's wife.*

"Why are you writing that down?" Chloe frowned at him. "Dellyn and Bonnie had drifted apart, that's all. Since Dellyn got back, she's had all she could handle with the house and stuff."

"I'm going to talk with Bonnie's husband tomorrow." Simon Sabatola had been in the resort town of Lake Geneva, near the Illinois border, when his wife died. "Do you think Dellyn was OK to leave alone?"

"She's not alone. Libby's there."

"My cousin Libby?" Roelke blinked. "How does Libby know Dellyn?"

"Dellyn's in our writing group. She's working on a children's book."

Roelke digested that unexpected tidbit. "Is that how you know Dellyn, too?" He knew Libby had talked Chloe into attending her writers' meetings.

"Dellyn works at Old World. She's in charge of all the gardens." Chloe flicked a box elder bug from her jeans. "She'd asked if I'd come over today and look at some antiques her parents left behind."

Roelke watched fireflies blinking in the twilight. This was one of his favorite times of day, in one of his favorite times of the year. The air was still. A few bats swooped overhead. "I just need to know you're OK," he heard himself say. "I hate that you got caught up in something to do with … you know. This."

"A suicide?" Chloe asked. "It's OK to say the word. And this is about my friend, not me. I'm better now."

He wanted to believe her. But he didn't understand suicide. Never would. And without understanding, he didn't think he could ever *not* worry about Chloe. She had been crawling out of a deep depression when he met her. How could he ever be sure she wouldn't slide back to that dark place?

"Roelke." She put one hand on his arm, and he felt an electric tingle. "Are *you* OK?" she went on, clearly oblivious of the effect she was having on him. "Is this the first time you've been called to a suicide scene?"

"I wish," he said curtly. His first case had been a beautiful fifteen-year-old girl in Milwaukee who'd lain down on her pink-canopied bed and shot herself in the head. She'd been one of the few dead people he'd seen who did *almost* look as if she was sleeping, with nothing but a small neat hole in her right temple and a little brain matter spilling onto the pillow to argue against it. His second case had involved a guy in a convertible sports car who drove into a tree at 120 mph. Not much left to find of driver or vehicle after that. Of course, that was still better than the guy who—

"Roelke?"

"If you ever feel that way again, for the love of God, don't use a car. It doesn't always work, and—"

"Roelke, stop it!" Chloe jerked away from him. "I said, I'm *better*. I'm not as fragile as you seem to think."

Maybe. Maybe not. "I don't accept suicide," he said.

Her eyebrows rose. "What does that mean?"

"There's something about Bonnie Sabatola's death that just feels … wrong, somehow."

She sighed, and sipped her drink again. She looked more sad than she had when Roelke had arrived. Great. Just the effect he'd wanted to have.

"I imagine that it always feels wrong when someone so young dies," she said.

"Yeah, but …" He drummed his thumb on the arm of his chair. "But what?"

"I don't know," he admitted. "But could you maybe sound Dellyn out about Bonnie? I mean, they must have spent a little time together, right? They had to handle things after their parents died. Could you ask Dellyn if Bonnie had seemed depressed or something?"

Chloe's mouth twisted with distaste. "I'm not going to pry into her family life, especially right now."

"You're going to see her anyway, aren't you?" Women always did that after someone had a loss. They took over casseroles and stuff like that. Roelke's grandma had always kept something ready in the freezer.

"Well, sure," Chloe said warily. "I'm going over tomorrow morning."

"So, just let me know if she says anything about Bonnie. Her state of mind. That's all I'm asking." Roelke stood, feeling clumsy. "I gotta go. Thanks for letting me come by."

She stood too. "Geez Louise, Roelke. You don't have to thank me for *that*."

He placed one palm on the porch railing. It wobbled. He should come back with his toolbox. "I don't want to assume anything. Not with … Not until you decide what you want."

Even in the fading light he could see color stain her cheeks. "I haven't even agreed to see Markus, Roelke. I didn't know he was coming to Wisconsin, and I don't know what—if anything—I'm going to do about it. It doesn't have anything to do with … us."

But there is no 'us,' Roelke thought. There might have been. There almost was. In fact there *had* been, one glorious afternoon in June. But not now.

"Right," he said. "We'll stay in touch." He thought he'd hit the right note with that. Calm. Cool. Leaving things open.

Then he ruined his exit by putting his palms gently on her cheeks. She seemed OK with that, so he bent his head to kiss her. A real kiss, the one he'd been fantasizing about.

At the last second, he remembered that Chloe's Swiss ex had flown halfway around the world to find her.

Roelke kissed Chloe's forehead. Then he headed home.

———

Chloe was still sitting in the lawn chair on her porch, thinking about Roelke, when the phone rang. It might be Libby, or her best friend Ethan—calls she'd gladly take. It might be her mom—a so-so proposition. Or it might be someone she wasn't ready to talk to.

Indifferent, the phone kept shrilling. Chloe put her drink down, went inside, and grabbed the receiver. "Hello?"

"Chloe. Hello."

You lose, said a voice in her head. "Markus."

"How are you?" Markus's diction was excellent. Only a light *Suisse-Deutsch* accent revealed that English was his second language.

"Um, OK."

"We need to talk, Chloe. In person."

She felt the same spasm of panic that came every time he called. "I don't—"

"I've been in Wisconsin for a month already," he reminded her. "I've already used up half of my sabbatical. Just give me a chance. I don't want things to be this way between us."

Chloe watched a firefly through the glass as it climbed the living room window. Spark, dark. Spark, dark.

"I'll meet you anywhere," Markus said. "Any time."

Chloe clenched one fist. She had to get this over with. "This Saturday morning. Eleven o'clock. Pick a place in New Glarus."

"You don't need to drive over here. I'll—"

"Pick a place in New Glarus!" She'd rather drive an hour than allow Markus Meili to invade her own geography.

"The New Glarus Hotel," he said, the words breathy with relief. "They have great food. I'll see you then." He hung up quickly.

Chloe replaced the receiver more slowly. Her kitten, Olympia, barreled from the shadows and pounced triumphantly on the coiled phone cord. Chloe scooped her up and pressed her cheek against the soft fur. "Oh, Olympia. I think I just did something stupid."

FIVE

It rained in the night, just enough to leave the pavement damp when Chloe parked in front of Dellyn's place. Over the years Eagle had crept out to meet, although not yet engulf, the farmhouse. Fortunately, it stood on the south side of the village. Most commuters headed north/northeast to Oconomowoc, Waukesha, or Milwaukee.

Birds were singing their new-dawn songs. Chloe yawned, grabbed a foil-wrapped parcel, and climbed from the car. On a hunch, she skirted the front door and walked around the house. An enormous fenced garden stretched away from the back steps. Dellyn was on her knees behind a frilly row of carrots.

"Hey," Chloe called. She joined her friend. "I know you don't need banana bread, but—"

"I do need banana bread. Thanks." Dellyn got to her feet and pulled off her garden gloves. "What are you doing up at this hour? You have trouble making it to the morning meeting."

Chloe sighed. In the summer, Old World Wisconsin opened at ten every day. The morning briefing for interpreters started at 9:30—and yes, when she was required to attend, she did usually cut it close. "I wanted to see how you were doing. I figured you'd be up."

"I didn't get much sleep." Dellyn's eyes were red-rimmed and puffy. Her face looked thinner, as if she'd lost weight overnight. "But God knows there's plenty to do out here."

"This is an amazing garden," Chloe said. "You must harvest enough to feed Rhode Island." The garden was at least half an acre. Individual raised beds were arranged in neat grids and mulched with straw. Plastic markers anchored each row, genus and species noted with indelible black marker. A huge compost pile filled one corner. A large potting shed stood in another.

It was a master's garden … but it was also sliding toward chaos. Flowers needed staking or dead-heading. Burdock and knapweed poked among the vegetables. Bean poles leaned at alarming angles.

"My mom's two passions were Eagle history and gardening." A tiny smile twitched the corners of Dellyn's mouth. "When Bonnie and I were little, Mom always gave us each our own plot. We could plant anything we wanted. Dad even built us our own garden cottage." She pointed to a child-sized structure almost hidden behind a pea trellis. It was tired, and sorely in need of paint, but Chloe could imagine the two little girls' delight in having their own playhouse.

Dellyn surveyed the clumps of rhubarb, feathery asparagus fans, tomato plants bursting through cages, hilled potato plants. "Mom had already finished her planting when she died. I couldn't just let it go. She must be appalled, though. I can't keep up."

"No," Chloe said firmly. "I bet she smiles down every time you come out here."

Dellyn scraped soil from her knuckles with one fingernail. "I just need to hold my own until fall. There are shoeboxes full of seeds around here somewhere. Next spring I'll pick out some of her favorites and do something smaller."

"I've never had space of my own for a garden," Chloe said, "but I've got a little packet of hollyhock seeds tucked away. They came down from my great-grandmother."

"Did you notice mine?" Dellyn pointed toward the garage, where a wall of spectacular ten-foot-tall, rose-colored hollyhocks stood. "*Alcea rosa*. Thank God people like my mom save seeds from the old varieties. Puritans made teas of powdered hollyhock flowers to prevent miscarriages."

Chloe tried not to wince. "Every variety is precious," she agreed. She and Markus had discussed historic sites' role in preserving genetic material many times. Back before Chloe's miscarriage ended their relationship, anyway.

"My mom saved seeds to keep costs down," Dellyn was saying, "but she understood how important it was to preserve old varieties, too. She was a charter member of Seed Savers' Exchange."

"That's pretty cool." Seed Savers Exchange had been formed in the mid-seventies to document, save, and share seeds from garden plants that might otherwise disappear. Historic sites gardeners were active participants and big fans.

"After my parents' funeral, when I was trying to figure out if I'd come back to Eagle for good, I saw the ad for the head gardener position at Old World. I didn't really think I'd get hired. But I did."

"Everything your mom taught you no doubt helped you get the job," Chloe said gently. "It's like she was still taking care of you."

"Yeah." Dellyn fished in her pocket for a tissue, and wiped her eyes. "You want some coffee? I can take a break." She led the way to a pair of metal chairs against the fence. A red-capped Thermos sat on a low table between them.

"Thanks." Chloe poured herself a cup and took a grateful sip. "Listen, is there anything I can do for you? Help with the funeral arrangements?"

"Thanks, but no. The cops finally tracked Simon down—he was off on some business thing in Lake Geneva—and he came over last night. He's making all the plans." Tears welled up and over. Dellyn dug for another wad of tissues and blew her nose. "Sorry. I'm just so *angry* at myself. I had no idea Bonnie was having problems! How could I not have known?"

"She probably didn't *want* you to know."

Dellyn twisted her fingers together. "A few days ago I came home from work and found a carton sitting on the kitchen table. Spooked the hell out of me, actually. But inside was a stack of my mom's old garden journals. Bonnie had taken them after our folks died."

"Did she leave a note?" Chloe asked.

"Yeah. All it said was 'You should have these.'" Dellyn's voice was flat. "It pissed me off that she'd left the box while I was at work, like she didn't even want to talk to me. But now … *Dammit!* Why didn't I just pick up the phone?"

"Did Bonnie ever act as if something was bothering her?" Chloe mentally cursed Roelke for asking her to pry.

"I don't know. She'd changed so much from when we were kids." Dellyn hunched over, elbows on knees. "I lost my parents without having a chance to say good-bye. I should have made more of an effort to reach out to Bonnie."

"She probably didn't want to add to your burdens." Chloe sipped her coffee. "Do you and Simon get along OK?"

Dellyn straightened again, and shrugged. "Bonnie is—was—only a year older than me. We were really close until she got serious about Simon. They got married when she was eighteen. I resented him. I would have resented whoever she married, I guess. It seems stupid now."

"Did he try to get to know you?"

Dellyn added a splash of coffee to each of their cups. "He and Bonnie actually invited me to come on some of their dates. We went to the county fair, and to a couple of concerts. There aren't a lot of guys who would let his fiancée's little sister tag along."

A bluebird landed on the fence nearby, considered his options, and flew off. "No," Chloe agreed.

"And then after they got married, everything just seemed … weird. Simon was older than Bonnie, and already had this high-powered career." Dellyn gestured vaguely toward the garden, and the open land beyond it. "Dad farmed until I was ten. That's when he sold off some acres, and the houses up the way got built. And he and Mom lived and breathed history. So it seemed sorta bizarre to visit Simon and Bonnie at their place, all ultra-modern. It was like she had … I don't know, turned her back on her roots or something." She made a derisive noise. "That sounds so cliché."

"People change," Chloe said, and winced. "Now *that* was a cliché. Sorry."

Dellyn waved one hand in an *It doesn't matter* gesture. "We had a pretty big fight. Me and Bonnie. Right before I left Eagle."

"What about?" Chloe imagined Roelke going rigid, ready to pounce on any new tidbit of information, and made an effort to banish him from her brain.

"I didn't like how she was acting. Hardly ever sparing a minute to visit Mom and Dad. Behaving like she was too good for us. Always dressing like she was going to the opera or something." Dellyn sighed. "After that, I'd see her when I came home to visit ... everything all polite on the surface."

Sorry, Roelke, Chloe thought. She wasn't going to come away with an ounce of information about what might have been troubling Bonnie.

"But I've been back for over two months now," Dellyn was saying. "I had plenty of time to mend fences. And I didn't. I didn't even try."

Chloe hated the bleak look in her friend's eyes. "Do you want me to call in to work for you? I could take the day off too." Chloe hadn't gotten off to a great start with Old World Wisconsin's director, and she was trying hard to stay off his radar. But since the historic site was open seven days a week, she and Dellyn did have some flexibility with their hours.

Dellyn shook her head. "No, I'm going in. The gardens are producing big time right now, and I'm already behind. And Harriet—my top volunteer—is coming at eleven."

Chloe nibbled her lower lip. She sensed something brittle in Dellyn. She was afraid her friend might snap.

"I need to keep busy," Dellyn said simply.

That, Chloe understood. "Well, I'll help you all I can." She gave Dellyn's hand a quick squeeze, then stood. "I better get going."

"Got just a minute?" Dellyn cocked her head toward the house. "I found a copy of the article I was telling you about. You'll get a kick out of it."

Chloe followed Dellyn out of the garden, latching the gate behind them. "Right after I got back to Eagle, I got a call from someone I knew when I was a kid," Dellyn said over her shoulder. "Valerie Bing grew up in Eagle, and went to school with Bonnie. Anyway, she'd written this piece about the Eagle Diamond."

The back door opened directly into the kitchen, which was decorated in the regrettable 1970s-fave motif of mustard yellow, burnt orange, and avocado green. Dellyn led the way into what had likely been intended to serve as a ground-floor bedroom in the era when people commonly had elderly parents living with them. The room was lined with bookshelves and file cabinets—not to mention a few stacks of boxes that hinted of more stuff collected in the name of preserving Eagle's history. On the large desk, spiral notebooks and stacks of files surrounded a huge manual typewriter.

"Valerie had talked with my folks while she was doing research," Dellyn said. "The article was published in *Wisconsin Byways* right after they were killed. She sent me a lovely card, and a copy of the magazine." Dellyn scanned the desk, then frowned. "I *thought* I'd left it out for you." She began lifting folders, peering under piles. "What on earth did I do with it? It was right here." She finally dropped into the desk chair, rubbing her forehead with the heels of both hands.

"You just had a huge shock," Chloe said gently. "I'd be worried if you *didn't* feel scattered. You'll probably put your hand on the article as soon as I drive away."

"Yeah, I'm sure you're right." Dellyn sighed. "I was rummaging around in here for most of the night." She picked up a cheap notebook, the bound kind with a black-and-white marbled cover, dog-eared and dirty. She opened it almost reverently.

Chloe leaned over Dellyn's shoulder. "Was that your mom's?"

"Yeah. She didn't keep diaries, but these old journals are almost as good. She started them in 1942, the year she and Dad got married. She skipped the year Bonnie was born, but otherwise she was faithful."

Chloe leaned close as Dellyn leafed through smudged pages. Mrs. Burke had recorded everything she'd planted by both common and Latin name, with addendums about pests, weather, and harvest. But the entries were as much folklore as science. *Eugenia Miller gave me a new basil plant and a recipe for cucumber and tomato salad.* And, *SSE's 'Grandpa Ott's' morning glories bloomed for the first time this morning. A luscious deep purple. Must save enough seed to give some to Sonia.*

"What a treasure," Chloe said softly. "When my grandma died, I got her file box of recipe cards. Half of them are for foods I'd never fix—Jello-and-mayonaise salad, stuff like that—but there's more *her* in those cards than in any object."

Dellyn set the notebook aside, and reached for a file folder. Opening it, she revealed a stack of whispery onion-skin paper, all covered with typewritten notes. "And these were my dad's."

"*October 14, 1963,*" Chloe read aloud. "*Mrs. Harrigan gave me a black dress that her grandmother wore on her wedding day, June 18,*

1890." Chloe stepped back so she could regard her friend. "So he *did* keep records! That will help a lot as we work through all that stuff in the attic."

"Thank God for small favors." Dellyn looked at her watch. "If you're going to make it to morning meeting, you better get going."

SIX
1876

"He likes you, you know."

Clarissa Wood paused, pushing hair from her forehead with one wrist. She had a roast in the oven, and peas and potatoes on the stove. "Who?"

Her husband snorted. "The German. He makes calf eyes at you whenever he thinks I'm not watching."

"He just likes my cooking," Clarissa said lightly. She cracked the oven door, and a new wave of heat shimmered into the room. She hoped that would excuse any flush staining her cheeks. Charles was a good man. A good husband. Still … it had been a long time since he'd looked at Clarissa the way Albrecht looked at her.

"I think there's more to it than that." Charles stepped behind her, and Clarissa felt a whisper of unease. Then he surprised her, wrapping his arms around her, holding her close.

Clarissa leaned her head against his shoulder, smelling sweat and dirt, the cheap cotton shirt rough beneath her cheek. "Perhaps," she admitted. "But he's harmless. A young man who hasn't yet found a good woman of his own. We're lucky he's willing to work for you." She and Charles only rented the land they were developing. They were saving every penny toward buying the lot. A Yankee workman would have asked twice what they were paying Albrecht.

"I suppose so," Charles admitted. He sounded distracted. He pressed his mouth against the side of her neck. Then he reached for her hand, tugged.

"Let me at least take the roast from the oven!" Clarissa protested, but she laughed. If her husband's dinner scorched, he'd have no one to blame but himself.

SEVEN

"Got a minute?" Chief Naborski asked.

"Sure." Roelke followed the chief into his office. It was shift change again. The older man liked to catch up with whomever was coming on duty. He always posed his request as a question, though. Not an order.

Chief Naborski dropped into his chair. He refused to purchase anything that swiveled or rolled; he liked chairs he could tip back on two legs, which he did now. "Fill me in on the suicide. Have you talked to the husband?"

"Simon Sabatola." Roelke settled in a chair in front of the desk. "Not yet. He was playing golf in Lake Geneva with a client. Some business thing." He resisted the urge to roll his eyes. The idea that playing golf on a summer morning qualified as work was beyond his experience. "It took awhile for the local guys to track him down. Sabatola's office, and the client's office, knew about the golf outing but didn't know which course. I'm going to talk to Mr. Sabatola today."

"Good." Chief Naborski ran a hand over his buzz-top. He was a stocky man, plain-spoken, fair with his officers and with the public.

"I've got a funny feeling about this one."

"Suicides are never easy." The chief shook his head. "Hard to tell what finally pulls the trigger, so to speak. Money problems. Relationship problems. Or who knows what else."

"Yeah." Roelke thought about that. Money and marriage. Tricky things to investigate. But he was going to try.

"Different topic. Everything set for your first Movie Night?"

"All set." Roelke had proposed a summer series of free, family-friendly movies in the village park. His theory was simple: kids watching a movie were not bored and, therefore, not getting into trouble. He'd written a grant that pulled in some state dollars, and gotten approval from the village board.

"Lined up all the help you need?"

"I've got volunteers from the Lions Club, American Legion, the Fire Department, and the Kettle Moraine Snowmobile Club."

"Good. One more thing." Chief Naborski gave him a level gaze. "Wasserman's retiring."

Roelke felt every cell quiver, like a hound catching a scent.

"So there's going to be a permanent, full-time slot opening up," Naborski said. "Patrolman II. Earns $7.40 an hour."

Which would be a nice bump from Roelke's current Patrolman I status, at six bucks an hour.

"We're not going to open the search to outside applicants," the chief was saying. "Not when I've got two good part-time officers already waiting."

Two good part-time officers, Roelke thought. Me and Skeet.

Naborski twiddled a pen in his fingers, like a cheerleader with a miniature baton. "It's out of my hands, of course. The Police Committee will handle it. Get your application to the Village Board by next Wednesday."

"Will do." Roelke realized that his right knee was bouncing up and down with suppressed energy. He forced it into stillness.

Chief Naborski let the front of his chair bang to the floor, his end-of-conversation signal. "Any questions?"

"No sir," Roelke said. But there was one more question. It clanged like a bell in his brain as he left the chief's office, checked his duty belt, told Marie where he was going, and headed out.

If Skeet wins this job, Roelke thought, what the hell am I going to do?

———

Simon Sabatola lived outside the village. The short drive gave Roelke time to consider strategy. Putting Sabatola on the defensive would probably accomplish nothing. Good cop, then. I am your friend.

Roelke felt his eyebrows rise as he turned into a long, winding drive. The place looked like an estate, better suited for suburban Chicago than rural Wisconsin. The grass was the uniform lush green that signaled the regular arrival of a lawn service team with power trimmers and tanks of herbicide. Flower beds lined the drive, filled with a few plants he recognized—roses, day lilies, hydrangeas—and a lot he didn't. No dandelions or dead blooms in sight.

The house itself was a modern chalet. Roelke parked beside a gleaming black Lincoln Town Car. When he knocked on the front door he half-expected a maid or uniformed butler to answer. Instead, a small man in an expertly cut navy-blue suit appeared.

"Mr. Sabatola?" Roelke asked.

"No, I'm Edwin Guest. I work for Mr. Sabatola." Guest paused, eyebrows raised expectantly.

Roelke introduced himself. "I'd like to speak with Mr. Sabatola."

Guest hesitated. He was balding, and had a thin face and pale eyes, with no particularly memorable features. Roelke wondered if rich people looked for that when they hired people.

Finally Guest ushered him inside. "I'll see if Mr. Sabatola is available."

"I'll wait until he is." Roelke smiled pleasantly.

Guest disappeared. Roelke used the pause to take impressions of the house. The décor favored leather and steel, with splashes of color provided by large abstract paintings on the walls. Roelke stared at one particularly vivid piece, trying to make sense of the primary colors slapped on the canvas. What did people see in this stuff? It probably cost a fortune, and Libby's young son could have—

"Officer McKenna?" A man entered the hall from a side room. "I'm Simon Sabatola."

Roelke shook the widower's hand. Simon Sabatola stood over six feet, with broad shoulders and a firm grip. At first glimpse, he had a commanding presence. His eyes, though—they were red and swollen, full of shadows, full of pain.

"I'm terribly sorry for your loss," Roelke said. "And I'm sorry to intrude at such a difficult moment. I hope you can understand that I need to ask a few questions."

Sabatola ushered him into the living room. "Would you like anything? Coffee?"

Roelke declined the coffee, and perched on the edge of a black leather sofa. Sabatola sank into a matching chair. A framed wedding portrait of Simon and Bonnie Sabatola sat on a glass end table beside him. She'd posed snuggled against her husband, chestnut hair arranged in curls, face glowing with joy beneath her bridal veil. Roelke felt a tightening in his chest. She was—had been—stunning.

"Have you learned anything about my wife's death?" Sabatola asked.

"I have no new information," Roelke said carefully. "As I'm sure you were told, your wife died by a self-inflicted gunshot wound." He paused. Some people in this situation wanted all the details. Some wanted none.

"It still seems so... unreal." The other man's eyes filled with tears. "I keep thinking it's all a mistake."

Roelke never knew what to do with men who cried. He avoided Sabatola's gaze for a moment, giving the other man time to compose himself. "I can only imagine the shock, sir. But... had Bonnie seemed distressed lately?"

"No, nothing like that." Sabatola spread his hands, palms-up, in a gesture of bafflement. "I mean... obviously she must have been upset about *something*, or she wouldn't have done such a thing. But whatever it was, she managed to hide it from me."

"Was she being treated for depression?"

"No."

"Forgive me, sir, but I need to ask. Had the two of you been having marital difficulties?"

"What? No!" The other man looked shocked. "Our marriage was perfect." He rubbed his eyes with his fingertips. "I knew the moment I saw Bonnie that she was the one for me."

"What did your wife do?"

Sabatola blinked. "Do?"

"Did she have a job? Do volunteer work? Have a hobby?"

"Bonnie chose not to work, after we married." He leaned over, arms on his knees, too restless to sit still. "She sometimes did charity work. She loved to cook, and to garden."

Roelke thought of the huge garden he'd glimpsed at the Burke house. It wasn't surprising to think that Bonnie had a green thumb. "Did your wife keep a diary?"

Sabatola shook his head. "I went through her things after I got home last night. I didn't find a diary, or a letter, or anything else to explain what she did."

Roelke flipped open his little notebook so he could jot down key points. "Your wife shot herself with a 9 millimeter Smith and Wesson, Model 39. The gun was yours?"

"Yes. We only had it for self-protection. I never dreamed Bonnie …" He swallowed visibly.

"I understand you were golfing?"

"Yes." Simon Sabatola stood abruptly and walked to a bar that stood near the back corner of the room. He used tongs to put a few ice cubes in a glass, then added a splash of whiskey. "I beg your pardon," he said, as he seated himself again. "I'm not an alcoholic. But a little Glenlivet does help."

"No need to apologize, Mr. Sabatola."

Sabatola sipped before resuming the conversation. "Anyway, I was in Lake Geneva, playing a round with a man I hope to do business with. A parts manufacturer."

"You work for a company called AgriFutures?"

"I do." Sabatola nodded. "My stepfather started the company forty years ago, in Elkhorn. After he passed away we probably should have moved the company to Chicago. But my wife's family was in Eagle ... well, you know that, of course. She didn't want to leave Wisconsin."

"So you put family first."

"It's always a balance," Sabatola said. "I'm going to be named CEO of AgriFutures soon. Bonnie and I had always dreamed of that. Now ... it hardly seems to matter." He took another drink of whiskey—more of a gulp, this time. When he put the glass down on a marble coaster, his gaze lingered on the wedding portrait. Fresh tears glistened in his eyes.

Roelke closed his notebook, and decided to edge into deeper waters. "Mr. Sabatola, I'm sorry to say that I've seen other cases like this. I hope you don't blame yourself. Sometimes women have everything they could ever want, and still ..." He let the sentence trail away.

"Bonnie did have everything." Sabatola tossed back another gulp of whiskey. "Everything any woman could dream of."

Roelke shook his head sadly. "Thank you, Mr. Sabatola. I'll be in touch if I need to speak with you again."

"I'll be back in the office tomorrow. I couldn't face it today, but ... I find that rattling around this house is even worse." Sabatola looked around the living room—stylish, cold, empty. "I don't know what I'm going to do without her. I just can't imagine coming home from work and her not being here."

Both men stood. "I'll call my secretary to show you out," Sabatola said. When he left the room he took his whiskey with him.

Roelke waited for the promised escort, not realizing until Edwin Guest appeared that he'd already met Sabatola's secretary. "Thank you," Roelke said when they reached the door. Guest nodded.

Once outside, the door firmly closed behind him, Roelke sucked in a deep breath and blew it out again. He knew better than to admit it to Libby or Chloe, but male secretaries—or nurses, or flight attendants—made him uncomfortable. He wasn't proud of that, but there it was.

He could almost hear Chloe calling him a Neanderthal. That pushed his thoughts to the last time he'd seen her. For a moment he'd forgotten about Alpine Boy. For a moment, it had been just him and Chloe, picking things up right where they'd left off before her stupid Swiss ex had popped up.

You need to be thinking about Simon Sabatola, not Chloe, Roelke chided himself. He drove a mile and pulled over. He wanted to flesh out his notes while the conversation was still fresh. Once he'd done so, he stared at the page. Simon Sabatola had not been able to offer any explanations for Bonnie's suicide. Had Bonnie truly been such a skilled actress? Or had Sabatola's business trips and aspirations blinded him to the fact that his wife was struggling?

Still, the widower had obviously been in real pain, experiencing deep grief. He may not have been a particularly attentive husband … but he'd loved Bonnie.

Roelke slipped his notebook away. He wasn't finished with Simon Sabatola. Next step: a visit to AgriFutures. Roelke was planning to attend Bonnie's funeral, too, with eyes and ears wide open.

EIGHT

"This," Chloe muttered, as she turned into the village of New Glarus on Saturday morning, "was a big mistake." She already felt emotionally assaulted. The area had been settled by Swiss immigrants in the 1850s. Now, tourism based on Swiss heritage was a huge part of the town's economy and identity. Many of the commercial buildings resembled Swiss chalets. Canton flags hung proudly from poles. Signs identified the Swiss bakery, the Swiss embroidery factory, the Swiss pharmacy and imports store.

Chloe inched her Pinto into a parking spot on Main Street and sat clenching the steering wheel. She hadn't wanted to invite Markus into her world, but coming into his was just as brainless. Finally she took a deep breath, pried her fingers free, and climbed from the car. She wasn't going to run away with her proverbial tail between her proverbial legs. She had a firm plan established: Meet her ex, say some things that needed to be said, and turn her back on him. Forever.

The New Glarus Hotel was a village landmark. The big frame structure, originally known as the Glarus House, had been welcoming hungry travelers for well over a century. Chloe walked into the dining room twenty minutes early. She wanted to choose her seat; wanted to see Markus before he saw her. She wanted to have the few seconds—as he approached the hotel, entered the dining room, scanned the room—to see how she felt.

Markus didn't give her the chance. He already sat in a booth in the sun porch that overlooked Main Street, watching her.

Lovely.

Despite her intention to be cool and aloof, she stopped moving. For a year, now, Markus had been her past. She'd worked hard to construct a new life here in Wisconsin. Without him. But here he was.

"You can sit anywhere," a waitress called.

Chloe made her way to the booth. Markus got to his feet, looking as if he might make physical contact—a hug, perhaps a friendly kiss. She slid quickly onto the vinyl bench.

A young woman wearing an outfit that suggested a Swiss dirndl, with *Tess, Trainee* printed on her nametag, appeared at Chloe's shoulder. "Um, do you want coffee?"

"Please."

The waitress splashed coffee into the mug with such vigor that some slopped into the saucer. "Oh, sorry! Do you, um, need time with the menu?"

Chloe shook her head. "I'll just have some toast."

"We're only serving off the lunch menu now," Tess said apologetically.

Chloe ground her teeth, looked at her choices, and ordered *Kaesechuechli*—a cheese pie served with fruit. Markus asked for *Wienerschnitzel*. Tess nodded, started to walk away, returned and snatched up the menus, left again.

"I thought you might not come," Markus said.

"I almost didn't." Chloe became aware of the music being piped into the dining room, a lively Swiss folk collection with plenty of yodeling that hit her nerves like a band saw.

"You look good."

"Thanks." He did too, actually, although she didn't feel like saying so. Markus Meili was slightly built, with a wiry strength that made him at ease handling draft horses and oxen and hogs. His face was still interesting, rather than handsome, although his gray eyes were more watchful than she remembered. His wavy hair was still thick as ever. Still worn a little long. Still displaying a tendency to fall forward across his forehead. It asked—begged, really—to be smoothed back. Chloe's fingers twitched with silky remembrance. She slid them under her thighs, pinning them against the seat.

"How are you?" he finally asked.

Chloe pulled her hands free again, reached for the tiny pitcher of cream, and carefully poured a generous dollop into her coffee. "I'm good."

Markus pushed his mug aside and placed both palms on the table, leaning closer. "All right, look," he said quietly. "You don't want to chat. So let's just say what needs to be said." He paused, raking his own fingers through his hair. It was a gesture both forgotten and so viscerally remembered that for a few seconds Chloe couldn't breathe.

Markus held her gaze. "I screwed up."

"Yeah. You did. Big time."

"I made a mistake—"

"A mistake?" Chloe hissed. She didn't want to touch his hair anymore. "You asked me to move to Switzerland, Markus. I turned my life inside out to do that. We were happy together for over five years. Then I had a miscarriage, and three days later, you told me to pack my bags. It was inhuman. And you call that a *mistake?*"

Tess returned, deposited their plates, marched away again.

Markus swallowed visibly. "You have every right to be angry—"

"Damn straight."

"There's no excuse for what I did. The only explanation I can give is that … well, I panicked."

Chloe regarded him coldly.

"We'd never even *talked* about having a family. I didn't even know you were pregnant, and—"

"I didn't know I was pregnant either," Chloe snapped. An elderly, frizzle-permed woman at a nearby table turned her head, eyeing them with interest. Chloe forced her voice down a few decibels. "Did you think I'd gotten pregnant on purpose? You thought I was trying to trap you or something? Was *that* it?"

Markus sighed heavily, picked up his fork, put it back down. "I didn't know what to think."

"How could you even *consider* that I'd do something like that?" The odors of coffee and melted cheese seemed suddenly sour, making Chloe feel nauseated.

"Chloe, I—"

"You know what? I'm outta here." She wriggled from the booth.

Markus scrambled after her, and grabbed her wrist. "*Please* don't go. Just hear me out."

Chloe jerked her arm free. For a few moments they stood like that, face to face. Chloe contemplated hitting him, telling him to kiss her ass, walking away forever.

Instead she sank back on the bench. The elderly woman hitched her chair to one side, so she'd have a better view.

Markus slid back onto his seat. "I'm *sorry*. I know that sounds empty. I know it doesn't change anything. But I've needed to say it. I treated you horribly, and I'm very sorry."

Chloe looked out the window. On the street below a man in a red car was blocking traffic while he tried to parallel park in front of the hotel. Chloe watched as he see-sawed gingerly back and forth for several minutes before giving up and driving on. Finally she looked back at Markus. "Why now? All this happened a year ago. Is there a reason you're here right now? Because your timing sucks, Markus. It really sucks."

"I saw mention of your hire in the ALHFAM magazine."

Damn professional journal. Editors had no right to publicly spew people's personal information, even in the living history, farm, and agricultural museum community.

"It seemed like it was meant to be. I'd already been talking with Claude—you remember Claude?"

"I remember Claude," Chloe said through gritted teeth. Claude was Markus's boss at Ballenberg, the huge open-air museum in Switzerland where he worked. And where she had, once, worked also.

"We'd been talking about me coming over here, doing some fieldwork. Many Swiss emigrants ended up in Wisconsin—there are still some old-timers in New Glarus, and Monroe ... we were hoping someone might even still have some old-breed livestock."

His eyes sparked with the enthusiasm she remembered. "Genetically, finding a new population here would mean—"

Chloe glared at him as understanding dawned. "You *prick!* You didn't come here to talk to me, you came here to look for goats!"

Markus sobered. "All I meant was that I was able to get Ballenberg to pay my travel expenses, and approve a two-month leave." He leaned back and studied her. "I've never gotten over you, Chloe. The more time went by, the more I realized that I still … that I still have feelings for you."

Chloe pulled a napkin from the silver dispenser and began folding it into tidy triangles. "So what, you think you can pick things up where we left off? I'm supposed to just forget everything you put me through? It's not that easy."

"Of course it's not that easy." Markus rotated his coffee mug a neat quarter-turn. "But I'll be in Wisconsin for another month. I would like very much to spend some time with you."

Tess appeared and stared with dismay at their full plates. "Is something wrong with the food?"

"Absolutely not," Markus assured her. "It's as good as I could get at home in Brienz. Be sure to tell the chef." Tess beamed, and disappeared again.

Chloe watched her leave before turning back to Markus. "I don't think it's a good idea for us to spend time together."

"Is there someone else?"

I wish I knew, Chloe thought, pausing from her freestyle origami. "Maybe."

Something flickered over his face. It took her a moment to decipher his expression as regret. She had once thought she knew his every nuance. Regret—that one was new.

"Just give it a chance," he said. "Please, Chloe. We were good together. Let's just see if we …" He lifted one hand, palm up. Another forgotten/familiar gesture. They were coming back now—all the intimacies, all the shared experiences, all the memories. All the things she'd spent a year trying very hard to forget.

"We can start small," Markus said. "I need to visit Old World Wisconsin. Will you show me around?"

"Absolutely not."

He blinked. "Why not?"

"Because I don't want to."

"But I must visit! Claude expects me to learn about your breeding program!"

"Oh, come on. We don't even have a Swiss farm."

"It doesn't matter. Old World Wisconsin is one of the best-known American historic sites among agricultural historians."

"Fine. Call the site and ask to speak with the head farmer. He'll show you around."

"And I'll need to see whoever manages your garden program."

"Gardens?" Chloe felt her brows rise.

"Some of my funding for this trip came from a … what's the word? Consortium? A consortium of European historic sites doing research on heirloom plants. They want to know what species and traditions might have crossed to North America."

"Begin with the farmer," Chloe said firmly. "Our head gardener's sister just died. And she only started this past spring, anyway. I don't know how much she'll be able to tell you."

"I really want to see the site through *your* eyes."

"That's not gonna happen."

He chewed his lower lip for a moment. "All right, how about this. I just got an invitation to visit an elderly couple, Johann and Frieda Frietag, on Monday. They are evidently quite frail, but still living on the farm his great-grandfather built. There's a tiny cheese factory on the grounds, and I want to talk with them about livestock and vegetables. Why don't you come with me?"

"No."

"Why not?"

"I have to work. Staff meeting." It was even true. Director Ralph Petty started each week by convening the few Old World Wisconsin employees with permanent status.

"Their granddaughter said they make an old variety of green cheese," Markus said, with the air of offering a tantalizing treat. He knew how interested she was in historic food traditions.

Chloe didn't like being manipulated. "I don't care."

"And Frieda is an expert at embroidery."

Chloe glared at him. He knew how interested she was in historic textiles, as well. They had done this many times in Switzerland—visited some elder, learning what they could about traditional folkways.

"Please, Chloe. *Please.*"

Maybe it was the humble tone to Markus's plea. Maybe it was a reflexive response to five years of shared history. Or maybe it was the permed lady's tiny, encouraging nod. For whatever reason, Chloe heard herself mutter, "Oh, all right."

NINE

Roelke had no trouble finding the number he wanted in the phone book. It took much longer to scrape up the courage to dial. He was pulling the receiver from his ear with relief when he heard a woman's breathless voice. "Hello?"

"Peggy? This is Roelke McKenna. I don't know if you remember me—"

"Roelke? Of *course* I remember you!" Delight replaced Peggy's initial surprise. "Biology, English Lit … and we had the same study hall our senior year, remember? How are you doing?"

"Well, thanks." Roelke began drawing tiny triangles on the scrap of paper where he'd scrawled Peggy's number. "And, um, how have you been?"

"Good, Roelke. Really good. What brings you calling now, stranger?"

Peggy MacDonald, plump and perky, had had a crush on him all the way through high school. Roelke really hoped he wasn't screwing the pooch by calling her now. "I was hoping you could help me out with something. I've heard you work for an investment company."

"I do. Our office is in Lake Geneva."

"That's impressive," Roelke said, and meant it. Math was not his thing. "Did you know I'm a cop?"

"Oh, yes."

"Well, cops don't earn a whole lot." Especially part-time beat cops in a small village. "But I've been saving for years, and—"

"Oh, good for you! Let that compounding interest work."

"Right," Roelke said. "I've been thinking about investing some of it. I'm young enough that I can handle something with a bit of risk, wouldn't you say?"

"Absolutely!"

Roelke, who had no intention of ever risking a penny of his savings, glanced at his notes. "I'd like to invest in a local company. Something that provides jobs around here."

Peggy's voice grew thoughtful. "You'd have lots of choices in Waukesha, of course."

"Let's stay out of Waukesha city, for now. Is there anything more rural, or in a smaller town?"

Peggy named several companies. Roelke said "Hmmn," or "Well, maybe," to each. Finally she said, "There's always AgriFutures, of course. It's a publicly traded company."

"That one's down near Elkhorn, right?"

"It's quite a local success story," Peggy said. "A struggling entrepreneur came up with a new piece of farm equipment. Was granted a patent, got whatever it was built, and started pounding the pavement."

"I kind of like the idea of investing in a company that makes stuff for farmers. I could do it in honor of my grandparents."

"Roelke, that is so sweet!"

"But here's the thing," Roelke said quickly. "I find the whole idea of investing a little ... intimidating. I mean, how can I know if the company is really stable?"

"AgriFutures has been a powerhouse as long as I've been in the banking biz," Peggy assured him. "It's a big player on the international market. They've been adding jobs steadily."

"Hmmn."

"They've also given a lot to the community. A big donation to the library, playground equipment for schools, stuff like that. Would you like me to do some research for you?"

"That would be great!" Roelke said. "I'd be glad to hire you."

"Oh, Roelke!" Peggy said, in a mock-scolding tone. "I'd never take money from an old friend like you! Give me a few days, OK? I'll let you know what I find out."

"Thanks, Peggy. I really appreciate your help."

"You know, I still get back home almost every weekend," she said. "I like to check on my folks. Maybe we could get together for lunch or something."

This was just what he'd hoped to avoid. Well, she was doing him a huge favor; the least he could do was buy her a meal. "Sure," he said. "We can do that."

"Oh, goody!" she chirped. "I'll be in touch!"

———

"Idiot," Chloe muttered as she drove north from New Glarus. "Idiot, idiot, *idiot*." She was glad she'd promised to help Dellyn with the antiques in her parents' attic that day. She didn't want to be alone, with nothing to do but wonder why on earth she'd agreed to spend more time with Markus.

When she got to Dellyn's place she walked around the house and checked the garden. Empty. She retraced her steps and knocked on the screened door in front. "Hello?" she called. "Dellyn? It's Chloe."

"Come on in," Dellyn called. "It's open."

As Chloe stepped inside Dellyn came downstairs looking hot, grubby, tired, and sad. "I was up in the attic."

"Well, reinforcements have arrived. Lead on."

Once back in that oven-like space, Dellyn captured a few damp, stray strands of hair and re-did her ponytail. "These heirlooms aren't tagged or numbered," she explained. "I was trying to start with an inventory."

"Good plan," Chloe agreed, trying to sound hearty. "We can number each carton as we go."

They worked steadily for some time. Chloe was just retucking the flaps on the sixth box when a woman's voice drifted up the stairs. "Yoo-hoo!"

Chloe looked at Dellyn. "I didn't know anyone actually said 'yoo-hoo' anymore."

"It's my neighbor. Come on. She won't leave until we come down."

"Do you want her to leave?"

"I shouldn't have said that." Dellyn sighed and turned away.

Downstairs, Dellyn made the introductions. "This is my Aunt Sonia Padopolous. Sonia, my friend Chloe works at Old World with me."

"Nice to meet you," Chloe said. "You're Dellyn's aunt … ?"

"Oh, not by blood, but I've known Dellyn since she was in diapers." The plump woman held a picnic basket in one hand. She wore lavender polyester shorts, a frilly cotton blouse—both a little too tight—and short white socks with thick-soled tennis shoes. Her cropped hair was the flat red of a bad dye job. Chloe guessed she was probably in her mid-sixties.

Sonia turned to Dellyn. "Honey, I brought over some fried chicken and cole slaw. And my Oatmeal Gems."

"Thanks. I'm not hungry, though. You've got to stop bringing things over."

"You have to eat," Sonia said firmly. She marched into the kitchen and insisted on setting the kitchen table right that minute.

Dellyn took a pitcher of cold tea from the fridge. Chloe accepted a tall, sweating glass gratefully. She fended off the offer of fried chicken by explaining she was a vegetarian, but tried to make nice by taking a large helping of cole slaw.

Roelke's disapproving voice echoed in her mind: *Coffee and cole slaw? It's two o'clock in the afternoon. You need protein.*

Lovely. Now both of the problem men in her life had intruded into the day.

"So," Sonia said. "You work at Old World too? Are you one of those guides?"

"We call them interpreters," Chloe said. "But actually, I'm curator of collections."

"Chloe's not a Jill-come-lately to the history world, like I am," Dellyn said. "She actually knows what she's doing."

"Sort of, anyway." Chloe took a bite of cole slaw, and strangled a cough. Good Lord! How could someone ruin cole slaw? She grabbed her glass of tea and gulped.

Sonia didn't seem to notice. "Dellyn's parents would have loved you, then. They knew everything there was to know about Eagle history."

"Speaking of that, I've got Valerie's article about the Eagle Diamond I was telling you about, Chloe," Dellyn said. She got up from the table and, behind Sonia's back, slid a napkin-wrapped chicken leg into the trash can. Then she grabbed a few stapled pages from a stack on the counter, and handed them to Chloe.

"I knew you'd find it," Chloe said, as she wondered how she might discreetly dispose of her cole slaw.

Dellyn slid back into her chair. "I didn't find it. It made me so crazy that I finally went to the library and dug out the magazine, and made a photocopy."

Sonia reached across the table and patted Dellyn's hand. "Hon, you've had two terrible shocks in a row. I'm not surprised if you're feeling a little punky. Now, what's this about the Eagle Diamond?"

"You know the story?" Chloe asked.

Sonia rubbed at an invisible spot on her fork. "Everyone around here knows the story. But it's just a legend." She slid a plate of cookies toward Dellyn. "Have a couple of my Oatmeal Gems."

Dellyn's face was tight as she dutifully took a cookie. Chloe looked from her friend to the neighbor, trying to figure out the vibes. Aunt Sonia was eccentric, but aside from her cooking, seemed harmless. Dellyn, though, was acting uncharacteristically wired.

"I hear the mailman," Dellyn said. She slid from her chair and headed toward the door. Chloe watched with admiration as Dellyn slid her cookie into a pocket of her shorts. She was good at this hide-the-food thing. Chloe still didn't know how to ditch the slaw without being obvious, so she steeled herself for one more bite of the vinegar-and-pepper-with-a-bit-of-cabbage mess, washed down with another gulp of tea.

By the time Dellyn returned to the kitchen, Sonia had finished her own meal. "I've got to run on home," she said. "Still no word on the service?"

"They had to do an autopsy, remember," Dellyn said stiffly. "That slows things down. But Simon is planning a memorial for Tuesday. If we have Bonnie's body by then, we'll bury her. If not, we'll have a private burial when we can." She leaned against the counter and folded her arms. "Thanks for stopping by, Sonia."

Chloe waited until she heard the front door close before scraping the remnants of her meal into the garbage. "I don't mean to be rude," she said, "but this food is inedible."

Dellyn began flipping through the stack of envelopes she'd retrieved from the mail slot. "Yeah. She's a horrible cook."

"Tell me if I'm being too nosy, but … well, you didn't seem happy to see a friendly neighbor."

"I wasn't." Dellyn began tossing envelopes aside. "Condolence card, bill."

OK, Chloe thought. Dellyn doesn't want to talk about Sonia Padopolous.

"Two condolence cards. Bill." Suddenly Dellyn went very still.

"What is it?"

Dellyn slowly turned an envelope toward Chloe. It was addressed to Dellyn Burke in blue ink. And in the upper left corner, written with the same pen: *B. Sabatola.*

Chloe stared. "Oh my God."

"It's from Bonnie. Do you think I should open it?"

"Well … yeah, I do. Maybe it will explain why she felt she needed to kill herself."

Dellyn unfolded the paper, read it, and handed it to Chloe. The note was frustratingly terse. *Dellyn, I'm so sorry. I just can't face it anymore. Love always, Bonnie.*

"Is this your sister's handwriting?" Chloe asked.

"Yes." Dellyn's eyes welled with tears. "But she didn't explain anything! How could she send me a note like this, but not tell me *why?*"

Chloe put an arm around her friend's shoulders. "I imagine she was doing the very best she could, and that she was completely out of emotional energy. Depression does that to a person."

"I'm trying not to be angry at her. But I can't help it."

"You're entitled to your feelings. Just remember that even in the end, she was thinking about you. She wanted to apologize to *you.*"

"I guess." Dellyn snuffled. "Yeah. I suppose it's something." She drew a deep, shuddering breath. "I better call Simon, and let him know this came. Maybe he got one too."

"The cops'll want to know about it, too."

Dellyn blinked at her. "The cops? Why?"

Chloe growled silently at Roelke. "I think they just like to know all the details on cases like this. So their files are complete."

"That's the least of my concerns. I need to call Simon."

60

Chloe sat back at the table as Dellyn punched in the numbers on the wall phone. "Simon? It's—yeah, it's me." She told him about the letter. "Did you get one too? ... Yeah, I'll wait." She put a hand over the receiver and said, "He hasn't gotten his mail yet." Dellyn stared blindly out the window for a few moments, and then turned her attention back to the phone. "No? ... Sure, I'll bring it right over. See you in a bit."

"He wants to see it?" Chloe asked.

"Yeah. He hasn't gotten, or found, any message from Bonnie." Dellyn ran a hand over her hair, looking around the kitchen. "I need my car keys. They're around here somewhere ..."

"They're right here." Chloe retrieved the key ring from behind the napkin holder. "Are you OK to drive? I could take you, and just wait in the car."

"Thanks, but I'm OK." Dellyn shaped her mouth into a smile. "And thanks for the help this afternoon, too. I really appreciate it."

"I'll tell you what," Chloe said. "How about if I stay here, and keep working until you get back? I've got nothing better to do."

"Really?"

"Really," Chloe said. "As pathetic as that sounds."

"Be my guest, then. If you need to leave before I get home, just pull the door closed behind you."

Chloe waited until she heard Dellyn's car back from the driveway before reaching for the phone and punching in Roelke's home number. No answer. She tried the station's non-emergency number. No answer there either, and she hung up before the call switched to the county line. Well, this really wasn't her business anyway. Dellyn would probably tell the cops on her own. Bonnie had mailed a suicide note, evidently just before driving to the trail and killing herself. Case closed.

The best thing she could do for Dellyn was get back to work in the attic. The thought of ascending back into that purgatory of heat and dust and clutter made Chloe break out in a sweat. *Some friend you are,* she berated herself, and forced herself to move.

She spent a good hour in the attic before retreating back to the kitchen. After rummaging in the fridge, Chloe settled back at the table with a slice of the banana bread she'd brought the other morning—which she knew was quite edible, thank you—and a glass of tea. Valerie Bing's magazine article about the Eagle Diamond lay beside her plate. The headline declared, "A Mystery Endures in Eagle." Idly, Chloe began to read.

TEN
1876

ALBRECHT WIPED HIS FOREHEAD with his elbow. He was digging through clay, now. The well shaft smelled rank with his effort, and his eyes stung with sweat. His shirt was soaked. His kerchief was soaked. Even his hat was soaked. He pulled his canteen from the bucket where he'd left it, and gulped greedily. The water was warm and tasted of tin.

"You stopping?" Charles hollered down the shaft.

Albrecht hadn't planned on stopping yet, actually. He had the energy to send up a few more buckets of earth, and to unload the buckets of limestone Charles sent down to line the shaft. But the irritation in Charles's tone snapped Albrecht's patience in two.

"*Ja,*" he yelled back. "I'm coming up." He began the climb toward sunlight.

Charles was waiting for him, chewing a piece of grass, squinting. "I'll go down again," he said, as Albrecht flopped on the grass. "I'm not ready to quit."

Albrecht watched Charles descend into the hole, then looked toward the garden. Clarissa had made good progress; a wide swath of raw, new-turned earth had been exposed. Clarissa herself was nowhere in sight. Good, he thought. He hoped she'd gone inside, out of the sun, and was taking a rest.

Charles probably never thought to ask his wife if she needed a rest. Just as he hadn't thought to ask if Albrecht minded staying a while longer. Now that the shaft was so deep, one man was needed on the surface to handle the winch and dump the buckets of earth sent skyward. Albrecht flexed his shoulders, trying to ease their ache.

"Mr. Bachmeier?"

Albrecht scrambled to his feet so fast he almost lost his balance. "Mrs. Wood!"

"I thought you might like some switchel." She still wore her bonnet, but so close, he could make out her face beneath the brim.

"Thank you, ma'am," he said. He sipped slowly, savoring the tang of apple vinegar-and-water; savoring even more the chance to stand so close to Clarissa. She smelled of sweat too, but hers was somehow sweet.

Finally, the tin cup was empty. He handed it back with reluctance, hoping his fingers might brush hers. They didn't.

"It looks like your garden is coming right along," he said, feeling a little desperate.

She smiled. "Oh, yes. I can't wait to start planting. Vegetables, of course, but I must have flowers too."

She's a good woman, Albrecht thought. A good helpmeet. He tried to think of something else to say, but Clarissa was already turning away.

ELEVEN

CHLOE DRAINED THE LAST of her tea as she finished the article. Interesting stuff, although she was curious about the woman mentioned. Clarissa Wood had become a widow some time after the Eagle Diamond had been found, but when? How? *Wisconsin Byways* was a glossy magazine intended for a general audience. No handy footnotes.

Well, Mr. Burke had compiled a file on the diamond, right? Dellyn wouldn't mind if she looked through his records. Besides, the office was at least twenty degrees cooler than the attic. With the article in hand, Chloe made her way into Mr. Burke's office.

An hour later she admitted defeat. She'd fingered her way through all the file cabinets, poked through stacks of cartons crammed with more file folders, and skimmed the ledgers. She hadn't seen anything labeled "diamond" or "Eagle Diamond" or "Wood."

Chloe glanced at her watch. Libby had invited her over for a cookout that evening, and she'd frittered away most of the afternoon. Time to leave a note for Dellyn, who had evidently been waylaid at her brother-in-law's house, and am-scray.

As Chloe walked from the room she picked up the article again, skimming the columns of text … and abruptly, another name caught her eye: G. F. Kunz. She'd seen that name during her search of the files … hadn't she? Somewhere?

She was tempted to forget it, but that nagging sense of familiarity plunged her back into the search. Twenty minutes later she found the remembered file—thankfully, in one of the cabinets, before having to manhandle the heavy cartons again. "I knew it!" she announced, rather impressed with herself. Not too long ago, when struggling with depression, she'd had trouble remembering what she'd had for breakfast on any given day. This was no small achievement.

The Kunz folder was flat, containing only a single document. Chloe read the letter and whistled. The information it contained predated the Eagle Diamond's theft, but was significant historically. Dellyn would be tickled.

Chloe left the file on the kitchen table with a scrawled note: *Fun find for the day. Hope all went OK with Simon. I'm heading to Libby's for a cookout supper. Come on over if you'd like company.*

———

When Roelke arrived at Libby's house that evening he was surprised to find Chloe reclining in a lawn chair, sipping wine. That's OK, he told himself. It's cool. After all, he'd been the one to introduce Chloe to his cousin. At the time it had seemed like a good idea. These days, he wasn't so sure. After his aborted attempt to kiss her, things might feel … awkward.

But Chloe greeted him pleasantly enough. The temperature was dropping, shadows had stretched across the back yard, and a light breeze kept most of the mosquitoes away. Libby's two kids were at a neighbor's house, which meant grownup conversation could reign. Maybe this would turn out to be a good evening.

Libby, as usual, turned out a feast with what appeared to be minimal effort. "Is your burger OK?" she asked Chloe, once everyone had been served.

"Amazingly good," Chloe said, with obvious sincerity. Libby had grilled a portabella mushroom cap for her, topped with a thin slice of smoked gouda cheese. "Did you put hickory chips in the coals?"

"Hickory shells." Libby extended her legs and crossed her ankles. "They have more oils than the wood."

"The word 'fanatical' comes to mind," Roelke said. He rolled his eyes, because his cousin would suspect something was up if he didn't needle her. But as far as he was concerned, Libby could add frankincense and myrrh to the coals if it meant that Chloe ate a good meal. For a vegetarian, she didn't pay enough attention to nutrition.

Chloe licked mushroom juice off one of her fingers. "If these are the results, she can be as fanatical as she wants."

Libby got up to check whatever she was grilling for dessert. She was three years older than Roelke, practical and self-assured, and occasionally too all-knowing for her own good. But this old ranch house in Palmyra, worn and toy-strewn, felt much more like home than his own tiny apartment several blocks away.

And he really, *really* wanted to stay where he could come by Libby's place whenever he wanted. "There's a position opening up," he announced. "EPD. Full-time."

"Hey, that's great!" Libby said.

"Yeah." Roelke nodded, and tried what he hoped was a casual glance in Chloe's direction.

"That *is* great," she said. "I'm sure you'll get it."

He rolled his shoulders. "Well, I'm not sure. There are two of us going up for it. Me and Skeet Deardorff." Roelke began tapping the arm of his chair with his thumb. "Skeet's got as much experience in Eagle as I do. He's taking extra classes. And he's never given anyone in Eagle a speeding ticket."

Libby blinked. "What?"

"He lets anyone with an Eagle address off with a warning." Roelke and Skeet had debated that approach many times. "They're paying our salary, man," Skeet would say. Roelke insisted that equity in every detail was the only way to go. Now, he tried to remember if he'd ever ticketed anyone on the Police Committee for speeding.

"Roelke? Hey, you." Libby snapped her fingers. "Don't obsess about it now. You're a good cop." She got up to check the grill.

Chloe smiled at him. "And you'll do great at the interview."

God, she was beautiful. Roelke didn't like needing to compete—for the job he deserved, or for a place in Chloe's life—but when she smiled like that, he felt as if anything was possible.

"Ah, perfect." Libby pulled some fruit kabobs from the grill, and served them on small plates. Pineapple dusted with coconut, and some yellowy-orange fruit Roelke couldn't identify. Mango, maybe? The skewered fruit provided the perfect treat to end a hot day, warm and crusty outside, juicy and sweet inside. The last of his tension leaked away.

"Anyone want a beer?" Libby helped herself to a Leinenkugel from the cooler, then turned to Chloe. "Did you talk to Dellyn today?"

Roelke felt his sense of calm head for the hills.

"I was at her house this afternoon," Chloe said. "I'm helping her with a bunch of old stuff her parents left in the attic."

"How's she doing?" Libby poked a lime wedge into the bottle.

Chloe shot Roelke a sideways glance. "She's OK, I think, considering."

"Did something happen?" Roelke asked, trying really hard to sound mild.

Chloe told them about the letter. "Poor kid," Libby muttered.

"I'd like to see that," Roelke said at the same time.

Chloe squirmed. "Well, I told her to call you about it. Bonnie's husband wanted to see it, though."

"I hope they don't destroy it." Roelke gazed blindly over the lawn, thinking.

Libby frowned. "What difference does it make? The poor woman committed suicide, Roelke. I know that pisses you off, but you can't change it."

A chipmunk darted to the edge of the patio, packed his cheeks with seeds spilled from one of the bird feeders, and raced away. "Something feels funny about this one," Roelke muttered. "I'll talk to Dellyn about it."

Now Chloe was frowning at him, too. "Do you really need to make Dellyn talk through everything all over again?"

Well, hell. Roelke considered his options: back away, or dig a deeper hole. Something compelled him to cling to his metaphorical shovel. "Will you two come on a drive with me?" he asked.

"Why?" Libby ran a hand through her short-cropped hair, eyeing him with suspicion.

"Where?" Chloe asked, with equal suspicion.

It belatedly occurred to Roelke that asking Chloe to help him dissect Bonnie Sabatola's last earthly moments was quite possibly the worst idea he'd ever had. "Never mind," he said. "Forget I said anything."

"OK," Libby said. "Listen, Justin just joined a soccer club. He wants to do it, but the poor kid isn't as athletic as some. His first game is a week from Sunday. Want to come to his first game and help cheer him on?"

"Of course," Roelke said. He tried to fill the gap left by Justin's asshole father, who was more absent than not.

"Me too!" Chloe said, which was a surprise, but a good one. "Sounds like fun." She glanced at her watch. "I really need to hit the road."

Roelke walked her to her car. He considered trying to kiss her again, but the moment just didn't seem right.

Libby was carrying dishes inside when he rejoined her. "I need your help," he said. "Let's go for that ride. It won't take long."

Libby insisted on putting the food away before leaving, but twenty minutes later, the two of them stood at the head of the White Oak Trail.

"Why are we here?" Libby gave Roelke her *I am not amused* look.

"An experiment. I'm going to head in a ways. I want you to walk the trail until you reach me, and count your steps."

"Roelke—"

"Holy toboggans, Libby, do you think I'd bring you here if it wasn't important?" He turned away and jogged to the spot where he'd found Bonnie Sabatola's body. In the canopy overhead, songbirds warbled the day's final songs. No evidence of the violent death remained. How many children had skipped unknowingly over this spot? How many hand-holding couples had wandered past?

Libby joined him a few minutes later. "Two hundred and thirty-two steps," she announced flatly. "Now, what the hell was all that about?"

Roelke told her about Bonnie Sabatola's instructions. "She said she'd be three hundred paces up the trail. I reached her in one-eighty-seven, but I was running. I wanted to calculate a woman's pace. According to Bonnie's driver's license, she was five-feet-seven."

"About my height."

"Exactly. But you didn't get even close to three hundred paces. Besides that, she said her wallet would be on the wheel of the car. Instead, I found it by the trail."

"Let's get out of here," Libby said. She turned and started walking back toward the parking lot.

Roelke followed her. For a moment neither one spoke. Finally he said, "I just want to understand what happened."

"Are you trying to understand the last minutes of Bonnie's life?" Libby asked. "Or are you trying to figure out what sent Bonnie to that trail in the first place?"

Libby had a habit of out-thinking him. He hated when she did that. "Well, first of all," Roelke said, "I want to know what pushed her over the line. Someone must have done something to make her feel the way she did."

"Dellyn wasn't aware of anything going on. If Bonnie's sister didn't know about any problems, and her husband says he didn't know, what can you possibly do now? Even if Simon was having an affair or something, that's not a crime."

"I know," he admitted. "And maybe I'm way off base. But something doesn't add up here. What if someone *was* abusing or threatening Bonnie Sabatola in a criminal way? Isn't discovering that worth some effort?"

Now Libby looked away. She had some experience with domestic abuse. After her husband's first punch she'd left him, gotten a restraining order, and started divorce proceedings. But lots of women weren't as strong-willed as Libby.

They reached the parking lot. Libby didn't speak again until they'd climbed into his truck and left the trailhead behind. "Roelke," she said quietly, "if someone was brutalizing that woman, physically or emotionally, I hope you find some way to nail his ass to the wall."

"Thank you."

"But I also think that you're wasting your time obsessing about Bonnie's last moments."

"I'm not obsessing!"

"All I mean is, you'll never understand what she was thinking. What she was feeling. You'll never know why she said three hundred steps, and only went two hundred and thirty. I worry that . . ."

She sighed. "Shit, I'm not your mother. I just don't want you to make yourself nuts, OK?"

He thought about that, and reluctantly conceded that Libby had a point. He'd been on suicide calls before without feeling a need to get inside the head of the person just before they did the deed. Examine the scene, piece together motive from a letter or those left behind—sure. No more.

But something about this case was haunting him. And even he could figure that one out. Bonnie Sabatola's was the first suicide call he'd taken since he'd met Chloe. Since he'd learned that Chloe had, not so long ago, been in some dark emotional pit herself.

"OK," he said, as he turned onto Libby's street. "I will never know exactly what happened on that trail back there, or what Bonnie Sabatola was thinking in her last moments. I will stop wasting time trying to figure it out."

"Good."

"But I'm not done trying to find out if she was being abused or threatened, at home or elsewhere," Roelke added. "Not by a long shot."

———

That night Chloe wandered in circles, played with Olympia, tried to read a book. Finally she called her best friend. "I think I screwed up," Chloe told Ethan, a buddy from her forestry school days at West Virginia University. "Twice, actually."

Small silence. "What did you do?"

She pressed the telephone to her ear, wishing they didn't have half a continent between them. "First I met Markus. Then I agreed to go visit an elderly couple with him."

A longer silence. Then, "How was it to see him again?"

"Freaky."

"He's there just on business?"

Chloe leaned back in the big brown chair in her living room. "No. He says he still has feelings for me. He wants to try things again."

"It took him long enough to figure that out."

"No kidding."

"Do you still have feelings for him?"

"I don't know." Chloe closed her eyes. "Mostly I just feel pissed off. All those months when I would have given anything for a phone call from Markus, and then, *finally*, just when I'm putting it all behind me ..."

"What about you and that cop with the funny name? Are you still seeing him?"

"Sort of. Not really. I don't know." Chloe used one finger to stroke Olympia, who had jumped into her lap. "Ever since I told him about Markus, things have been really strained. He was over here the other evening—"

"Yeah?" Ethan sounded pleased.

"It's not what you think. He was here on business. Sort of."

Ethan groaned.

"Don't freak out. It's nothing that involves me." Chloe told Ethan about Dellyn and Bonnie. "Roelke's investigating Bonnie's death. He just wanted to ask me about Dellyn." And he almost kissed me, she thought. Almost.

"Are you doing OK?"

"I'm OK," she said resolutely. "But I don't have a clue what I'm going to do about Markus."

He sighed audibly through the wire. "What do you *want* to do? What do you want, period?"

"I just—I think I just want some stability in my life. I'm thirty-two years old, for God's sake. Isn't it time I had a savings account, and a stable relationship?"

"Do you think Markus or Roelke could offer you those things?"

"I don't want any man to take responsibility for my savings account. As for the other..." Chloe let the thought dangle. "Honestly? I have no idea. I don't know that I could ever trust Markus again. And Roelke can be a nut job at times."

"Maybe neither one of them is right for you."

Chloe didn't want to think about her tangled love life any more. "How about you and Chris? Everything OK on your end?"

"He's good. We're good. Celebrating three years together next month."

"Good for you. I'm glad somebody's life is stable."

He laughed softly. "Things will work out for you, Chloe. Whatever ends up happening between you and Markus... maybe you needed to see him again. You two ended things so abruptly, there was bound to be a lot of stuff left unsaid."

"Or maybe talking to him is the verbal equivalent of pressing my hand down on a hot stove just when the first burn was starting to heal." Chloe switched the phone to her other ear. "Ethan? Thanks for listening."

TWELVE
1876

"I'M COMING UP!" CHARLES shouted.

Albrecht frowned. Charles had only descended into the well a few moments ago. "What's wrong?"

"Nothing! Just tend the rope."

Albrecht made sure the windlass was secure. Maybe Charles had decided he was hungry, and wanted his mid-day meal.

Clarissa was on her knees, planting seeds in her new garden. Her hand cultivator obviously needed sharpening. And did she know that she might get only five or six weeks before first frost? Perhaps he should say something to her. Offer some advice. He was a novice well-digger, but he knew plants.

Then Charles clambered up from the depths of the well. Albrecht offered a hand and helped pull him the last foot or so. "You're stopping for dinner?"

"No." Charles pulled something from his pocket. "Look at this. Ever see anything like it?"

Albrecht squinted at the yellowish stone. "No."

"Me either." Charles spit on the stone, then rubbed mud away with his thumb. The stone grew shiny, even sparkled in the sunshine.

Albrecht took the stone from Charles's palm and scraped it with a fingernail. "Hard, too."

"Clarissa!" Charles called. He took the stone back and curled it into one fist.

His wife left the garden and joined the men. "What is it?"

"Something pretty." Charles grinned, and gave her the stone.

Clarissa's face softened into a smile that made Albrecht's heart ache. "It *is* pretty! I'll wash it up and put it on the windowsill."

"We'll dig for another hour or so before stopping for dinner," Charles told her. He slapped Albrecht on the shoulder. "Let's get to it."

Clarissa's smile dimmed. She slipped the yellow stone into her apron pocket, and nodded. "I'll have it ready."

The man is a fool! Albrecht thought. If *he* ever had the chance to put such a smile on Clarissa's face, he surely wouldn't cut the moment so short!

"You want top-side, or down below?" Charles asked.

"I'll go down," Albrecht said. As he backed into the hole, the last thing he saw was Clarissa, back on her knees in the garden. But in his mind, he could still see her delighted smile.

He'd give anything to bring a smile like that to Clarissa Wood's face.

THIRTEEN

On Monday, Roelke dropped his application materials off with the village clerk on his way into work. Step one. Done.

When he got to the EPD, Chief Naborski called him into the office. "We've got autopsy results for Bonnie Sabatola," he said, and pushed a piece of paper across his desk.

Roelke skimmed the report. Trajectory of the bullet was consistent with what the scene had suggested. Stippling on the skin confirmed that Ms. Sabatola had pressed the muzzle of the gun against her throat. The ME did find old bruises on Bonnie Sabatola's arms consistent with a man's hands, but no evidence of broken bones. The only medical records he'd been able to find pre-dated her marriage.

"She hadn't seen a physician in *any* capacity since her marriage?" Roelke frowned. "That doesn't feel right."

"Any records of 9-1-1 calls?" Naborski asked him. "Any relatives shed light on what was going on?"

"Nope." Roelke tapped his thumb against the chair. Bonnie had never called for help, never reported her husband, never been treated for unexplained injuries. He'd checked.

"You come up with anything when you talked to the husband?"

"The guy is pretty shook up. No way's he faking that. But ..."

"But?" The chief tipped his chair back and regarded Roelke.

"I'd like to push a bit more."

"Why?"

"It's a gut thing," Roelke said. "Something's off. Just because a guy grieves for his wife doesn't mean he didn't knock her around before she died."

The chief shook his head. "Unless you can prove false imprisonment or something, you're going to have a very hard time getting anything to stick."

"I know," Roelke admitted. "But I'm not ready to let go. I'll take Sabatola the autopsy results, for starters. If I want to talk to anybody else after that, I'll do it on my own time."

The chief's chair banged back down on the floor. "OK," he said. "Just don't let it get in the way of your primary duties. Eagle residents expect to see their officers patrolling the village."

Residents and the Police Committee, Roelke thought, as he left the chief's office. Roelke paused, then opened his locker. The small photo of Erin Litkowski, a pretty redhead, smiled serenely down from the photo frame on the shelf. She'd cut all ties with family and friends and simply disappeared—all because of her asshole husband-turned-stalker. After learning that Erin had gone underground, Roelke had done some extra reading about abusive spouses. He'd seen them, certainly. But the books had helped him get inside the abusers' heads. Sometimes that helped him spot trouble before somebody ended up in the ER. Or worse, the morgue.

But not this time, he thought. He slammed his locker door and headed out.

———

Markus had asked Chloe to meet him at The Swiss Historical Village Museum, which was operated by the New Glarus Historical Society. He was waiting in the parking lot, and bounded over when he saw her car. "Isn't it a beautiful day?" he exclaimed. "I've more-or-less been headquartered here during my sabbatical. Have you toured the museum? No? I'll take you around some time. The story of the Swiss community here is extraordinary."

They drove to the Frietag farm in the Ford Fairmont Markus had rented for his stay. A child might have created the landscape with her smallest box of crayons: blue sky, white clouds, green fields, red barns.

"How was your staff meeting?" Markus asked.

"Painful as ever. We're getting audited." Ralph Petty, the site director, had been near apoplexy about it.

Markus frowned. "Audited?"

"It means 'investigated,' sort of. Evidently some nice folks think too much money has been funneled to Old World over the past few years. People within the historical society think more should flow to other historic sites and other divisions. And a state legislator has a bug up his butt about getting state historic sites moved into the division of tourism." She shuddered, picturing some gung-ho official morphing Old World Wisconsin into an old-timey theme park.

"That would not be good."

"No."

"Well, try to forget about it for now. This will be fun." Markus slowed to let a couple of motorcycles blitz past. "Johann and Frieda were born here in Green County, but English is their second language. Once the last of these elders pass on, *Bernertüütsch*—the Glarner dialect—will disappear. Help me watch for the turn, OK? You can't see the house from the road. Look for a red mailbox with 'Frietag' painted on it."

"Sure."

"The community is very protective of them. Johann's health is quite bad. I was in New Glarus for weeks before the folks at the historical society decided I was worthy of meeting them. Then it took me some time to connect with them. No telephone. I had to work through their granddaughter, Martine." Markus flashed her a grin. "Don't you love the sound of that?"

Chloe managed a small smile. "Do they have goats?"

"If I'm lucky. The earliest immigrants were primarily laborers in Switzerland, not farmers, so nothing goes back that far. But the settlers purchased cows and chickens upon arrival. And Swiss people continued to come. I might find some old-breed animals. OK." He flipped on his turn signal. "Here it is."

Johann and Frieda Frietag lived in a small frame farmhouse—perhaps 1870s, Chloe thought, although several haphazard additions had changed the profile. As Markus parked the car a woman about Chloe's age stepped outside. She was big-boned and muscular. "Mr. Meili?" she said cautiously.

"Please, it's Markus." He gave her one of his warm grins.

Chloe stepped forward. "And I'm Chloe Ellefson."

The other woman's posture visibly relaxed, and she extended a hand. "I'm Martine." Her grip was too strong, but obviously welcoming. "I live about a mile away, over that hill on my folks' farm. But I keep an eye on things."

"It's kind of you to let us visit," Chloe said.

Martine made a wry gesture. "I get calls for Gran and Grandpa all the time these days, and I almost always say no. I had to tell the historical society not to give our names to just anyone wanting to do research. Gran and Grandpa love company, but they both tire easily."

"We'll keep our visit short," Markus promised.

"I'd appreciate that." Martine shook her head. "The vultures are circling. I've found developers trespassing on our property. Someone writing a book spent ten minutes trying to impress me with how important he was, and how I was obliged to let him come interview my grandparents. And just this morning an auctioneer called me and offered to come 'assess the household.'" She made air quotes with her fingers. "For only a nominal fee."

Bastards, Chloe thought. "I'm so sorry."

Martine gave a small smile. "I *am* interested in preserving what my grandparents know about agriculture. I've been learning to make cheese the old way, and Gran knows everything there is to know about gardening." She nodded at Markus. "So when you called and said you were from Ballenberg, and that you had a friend from Old World Wisconsin who would come also … well, that appealed to me."

So, Chloe thought, Markus mentioned me to Martine before he even asked me to come. Chloe looked at him with raised brows.

Jerk. He gave her a tiny, apologetic shrug, looking only slightly abashed.

Martine led them through the house to the kitchen. The room was hot enough to take Chloe's breath away, but also welcoming in a cluttered and comfortable way. "Gran?" Martine said. "Here are the visitors I was telling you about."

A tiny wren of a woman with stooped shoulders turned from an iron-and-enamel wood cook stove. Speaking Swiss, Markus made introductions. Frieda beamed at him, then turned to Chloe. "*Gruetzi!*"

"Hello," Chloe said. "I'm afraid I'm not fluent in your first language." She'd tried hard to scour all things Swiss from her mind, and her command of the language was rusty at best.

"No matter," Frieda assured her. "I'm glad you're here."

Chloe was completely disarmed by the genuine pleasure in Frieda's eyes. I love my job, Chloe thought. Some of her irritation at Markus faded. It had been arrogant of him to presume she would come … but he did know her well.

"Grandpa is upstairs," Martine was saying. "He's having a good day, so we'll go say hello." She led the way up a steep and narrow staircase. Frieda followed, clutching the banister tightly.

Johann Frietag was propped on pillows in a bed that might have been made a century ago, tucked beneath a quilt made of fabrics almost as old. He was a thin man, with the large hands of a farmer and glasses that seemed too big for his face. Each breath was labored, audible.

Martine got everyone settled into chairs near the bed, and made the introductions. Johann grinned, and Chloe glimpsed the young man he'd once been. "People used to call me an old coot," he told them. "Then some lady from the historical society came out a year or so ago. Talked about how important it is to preserve the old ways. All of a sudden I'm a somebody important." He looked pleased. "She called Frieda and me 'vessels of tradition.'"

"That's a fancy way of saying that we're old," Frieda said dryly.

With the Frietags' permission, Markus started a small tape recorder and began asking questions. Chloe was content to just *be*. She felt a certain peace in this place, which was indescribably welcome. Johann and Frieda were delightful. Their speech was slow and sing-songy, rich with the Glarner inflection Markus had spoken of, and sprinkled with bits of dialect. Chloe caught the word *gulli*—rooster—when Markus asked Johann about his livestock.

Finally Martine said quietly, "That's enough."

"Why, this young man and I are just getting acquainted!" Johann protested.

"You need to rest now, Grandpa," Martine said firmly. "Perhaps Markus can visit again."

Markus nodded. "I'd like that."

"All right, then," Johann conceded.

Frieda gently tucked the quilt around her husband. For a moment the two gazed at each other, communicating with a silent intimacy. Then Frieda kissed him on the forehead. "Rest," she whispered, and he closed his eyes.

When she saw Chloe watching, the old woman smiled. "We've been married for seventy-one years," she whispered.

A hand squeezed Chloe's heart. She felt sympathy for this woman facing the loss of her husband of seventy-one years. She felt envy, too.

Johann was snoring lightly as they all trooped back down to the kitchen. Martine gestured to the table, which was already set for a meal. "Please, sit down. Grandma wanted to serve you lunch."

Frieda bustled about the kitchen for a few more moments, filling bowls and carrying platters to the table. "*Chabis*," she said, setting a bowl of cabbage salad at Chloe's elbow. "And fried chicken. And *spaetzle*."

"What a feast!" Markus said, with the sincere enthusiasm that always melted elderly hearts.

Then Martine passed a plate of something that resembled cheese, but was green. "*Grünen Schabzieger*," she said, with a mischievous grin. "The American name is 'sap-sago.' It used to be common locally, but no one but us makes it anymore."

Chloe took a helping of the hard cheese. Everyone watched while she tried it. It had a strong flavor, but she pronounced it delicious.

Frieda nodded with approval. "The old Swiss folk used it to treat stomach troubles."

"A few months ago, when Grandpa started failing, he was reminiscing about eating sap-sago as a boy," Martine said. "So Gran and I tried a batch as a surprise."

"Now," Frieda said, "the *Bierabrot*."

"Oh—I love *Bierabrot!*" Chloe carefully avoided looking at Markus. Swiss pear bread, moist and dense, had been a special Sunday-morning treat when they'd lived together in Brienz.

After the meal everyone went outside. Chloe heard bells clang with the placid movement of cows grazing on the steep hill behind the barn. The audible memory of glorious days in the Alps was so strong that she put a hand over her chest, expecting to feel her heart fluttering. This time she dared a glance at Markus. He nodded.

Frieda gestured. "There's the *Käsehütte*."

The cheese hut was a small frame building, nondescript except for a gleaming and obviously new coat of white paint. When they all trooped inside, Chloe's mouth opened. "This is *amazing!*" The building was frozen in time.

"When I was a kid, Grandma still did her laundry in here." Martine patted the iron cauldron built into a brick casing.

"Johann and I made cheese in here every day for over thirty years," Frieda added.

"We've started making Emmentaler cheese again," Martine said. She touched an enormous copper kettle hanging from a heavy beam. "After it cooks here, and we cut the curds, we use that pulley system to haul the curds over to the pressing table."

Markus ran his hand over grooves in the old table. "These allow the whey to drain from the curds?"

Frieda nodded. "Into a bucket. Nowadays they say that whey has a lot of protein. Cheesemakers can sell it. We used to feed ours to the hogs!"

"A century ago, lots of farms around here had their own little cheesemaking operation," Martine explained. "Maybe four or five farmers would bring their milk. Most of the little factories were gone by World War II. Gran and Grandpa kept theirs going, even when they just made cheese for themselves."

"Your cows are Brown Swiss?" Markus asked.

"We've only got the two now," Frieda said. "Years back, we also had some milking shorthorns. But Martine's thinking about expanding the herd." Her delight was obvious.

"My dad and his brother, and my older brothers … they have no interest making cheese," Martine said. "Our farm over the way is completely modern, with a herd of Holsteins. I work there too, but I don't want to see our family's heritage lost. Gran and Grandpa and I have been kicking around the idea of keeping the *Käsehütte* going. The cool cellar where they used to store the cheese is still standing, too. I think there's a market for cheese made in small batches, Sap-sago and Emmentaler and baby Swiss."

"Martine is our vessel of tradition," Frieda said.

"*Wunderlicher* is more like it," Martine said, and for just a second Chloe thought she saw something sad flash in her eyes.

But Frieda flapped a hand at her granddaughter, and said to Chloe, "Martine has acted in the Wilhelm Tell Festival since she was a little girl. And she's learned archery."

"I compete in *Schützenfests*. Next up is *Volkfest*, when New Glarus celebrates Swiss independence. Having women compete probably strains tradition, but I like the challenge." Martine took her grandmother's arm. "You've been on your feet long enough, Gran. Why don't we stop the tour here for now."

"When you come back, I'll show you my garden," Freida promised Chloe, as they headed for the car. "And my embroidery."

Once farewells were said, Chloe and Markus headed back to New Glarus. Several miles passed in silence. Finally Chloe admitted, "I enjoyed that."

"The Frietags are wonderful people."

"That green cheese was wild," Chloe said. "Have you seen that before?"

"It's still made in Glarus, I think. Probably goes back a thousand years." He shook his head. "Kids learn in school that the rainforest is full of medicinal plants, but no one thinks to wonder if the cure of some disease might be growing in some old woman's garden down the road."

"That's why we do what we do." Chloe enjoyed a moment of self-satisfaction. Then she remembered something she wanted to ask. "What does *Wunderlicher* mean?"

"It means, 'an odd one.'" Markus scratched his knee, considering. "I suppose Martine meant she likes to spend time with her grandparents, learning to make cheese and Swiss dumplings."

Chloe wriggled on the seat, tucking one foot beneath her. "Well, I don't see anything odd about that."

"You wouldn't." Markus laughed. "I imagine any old Glarnese farmer might stop by that farm and feel completely home." He shoved his hair back, keeping one hand on the steering wheel. "And meeting the Frietags with you ... well, it felt like old times."

It did, a bit. Chloe poked at her feelings with a ginger finger. Today's plunge back into Swiss history and culture had been less difficult than the first, when she'd met Markus at the New Glarus Hotel. It was a relief to think she might have gotten past the worst of their bad breakup, and her lingering aversion to all things Swiss. There was much to cherish about her time spent in Switzerland.

Markus glanced at his wristwatch. "We could still make it to Old World this afternoon. Any chance we could go see the farmer there?"

Chloe watched a bicyclist struggling up the hill as she considered. She did not want Markus at Old World ... but he was clearly going to visit, with or without her. It felt churlish to refuse to so much as introduce him to the farmer. She blew her breath out slowly before once again saying, "Oh, all *right.*"

FOURTEEN

ROELKE PULLED INTO A parking lot behind a sign that said **Agri-Futures—Helping the World Grow!** The office building was an imposing black box with big windows reflecting the sun, perched on a hill outside of Elkhorn. In the green expanse on either side of the front walk stood enormous machines—a tractor on one side, a combine on the other.

Roelke pictured the Farmall A tractor that had served his maternal grandparents for decades. Roelke had driven it many miles himself during summers on the farm, up and down the cornfield, looking down to be sure the cultivator hoes were scratching up weeds instead of corn plants. Sixteen horsepower on the drawbar and eighteen on the belt, with twenty-one inches of clearance. If it rained, he got wet. If he wanted to hear music, he whistled. That old Farmall would just about fit into the wheel well of one of these monsters.

Well, times changed. Roelke still thought about his grandparents' farm. A lot, actually. But he had no wish to become a farmer. None at all.

AgriFutures' lobby was an atrium extending up half a dozen stories. A middle-aged woman with dark hair and a conservative suit sat at a sleek desk situated fishbowl-like in the center of the sunny column. Roelke offered his friendliest smile. "I'm here to see Mr. Sabatola, the vice-president."

"We have two vice-presidents," she said, sounding well rehearsed. "Simon Sabatola heads the equipment division. Implements and machinery. Alan Sabatola, the chemical division. Pesticides, herbicides, and fertilizers. Whom do you wish to see?"

"Simon."

"Do you have an appointment?"

"No," Roelke said politely. "But I need to speak with him."

She hesitated for only a moment. "Sixth floor."

He thanked her and headed upstairs in the elevator—all glass, with a view of both the atrium and the lawn behind the building. More equipment was parked with casual care, like sculptures outside some museum of modern agricultural art. Roelke almost heard his grandfather snorting with derision.

The elevator slid to a silent stop, and opened into a reception area where Edwin Guest, Simon's fussy little secretary, was talking on the telephone. "That's not the way I ... no. We can't apply for the patent until I'm sure that this is the way I want—" He noticed Roelke, and terminated the conversation abruptly. "I'll have to call you back."

Then he fixed Roelke with a look of prim disapproval. "Mr. Sabatola's schedule is very full today. And on his first day back after the tragedy..." Guest let the sentence fade away.

"I'm very sorry to intrude again," Roelke assured him.

Guest made a show of leaving Roelke waiting while he disappeared into an inner office. The reception area furniture was a unique fusion of Danish modern and farm, with stylized tractor seats for chairs, and even floor lamps fashioned from cultivator prongs. Huge images of agricultural machinery, brilliantly lit and photographed, filled the walls.

Weird shit. Roelke turned from what AgriFutures probably called AgriArt, and studied Guest's desk by the window. A light was blinking on the phone. A stack of closed file folders stood neatly on one corner. An electric typewriter hunched under its dustcover on a side table. The personal touches were minimal: a tray holding several pots of African violets and a calendar with a photograph of a German shepherd. Normally the dog calendar would have forced Roelke to raise his opinion of the secretary a notch, but the African violets canceled that out.

Notations on the calendar were made in fine-tipped pencil, precisely lettered. Roelke studied the coming week. Tuesday: *Funeral.* Wednesday: *Conference call—Taiwan. R & D presentation. Board meeting.* Thursday: *Mtg. with legal re patent application. Mtg. with Patterson re 2nd quarter numbers. Roxie's R., PM.*

Roelke paused. Roxie's R? The name might refer to anything or anyone, but something niggled at his brain...yes. There was a tavern on the outskirts of Elkhorn called Roxie's Roost. He'd never been there, although he'd driven past it a few times. A typical small

Wisconsin tavern, nothing flashy. It was hard to imagine Edwin Guest stopping there for a burger and beer on his way home.

The door to the inner office was still closed. Roelke lifted the calendar page with a fingernail and tipped his head to glance at next week's schedule. More precise and often cryptic references to conference calls, meetings, reviews. And on Thursday, once again: *Roxie's R*. Well, hunh.

The doorknob rattled. Roelke stepped away from the desk before Guest reappeared. "You may enter," the secretary said, gesturing Roelke toward the inner office.

Simon Sabatola was already on his feet, coming around a massive desk with hand outstretched. His eyes were bloodshot. "Officer McKenna. Have you found any more information about Bonnie's death?"

"No, sir, but I've got the death certificate and autopsy results for your wife," Roelke said, as gently as he could. "Perhaps we could sit down?" He gestured toward a cluster of furniture at the far end of the huge office. He had his doubts about Sabatola, but nobody should have to hear "autopsy" and "your wife" in the same sentence.

Sabatola's face seemed to lose what little color it had, and he dropped into one of the leather chairs.

Roelke sat on the sofa. "All the report really does is confirm what we already knew. Your wife died of a self-inflicted gunshot wound. There were no signs of other physical distress of any kind." Except the bruises. But Roelke was holding on to that tidbit, for now.

Sabatola closed his eyes and bowed his head. It took several moments for him to look up again. Finally he seemed to make a concerted effort to focus. "Thank you."

"You're free to make whatever plans you wish for burial."

"Tomorrow," Sabatola said. The word was barely audible, and he cleared his throat. "I've already talked with the priest at St. Theresa's, in Eagle. Tomorrow, at two o'clock."

"I understand that Dellyn Burke received a letter from her sister in the postal mail. Have you received one as well?"

Sabatola looked startled. "No, I—I'm afraid not."

Roelke pulled his little notebook from his pocket. "I also hoped to get the names and phone numbers of some of your wife's friends."

"Is this really necessary?" Edwin Guest snapped from the doorway.

Roelke turned his head, eyebrows raised. "I am speaking with Mr. Sabatola."

Guest tried to stare him down. Roelke didn't let him. Guest looked physically fit—probably compensating for his short stature and receding hairline—but he was in no position to take control.

"It's all right, Edwin." Sabatola sounded weary. "Officer McKenna is just doing his job. You can wait outside." When the door shut he turned back to Roelke. "Don't mind Edwin. He's worked with me for years."

"I understand," Roelke lied. He understood nothing about the relationship between a male secretary and the vice president of an international company. "And I wish my intrusion weren't necessary. Now … can you give me contact information for any of Bonnie's friends?"

"Well, let's see." Sabatola studied the wall, as if a list might magically appear. "I know her best friend from high school lives in Guatemala now. Otherwise ... well, I really didn't pay much attention to Bonnie's friends."

"I can imagine that a job like this—" Roelke waved his hand vaguely—"would consume most of your waking hours."

Sabatola's tone turned confidential. "Actually, I was afraid she was getting too cut off from her old friends. But she took a great deal of joy in our home." He sighed. "I'm sure it must seem that I was a poor partner."

Damn straight. "Not at all."

"AgriFutures is an international company, and we're experiencing explosive growth. My stepfather—he started AgriFutures, back in the fifties—died of lung cancer recently. Our Board of Directors hasn't made the formal announcement yet, but I've been groomed to become CEO. My half-brother is younger, and doesn't know the business as well. These past months have been intense." He sighed. "But if I hadn't worked late so many evenings, perhaps Bonnie ..."

He rose abruptly and walked to the window.

Roelke stood too. "It's always a difficult thing, trying to balance work and family."

Sabatola gestured toward the mega-monsters on the lawn below. "Those machines represent the future of agriculture. And not just here in the States. The industrialized world needs to find ways to help third-world countries feed their people. AgriFutures is taking a leadership role in tackling world hunger."

"Ah," Roelke said. Usually a helpful prompt.

"We're working on a new spring-loaded tiller designed for areas where people are still farming by hand. If one tine strikes a stone or root in the soil, the others continue to work at the correct depth. The main frame will be the strongest in the business, adaptable to a variety of conditions."

"I helped out some on my grandparents' farm when I was a kid," Roelke said. "We probably could have used one of those."

"In most parts of this country, agricultural innovation is an ongoing process. But in many third-world nations, desperate farmers are barely surviving. They don't have time to evolve gradually. One machine like our new tiller could revolutionize the economy of an entire village."

"It sounds exciting," Roelke said obligingly. "But... how can those struggling farmers afford a new tiller like that?"

Sabatola waved one hand dismissively. "They can't directly, of course. But we're building a strong global network that includes investment companies. We're partnering with people who have the vision to see the potential rewards inherent in aiding developing nations."

"Ah," Roelke said again.

Sabatola gestured toward one of the enormous combines below. "Impressive, aren't they? Those machines have a beauty all their own."

Beauty? Now, that was pretentious crap. "Everything is very... big," Roelke said.

"Our unofficial motto is 'Get big or get out.'" A smile briefly softened Sabatola's face. Then he shoved his hands in his pockets. "Forgive me. It's just that..." He nodded toward the lawn. "All I have left right now is my work."

Roelke wondered what Bonnie's parents, who had worked the kind of small family farm now being overtaken by factory farms that needed equipment on this scale, had thought of their son-in-law's line of work. Mr. Burke had likely owned a tractor much like the one Roelke had learned to drive on his grandparents' farm.

"I'll let you get back to work, sir," Roelke said. "Thank you for your time."

———

Chloe and Markus reached Old World Wisconsin an hour before the site was due to close. "I know the farmer will be at one of the Finnish farms to milk the cows just after closing," she told him. "We can walk out."

"Let's loop through the site," Markus said. In response to her startled look, he shrugged. "I've studied maps of the grounds. I'd really like to see the farms."

"OK," she said. "Let's go."

They walked first through the Crossroads Village, where visitors were drinking root beer at the inn, exclaiming over goods in the store, playing croquet, participating in a temperance rally. The interpreters—those underpaid and underappreciated educators who donned period clothing and spent their days interacting with the visitors—kept toddlers from touching hot stoves, positioned their bodies between inquisitive adults and tempting artifacts, gave directions to the public toilets, and dispensed first aid to bee-sting victims. Markus was clearly impressed.

That bubbled into pure professional joy as they continued on to the German area. "Two *fachwerk* farmhouses? Your vernacular architecture collection is amazing! That's a Plymouth Rock chicken? That mower is a reproduction?"

He had wanted to see the historic site through her eyes. Instead, Chloe was seeing it through his … which reminded her how lucky she was. Few outdoor museums in the country were as large, as well interpreted, as wisely located. Old World Wisconsin's farms and crossroads village, comprised of structures moved from all over the state and painstakingly restored, were situated within the Kettle Moraine State Forest. Prairies, woods, and kettle ponds provided a natural visual buffer to modern intrusions.

"You can see the Norwegian and Danish farms another day," Chloe said finally. "We need to catch the farmer before he's done for the night."

Slapping at mosquitoes, they walked a nature trail to the Ketola Farm, a Finnish homestead restored to its 1915 appearance. Chloe introduced Markus to the historic farmer, a laconic blonde-bearded man named Larry. Markus asked questions about the stump fence, the reproduction root cellar, the DeLaval cream separator, the young steers bellowing for attention in the pasture. In the big dairy barn, he ran an appreciative hand over a Jersey's rump. "Do you get enough milk to support the site's food program?"

"Well, pretty much," Larry said. "Cheese, butter, milk for cooking … it starts right here."

Markus grinned. "You've managed the ideal! Most sites have to set things up for show. It's so much harder to actually make an agricultural system work as it should—to make the farm exhibits self-sufficient."

"Oh," Chloe said softly. Markus shot her a quizzical glance, and she waved a hand to say, *No, nothing.* But it wasn't nothing. For just a moment she'd felt a flush of the old affection, the old admiration for Markus's energy, the old comfort of a shared passion for living history. For just a moment she had forgotten all the ugliness.

Which was unsettling. "I'll wait outside," she announced. She turned her back on the men, left the barn, and walked across the farmyard.

The interpreters had locked the sauna when they left for the day, but Chloe had a key and she let herself inside. It was her favorite building on the site, and she sank onto one of the benches in front of the fire pit. The building smelled of smoke because the interpreters sometimes built a fire, heating rocks before splashing them with cold water to demonstrate the old Finnish ritual of steam baths. Chloe closed her eyes.

Most of the historic buildings on the site gave her jumbled impressions, the mix of emotional residue that built up in layers over time. Not this one. She could sense the Finnish women who had once found respite in this tiny room; could feel their calm, their sense of safe respite, the strength they called *sisu*, emanating from the fibers of wood and stone.

Perhaps ten minutes later she heard tires crunch on gravel outside, the slam of a car door, then tentative footsteps in the entryway. Dellyn poked her head around the inner door. "Hey," she said, her eyebrows arching toward the headscarf that covered her hair. She wore her usual on-site garb: long black skirt, faded blouse, dirty apron. "Um ... why are you sitting in the sauna?"

"It's peaceful in here," Chloe said. "The Finnish women came in here together, you know? And not just to bathe. They even came in here to give birth. I can picture this building as it was for them, clean and safe and warm." She shrugged, a little embarrassed. "Sitting in here helps me calm down."

Dellyn sank down on the bench beside her. "Do you need to calm down?"

Chloe reminded herself that Dellyn's problems were much bigger than her own. "Mostly I'm here because a guy from Ballenberg is talking to Larry in the barn."

Dellyn circled one hand in a *Keep going* gesture. "And ..."

"He's an old, um, acquaintance."

"It's your ex, isn't it! The guy you lived with in Switzerland."

Chloe sighed. She'd never mentioned her personal past to Dellyn, but the historic sites' community was like any other. "Yeah."

"Are you OK?"

"I have no idea."

"Sorry."

"Thanks. But how are you? How did things go with Simon?"

"Oh ... all right, I suppose. Bonnie's letter shook him."

Chloe leaned back against the next higher bench. "Bonnie didn't send him one?"

"Nope. I think that really hurt him. We sat and talked for a while. It was the nicest he's been to me in a long time."

Chloe tried to weigh that statement against the brooding questions in Roelke's eyes whenever Simon Sabatola's name was spoken. Should she try to warn Dellyn against him? But on what grounds? For now at least, she told herself, keep your mouth shut.

Dellyn picked up the dipper used to sprinkle cold water on the stones, and smacked the ladle against one palm. "Simon's going to take me out to dinner. He said we'd both do well with a change of scene for an hour or so." She sighed. "I think he would have made a good brother-in-law, if I'd just let him."

"I wish you weren't so hard on yourself."

"Let's talk about you for a while. So, who's this Swiss guy?"

Chloe was spared further discussion of her tumultuous love life as the sound of male voices drifted through the open door. She scrambled to her feet. She'd let Markus invade her site. No way was she letting him inside her sauna. She grabbed Dellyn's wrist and towed her outside. Chloe didn't make the introductions until the door was safely locked behind them.

"I'm glad to meet you," Markus told Dellyn. "The gardens are fantastic! May I come back and talk with you about your heirloom varieties?"

"Um … OK," Dellyn said.

Chloe let them make arrangements to meet. "I have to be in Madison that day," she lied blithely, when Markus tried to include her.

Dellyn shrugged. "No problem. Listen, I've got chores to finish. Chloe, I'll see you later."

"Yeah," Chloe said, hoping that wasn't code for "Chloe, I'll want all the details later." She touched her friend's arm, "Oh—Dellyn? What did you think of that file I left on your kitchen table on Saturday?"

Dellyn looked blank. "What file?"

"The one marked 'G. F. Kunz.' Kunz was referenced in that article about the Eagle Diamond you gave me. He was an appraiser from New York, and in 1883 he wrote a letter to some jeweler, saying the diamond was worth about seven hundred dollars. I found the file in your parents' study, and left it out on the kitchen table for you."

Dellyn pinched her lips into a tight line for a moment. "If you left it out, I must have seen it, but …" She thumped the hoe she

102

was holding against the ground several times. "I don't even remember. I swear, Chloe, sometimes I think I'm truly losing my mind."

"You're on overload, that's all." Chloe wished that she'd never mentioned the stupid file. "Don't worry about it."

"I'm sorry," Dellyn said to Markus. "It was nice to meet you, but I've got to spread ashes on the cabbage plants before the moths eat them." Blinking fiercely, she strode toward the garden.

Markus shoved his hands in his pockets, watching her go. "Is she all right?"

"Her sister just died," Chloe reminded him. Something she couldn't quite put her finger on was making her uneasy. "But I'm starting to wonder if something else is going on, too."

FIFTEEN

"Pardon me," Roelke said politely, as two young women wearing long dresses pushed through the tavern door.

"No problem!" one of them said, with a big smile. Her green-and-white striped dress was fancy, with what must have been a pillow somehow stuck on her butt to hold out a froth of ruffles. Her companion was dressed as if she was one step away from the poorhouse: a patched skirt, a faded blouse, an equally sun-bleached headscarf tied over her hair. That one fished car keys from the cloth-covered basket over her arm, and the two made their way to the parking lot.

Roelke watched them go. Since coming to Eagle the previous year, he'd gotten to know the local bar scene. He knew which tavern attracted a low-key family crowd; which bar was most likely to attract trouble. Same as on his Milwaukee beat. But he'd never experienced a place like Sasso's. Often half of the patrons wore some kind of historic costume. "Period clothing," Chloe had once corrected him. "Costume implies something superficial."

Whatever that meant.

Roelke stepped inside. The taproom was crowded with Eagle residents and Old World interpreters, all relaxing at the end of the day with a cold one and, perhaps, a basket of fish and fries or a burger. Roelke caught the owner's eye and nodded—the man had a good relationship with the local cops. He ran a clean place.

Tonight looked much like any other evening. Roelke was pulling a double shift, so he'd be just as happy if things stayed quiet. He strolled through the crowd, Seeing and Being Seen. He asked for one kid's ID, and the young man triumphantly proved that he was, indeed, legal. Barely, but that still counted.

"Happy birthday," Roelke said. "You're not going to ruin your night by driving home, are you?"

"Nope," the kid said. "I'm drinking. He—" he pointed to his friend, who was nursing a fizzing soda—"is driving."

Roelke grinned. "Have a good evening, then."

He made a looping saunter through the crowd. No sign of anyone drinking to excess. No sign of anything problematic at all.

Then, just as he was turning to wind his way back to the door, he caught a glimpse of someone pressed against the wall. Something in Roelke's chest hitched, like a knot being tightened. Chloe's back was to him, but Roelke recognized that waterfall of blonde hair, the slope of her shoulders, the thin fingers wrapped around the stem of a wine glass. He changed course.

Chloe's companion was a stranger, a wiry man with light brown hair, a narrow nose, and a focused gaze that didn't leave Chloe's face even when he drank from a stein of dark beer. As Roelke approached the man said something inaudible. Chloe laughed, a rippling peal that seemed to come from some deep, joyful place inside.

Damn it. Roelke stopped behind Chloe. If he wasn't on duty he might have put a hand on her shoulder. But he was, so he didn't.

The stranger saw him first. A look of surprise chased the good humor from his face. "Yes, officer?" he asked politely. He had a slight German accent. "*Suisse-Deutsch*," Chloe had once corrected him.

Whatever the hell that meant. Roelke spoke with equal politeness. "Good evening."

Chloe whirled. "Roelke! I—um—are you on duty?"

"I'm not in the habit of socializing in uniform."

Her cheeks flushed. "Um … Roelke, this is Markus Meili. Markus, this is my friend Roelke McKenna. He works for the Eagle Police Department."

Meili offered his hand. "Pleased to meet you." His tone was still cordial, but his eyes narrowed, clearly assessing.

"Likewise," Roelke lied, doing some hard assessing of his own. So. This was the Swiss ex. Chloe had gone from 'I don't know if I'm even going to see him' to 'Oh, Alpine Boy, that's so funny' at lightning speed.

"We were just … that is, Markus wanted to see Old World," Chloe said. "I introduced him to the historic farmer and then we, um … we decided to—you know. Stop for a bite."

Roelke waited a beat, letting the silence become uncomfortable. Then he said, "Have a pleasant evening," in his best cop voice, the one he pulled from his back pocket when people were acting like assholes, and walked away.

———

"Is that the guy?" Markus asked.

Chloe commanded her fingers to loosen their death grip on the wine glass. "What guy?"

"The 'maybe' guy."

"What makes you say that?"

"Because I *know* you, Chloe." Markus sighed. "Look, we should at least be honest with each other."

Damn the man, Chloe thought. She considered demurring again—what Roelke McKenna did or did not mean to her was none of her ex's business—but decided that she'd only sound petulant. "Yeah," she said finally. "That's the guy."

"A policeman?" Markus asked, almost to himself. He looked utterly perplexed.

Chloe drained her wine, leaned over, and deposited the glass on the bar. "I gotta go."

They said good-bye in the parking lot. "This was nice," Markus said. "And we have a return trip to the Frietags to look forward to."

Chloe shrugged. "Well … I don't know. Dellyn should be the one to go with you."

"Maybe," he said softly. "But I'd rather take you."

Chloe took a small step backward. Sasso's parking lot, with its steady stream of Old World staff, was the last place she wanted Markus to make a move. "I *said*, I don't know. Give me some space, will you? I'll think about it."

Moments later Chloe watched his rental car crawl from Sasso's parking lot. Well, shit. Her last words to Markus Meili had sounded petulant and shrewish.

So what? she asked herself. She didn't know if she wanted to go on another excursion with him. And yet ... part of her *did* want to go back to the farm with him. Part of her *did* want to try to recreate their past, the shared camaraderie—the easiness that had briefly taken over this evening.

And that part scared her witless.

She slid into her Pinto and slammed the door with unnecessary force. Then she rested her elbows on the steering wheel, and her face in her hands. Taking Markus to Sasso's had been royally stupid.

She hadn't planned to take Markus to Old World, and she had. And then when he suggested dinner ... well, it seemed rude to refuse. The site tour had given them something to talk about over their meal. And when they'd relinquished their table to waiting diners, and Markus had suggested a nightcap, something made her agree.

A sharp rap on the car window jerked Chloe back to the moment. A young man wearing a straw hat, linen shirt, and wool trousers held up with suspenders stood by the car. She rolled the window down.

"You OK?" he asked.

One of the interpreters. From the German area, wasn't it? "Yeah," Chloe said. "Just a headache. But I'm fine."

"OK, then," he said, and sauntered on to his own junker. People didn't go into historic sites work for the money. But they are kind, Chloe thought. They take care of their own.

And that made her think about Dellyn. Her friend Dellyn, who was struggling with far worse problems than *she* was.

Chloe stared blindly out the windshield, letting something that had been nagging at her subconscious wiggle to the foreground. As it did, she felt another flicker of unease. It seemed odd that Dellyn didn't even *remember* seeing the file Chloe had left out on her kitchen table. Misplacing it, as she had done the original article about the Eagle Diamond—maybe. But to not even remember seeing it …

Chloe fished her key from her pocket, and turned it in the ignition. If she took the more easterly route home, she'd drive right by Dellyn's place.

Five minutes later she parked on the street in front of the Burke house. Twilight had muted the evening, but a lamp burned in the front window. Chloe marched up to the porch and rang the bell.

The chime was met with only silence. She rang again, waited. Nothing. Well, Dellyn had said Simon was taking her to dinner. Maybe she was still out. The free-standing garage was windowless, so she had no way of checking for Dellyn's car.

Or … maybe Dellyn *was* home, and finding solace in her mother's garden. Chloe hurried around the house. The garden was empty, but a light glowed from the old barn beyond it. Maybe Dellyn had decided to poke through whatever had been stashed there. She was probably looking for artifacts to display in the Garden Fair.

Chloe skirted the garden. The barn door was ajar, and she slid inside. The building still smelled faintly of musty hay and manure. Several bare bulbs cast a yellow glow on stalls now filled mostly with furniture—a chest of drawers, a huge china cabinet. A long wooden counter, perhaps saved from an old store, had been shoved against the closest wall. An anvil, and a variety of black-smithing tools, stood in front of it.

Geez Louise. It would take some digging to excavate the agricultural tools Dellyn hoped to find.

There was no sign of Dellyn. One of the far corners had been walled off—perhaps an office or workroom of sorts?—and Chloe headed in that direction. "Hello?" she called.

The lights went off.

Chloe froze mid-sentence, mid-stride. OK, she told herself. No need to panic. Maybe some faulty old circuit had shorted out. She instinctively summoned Grandma Ellefson from memory's murky depths. *There's nothing here that wasn't here in the light,* she used to say, when Chloe or her sister got spooked of the dark.

Then Chloe heard a faint scrabble of sound, off to her left, near the back wall. The fine hairs on the back of her neck quivered to attention.

Get a grip, Chloe ordered herself. Maybe Dellyn had made the noise, and was standing in frozen stillness too, equally spooked.

"Hello?" Chloe called again. At least she'd intended to call. The word came out as more of a quivering croak.

No answer. Chloe chewed her lower lip. OK, *still* no reason to panic. She'd probably heard a critter. Raccoon, porcupine, or even an owl.

But there was no reason to speculate. Her eyes were adjusting to the gloom. All she wanted to do was get out of the barn. Preferably without tripping over some artifact and impaling herself on a sickle.

She'd taken several steps when she heard a wooden creak. Close. Behind her. As she whirled something hard skimmed the side of her head and slammed into her left shoulder. Her knees buckled. The floorboards smacked her, hard. Chloe landed on hands and knees. Force kept her going, onto one shoulder and hip. "Ow!" she yipped. Something ripped into her arm.

Footsteps retreated toward the door.

Tears scalded Chloe's eyes as she struggled with pain, and with shock ... and finally, with the understanding that someone had actually attacked her.

———

After leaving Sasso's, Roelke stopped at the station to use the can, have a soda, and work on his daily report. He kept good notes, but it was hard to be neat when scrawling on a clipboard in the car. Thorough reports might make the difference to the Police Committee. Besides, he liked things tidy.

He recorded the swings through the village park and schoolyard—no sign of trouble—and the speeder he'd pulled over. He made a terse entry about the bar checks, ending at Sasso's.

Where Chloe had been laughing it up with her ex. He left that part out, but was glaring at the report when someone banged on the door.

Roelke frowned. Once regular office hours passed, people usually called if they needed help. He set the clipboard aside, hurried to the door, and jerked it open.

Jesus. Chloe stood there, her blouse torn, eyes brimming with tears.

Something inside of Roelke went very still, and hot, and hard. That *bastard.*

"Um, Roelke?" Chloe quavered. "Someone hit me."

"Come inside." He put a hand on her shoulder, guiding her as gently as he could while filled with fury. He looked beyond her—her car, no one else in sight—before closing the door. "What did he do?"

Chloe dropped into the chair he indicated. "He hit my shoulder. But I was turning around. I think he was aiming for my head. If I hadn't been turning, he would have hit me on the head."

"Were you still at Sasso's?" Roelke asked. He wanted witnesses.

"What? No!" Chloe blinked, and sniffed. "I was in Dellyn's barn."

"What were you two doing in Dellyn's barn?"

Chloe wrinkled her forehead at him. Then something dawned in her eyes. "It wasn't *Markus*, you idiot! I don't know who it was." She told him what had happened.

With a stab of regret, Roelke let go of the mental movie that starred him, cop extraordinaire, arresting Markus Meili for assault. "How badly are you hurt?"

"Not badly." Chloe moved her left shoulder gingerly, then examined her scraped palms. "I was scared more than anything else." She took a deep, shuddering breath. "Now I'm mostly pissed."

"Come with me." Roelke towed her into the bathroom, where he carefully washed her hands and coated the abrasions with antiseptic. Next he bandaged a bad cut on her right arm, holding his breath, fingers tingling as he reached through her torn shirt. "What did this? Did you fall against something metallic?"

"Just the rough edge of a stanchion, I think."

"Did you hit your head when you fell?"

"No."

No fear of tetanus or concussion, then. Roelke exhaled slowly. "OK. Let's go back in the office."

He ushered her back to Marie's empty chair, and he dropped into the one the officers used. "You have no idea who hit you?"

"No, I told you! None at all. It was dark, and I got spooked. I was turning to get out of there when something slammed down. It brushed right by my ear—" Chloe gestured—"as I turned. Then it hit my shoulder so hard I fell."

"Was it a fist?"

She sucked in her upper lip, thinking. "Something harder, I think."

That was bad. A fist might suggest that Chloe had startled someone who didn't belong there, but had no real intention to cause bodily harm. "Are you sure it was a guy?"

Chloe closed her eyes for a moment, then shook her head. "No, I can't be sure. He hit me really hard. But I guess it could have been a woman."

Roelke's right knee jiggled up and down. "Can you think of any reason why someone would be in Dellyn's barn? I'm trying to figure out what this person was after. And why he—or she—didn't just wait and let you leave, instead of attacking you."

"The barn is packed with all kinds of antiques."

"How valuable?"

"I have no idea! I'd never been in there before tonight."

Roelke stood, and extended a hand to Chloe. "Come on," he said. "Let's go see if Dellyn is home."

SIXTEEN

CHLOE STRUGGLED AGAINST ANOTHER spasm of unease as Roelke banged on Dellyn's front door. Still no answer.

"Let's go take a look at the barn," he said.

Roelke had Chloe wait outside while he searched the building. It seemed to take a long time. She stood with arms crossed, clutching her elbows. At least the lights were back on.

Finally Roelke poked his head out the door. "All clear. Come show me where you were."

Chloe stepped inside. The lights were doing their yellow best to dispel the shadows.

"Two switches," Roelke told her. "One by the door, one in the feed room. Evidently whoever was here turned on the lights when he came in the main door, and then turned them off with the feed room switch when he heard you come inside."

And then crept up on me, Chloe thought, and attacked. She felt a flicker of remembered fear, but just a flicker. She hoped that wasn't only because Officer Roelke McKenna, über-cop, stood beside her. She wasn't big on the whole distressed damsel thing.

"And where were you when he hit you?"

Chloe pointed. "Right here. He knocked me against that stanchion." She pointed to a vertical wooden post.

Roelke crouched to examine it. "Here's what ripped your shirt." He pointed to a large knothole on one edge of the post. The bottom tip of the C-shaped curve that bordered the hole was sharp, and still held a couple of cotton fibers.

Chloe swallowed hard. "I'm glad my head didn't hit that."

Roelke played the beam around the cluttered aisle. He abruptly muttered something unintelligible and brought the light to rest on something on the floor nearby.

"Oh my *God*," Chloe whispered. She crossed her arms over her chest again, grabbing her shoulders, warding away any remaining evil. A primitive and obviously homemade hand cultivator lay in the sphere of light, a heavy wooden handle with a wickedly pointed curve of iron attached at the head. Used while kneeling in a garden, it would simply be a handy tool to dig holes or hack at deep-rooted weeds. But used as a weapon … "He could have killed me with that thing!"

"Yeah," Roelke said grimly. "Don't touch it." He crouched and carefully eased the cultivator into an evidence bag he pulled from a pouch on his belt.

"What's that—wait, turn it over again." Chloe crouched too, compelled to get a closer look. She pointed to the tip of the wooden handle, which was carved with a flower. "It looks like a rose. That bastard attacked me with a piece of folk art!"

"Hunh."

Chloe stared at the cultivator, struggling with a sickening slough of emotions. Someone had once lovingly taken the time to personalize the tool—perhaps some farmer's gift for his wife, the rose chiseled out on long winter evenings?

"I turned as he was swinging," she said again. "I think the handle hit my shoulder. But if I hadn't turned..." She couldn't even finish the sentence. If she hadn't turned, if that sharp blade had—

The barn door they'd left half-open banged against the wall with a sudden crash that made her flinch. "What's going on here?" Dellyn demanded, as she stepped into the barn. "Chloe? And Officer McKenna? Oh, God. What now?"

Chloe stood to greet her. "I stopped by to see you awhile ago. I thought you might be in the garden, and when I went to look..." God, she hated having to add more burdens to Dellyn's basket! Nothing for it, though. She told Dellyn what had happened.

Dellyn gasped, and pressed one hand over her mouth. "Are you all right?"

"Fine," Chloe assured her firmly. "Really. I'm fine."

"But—"

"Miss Burke, may we go into the house?" Roelke asked. "We might be more comfortable talking there."

"Um...sure." Dellyn led them outside. Once the barn door was closed, she slid a wooden latch into place.

"No lock?" Roelke asked.

"Never has been. Back when my folks were farming, we had a watchdog. They never replaced the last dog when he died."

They trailed silently to the house, where Dellyn ushered them inside. "Come on into the living room."

116

The room was crowded with a mix of antiques and pieces that might have been comfortable and fashionable thirty years earlier. Framed photographs of people—tintypes, CDVs, cabinet cards, blurry snapshots, a Polaroid or two—covered most of the walls, but a huge canvas hung over the sofa. Oil paints captured an ocean storm, restless waves beneath a dramatic skyscape, with just a hint of rocky shoreline. Chloe's eyes widened. "Is that one of yours?"

Dellyn nodded. "I've been reluctant to change much in the house, but I did hang a couple of paintings. Please, both of you—have a seat."

Roelke settled stiffly on the edge of one chair. "Miss Burke, how long were you away from the house this evening?"

She stared at a clock, considering. "A couple of hours. Simon picked me up at six."

"Can you think of any reason why someone might want to harm you? An ex-spouse, angry boyfriend, anything like that?"

"No!" Dellyn looked bewildered. Chloe slid closer and put a comforting hand on her friend's arm.

"And can you think of any reason why someone might enter your barn?"

"Of course not!"

"Chloe—Miss Ellefson—tells me that your parents collected a lot of antiques. I'm guessing that some of them might be valuable."

Dellyn spread her hands. "I don't really know for sure yet. But you saw what was in the barn. Aside from some old tools, it's mostly stuff too big to carry. Besides, my parents weren't senile! I'm *sure* that if they did have anything of particular value, they would have kept it in the house."

"I've been helping Dellyn create an inventory," Chloe added. "We're a long way from a good assessment, though." She turned to her friend. "Maybe someone is trying to find something they donated to your parents for the historical society. People can go nuts over family heirlooms." She knew that all too well. She'd taken her current job believing that working with objects would be more peaceful than the constant stress inherent in overseeing interpretive programming at an historic site. *That* brilliant hypothesis had proved wrong, wrong, wrong.

"Well, I suppose it's possible," Dellyn said. "If so, I have no idea who it might have been, or what they were after." She jumped to her feet and began to pace.

Roelke asked, "Who else might know if your parents had collected something particularly valuable?"

"They were movers and shakers with the local historical society. Probably everyone in the village knew they'd been collecting stuff from Eagle residents for years."

Roelke pulled his little notebook from his pocket and made a few notes.

"There is …" Dellyn began finally, then halted. "No. It's just too ridiculous."

"What is?" Chloe asked.

Dellyn perched back on the sofa. "Well, this is going to sound crazy, but … Officer McKenna, have you heard of the Eagle Diamond?"

Roelke's eyebrows rose. "The what?"

"This guy was digging a well in 1876, and he found a diamond. It was the biggest diamond ever found in North America, at least at that time. The well was up on the hill on Highway 67, near the water tower. That's why they call it Diamond Hill."

Roelke's expression suggested that he had never heard anyone call it that. "And this has to do with Chloe getting attacked … how?" His knee began to piston.

"The guy who found it gave it to his wife," Chloe said. "Some time later, she hit hard times, and sold it. She got ripped off, but that's beside the point. The diamond ended up on display at the American Museum of Natural History. Then in 1964, this guy named Murph the Surf stole it."

"Murph the Surf?" Roelke repeated. "You're kidding, right?"

"It happened," Dellyn insisted. "He broke into the museum one night and stole a bunch of gemstones. Most of them were recovered, but the Eagle Diamond never was."

"Miss Burke, I still don't see—"

"So, most people assume the Eagle Diamond was cut down into smaller pieces, and sold, and therefore will never be found. But there's no proof of that." Dellyn picked up a sofa pillow and hugged it against her stomach. "And ever since I've been back, I've had trouble keeping my hands on anything related to the story. I left an article about it out for Chloe, but when she visited the next time, I couldn't find it."

"You've had a terrible shock," Roelke reminded her.

She waved that away with a flick of her hand. "Then Chloe found a document—a letter reporting on the first real appraisal of the diamond, done back in 1883."

"I did," Chloe affirmed. "I left the file out in plain sight for her, on the kitchen table."

"But I never saw it," Dellyn insisted. "I didn't know anything about it until Chloe asked me about it."

Roelke jotted something in his notebook. His face was expressionless.

"My dad planned to write a book about the Eagle Diamond, and he'd been gathering information for years. I've been going through my mom's garden journals, and … well, they made me feel close to her, you know? So earlier today I decided to look at my dad's box of files about the diamond."

Chloe looked at Dellyn. "And you can't find it."

"No. And I tore his office apart."

"I did a quick search last week, too," Chloe said. "Nothing but the letter from the appraiser, which was filed under his own name. Maybe his Eagle Diamond files got tucked away in the attic or something, though. We've hardly scratched the surface up there."

"But why? The attic was just for storage. My dad did all of his writing, articles for the newsletter or whatever, in his study."

Roelke cleared his throat. "Do you think your parents had this diamond tucked amidst all the other Eagle memorabilia?" His tone was more polite than Chloe would have credited him with.

"I don't really think they had the Eagle Diamond," Dellyn said quickly. "But what if someone else thinks they did? Or even that my dad had found some new information about it?"

No one seemed to know how to answer that. "Thank you for sharing all this," Roelke said finally. "It's often impossible to know what might be helpful. But let's focus on practical matters. Miss Burke, do you lock your doors when you leave the house?"

"Well … this is *Eagle,* for God's sake! I can't say I worry about it all the time."

"You need to worry about it," Roelke said crisply. "Did you change the locks when you moved in?"

"Change the locks?" Dellyn looked bewildered. "No."

"Do you know who else might have a key to your place?"

"My neighbor does. Sonia Padopolous. She and my mother were good friends."

"I'll follow up on that."

"If you talk to her, say no if she offers you anything to eat," Chloe murmured. It was probably an inappropriate comment, but... really. The woman had no taste buds.

Roelke frowned at her, then asked Dellyn, "Anybody else?"

She shook her head. "No. I mean—well, Bonnie would have had one."

Roelke made another note, his face impassive. "Miss Burke, I encourage you to call a locksmith. Change the house locks, and get padlocks for the barn."

Dellyn rubbed her temples. "Chloe, I'm *really* sorry for what happened to you—but it had to have been just some kid. Someone playing a prank, or out on a dare."

"But here's the thing," Chloe said. "He came at me from behind. He *wanted* to attack me. I was on my way out of the barn when he knocked me down. If I startled some kid, isn't it more likely that he would have bolted, or hidden until I left?" The vision of that cultivator seemed branded into her brain. I could have been killed, Chloe thought. I could have had my skull cracked in two like an egg.

Dellyn flopped back against the sofa. A car passed on the street out front, its radio cranked up so loud that the pulsing bass thrummed through the room.

Then Roelke stood, tucking away his notebook. "Before I go, I'd like to take some photographs in the barn. I'll need to take that cultivator with me, too. And I want to look around outside."

The two women waited on the back step as Roelke fetched a camera from the squad car. Ten minutes later, he emerged from the barn and inspected the yard, the garden, and the outbuildings. The harsh beam of his flashlight sliced back and forth through the night.

"I don't *freaking* believe this," Dellyn muttered. Chloe squeezed her hand.

When Roelke rejoined them he reported, "I didn't see anything out of order. But you need to be attentive. Call us if you see anything, or find anything amiss."

They walked back around the house. "Dellyn, why don't you stay at my house tonight?" Chloe suggested. "I'd really love to have you."

Dellyn shook her head. "I am burying my sister tomorrow."

Chloe put an arm around her friend's shoulder. "I know. But it doesn't matter if you wake up here, or at my place."

"This is my home. I won't be spooked out of it."

Chloe tried to think of a reasonable argument, and came up with diddly. No way to change Dellyn's mind without risking alienating her altogether. "I'll come by in the morning, then."

"No need," Dellyn said, her tone weary. "I'll see you at the service later."

Chloe turned to go, but Roelke paused. "Miss Burke. Have you thought any more about what might have been troubling your sister? Any new ideas?"

Dellyn sighed. "I don't *know* what was bothering her. I already told you that."

Chloe struggled to maintain her composure until she and Roelke had settled into the squad car again and watched Dellyn disappear back inside the house. "What was that for?" she demanded.

He turned the key in the ignition. "What?"

"That last question! Do you think Dellyn wasn't upset enough about what happened tonight without bringing up Bonnie again?"

Roelke checked his mirror and pulled into the road. "Sometimes people remember things a day or two after a crisis. Details that didn't come to mind right away."

"But what does it matter? Do you think Dellyn doesn't feel terrible enough? Geez!"

"I want to know why Bonnie Sabatola did what she did," he said stubbornly.

Everything that had been pushed away in the last hour—Markus and the awkward introductions at Sasso's and her own muddled feelings—roared pride-like back into the car. Whatever sense of safety and calm Roelke's presence had given her evaporated.

"Maybe you are letting your friendship with Dellyn get in the way of thinking clearly," he said. "She's overwrought."

"Get in the way of thinking clearly?" Chloe echoed incredulously. "You're criticizing me for trying to take care of a friend? A friend you're dismissing as 'overwrought'? You self-righteous jerk! Why not call us both 'hysterical females' and be done with it?"

"There's nothing wrong with trying to take care of a friend. But this is police business."

"Well, it's personal business to me. Dellyn is my friend. She doesn't have anyone else right now."

"She has other friends." Roelke pulled up behind her car, in front of the police station. "Libby, for one."

Chloe shook her head. "You know what? This is the stupidest argument we've ever had."

"I think you like feeling important."

"I—*what?*" She gaped at him. "Maybe I just like having a woman friend in my life, Roelke. Ever think of that?" She'd never parsed it quite that way, but it was true. At West Virginia University's forestry school, most of her friends had been guys. She'd gotten along fine with the small group of museum studies students she'd gone through grad school with, men and women, without hooking up with any one in particular. In Switzerland, her social life had revolved around Markus and his friends. Libby was great, but she was Roelke's cousin, first and foremost.

Roelke pressed his knuckles against his forehead. "Chloe—"

"Dellyn is my friend, and I'm worried about her. I'm afraid she might end up depressed herself."

"I don't want that to happen," Roelke said, in a patronizing tone that could not have been calculated to annoy her more. "But I still have a job to do. When it comes to that, you need to back off."

"*You* need to back off," Chloe snapped. "And leave Dellyn alone." She scrambled from the squad car and slammed the door. She was aware of Roelke watching as she unlocked her own car, slid inside, started the engine, and pulled away.

"Neanderthal," she muttered. She drove down Main Street carefully. She wouldn't put it past him to ticket her for going two miles over the limit.

When she reached Dellyn's house she braked and pulled over. She briefly considered knocking on her friend's door again.

But … no. Dellyn wanted to be alone. And Chloe understood the feeling of being besieged; of knowing that the last tattered scrap of the energy needed to interact with other homo sapiens was about to disintegrate.

That was a big part of why Chloe wanted to help. She knew how it felt to be broken. She knew how it felt to be alone. She knew how it felt to try, and try, and try, and still feel every sense of mastery over her own life drift away.

And when Chloe had hit the sucking muck at the absolute bottom of her personal well, one person had saved her: Ethan, her best buddy, who had put his own life on hold long enough to get her firmly started on the long climb toward daylight.

A lamp blinked on in the attic window. Dellyn, back to work on the artifact inventory.

Chloe had never known how to thank Ethan for helping her. Until now. "You're not all alone," Chloe whispered to Dellyn.

Then Chloe pulled back on to the road. As she left Eagle she realized that her hands ached, and she loosened her death grip on the steering wheel. "No way I'm backing off, Officer McKenna," she muttered. "No frickin' way."

She knew Roelke would do everything possible to track down whomever had attacked her in the barn. That was police business, and she was happy to leave it to him. But she also doubted that he'd give any credence to Dellyn's theory about the Eagle Diamond.

Might someone actually be searching for the diamond? Or even information about the diamond? It was hard to imagine. But criminals weren't the brightest bulbs in the box, now, were they? Besides, what mattered most was that *Dellyn* believed it possible. And Dellyn needed to have someone on her side.

"OK," Chloe told the windshield. "Time to learn more about the Eagle Diamond."

First, she'd need to keep helping with Dellyn's inventory project. Perhaps they could unearth her father's missing files about the diamond. That would provide some comfort, and probably shut the whole stranger-seeking-diamond theory down cold.

Second, she'd look for more information about the diamond herself. She was a curator; she knew research.

Chloe slowed as she reached the outskirts of Palmyra. Suddenly she flipped on her turn signal. "And third, talk to Libby," she said. Two minutes later she knocked on Libby's door.

Libby's eyebrows raised in surprise when she saw her visitor. "Chloe!"

"Sorry to drop in unannounced," Chloe said. She could hear Libby's son complaining about something from the next room. "I was driving by, and just have a quick question. Would it be OK if I invited someone else to come to our next writers' meeting?"

"Justin, I want the Legos picked up, and the whining to stop, by the time I get back there," Libby called over her shoulder. Then she turned back to Chloe. "Who do you have in mind?"

"A friend of Dellyn's. Her name is Valerie Bing. She recently moved back to Eagle from … well, I don't know, from someplace. She's trying to get established as a freelancer. She just had an article about the Eagle Diamond published."

Libby regarded her. "Is Roelke going to be pissed at me if I say yes?"

"I can't imagine that Roelke would be at all interested in our writers' group meeting."

Libby snorted with laughter. "Fair enough. Sure, go ahead and invite her. Just phrase it as a one-time thing, though, until we see how everyone gets along."

Done, Chloe thought, as she headed back to her car. She didn't need to wait for Roelke to decide if Dellyn's problems were worth exploring. She could do some exploring on her own.

SEVENTEEN

ROELKE'S PHONE WAS RINGING as he trudged up the stairs to his apartment that night. "Jesus," he muttered, fumbling for his key. It was after midnight. One of the part-timers, a new kid, was on duty. If he's asking for help on something stupid, Roelke thought, I will not be happy.

When he finally grabbed the receiver, though, a lazy voice greeted him. "Cow-boy!"

"You need new material," Roelke told Rick Almirez. His oldest buddy from his Milwaukee PD days frequently chastised Roelke for trading in the city for cow country. "What's up? And why the hell are you calling so late?"

"I've been trying for hours. Figured you'd get off shift sooner or later." Rick didn't sound even mildly chagrined. "Joe Dawson's getting married. Third Saturday in September. He wants the band to play at the reception."

"*Our* band?" Roelke loved playing blues and jazz with a few other cops. They called themselves The Blue Tones, and practiced every month. But honestly, they weren't that good.

"Yes, our band, nimrod. Evidently Sharon is preggers. Thus the haste."

"We should squeeze in some extra practice."

"Oh, yeah. Can you make it next Saturday?" The question was punctuated with a faint woosh of expelled air.

Roelke pictured Rick, sitting at his old Formica-topped kitchen table, phone in one hand, cigarette in the other. A sudden twist of melancholy hit Roelke in the chest. "Um … Saturday might be a problem," he said. "I'm on duty."

"So, get somebody to switch with you."

"I can't." Roelke sighed, knowing what was coming. "It's Movie Night in Eagle."

Brief silence. Then, "Movie Night?"

"Yeah. And it was kind of my idea, so I have to be there."

"Movie Night," Rick repeated, with a tone he might have used to say Hepatitis Night.

Well, Rick was an adrenaline junkie. No point in belaboring the topic. "See if the guys can do Sunday night," Roelke said. "I could make that."

"OK." Another pause, another whoosh of expelled cigarette smoke. "One more thing. Joe's leaving the force."

"No shit?"

"Sharon's folks offered him a job in the family business," Rick said. "A lumberyard, I think. Up by Tomah."

"Well, hunh."

"You know what that means. There's going to be a vacancy opening up."

Roelke's knee began to bounce up and down. Fast.

"I talked to the lieutenant about it," Rick said. "Off the record. He can't make any promises, but he did say he'd be pleased if you applied. Said he'd look for your application."

"Rick—"

"Just think about it," Rick said. "Everybody would welcome you back, McKenna. But the clock's ticking. They want to move on this thing. Application deadline is end of the week."

"*Rick*—"

"You might not get another chance like this!"

"A permanent position just opened up here. I've already put in for that."

"Are you sure you're going to get it?"

"No."

"So, put in for the Milwaukee job too, all right? That's all I'm sayin'."

Roelke sighed. "All right," he heard himself say. "I'll think about it."

After hanging up the phone, Roelke scrubbed his face with his palms. He didn't *want* to go back to Milwaukee. But it felt good to be want*ed*.

The Eagle Police Department was only four years old. The officers all got along well enough. Usually, anyway. But they were a collection of mostly part-timers, some kids trying to break into police work, a couple of vets trying to ease into retirement, one detective from Waukesha who picked up stray patrol shifts in

Eagle to earn extra cash. The person Roelke liked best was the chief. But the chief was his boss, not his friend.

"Well, hell," he muttered. He stamped down the cramped under-the-eaves corridor to his miniscule kitchen, opened the fridge, and stared at the shelves with disapproval. He never kept beer at home. But every once in a great while, he wished he did.

Just as every once in a while, he wished he'd never left the MPD. He missed shooting the shit with Rick every day. Missed hanging out with guys he'd gone through the academy with.

Roelke poured himself a glass of apple juice and looked out the kitchen window. Beyond the exterior staircase to his apartment, which was a total bitch to shovel in the winter, was a parking lot. Nothing to see at this hour except his truck and a dumpster.

"I *like* working in Eagle," he muttered.

But that wasn't the problem. The problem was that he seemed hell-bent on screwing himself out of the permanent position. Something about this Sabatola case was making him nuts. He was losing perspective. Just when he should be hunkered down, playing everything by the book, not giving Chief Naborski a single moment's pause.

And then, of course, there was Chloe. He was doing a pretty good job of screwing his chances with her, too.

He thought about his dad, and his brother Patrick. Both of them had self-destructed. Roelke had always tried to hold himself above their examples. And despite his momentary longing for a cold one, he didn't have their problem with alcohol.

But there was more than one way to self-destruct. If anyone should know that, a cop should.

EIGHTEEN

"What's eating you?" Marie demanded.

Roelke slammed his locker door. "What do you mean?"

"You've been barking at people all morning," the clerk said.

"No, I haven't."

Marie held both palms toward him in surrender. "Right. Have it your way." She swiveled back to her desk.

Great. Pissing off Marie did not bode well for anyone at the EPD, most especially a part-timer trying to win a full-time slot. "Marie," he began.

"Chief needs to present bids on new tires for the squad car," Marie said. "I've got to get this written up."

Well, hell. Roelke grabbed the squad keys and left. As he drove down Main Street, he realized that his fingers ached. He was clenching the steering wheel like a terrified first-time driver.

Well, hunh. Maybe something *was* eating him.

Five minutes later he climbed the front steps of a small brick ranch house, just north of Dellyn Burke's place. Clouds of flowers lined the walk, and spilled from a dozen or more hanging baskets. No wonder Sonia Padopolous and Dellyn's mother had been friends.

The front door was open, but no one answered his knock. He was about to try again when he heard faint chords of … something vaguely musical. He followed the sound around the house.

A plump woman wearing a lavender sweat suit and Keds sat in a lawn chair, strumming a ukulele. "When the red, red robin comes bob-bob-bobbing along," she sang, evidently to the robin splashing in a cement birdbath nearby.

OK, this was a first. Roelke waited until the song ended before coughing politely. "Mrs. Padopolous?"

"Oh!" Sonia Padopolous jumped to her feet, her eyes wide. The expression that chased the surprise aside, though, was not fear, or even wariness. Instead, a look of … regret, perhaps resignation, shadowed her eyes. Her shoulders slumped.

He waited for her to speak. She didn't. "I'm Officer McKenna," he said finally. "I got called to your neighbor's house last night. A friend of Dellyn Burke's startled a prowler—"

"A prowler? At Dellyn's? Last night?" The color drained from the woman's face, leaving two artificially pink blots of blusher on her cheeks. She stood with the instrument dangling from one hand.

Something not quite right here, Roelke thought. "Might we step inside?" he asked politely.

Mrs. Padopolous ushered him into a spotless kitchen. "You go through there and have a seat in the parlor. I'll get you a snack."

Roelke remembered Chloe's warning. "No thank you, ma'am," he began, but she flapped her hands in a shooing motion. He watched her bustle about the kitchen with what seemed to be an excess of movement, avoiding his gaze. Was it better to keep an eye on her, or to keep things friendly and obey her command? Friendly, for now. He kept going.

In the living room, Roelke took a quick look around. Paperback romance novels filled two bookcases. A vase of red silk roses stood on an end table. A card table in the corner held a partially completed jigsaw puzzle of some European castle.

Sonia Padopolous had time on her hands. She was lonely. And she dreamed of people and places far beyond Eagle, Wisconsin.

No pictures of grandchildren graced the walls, but a framed portrait on the credenza showed a much younger Sonia posed with a trim, dark-haired man. A flag folded with military precision and encased in a triangular glass-topped box sat nearby, next to a black-and-white photograph of a man in army uniform, circa World War II.

"That was my husband," Sonia said behind him. "He survived the Battle of the Bulge, came home, and died of the flu five years later. Here." She held out a plate of cookies.

Roelke accepted one oatmeal cookie and a napkin. "How long have you lived next door to the Burkes?"

She perched on a chair upholstered with huge mauve flowers. "Since nineteen forty-six. Loretta—that was Dellyn's mother—and I hit it off right away."

"So you've known the family well."

Sonia pulled a tissue from a decorative container, and used it to polish the base of a brass table lamp by her chair. "Well ... I watched

Loretta's girls grow up. My heart just breaks for Dellyn. One tragedy after another."

Roelke nibbled his cookie, and almost choked. Perhaps Mrs. Padopolous had mistaken salt for sugar? He coughed into his napkin, and tried to keep his voice steady as he said, "Bonnie's death must have been especially difficult."

Mrs. Padopolous rubbed fiercely at an invisible spot. "Yes."

Roelke tried to decide the best way to encourage confidences. "I was the first officer on the scene," he told her. "And I don't mind telling you, I can't quite shake what happened. Did you have any inkling that Bonnie was depressed?"

She began to cry. After a moment she sank back in her chair, and used another tissue to blot her eyes. "I *should* have known. I blame myself for what happened."

That seemed harsh. "Why do you say that?"

Sonia tore a corner from the tissue and rolled it into a tiny ball. "A few weeks ago, Bonnie came to see me."

"Did she seem distraught?"

"No, but ... Wait just a minute." Sonia disappeared, and emerged from the kitchen a few moments later with several folded pieces of cloth. "She gave me these. That's Loretta's work."

Roelke accepted what appeared to be dish towels, each sturdy white rectangle embroidered with a different flower. Some were familiar—pansies, daisies, lilies of the valley—and some were not. But he had no idea why Mrs. Padopolous was upset. Not even a clue. You may win that full-time slot with the EPD, Roelke told himself, but you obviously are not detective material.

"Bonnie said she wanted me to *have* these."

"Ah." A light finally flickered on in Roelke's brain. He laid the towels on the coffee table with due reverence. "She was distributing favorite possessions."

"Right." The older woman nodded fiercely. "Only I thought she was ashamed of these. Of me. Of her mother, even." Tears brimmed over again. "But that poor child was struggling."

Roelke's job often put him in proximity of weeping women, but it never got easier. "Some people get very good at hiding their feelings," he told her.

"Her mother was concerned. Had been, anyway. She wasn't real happy when Bonnie married Simon Sabatola."

"And ... why was that?"

Mrs. Padopolous tugged at one nylon knee-high, which had pooled around her ankle. "Well, people don't like to say so, but class matters. Simon was already a big executive. The Burkes were plain folks."

Roelke remembered Sabatola's home—the leather, the chrome, the oil paintings. "I see."

"I think Loretta was afraid that Bonnie would get spoiled by all that money."

"And did she?"

"I wouldn't say *spoiled*." Mrs. Padopolous exhaled a long sigh. "All I know is that she got more and more ... distant. I asked her over and over to bring Simon by for dinner, but she never did."

Perhaps that was Simon's influence, Roelke thought. Or perhaps Bonnie didn't dare bring her husband to Aunt Sonia's for an inedible meal.

Mrs. Padopolous dug the fingers of both hands into her hair. "I think she was depressed. It can just sneak up on a person, you know."

Roelke didn't know. He wanted to *never* know. "Did you ever happen to see any uncomfortable exchanges between Bonnie and Simon? Did he ever mistreat her?"

She shook her head. "He treated her like spun gold."

Roelke turned that tidbit over in his mind.

"Maybe some of his people were surprised that he chose to marry a farmer's daughter, but I never was. Bonnie was a beauty, but it came from the inside. She used to run in and out of this house like it was her own, and let me tell you, she was the sunniest girl you can imagine."

Sonia pulled a blue photograph album from a shelf, the kind with pocketed plastic sheets inside to hold pictures. She flipped to a page near the end, then pivoted the book so he could see it. "Here," she said, tapping one snapshot. "Here's Bonnie and Dellyn, back in the day when I was the local 4-H leader."

Roelke stared at a fading snapshot. He recognized Dellyn in the grinning girl on the right, proudly holding a red ribbon. A lovely girl, with features similar but more defined, posed on the left with a chicken in her arms. She was beaming.

So … how had everything gone wrong? Had Bonnie struggled to live up to the expectations that came from becoming an executive's wife? Had she struggled to gain acceptance from the women in her husband's circles? To be a charming hostess? To make polite small talk at cocktail parties?

"She had a dazzling smile," he said. "I expect that's what caught her husband's eye."

"Likely so," Sonia Padopolous agreed. "Dellyn has it too. She did, anyway."

Had those last words held a touch of ... what, anger, bitterness? Roelke made sure his cop-face was in place. "Dellyn hasn't had much to smile about lately, I suppose."

"I haven't seen much of her since she's been home." Sonia pulled the album from Roelke's hands and slid it onto the coffee table.

"Ah. Mrs. Padopolous, were you at home yesterday evening?"

"No. I was at a baby shower at my cousin's place in Mukwonago."

"Have you ever seen a prowler around here? Had any break-ins?"

She shook her head vehemently. "Never in all the years. But I'll double-check my doors tonight. And I'll stop over next door. See that Dellyn's really all right."

Dellyn Burke might not thank me for inspiring a carry-over, Roelke thought. "Ma'am, do you live here alone?"

"Oh, yes. But I'm quite used to it. Nothing rattles me."

"Do you have any children? Someone you could call if you needed help?"

Sonia hesitated before turning an album page and gesturing toward another snapshot. This one showed her younger self surrounded by perhaps a dozen grinning kids. "These were my children. My 4-H family. My, we had good times!"

Which did not, Roelke thought, answer the question. "Well, ma'am, we're just a phone call away. Please call if you see anything suspicious in the neighborhood."

"I will," she promised brightly. "Thank you."

Roelke was almost to the door when he turned, smiling pleasantly. "Oh, just one more question. I couldn't help noticing that you looked ... *resigned,* perhaps, when you first saw me. Were you expecting trouble?" It was a shot in the dark but not, he judged, completely wild.

"Expecting trouble?" She began folding one of the towels. "Why, I can't imagine what you mean."

He waited. Waiting often made people uncomfortable. Often made them talk just to fill the silence.

But Sonia stayed silent. Roelke thanked her again, and let himself out.

Back in the squad car he made some notes, and then considered. He needed more information. And he knew where to get it ... if Marie was ready to forgive him. He liked Marie. He admired Marie. But the woman could hold a grudge.

First, though, he had a funeral to attend.

NINETEEN

CHLOE HAD TAKEN TUESDAY off. When her alarm clock shrilled at nine AM, she slammed the snooze button. Five minutes later it shrilled again, got slammed again.

Get up, she told herself.

No response.

She hid her face in the crook of one arm, staving away the growing brightness. Her brain insisted on cataloging her problems: someone had attacked her the night before, a good friend was grief-stricken and—perhaps—the target of more trouble, Markus had somehow wormed his way back into her life, she and Roelke had argued.

"But I am not depressed," she muttered. "And I am not going to *get* depressed."

Response came in the way of a nose-nudge from Olympia. Chloe opened her eyes and stroked the kitten under her chin. "And I have a furry little buddy."

The alarm blared again. This time Chloe turned it off and struggled to her feet. Her palms stung. Her shoulder ached, and now sported an enormous bruise. She rolled it again, tried a careful shrug. Everything still worked.

"And I have a job," she told Olympia's backside—the kitten was already racing to the kitchen, giddy with the prospect of breakfast.

But Chloe couldn't talk herself out of her funk. Being hit in a dark barn had scared the bejeebers out of her. Fighting with Roelke made her feel horrible. And she was getting seriously worried about Dellyn.

Dellyn had brushed aside Chloe's offer of company that morning. The hell with that, Chloe decided. After breakfast for her and the cat, she dressed and headed to Eagle.

When she got to the Burke place she sat in the car for a moment. Even in daylight she felt skittish being here. She flashed again on the sound of her attacker approaching. The shock. The pain.

But today is about Dellyn, she reminded herself grimly. That comes first.

She found Dellyn sitting in the garden with Harriet Van Dyne, her favorite volunteer. "You, too?" Dellyn said, when she saw Chloe. But she smiled.

"I brought a coffeecake," Harriet said, as Chloe joined them. "Dellyn and I were just talking about creating a blue memorial garden in honor of her mother and Bonnie."

"Blue was Bonnie's favorite color," Dellyn explained. "And my mom's too."

Chloe searched her limited mental data base of ornamental flowers. "Delphiniums? Phlox?"

"And lupines," Harriet added. "Definitely lupines."

Dellyn managed a watery smile. "Thank you both for coming. It really means a lot."

———

Eagle's yellow water tower—painted with an enormous smiley-face—loomed over the roof of St. Theresa Catholic Church. Roelke stared at the iconic landmark which was, he had learned yesterday, situated on Diamond Hill.

"The world is a very strange place," he muttered, and got out of his truck. He'd leave the historical stuff to Chloe and Dellyn. All he wanted to do was catch bad guys.

Which was why he was attending Bonnie Sabatola's funeral. He always attended the services for people killed while he was on duty, if he could. Sometimes he went in uniform, offering respect on behalf of the police department. Today he wore his best civvies. He was more interested in seeing than being seen.

The church reached perhaps half-capacity with mourners. Most of them looked like business acquaintances of Simon Sabatola, the men in expensive suits and the women wearing heels and dark dresses and lots of jewelry. Sonia Padopolous was there, and Roelke pegged a small contingent as Dellyn's Old World Wisconsin friends. No one had come in costume, which he'd half-expected, but their clothing was less formal. Several wore glasses with old-fashioned wire frames. One long-bearded man wore suspenders and waistless trousers that gave him a vaguely Amish look. Chloe was wearing a denim skirt and light blue blouse that looked great, Roelke couldn't help noticing, with her coloring. She sat beside an older woman.

Dellyn Burke and Simon Sabatola had settled in one of the front pews with Edwin Guest and a man and woman Roelke didn't recognize. Simon stared at his lap through much of the service. When the priest began talking about "the lovely light that was Bonnie Burke Sabatola," Dellyn's shoulders began to shake, and the sound of muffled sobs drifted through the hot and hushed sanctuary. Simon put his arm around Dellyn's shoulders. She leaned against him.

Roelke wished he had a better handle on Simon Sabatola. The man couldn't name a single friend of his wife's, or provide any real details about how she'd spent her days. Roelke was still inclined to pin an 'abusive husband' badge on the widower, despite his grief and tears. But … was that only because he'd found no other trigger for Bonnie's suicide, and the spouse was always the first place to look?

Roelke wanted to be thorough. He also wanted to be fair.

At the end of the service he followed the mourners to the fellowship hall and lingered at the end of the straggle of guests, listening, watching. When he finally reached the head of the receiving line he saw Dellyn's eyes widen in surprise. "Why … Officer McKenna!"

"I wanted to pay my respects." Roelke told her, and then offered his hand to Simon Sabatola.

To his dismay, Sabatola's eyes filled with tears. Again. Edwin Guest, without even meeting his boss's gaze, discreetly passed a fresh handkerchief into his hand. Then Guest stepped into the background again, silent and unobtrusive, gaze lowered.

That guy's borderline creepy, Roelke thought. Unless … was it possible that there was more to the relationship between Sabatola

143

and Guest than met the eye? If so, and Bonnie had found out ... Hunh.

"It was kind of you to come," Simon said, when he'd blotted his eyes. He turned to the man standing beside him. "Alan, this is Officer McKenna. He investigated Bonnie's death."

"Alan Sabatola," the man said, pumping Roelke's hand vigorously. He was mid-thirties, perhaps, with tired eyes. "I'm Simon's brother."

Half-brother, hadn't Simon said? Roelke chewed on that as he retreated against a wall. The two brothers settled at a nearby table with some of the AgriFutures crowd. People began to filter to the buffet spread on folding tables by the church ladies. Alan Sabatola's voice rose as he talked with a heavy-set guy. "We are positioning ourselves to increase the productivity of subsistence farmers all over the world! Branching out from pest management to crop genetics is essential. We're going to replace old cereal grains with higher-yield crops."

Roelke listened with some disgust. Couldn't business wait until the reception was over? Maybe an impromptu board meeting was underway. Simon, he noticed, never looked directly at Alan. The two men kept more than casual space between them.

"Hey." Chloe poked his arm with her index finger. "I saw you, and just wanted to say hi."

"Hi." He tried to gauge her pissed index while still keeping an eye on the Sabatola brothers.

She pleated her skirt in her fingers. "Listen, I'm sorry we quarreled last night. Would you like to sit with us?" She glanced toward the Old World people.

"No." That sounded terse even to his ears. He lowered his voice and tried to back-pedal. "I mean, not right now. Can I join you in a little bit?" Simon Sabatola said something to his half-brother that seemed to sit poorly. Alan's face set in hard lines. Discreetly, letting his body shield the gesture from most of the guests, Alan stabbed one index finger toward Simon's chest and said, "Stop it, Simon." Roelke didn't hear Simon's response.

Roelke suddenly realized he hadn't heard Chloe's response, either. She was gone.

Damn.

Before Roelke could decide if he should submit himself to introductions to the Old World crowd, Simon Sabatola stalked out the door. Then a skinny woman Roelke didn't recognize got up from a nearby table and followed. She paused at the door, glancing over her shoulder, and slipped out after Sabatola.

Well, now. Even more interesting.

Roelke followed the woman outside in time to see her hurry after Sabatola, who was striding away from the building. She wore a plain skirt and sandals with a white blouse that seemed too large. Her dark shoulder-length hair was worn straight, with heavy bangs. She didn't fit the rich-business-acquaintance set.

She caught up with Simon in the middle of the parking lot, and put a hand on his arm. Sabatola jerked away from the touch, but he did stop. Roelke fiddled with a pack of cigarettes he pulled from his pocket, keeping an eye on the unlikely pair. The woman seemed to be pleading with Sabatola, who responded with a vigorous shake of his head. The woman said something else.

"Not *now!*" Sabatola blazed. He turned his back on the woman and strode back toward the fellowship hall.

Roelke leaned against the brick wall, affecting complete disinterest as he pulled a lighter from his pocket. He didn't smoke, which put him in a distinct minority among cops, but this pretense let him linger unobtrusively in all sorts of places. Sabatola, head down and fists once again clenched, didn't even glance his way.

The skinny woman stood for a few moments, staring after him. Then she got into an old-model Dodge Dart, and drove away.

Roelke was still mulling that exchange over when the door opened again. Another woman stepped outside and immediately began scrabbling through her purse. She extracted her own pack of cigarettes, but further search failed, evidently, to produce matches or a lighter.

"Can I offer you a light?" Roelke asked. He normally didn't encourage anyone to smoke, but this wasn't the time for a talk about lung cancer.

"Thanks." She joined him, put a cigarette to her lips, and inhaled fiercely. She was about his own age, with a narrow face framed by reddish curls.

"It's a difficult time," Roelke said.

"Yeah." She took another drag. "Are you a friend of the family's?"

Roelke introduced himself. "I was on duty the day Mrs. Sabatola died."

"Oh, God." The woman hunched her shoulders, as if defending herself from the vision of what he'd found on the trail.

"Were you and Mrs. Sabatola friends, Miss ... ?"

"Sorry. I'm Mona Lundy. Bonnie and I were friends all the way through high school together, and we both worked at a dress shop in Elkhorn."

Roelke felt something quiver inside. Finally, finally. "How long did you work together?"

Mona considered. "A year or so, I guess. She quit after the wedding."

"Did she say why?"

"No. She just came in one day and gave notice." Mona stared at a dandelion straggling through a crack in the sidewalk.

"Perhaps with a big house to take care of … and the gardens …" Roelke made a *You know* gesture.

Mona shook her head. "Bonnie loved her job. She had a knack for finding just the right style or color for customers. And she told me that she wanted to keep working after she got married. 'Simon wants me to quit,' she said, 'but I can't imagine not contributing anything to the family finances.'"

Lie number one, Roelke thought. Simon Sabatola had said Bonnie had wanted to quit her job. "Did you keep in touch after Bonnie left the dress shop?"

"I never saw her again." Mona took one last drag, dropped the cigarette onto the pavement, and ground it out beneath the toe of one shoe. "We talked once or twice on the phone. After awhile, though, the maid or whoever it was always said Bonnie wasn't home. She never returned any of my calls."

"Do you happen to know if Bonnie kept in touch with any other high school friends?"

"No, she pretty much disappeared." A new tear began dragging another black streak down Mona's cheek. "And then ... this. Now I wish I'd tried harder to stay in touch."

Roelke expressed his regret, and traded one of his business cards for Mona's contact information. "Sure, I'll call if I hear anything else," she told him. "But I doubt if I will. All of us—Bonnie's old high school friends—lost touch with her years ago."

TWENTY

CHLOE SPENT THE DAY after Bonnie's funeral cataloging artifacts in one of the old trailers that, for the time being, housed part of the historic site's collection. She'd recently completed a proposal for a new collections storage facility, and the site director was working on raising funds.

For now, simply organizing collections was an ongoing task. Some of Old World's objects had been donated directly to the site; some had been transferred from the state's collection back in 1976, when the historic site opened. Interpreters were permitted to actually use only a small subset of the artifacts in any given house, and those items needed to be unobtrusively but clearly identified. The financial gods in Madison had not yet budgeted a computer for the site. Wrestling the mélange of records she'd inherited into a concise and useful form was a task that would keep Chloe busy forever, if she chose to stay that long.

After the site closed, and she was free to drive her car onto the grounds, she locked the trailer and went in search of Dellyn. Chloe found her friend dead-heading zinnias in the narrow beds around the Hafford House, once the home of a widowed Irish woman who had made her way in the world by taking in laundry. "Hey," Chloe said, as she walked into the yard. "Pretty flowers."

Dellyn straightened. "Did you know that the Aztec name for zinnias meant 'eyesore'?"

"Um … no, I did not know that." Chloe surveyed the beautiful rainbow of flowers—orange, yellow, purple, red. "What were the Aztecs so cranky about?"

"The name meant they treated eye problems with it. The Spanish did too. They called the plant *mal de ojos*. The name we use today came from a German guy named Dr. Zinn who helped promote the flowers as ornamentals." Dellyn pulled off a few more dead blossoms. "There's your bit of garden trivia for the day."

Chloe watched her work for a moment. "Can't the interpreters do that?"

Dellyn wiped her hands on her stained apron. "In theory. But they can't keep up with everything."

"Neither can you," Chloe observed. Dellyn's cheeks looked hollow. Dark smudges beneath her eyes looked like bruises. "Dellyn, I'm worried about you. Your mom's garden, the inventory of your folks' collection, the Garden Fair, all the gardens here … it's too much to juggle at the best of times. Which this isn't."

Dellyn stared over the rest of the Crossroads Village. "I don't know if I even want to be head gardener at Old World Wisconsin anymore."

This is not good, Chloe thought. She tipped her head toward a nearby bench. "Let's take a break."

For a moment they sat in silence, savoring the peace of the site after-hours. Chloe watched a monarch butterfly dancing over the flowers. Finally Dellyn said, "Part of me wants to succeed as historic gardener. Part of me wants to get the heck out of town. But if I left, what would I do? The only things I'm much good at are waiting tables and planting seeds and pulling weeds."

"That's not true!" Chloe protested. "First of all, any historic site or public garden would welcome your knowledge. And on top of that, you're an artist!"

"At the moment, I'm not anything," Dellyn said. "I was a second-rate painter and a second-rate daughter and sister. Sometimes I think I should just sell my house and everything in it, and use the money for some kind of practical training."

"Like what?"

"I don't know. I'm not sure I even care. There's got to be a way I can pay my bills and still have enough time and energy left over to paint on weekends." She sighed. "I'm just so tired."

"Dellyn … you buried your sister yesterday," Chloe said. "Please give yourself time. Don't make any big decisions right now."

"I guess I don't need to decide right this minute." Dellyn shaded her eyes with one dirty hand. "What about you? You're sure you're OK after what happened in the barn?"

"One whopper of a bruise, but no real harm done." Chloe didn't want to dwell on the attack. "How are plans for the Garden Fair coming along?"

"Pretty well, despite everything. Harriet is making labels for the produce displays." Dellyn wiped sweat from her forehead with her apron. "And the interpreters are excited about choosing their best heirloom vegetables to represent their farms."

"A little competition is a good way to stir up the summer doldrums." Chloe had worked at historic sites for a long time. For summer hires—college students, mostly—the job that had seemed so romantic and fun in April sometimes got tedious by muggy mid-summer.

Dellyn arched her back, stretching out a kink. "And I asked Nika to take a look for any artifacts in storage that might work well on display."

Chloe was used to people asking her intern for help. Nika was a workaholic with an encyclopedic memory. "I can think of ... oh." Her voice trailed away as a muffled roar broke the afternoon's peace. A moment later Site Director Ralph Petty rode into view on a red motorcycle. Chloe willed him to keep going.

He didn't. Instead, he parked behind her car and walked down the path to join them.

Dellyn stood to meet him. "Hi, Mr. Petty."

"Hello, Dellyn." The site director turned to Chloe and added coolly, "Miss Ellefson."

Chloe flashed him her brightest, most chipper smile. "Actually, I prefer Ms."

Ralph Petty frowned at her. "As you know, Miss Ellefson, the auditors arrive in a few weeks. You will likely be drilled on procedures and policies. I just left in your mailbox a memo containing several random accession numbers from our collection. It will be good practice for you to check your records and verify the location of each artifact."

Chloe ground her teeth together. Didn't she have enough to do without Petty's petty make-work projects?

"Leave the results in my mailbox," he was saying. "In a timely manner."

Prick. "Okey-dokey," Chloe said. She flashed another smile, just to throw him off balance.

The director turned back to Dellyn. "I haven't had a chance to tell you how sorry I was to hear about your sister."

"I appreciate that."

"I also wanted to tell you how wonderful the gardens look." He gave a broad gesture, indicating that he meant all of the site's many gardens, not just those at the Hafford House. "You're doing a wonderful job, Dellyn. Truly wonderful."

"Thanks," Dellyn said a little dubiously. Ralph Petty wasn't inclined to give effusive praise. Or any praise, for that matter.

Chloe tried the mental-signal thing again, this time aiming it at her friend: *Don't bring up the fair. Don't bring up the fair.* She didn't want a more prolonged conversation.

Her telepathy didn't work any better than it had the first time. Dellyn added, "Plans for the Garden Fair are coming along nicely. I've spent several days working through old newspapers from the counties our farms came from."

"I applaud your incentive, Dellyn. That's *exactly* the spirit we need around here." Petty looked at Chloe.

Yeah, yeah, Chloe thought, as she nodded in agreement.

"Chloe's helping with the collections stuff," Dellyn said quickly.

"Good. Nothing can happen without teamwork. Keep up the wonderful work, Dellyn. Miss Ellefson." He strode back down the walkway, mounted his cycle, and roared away.

Chloe looked at her friend. "You're making me look bad, Dellyn. You know that, right?"

"That was not my plan." Dellyn looked troubled. "I'm sorry Petty's taking this audit stuff out on you."

"Don't worry. He just doesn't like me."

"I heard that he tried to fire your butt."

"Well, yeah. He did." Chloe spread her hands. "But the powers that be intervened. I'm still here."

"Your life might be easier if you didn't go out of your way to antagonize the man."

"It's just so instinctive!"

"I don't want you to get fired." Dellyn's voice quavered.

Chloe felt absurdly touched. "Hey, I'll try harder with Petty, OK?" she said. "Look, I like my job. I *need* my job. I'm not going anywhere."

"Sorry. I get weepy over everything these days."

"It's OK, really," Chloe said. "But, um, listen, Dellyn? You look exhausted. You've laid the groundwork for the fair. Maybe you should leave things to your volunteers, and the interpreters—"

"I don't *want* to leave things to other people. I need a break from going through the things in my parents' house. I need a break from my own thoughts. I need something to keep me so busy I can actually sleep at night."

Chloe watched a metallic green beetle lumber across the gravel path. She knew better than to think she understood how Dellyn felt, or what was the "right" way for her to deal with her problems. "I'll help you, OK?" she said at last. "We'll get it done."

———

Roelke answered a couple of minor calls that afternoon, and got back to the station twenty minutes before Marie left for the day.

The chief's door was closed. Marie was preparing paperwork for court. The radio on her desk was tuned to a station that grated his nerves—Lord, was that really the Bee Gees?

He reminded himself that he needed to curry Marie's favor. Complaining about her music wouldn't help. "Hey Marie," he said.

"Hello." Her voice was clipped. She didn't look up.

OK, she was still pissed. He pulled up a chair and sat at her elbow. "Marie, I need your help," he said, hoping he sounded humble.

She stopped typing, turned her chair to face him, crossed her arms, and waited.

"I visited Sonia Padopolous yesterday. She lives—"

"I know where she lives."

Of course she did. Marie had lived in Eagle all her life. Unlike him. "She seemed nervous. Not about the break-in next door, I mean. Nervous to be talking to a cop."

"Probably because of Alex," Marie said promptly.

Roelke sent up a quick, silent prayer that Marie would never retire. "And Alex is … ?"

"Her son."

He felt his eyebrows rise. "Her son? I asked about children, and she most definitely did not mention a son."

"Alexander Padopolous." Marie nodded slowly. "I haven't seen him in years. He must be … oh, thirty by now. He raised hell when he was still living at home. Put poor Sonia through the wringer."

"What kind of hell?"

The straight line of Marie's shoulders eased a bit. "Teen stuff, mostly. Speeding, DUI. But some petty larceny, too. Shoplifting."

Well, hunh. Roelke thought that over.

"Last time I saw Alex was likely three or four years ago," Marie said. "Sonia and I were teaching Sunday School, and I dropped by with some curriculum materials. Alex was lying on the sofa with a beer can in one hand, watching TV. He looked like he hadn't showered in a week." Her nose wrinkled. "I could tell Sonia was mortified."

"Her place today was neat as the legendary pin," Roelke said, trying to project empathy.

"I told Sonia later that she needed to put her foot down with Alex. There was nothing wrong with that boy but pure laziness. He had a chip on his shoulder big enough to fell an ox." Marie tightened her lips for a moment. "Maybe it came from growing up without his dad around. That's hard on any kid. But enough was enough."

"What did she say?"

"Not much at the time. But within a month, Alex was gone. He moved up to Waukesha."

The phone rang. "Marie, thank you," Roelke said quickly. "I really appreciate your help."

She gave him an all-is-forgiven smile.

Roelke thought about what he'd learned. Sonia Padopolous, widowed young, left to raise a lazy, troublemaker son. Could Alex Padopolous have been the prowler at Dellyn Burke's place? The prowler who had chosen to attack Chloe, rather than slip away into darkness? Might Alex Padopolous have been looking for the Eagle Diamond?

It was a stupid idea. Absurd, even. And yet … not completely impossible, either. An article had recently been published about the missing diamond. Alex had grown up next to the Burkes. He would know they collected local history stuff. He would likely even know his way around the barn.

Roelke always kept personal notes on index cards. He liked the form, the ability to shuffle, the ease of pulling them in and out of pockets. He grabbed one and began to write.

Alex Padopolous
—still in trouble?
—possibly saw article in Wisconsin Byways?
—need to

The chief's door opened. Roelke hunched his shoulders like a child afraid of being caught writing a note in class.

"Nice work, son," Chief Naborski was saying, as he and Skeet emerged from the office. Naborski clapped Skeet on the shoulder.

Chief Naborski didn't dish up praise with a generous spoon. And shoulder claps—those were even more rare. Roelke's last bit of tangible praise from the chief had been accompanied by a disciplinary letter, after a complicated mess with Chloe and a missing antique back in June.

The chief nodded a greeting before disappearing back into his office. Roelke stared at the closed door. The muscles between his shoulders bunched. He wanted that full-time job. Wanted it bad. But Skeet was evidently doing what he needed to do to win it.

"Roelke," Marie called. She was holding the phone. "There's a couple of kids skateboarding on Chinaberry Circle. Mrs. Lennox is afraid they'll get hit by a car."

Chinaberry Circle was a cul-de-sac at the end of one of the quietest residential streets in the village. In the county, likely. But Mrs. Lennox called the station at least once a week. She'd once called for help after a junco stunned itself by flying into her kitchen window.

Maybe I *should* go back to Milwaukee, Roelke thought.

But … no. He'd thought that through. Made his choices. He was where he wanted to be.

"I got it," he told Marie, and reached for the car keys.

TWENTY-ONE

When his shift ended Roelke didn't really *decide* to drive to Chloe's house. He just sort of found his truck headed in that direction. Early evening's soft light muted the landscape's colors as he drove the twisting road through the Kettle Moraine.

When he pulled into Chloe's driveway, he was relieved to see only her old Pinto in the driveway. No sign of Alpine Boy. But … that only meant the problem was avoided, not erased. He set his jaw. Chloe needed to decide who she wanted to spend time with, dammit. Maybe he should just say so. He'd been patient. He didn't deserve to be—

Chloe stepped out on the front porch to meet him. She wore faded jeans and a shapeless red T-shirt, an off-hand combination that struck him as incredibly hot.

He struggled to keep his mind where it belonged. "Hey."

"Hey."

"Listen, I'm sorry I didn't call first, but … anyway. Can I come in?"

"I suppose so." Chloe opened the screened door and gestured him inside. "Watch out for Olympia. She has a habit of getting underfoot." Hearing her name, the kitten shot from the kitchen. Her trajectory altered when she spotted a fly banging against one of the windows.

"Why did you name her Olympia?"

"Olympia Brown was a Unitarian minister. I think she was the first woman to be formally ordained, back in the 1860s or '70s. She served in Wisconsin."

Roelke had never heard of Olympia Brown. Or Unitarians. He silently trailed Chloe into the living room.

The farmhouse Chloe rented was huge for one person, but it had finally taken on some identity: books on the shelves, a colorful rag rug on the floor. It was a curator's space—a canning jar on the windowsill held wildflowers, an old iron did bookend duty, and a painted trunk served as her coffee table. The personal items she'd chosen to display included a cobalt bowl of stones, a hummingbird's nest displayed in a crystal shot glass, a huge pinecone.

"Those can't be easy to dust," Roelke said, gesturing toward the treasures.

Chloe rolled her eyes. "Could you be any more German?"

Roelke ignored that, his attention caught by mementos of Switzerland—a cuckoo clock, a delicate alpine scene silhouette cut from black paper, several photographs that showed pretty chalets with overflowing window boxes. A record playing on the stereo suggested people in ethnic costumes dancing to the bouncy strains of fiddle and accordion. If someone starts yodeling, Roelke thought, I'm outta here.

Chloe dropped into her brown easy chair. "Did you want something?"

Roelke perched on the edge of her sofa. "Look, I don't like the way things got left the night you got attacked. And I didn't mean to ignore you at the funeral. I was watching Sabatola, that's all."

"Oh." She studied him for a moment. Some of the tension seemed to drain from her posture. "OK."

Relieved, Roelke leaned forward, resting his forearms on his thighs. "Listen, I'm keeping a sharp eye on Dellyn's place. The other guys are, too."

"Good," Chloe said fervently. "It makes me sick to think that Dellyn might stumble across whoever it was that tried to bash me in the skull."

"Yeah."

"I was about to start supper when I heard your truck," she said. "You want to stay?"

"What's on the menu?"

"Popcorn and Oreos."

"*Chloe*—"

"Oh, lighten up, would you?" She got up and headed toward the kitchen. "How about lentil stew and a tossed salad?"

He followed her. "I have known you to skip meals altogether," he observed defensively. "I wouldn't be surprised if—"

"Yeah, yeah." Chloe filled a pot with water and put it on the stove.

"Can I help?"

"No, thanks, I've got it." She disappeared behind the refrigerator door, then emerged holding a bulb of garlic and an onion.

Roelke leaned against the wall and watched her work. "Is Dellyn doing OK?"

Chloe used the back of her knife to sweep translucent bits of onion into a bowl. "She's running on empty. She's talking about packing up and moving away. Somewhere."

"I'm sure you'd miss her."

"I would." Chloe minced the final slices. "And it would be a terrible loss for Old World, too."

Roelke was still staring at Chloe's hands. Her fingers were long, slender, graceful even as they chopped the garlic. "Well, she's just a gardener, right?"

Chloe straightened. "Just a gardener? What's that supposed to mean?"

Oh, hell. "Nothing! It's just that … well, I'm sure Dellyn is a really *good* gardener, but lots of people are, right? If she did leave—I mean, I know you'd miss your friend—but it wouldn't be all that hard to find someone else to—"

"You have no idea what you're talking about," Chloe snapped. "Dellyn is in charge of a dozen gardens, which represent a variety of ethnic groups, 1845 to 1915. She has to know what varieties of vegetables Finlanders planted in the cutover up north, and what progressive Yankee housewives planted in the southeast corner of the state."

"OK, I get it."

"She needs to find and propagate heirloom varieties of vegetables and fruits and flowers for each specific garden. She needs to consider whether German-speaking immigrants from Pomerania planted their gardens differently than German-speaking immigrants from Hesse-Darmstadt. She needs to understand how to control pests using historical methods. She needs to work with the interpreters to be sure the gardens support the foodways program. And then she needs to develop programs to help visitors understand the implications of—"

"O-*kay!*" Roelke held up both hands. "I don't know what I'm talking about. I *get* it." And Alpine Boy, no doubt, would have gotten it from the start.

The awkward silence between them was broken by the tiny hiss of steam as the water on the stove began to simmer. Roelke's gaze fell on a line of bird feathers arrayed on a shelf of cookbooks. He picked up a crimson plume. Cardinal, surely. "Where did you get this?"

"The back yard. Why?"

"Did you know it's illegal to have songbird feathers in your possession?"

Chloe's eyes narrowed. Her mouth got tight. Her chin jutted forward. "Why are you being such an asshole?"

Roelke didn't answer. He had no idea why he was being such an asshole.

"I think you should leave now." She crossed her arms over her chest, the big knife still clutched in one fist.

Roelke opened his mouth, closed it again, and departed.

———

Once Roelke's truck had disappeared, Chloe turned off the stove. "Shit," she muttered. She paced for a few moments, then went to the telephone and dialed a familiar number. "Ethan? It's me. Did I catch you at a bad time?"

"No, it's good, actually. I'm probably going to get called out in the next day or so. Looks like we've got a bad one in Montana."

"Oh." Ethan was a fire jumper. Scary stuff. "Well, I just called to announce that I hate men."

Pause. "Does that pronouncement include me?"

Chloe pulled her feet up on the cushion. "Unless you are prepared to skip the fire, fly to Milwaukee tonight, drive out here, and marry me, then you, too are on my list."

"What's going on?"

"Roelke just left. I swear, Ethan, we can't get through a conversation without fighting."

"Why?"

OK, a person about to drop into an inferno didn't have time to waste on the extraneous. "He … he just doesn't *get* me, Ethan. He doesn't get what I do. I'm worried about my friend Dellyn, and Roelke just blew it off." OK, that wasn't quite fair. "He blew off the importance of her job, anyway. He has no idea …" Her voice trailed away as it occurred to her that Ethan, her dearest friend in the world, wouldn't understand the demands of Dellyn's job either. Chloe leaned her head back against the chair, and closed her eyes.

"How did you react to that?"

Chloe was beginning to wish she hadn't called. "Well … I may have overreacted. Just a little bit." She hadn't been fair. She didn't know the ins-and-outs of police work. Why should she be angry— or even surprised—because Roelke didn't understand historic site work?

"Listen, sweetie, I can't sort this out for you. If being with Roelke makes you happy, spend time with him. If it doesn't, don't."

"It sounds so simple when you put it like that."

Ethan laughed, his voice warm and comforting through the wire. "Easy for me to say, hunh?"

"Tell me about you. Tell me about the fire."

They talked for ten minutes more before hanging up. The world beyond her windows was blurring into blue-black shadows. Olympia had fallen asleep on the carpet. Chloe sat, thinking about Roelke and Markus. Thinking about Dellyn.

All through college and grad school, Chloe had taken a different summer job each year. She loved seasonal work. She loved heading to new places. Going to Switzerland had been the grandest adventure of them all. Markus had done a terrible thing by dumping her when she needed him most. But before her miscarriage, she had never felt a need to press for any kind of commitment, either.

Her miscarriage had started a hellish year, but she'd pulled herself out of it. With lots of help from Ethan, and even some from Roelke, she'd turned her emotional corner. She had almost lost her job at Old World Wisconsin ... but not quite. She and Ralph Petty would never get along well, but she was truly trying to get through probation, and to lock down the job for good. A real job. A permanent job, with health insurance and everything.

And sometimes, that made her feel old. Was she losing something special? Would having a stable relationship make her feel better about herself right now, or worse?

"I have no freaking idea," Chloe told Olympia. "Let's go make dinner." Before she could move, the phone's jangle made her jump.

"It's Markus," her ex said. "I wanted to give you one more chance to come along when I go back to see the Frietags."

The Frietags, some wise and wonderful elderly people. "Yeah," Chloe told him. "I'd like that."

TWENTY-TWO

THE NEXT MORNING ROELKE was in Waukesha by 8 AM, with a couple of hours free before his shift started. He parked in front of Alex Padopolous's last-known residence. The tired brick building had been divided into flats, but several catalogs bursting from one of the mailboxes said *Alex Padopolous, 1A* in the address line.

Roelke's knock went unanswered. No surprise there. If Alex Padopolous was still living on the wild side, there was a good chance that he was either hung-over at this hour or reluctant to open the door to a cop. Roelke banged again.

"He's gone."

Roelke turned and regarded an elderly woman shuffling down the sidewalk with the tiniest Chihuahua he'd ever seen. Her hair was in curlers, which wasn't as common on the streets as it used to be.

"Are you referring to Alex Padopolous, ma'am?" He joined her on the sidewalk, keeping a wary eye on the dog. Chihuahuas weren't called ankle-biters for nothing.

"Is he in some kind of trouble?" The woman pulled a pack of cigarettes and a lighter from her pocket.

"No ma'am. I just want to talk with him."

She lit up, inhaled, and blew a long plume of smoke. "Well, I haven't seen him for two days."

Two days, hunh? Roelke thought that over. "Is that unusual?"

"Oh, yes. Noisiest neighbor I've ever had. Usually he's booming his music at all hours, drinking beer on the porch with his buddies. I hope he's gone for good."

"Do you happen to know where Mr. Padopolous works?"

"Ace Auto Repair, two blocks down. I heard Padopolous lost his license for a while, had to walk to work." The woman shook her head. "Too bad there's a handful of taverns within walking distance, too."

"Thank you, ma'am," Roelke said politely. "I appreciate your help." He watched the woman resume her walk, with the Chihuahua pattering along beside her. Nosy neighbors, he thought. Gotta love 'em.

Next stop, Ace Auto Repair. It was a busy shop, with a car on all three lifts and every parking space full. Roelke's uniform brought the owner from a back corner, wiping his hands on a greasy rag. "Alex Padopolous?" he barked, in response to Roelke's question. "Shit."

"Is there some problem, sir?"

"Damn straight there's a problem. Hasn't showed up for work for the last two days. Didn't even call in."

The other mechanic on duty began loosening a Chevy's lug nuts with an impact wrench. Roelke shouted, "Has he been a reliable employee in the past?"

"Been late a bunch of times. Knew his way around an engine, though, so I've been willing to give him a chance. But this shit? Unless he's got a damn good excuse, I'm gonna fire his sorry ass."

"Thanks for your time," Roelke said. "I'll let you get back to work."

He headed back to Eagle. Alex Padopolous had been AWOL for two days. That meant he'd disappeared right about the time someone had almost killed Chloe in Dellyn Burke's barn.

Forty minutes later Roelke pulled back into Sonia Padopolous's driveway. Time to pay Mama another visit.

This time Sonia answered the front door, and greeted him with a startled "Oh!" She did not invite him in. Or offer him cookies, thank God.

Roelke gave her his polite cop smile. "I'm sorry to bother you again, Mrs. Padopolous. May I come inside?"

"Is something wrong?" She kept her body wedged in the small opening she'd created when opening the door.

"I don't know, ma'am. I had hoped to speak to your son this morning. But Alex's neighbors and his boss haven't seen him in two days."

"Why do you want to speak to Alex?" Sonia's voice quavered.

"I need to ask him some questions. When was the last time you saw him?"

"Saw Alex? Well, let me think." She stared over his shoulder for a moment, as if a response required a mighty effort. "A week or so ago, I guess. Closer to two. I was running some errands in Waukesha and stopped by his apartment."

"Have you spoken to him since then? Has he telephoned?"

She shook her head emphatically. "No. That's not unusual. He … he gets busy."

"Do you have any idea where he might be?"

"No."

"Do you have the names of any friends I might call?"

"No, I don't. I'm sorry. I—I really can't help you." Sonia closed the door. The deadbolt rattled, as if she feared Roelke might follow her.

Well, hunh, Roelke thought, as he headed back to the squad car. Sonia Padopolous was a terrible liar.

———

That evening, Chloe took one last look around the living room. Flat surfaces swiped with a dust cloth, kitten toys mostly returned to their basket—check. Fresh-baked cheese straws, chocolate-dipped strawberries, napkins, and wine goblets arrayed on the trunk/coffee table—check.

When Libby had talked Chloe into joining the little "wine and whine" writers' circle, she'd been dubious. To her surprise, she actually enjoyed the gatherings. At their last meeting Chloe had impulsively offered to host. It was the first time she'd hosted any gathering since leaving Switzerland. She didn't want to go nuts. But it would be nice if the evening went well.

Besides, Valerie Bing was coming. She and the writing group members would be getting acquainted, but Chloe wanted to find out what Valerie might know about the Eagle Diamond that had *not* made it into her article.

She slapped her palms on her jeans. "I think we're good to go," she told Olympia.

Olympia urped a hairball onto the carpet. Chloe had just enough time to clean up before the first car pulled into the driveway.

Fifteen minutes later the regulars were settled in: Libby, who earned her living as a freelance writer; Hilda, retired schoolteacher and poet; and Gina, a plump mother-of-three who wrote science fiction novels. "Is Dellyn coming?" Gina asked.

Libby shook her head. "I tried to talk her into it."

"How about you?" Gina asked Chloe. "Do you have anything to share this time?"

"No," Chloe said guiltily. She had been well into her first historical novel when she lived in Switzerland, but she'd burned it when she and Markus broke up. "Want a strawberry?"

Hilda looked over pale blue half-glasses reprovingly. "Writers write, Chloe. You can revise bad writing. You can't do anything with blank pages."

"I know." Chloe handed her a glass of Chablis. "Oh, look! That must be Valerie pulling in."

Valerie Bing was tall and willowy, with honey-colored hair clipped back with a red barrette. The barrette completed an *ensemble*: jeans so stylish they could only be designer, a scarlet linen jacket over matching tank, and red high-heeled pumps. *Very* high, Chloe thought, trying not to stare. And pointy-toed. Ouch.

"Welcome," Libby said, once introductions were made. "Glad you could join us. You're new to the area, right?"

"Newly returned," Valerie allowed, as she perched on the edge of an armchair. "I grew up near here. Eagle, actually. But I moved to Manhattan after college."

Gina wriggled, settling more comfortably into the sofa. "So, what brought you back to Wisconsin?"

"A divorce. And since you're no doubt wondering, here it is: Four months ago I was assistant editor at *Stylish Women* magazine. I also had a brand-spanking-new MFA in Poetry. Then my marriage fell apart, I was publicly humiliated, I ended up with nothing but a lot of student loans, and I moved back into my parents' house. Yes, my *parents'* house."

Libby, Hilda, and Gina met that recital with the raised eyebrows and blank expressions of people who have no idea what to say.

OK, Chloe thought. Inviting Valerie here was a bad idea. And it was *my* idea. Me, the new kid in the group, already on thin ice for never bringing any writing to share. And on top of that, this bristling urbanite seemed an unlikely source of detailed information about the Eagle Diamond. Lovely.

Libby broke the awkward silence. "Did you bring pages to share?"

"Two new poems. Chloe said you're a mixed-genre group."

"Two poems will suffice," Hilda said primly. "Let's get to work."

———

Roxie's Roost looked a little seedier than Roelke remembered it. The frame building could use a fresh coat of paint. The neon Blatz sign in the front window was missing its final two letters. BLA, the sign promised, with ironic humor. Roelke's old red-and-white Ford Ranger pickup didn't have an NRA or Ducks Unlimited sticker, just one for Milwaukee's Summerfest. But he gauged it inconspicuous enough to blend in anyway.

This will probably prove to be a huge waste of time, Roelke thought, as he opened the front door. He couldn't imagine Edwin Guest frequenting the place. And even if Guest liked to leave high business society behind and relax with a cold one every week, he wasn't likely to turn blubbering informant. The secretary would probably realize that Roelke had seen the notation on his calendar, get even more pissed than he generally seemed to be, and leave again.

Well, so what? Sometimes it was good to stir things up and simply see what happened.

Once inside Roelke took a quick visual survey. The L-shaped bar stretched most of the length of the dim room. A couple guys wearing the bright orange vests of road construction workers sat at the middle of the bar, arguing about the Milwaukee Brewers' chances of making the playoffs. A few patrons hunched over beers at tables. Five older women were engrossed in an animated game of Sheepshead. The room smelled of cigarette smoke and fried onions.

"Can I help you?"

Roelke turned toward the woman behind the bar, and hoped he hid his surprise. He'd seen her before. At Bonnie Sabatola's funeral. Arguing with Simon Sabatola in the parking lot.

Holy toboggans. This was already interesting.

"Sure," he told her. "Miller Draft. And a glass of water." He slouched toward the long bar, and took the stool beside the wall.

The woman filled a glass stein and put it down in front of him. Her eyes held no hint of recognition. And why would they? He'd been wearing a suit at the funeral, and now was dressed in his oldest jeans and a faded T-shirt. And at the funeral, this woman had clearly been interested only in Simon Sabatola.

Roelke fished a five from his pocket. "Are you Roxie?"

"That's me." She slid a dish of peanuts his way. "You new around here?"

Her words had the intonation of someone asking an obligatory question. She sounded tired. Looked it, too. Blue Christmas-type lights twinkled above the bar, but even in that sallow light Roxie had the look of a woman who'd lived hard. Her skin was crinkled, her eyes narrowed, her shoulders bowed.

"I live in Palmyra." Roelke echoed her tone of polite disinterest. Requirements complete, Roxie left him alone.

Roelke sat sideways on the stool, back to the wall, left cheek propped on his left hand. He consciously mimicked the posture of a thousand drunks he'd seen in too many bars, trying to drown sorrows real and imagined. And I do have a few sorrows of my own, he thought, as an hour inched by without anything else of interest presenting itself. His love life was in the crapper. His professional life might be too, if the Police Committee chose to give the permanent position to Skeet. If only—

The door opened. Roelke slid his gaze in that direction as Simon Sabatola sauntered inside. The screened door slapped closed behind him.

Sabatola! Not Guest. Curiouser and curiouser. Roelke looked back at the remains of his carefully nursed beer. Sabatola settled on the bar stool farthest away from him.

Roxie folded her arms and stood for a long moment, staring at Sabatola. Evidently she was still pissed about whatever they'd argued about in the parking lot. Finally, unasked, she poured a glass of whiskey and deposited it in front of Sabatola.

Roelke watched the pair for the next hour or so. Roxie tended to other customers as needed, but in quiet moments she gravitated toward the far end of the bar. Her back was to Roelke, but her posture remained rigid. Roelke couldn't make out anything over the increasingly boisterous conversation between the road crew workers, but from what he could see of Sabatola's face, the businessman wasn't nearly as upset about *whatever* as the bartender was.

So … what does that tell you? he asked himself. Squat, actually, interesting as it was. Sabatola was involved with this woman in some way. An affair? Roxie didn't seem like Sabatola's type—but maybe that was the attraction.

"Tens take Kings," one of the card players said loudly. Roelke watched a young woman across the room stack dirty glasses on a tray, thinking. Maybe getting it on with a struggling tavern keeper represented something exciting for Sabatola. And maybe Bonnie had discovered that. If Bonnie was already struggling with depression and marital problems, learning of an affair might have pushed her over the edge.

He had no way to prove that little theory, though. And last time he checked, adultery wasn't a felony.

Sabatola had tossed back at least three whiskeys before he needed to visit the can. As he passed Roelke, Sabatola paused. "Officer McKenna?"

Roelke sighed audibly, looked up, and made a show of registering surprise. "Oh—Mr. Sabatola! Excuse me, sir, I didn't realize it was you."

"What are you doing here?" Sabatola rotated the glass he still held. The ice cubes made a tinkling sound.

Roelke shrugged. "Just needed a drink, you know?"

"Why here?"

"Well, I live in Palmyra and work in Eagle." Roelke took a drink and wiped his mouth with the back of his hand. "Drinking in the communities where you're recognized as a cop isn't the best idea. Sometimes a guy just needs a quiet beer. Without being judged for it, you know?"

Sabatola leaned one elbow against the bar. "I'm with you there." He tossed back the last of his whiskey and snapped his fingers in Roxie's direction. "Something in particular got you troubled, officer?"

"Please—just call me Roelke. As for what's got me down ..." Roelke hesitated. He sometimes used pretense while on duty, but he'd never pushed anything this far. And Lawrence Olivier, he was not.

Roxie provided a brief reprieve as she silently poured another whiskey. Sabatola threw half of it down his throat without blinking.

That eased Roelke over his moment of doubt. He was used to dealing with drunks. Sabatola might not show it, but he *had* to be getting schnockered.

"Just a woman thing," Roelke said morosely. Then he looked up, oozing contrition. "Oh, God—my apologies. That was thoughtless. My little problems are nothing, compared to ..."

"No, don't worry." Sabatola waved one hand. "It's all right."

Roelke grabbed a peanut and crushed it in his fingers. "I just don't understand women!"

"None of us do."

"You try to treat them right, but sometimes they're just never satisfied."

Sabatola stared into his glass. Too far, too fast, Roelke berated himself. He planted his elbow on the bar and his cheek on his hand, striving for the "I'm too dejected to speak further" look.

The men in construction vests erupted into laughter. A very fat man wearing a biker's black leather came into the tavern and waddled to a table. "Sixty-one! Sixty-one!" a woman crowed triumphantly from the card players' table.

Finally Sabatola clapped Roelke's shoulder in masculine solidarity. "You're right," he said. "Women are never, *ever*, satisfied."

"Can you give me some advice?" Roelke asked. "I don't earn a lot of money. I like being a cop, but I've been thinking that maybe I should go back to school. Get some kind of degree. My girlfriend ... she's got a Master's degree, for Chrissake."

"What in?"

"Um ... what?"

"What's her degree in?" Sabatola asked patiently.

"History. She likes old stuff."

Sabatola smiled. "She may have an advanced degree, my friend, but it's in a useless field. You go back to school and study business. Something useful. Something where a guy can apply himself and get ahead. Work your ass off. One day you'll look around and realize that *no* one has anything on you." With that he downed the rest of the whiskey, slammed the glass down on the counter, and disappeared into the restroom.

Sabatola didn't speak to Roelke again, although he stayed at Roxie's Roost for another forty minutes. He left at ten PM sharp.

Roelke surreptitiously watched out the front window. He'd intervene if he had to, because no way was Sabatola fit to drive. But a car immediately pulled up. Sabatola got in. The car disappeared.

That explained why Edwin Guest had *Roxie's R.* written on his own calendar. Evidently Sabatola indulged in a weekly binge, and evidently Guest's secretarial duties extended beyond the office.

"Another beer?" Roxie asked.

Roelke hesitated, then nodded. "Sure." He didn't want another beer, but he also didn't want it to appear that his business here was done at the exact moment that Simon Sabatola left. "And another glass of water, too."

He hit the can himself, and got back to his stool just as Roxie was depositing the drinks. "Thanks," Roelke said. He fished out another bill and tossed it on the bar. "Keep the change."

Roxie pocketed the bill silently, regarding him. "So, you know Simon?"

"We've met. Can't say I know him well."

"How'd you meet him?" Roxie's voice was tight. With challenge? Or maybe just irritation? Hard to say.

Roelke gave her an even gaze. "I'm a cop. Up in Eagle. When Mr. Sabatola's wife committed suicide, I was first on the scene."

"Oh, Lord." Roxie looked away. "That must have been ugly."

"Yeah. So like I said, I hardly know him well. Have you known him long?"

Roxie blinked. "You could say that. We grew up together."

"Here in Elkhorn?" Roelke asked, trying to sound bored.

"Yeah. Me and Simon lived next door."

"So you must know Alan Sabatola too."

She hitched one shoulder up and down, as if shrugging both would take too much energy. "I never really got to know Alan. He's younger than Simon. Simon's mother left when he was eight. Just took off one day. After awhile Mr. Sabatola got married again. That's when Alan got born."

Roelke frowned, trying to reconstruct Sabatola's family tree. "So Simon's father—"

"Mr. Sabatola was Simon's stepfather. Simon's real dad died when he was a baby."

Roelke chewed that over. "Mr. Sabatola—Simon, I mean—gave me some good advice earlier. I would have figured a rich guy like that couldn't understand what a working guy like me has to deal with."

Roxie snorted. "Simon wasn't always rich, believe me. Before that farm stuff business took off, the Sabatolas were scraping by just like the rest of us."

"I wouldn't have guessed that."

"Yeah. They all moved into a new house on the other side of town. Very la-di-da. But we still went to the same high school. Me and Simon and Edwin."

"Yeah, I've met him too." Roelke took a drink, disinterested.

Roxie glanced over her shoulder, then called to the young woman he'd noticed earlier. "Kiki, honey? Check on them, OK?" She jerked her head toward the card players.

Kiki nodded. She wore her long dark hair loose, so it was hard to see her face clearly, but she looked too young to be working in a tavern. Let it go, Roelke counseled himself. Let it go.

Roxie leaned against the bar. "Edwin had it the worst. He and his family lived in their car for a little while. I remember one winter he got sick and if this old lady down the block hadn't taken him in and given him some herbal tea or something, and a place to rest … well, who knows. And a year or two after that he showed up in school wearing a pajama top instead of a shirt. All Goodwill had to fit him, I guess."

Ouch, Roelke thought. He didn't care for Guest, but he could easily imagine what adolescents would make of *that*.

"But he was real smart," Roxie was saying. "A science nerd, always getting good grades. And look at him now."

"Was Mr. Sabatola a good student, too?" Roelke asked. "I mean, I'm just a cop. I can't imagine taking over a big business like Agri-Futures."

"Mr. Sabatola rode Simon pretty hard," Roxie said. "Simon never was a genius or anything. But he studied a lot."

"Ah."

Roxie smiled. The change was abrupt and transforming. "I was a cheerleader," she told him. "I didn't make varsity. Varsity was full of snobs. But I made J-V. I was good, too."

"I bet you were." Roelke smiled back. It was painful to glimpse this woman as she must have been in those days. Pretty and full of energy. Edwin and Simon had climbed into big business. Whatever relationship Roxie still maintained with Simon couldn't change the fact that she ran a bar.

"Well, that was a long time ago." Roxie's smile, and the loveliness, faded as quickly as it had come. She went back to work.

Roelke left a generous tip and headed for his truck. Before starting the engine he paused. He felt fine, but he hated getting behind the wheel after drinking *anything* alcoholic. It was a personal policy thing. Maybe he should call somebody.

But who? Libby would have to arrange for child care to come get him. And Chloe ... well, no way was he going to ask Chloe to pick him up at a bar.

"I'm all right," he muttered. He'd take it easy. Stick to secondary roads. County Highway H, which sliced through farmland, would get him back to Palmyra. It was late—going on eleven—and there wouldn't be much traffic.

Roelke felt a flush of satisfaction as he pulled out of the parking lot. "Childhood buddies," he mused, as he headed northwest. Maybe Roxie had played a role in whatever troubles led Bonnie, with gun in hand, to the White Oak Trail that day. But he couldn't help feeling sorry for a woman who gloried in memories of the J-V cheering squad while serving drinks in a dingy bar.

Lights appeared in Roelke's rearview mirror as some idiot zoomed up behind him. A kid trying to beat his curfew, probably. The road ahead was clear. Roelke eased toward the right shoulder so Mario Andretti could pass.

Andretti didn't pass, though. Instead he flashed his high beams several times.

"Asshole!" Roelke muttered. Why the hell didn't the driver just—

Suddenly more bright lights appeared in front of his truck. Too close, too brilliant, blinding him. "What the fu—" Roelke began, braking hard.

The lights disappeared, front and back, and the rear end of Roelke's truck thumped off the pavement. He felt a flash of panic: he was losing control of the vehicle.

Some part of his brain knew he had only seconds to avoid a crash. The fear disappeared. In the dashboard's faint glow he stared at his hands on the steering wheel. He thought about which way to turn the wheel, flashing back to skid practices on icy parking lots with his dad; more practices at the police academy. OK, he thought. Turn wheel slightly right, not left.

It didn't work. The right front of the Ranger was on the shoulder now. The shoulder was too soft. It dropped toward the ditch too quickly.

I'm going to crash, Roelke thought. Should he shield his face, or keep both hands on the wheel? Shield his head. And lean away from the steering column. He'd seen what they could do to a driver.

Roelke let go of the wheel when the pickup lurched sideways. It slammed on its side. Continued to roll. I'm upside down, he thought with wonder, as the truck cab flipped on its roof. He had the sense that the truck was going to keep rolling, over and over and over.

Then the driver' side of the truck struck earth, and Roelke's head struck glass.

TWENTY-THREE

To Chloe's amazement, the evening was not a total train wreck. Valerie proved herself a skillful critiquer, stressing positives and presenting suggestions for improvement that left each author feeling energized instead of beaten down. No mean feat.

"Stay a few minutes, will you?" Chloe asked Valerie, as the others began tucking notepads and folders into tote bags.

Valerie slipped the file folder holding her poems into the leather briefcase she'd brought. "Thanks for inviting me," she said, when she and Chloe were alone. "Your call came as a total surprise."

Chloe began carrying glasses into the kitchen. "Well, like I told you on the phone, Dellyn Burke gave me your number. She showed me the article you wrote about the Eagle Diamond."

"Oh. That one." Valerie picked up the snack plates and followed her.

"I liked it!" Chloe assured her.

Valerie twisted her mouth in distaste. "Local history fluff pieces for *Wisconsin Byways* wasn't quite the direction I expected my career to take."

"Stuff happens."

"Yeah." Valerie picked up the last cheese straw and nibbled at one end.

Chloe hesitated. She didn't want to set Valerie off again. She also did not want to let the evening pass without trying for more insight into the Eagle Diamond stuff. "You knew about the diamond story because you grew up in Eagle, I assume?"

"Right. I was looking for something quick and easy. I pitched over the phone, and the editor jumped at it."

Olympia bounded into the kitchen and sniffed at a golden crumb of cheddar cheese on the floor before happily gobbling it down. Chloe hoped that the kitten would at least wait until Valerie left before she decided that tidbit didn't suit her delicate digestion. "I'd never heard of the diamond until Dellyn mentioned it. Did you find anything in your research to suggest that it might have somehow made its way back to Eagle?"

Valerie crouched on her red spike heels and let Olympia sniff her fingers. "Heavens, no. I did some legwork at the state historical society, but didn't turn up anything to suggest that. I don't think anyone has a clue what happened to the Eagle Diamond after it was stolen. Cut into smaller pieces and sold, almost certainly."

"What did you learn about the guy who found it? Any handy memoirs left behind?"

"Hardly. There's little to go on except newspaper accounts, and a photocopy of an appraisal."

Dellyn's parents must have provided the photocopy of Kunz's appraisal to the state historical society, Chloe thought. Good for them.

"No one interviewed Charles Wood about it," Valerie added. "Or the hired hand, either."

"Um ... what?" Chloe turned around and leaned against the sink. "There was a hired man? That wasn't in your article."

"I had a word limit, and the hired man wasn't important," Valerie said. She looked at Chloe with narrowed eyes. "Why all the questions?"

"Just curious." Chloe gave her a bright smile. "I love that kind of stuff. And since Dellyn's parents were so involved in the Eagle Historical Society, and I'm helping Dellyn sort through their things ... The story caught my attention. Must be my novelist brain, leaping into overdrive."

Olympia wandered away, and Valerie straightened again. "It was a shame about Mr. and Mrs. Burke. Dellyn's going through their stuff?"

"Yeah. In her spare time. It's slow going, I'm afraid." Chloe began rinsing plates. "So, what happened in Eagle after they learned the stone the guy found was actually a diamond?"

"Everyone thought it was just a lucky fluke. A geological gift, not to be repeated."

"Anything else pop up in your research? Any little tidbit that didn't make it into the article?"

Valerie spread her hands, showing a flash of brightly polished nails. Crimson, of course. "Sorry. Not a thing. A diamond was found. A woman got cheated. A jewel thief made a fortune. End of story."

Chloe walked her guest outside. They'd reached the car when Chloe suddenly thought of something else. "You went to school with Bonnie Sabatola, right?"

"We were in the same class. I was really shocked to hear about what happened."

"Were you good friends?"

"Not best friends, anything like that. But we had a small class. Everyone knew each other. Bonnie and I stayed in touch until she got married."

"What happened after that?"

"Nothing. I was in New York, and didn't make it to the wedding. I sent a gift, and she sent a thank-you, and that was that. I sent Christmas cards for a couple of years, that kind of thing. But I never heard from her again." Valerie opened the car door, and slid inside. She started the engine... and then she sat, staring through the windshield, making no move to put the car in gear. Finally she looked up through the open window. "Listen, I—I hope I didn't mess up the evening."

"No!" Chloe said, striving for hearty cheer. "Of course not."

"I don't like myself very much these days," Valerie said. "But I discovered tonight that I do still care about poetry. Thanks for that."

Chloe was still groping for a response when Valerie pulled away. Chloe watched her turn back toward Eagle, back to her old bedroom in her parents' house. If members of the Wine and Whine Critique Group were willing to let Valerie come again, it might be a good thing for her. But Valerie Bing had an edge that made Chloe nervous.

———

The next morning found Roelke in a room at the Elkhorn hospital, in a very bad mood. "I'm getting out of here," he told the plump young nurse who arrived to check his temperature and blood pressure.

"After the doctor makes his rounds—"

"No, as soon as my cousin comes to get me. I already called her." He gestured toward the phone beside the hospital bed.

The nurse frowned her disapproval. Roelke ignored her. He was no doctor, but he knew he was OK. Bruised, banged. He had a goose egg on the left side of his head, and seventeen stitches in his left arm. But he'd come out of the wreck in surprising good shape, thanks in part to his training and in part to his compulsion to plan for the worst. "You're such a friggin' Boy Scout!" Rick had hooted, the first time he saw the sheepskin covers Roelke had added to his lap belt and shoulder harness.

If he hadn't, Roelke thought now, the bruises left by the belt would be worse. And his headache was much better today. That was all that really mattered.

Twenty minutes later, dressed and dozing in the bedside chair, he heard Libby's voice in the corridor. "I *am* immediate family! Just tell me where he is!"

"Jesus," Roelke muttered.

Libby burst into the room. She wore old jeans and a purple tank top and running shoes. For a moment she looked ready to fling her arms around him. He braced for the onslaught. She stopped herself just in time. "Oh my God. Are you OK?"

"I'm OK. I look worse than I feel. Where are the kids?"

"At a neighbor's house." Libby scanned his face, his arm. "Oh God, Roelke. I've always been afraid something like this would happen."

"I was off duty, Libs. I didn't get shot. I got run off the road."

Libby still looked stricken. It wasn't a good look for her. "Did they get the driver?"

Roelke started to shake his head, but quickly switched back to verbal communication. "No. The guy—whoever it was—kept going. It was probably some drunk. Or some kid. Or some drunk kid." He didn't mention that there had been two drivers at the scene of the accident. One behind, one who came at Roelke's front, seemingly out of nowhere. Neither had hung around.

Libby pinched her lips together for a moment. "If anything ever happened to you—"

"Nothing's going to happen to me," Roelke growled. "Come on. Let's get the hell out of here."

Once settled into Libby's car, Roelke leaned his head against the rest. "Take H, OK? I want to look at the crash site." The day was cloudy, thank God, since his sunglasses were in his truck, which had been towed to a garage. God, his *truck*.

She shot him a disapproving look. "I really think we should—"

"You can take me to the scene, or I'll drive back by myself."

He'd gone off the road in the farming community of Sugar Creek. He spotted the residue of his adventure beside a cornfield. Some broken glass glinted in the sun—mirror, most likely. Vegetation was crushed from the shoulder to the bottom of the ditch.

Libby pulled over and they both climbed from the car. "I went off here," Roelke pointed, "then rolled. Three-quarters of a full rotation."

Libby reached for his hand and squeezed.

"It's strange," Roelke mused. "I had this clear sense that the truck was going to roll many times. But I don't know where that came from. The ditch isn't that deep."

Libby unpinched her lips long enough to say, "I imagine everything was a blur."

"It wasn't, though. Everything must have happened really fast, but it didn't *seem* like it. And I didn't hear anything, although the truck must have made a lot of noise as we banged over. But I was thinking clearly."

"Come on." Libby tugged his hand. "Let's get you home."

"Give me a minute." He pulled free and walked into the middle of the empty road. He looked in both directions, trying to overlay his memories on the geography.

"I was heading north, right down there, when this vehicle zoomed up out of nowhere," he said. "Right on my ass. I eased over, hoping the guy would pass, but he didn't. Just flashed his high beams. They hit my rearview mirror."

"Jerk," Libby muttered. Her posture was tight, as if ready to spring. If the driver showed up right then, Roelke had no doubt Libby would take him down.

He tried to focus. "Then, while I was dealing with that, brights hit me from the front. I swear, they seemed to come out of nowhere. I was already right next to the shoulder. I swerved, trying to get away from the other car. That's when I went off the road."

He frowned, trying to figure out where the car in front had come from. Nobody would be stupid enough to drive down County H in the dark with no lights on, would they? Well, if the driver hadn't been driving south on H, he must have been ...

"*There.*" Roelke pointed. The accident had happened just after he'd passed the junction of Sugar Creek Road, which hit County H from the west; and just before Schmidt Road bisected H from the east. The angles of the three roads formed a small triangle of unclaimed ground on the west side of County H, filled with trees and shrubby vegetation, tall and dense.

"I think the bastard was sitting on Schmidt, right there, as I was coming up. He pulled out onto H without any lights on, then hit his brights." Roelke turned again. "And whoever was on my tail must have turned onto Sugar Creek after the other guy went by. I remember the lights from both vehicles disappearing, right as I started to roll."

Libby's eyes went wide. "Are you saying somebody did this on *purpose?*"

Roelke chewed that over. It may have all been a bad combination of unrelated events. But if someone had wanted him to crash ... this would be a place to try it. And if it *was* deliberate, and aimed at *him,* the person responsible must have known that he'd be driving north on County H, right then; must have known he'd be leaving Roxie's Roost and heading home.

"Roelke?" Libby demanded.

"Just give me a minute." He thought back to his conversation with Roxie. He'd lingered at the tavern long enough for Guest and Sabatola to come up with the plan and get into place.

But it would have taken two drivers to pull off the maneuver. Driver A had climbed up on his tail, and flashed his brights to signal *Yes, this is McKenna.* Then Driver B pulled out and flipped on his brights. Had Sabatola been sober enough to handle a vehicle?

"*Roelke!*" Libby snapped. "You think this was deliberate?"

"It may have been," he admitted. "Now that I'm here, and can see the lay of the land, it all stacks up."

"Well, call the sheriff's office as soon as we get home. Let them handle it."

Roelke sighed. He'd already given a statement to a Walworth County deputy. Roelke had pulled himself together enough to tell the deputy that he was a cop. Then he described the crash itself. Yes, another vehicle had run him off the road. No, he hadn't gotten a good look at the vehicle, much less the driver. It had been dark. The other vehicle had been driving with high beams on. It had all happened fast.

"I can't do that," Roelke told his cousin.

"Why the hell not?"

A station wagon appeared from the north. Roelke pulled Libby farther onto the shoulder and waited for the car to pass. Then he said, "I'd been drinking."

"*What?*" Libby stared at him, mouth open. "Have you gotten stupid all of a sudden? What were you *thinking?*"

"Long story. It was a work thing." Unofficially.

The grim look in her eyes didn't fade. "How much did you have?"

"A couple of beers."

She blew out a long breath. "That's not a lot."

"I know. And I *felt* like I was OK." Roelke winced as he said it; wasn't that what every drunk driver believed? How many idiots had said those very words to him after getting pulled over for weaving all over the highway? "But … I may have been impaired."

Libby crouched beside the gravel shoulder and watched the corn grow for a few moments, rubbing her temples. After a moment Roelke sat down beside her.

Finally Libby said, "From the way you described what happened, it doesn't sound like you were impaired."

"But after my dad … and Patrick …" His father and his brother. Both drunks. Roelke savagely pulled the head from a Queen Anne's Lace plant. "The thing is, maybe I would have been able to keep the truck on the road if I hadn't been drinking."

"Your reaction time might have been a tiny bit slowed," Libby allowed. "But that probably didn't make any difference."

Maybe not. But Roelke had broken his own commandment. He'd never be completely sure of anything. And no way was he going to take that to the Walworth County guys.

Was it a coincidence that he'd been run off the road so soon after leaving Roxie's Roost? Simon Sabatola might be a piss-poor excuse for a husband, and Edwin Guest might be a fussy prig, but would either of them deliberately cause an accident? And if so, *why?*

Roelke didn't know. But he was royally pissed, and he was going to find out.

TWENTY-FOUR

CHLOE'S PHONE BEGAN RINGING the next morning while she was unlocking the trailer that served as her office. She wrestled her way inside and grabbed the receiver. "Hello?"

"Chloe? It's Libby."

Libby? Oh, God. *Roelke*. Had he been shot? Stabbed? "What's wrong?"

"Roelke's fine," Libby said quickly. "But he was in an accident last night. Rolled his truck. I didn't trust him to tell you himself, and I figured you should know."

"But he's OK?"

"Some bruises, some stitches. He's at home and grouchy."

Chloe blew out a whooshing sigh. It took conscious effort to relax her stomach muscles, and to loosen her grip on the phone. Something to think about later.

"I do have another bit of news," Libby said. "I called a friend of mine in New York this morning. I've done a bunch of freelance stuff for *Rural Lifestyles* magazine, and the copy editor and I have gotten friendly. Anyway, I asked if she knew anything about Valerie's abrupt departure from the city."

"Learn anything new?" Chloe asked, then immediately felt a spurt of self-disgust. She earned her living, in a general sense, by poking into the lives of the long-dead. Prying into those of the living—that didn't feel so good.

"Valerie's ex is a senior editor." Libby named a huge book publishing company. "Valerie accused him of infidelity when she filed for divorce. Evidently she went public in a big way. Her ex was known as a playboy, so probably the only person surprised by his affair was Valerie. Anyway, he got pissed. Threw a lot of mud her way. And in the end, Valerie got out-lawyered."

Chloe poured water into the little coffeepot on the counter with one hand, thinking that over. *I've got nothing left but student loans*, Valerie had said. And, *I don't like myself very much these days.* "Thanks, Libby."

"You want to tell me what all this is about?"

Chloe sighed. "It's probably about me being stupid."

"Your prerogative," Libby said. "Listen, though, will you be seeing Dellyn today? I've tried calling her several times in the past few days, and I never catch her."

"Her Garden Fair is tomorrow and Sunday," Chloe explained. "She's been putting in extra hours on that."

"Let me know if there's anything I can do," Libby said. "I'm worried about her."

———

Roelke was lying on his sofa that afternoon, listening to Duke Ellington's *Sophisticated Lady* and thinking about his accident, when the phone rang. "That better not be work," he muttered. He had the day off. He was in no mood to get called in. Without sitting up, he groped for the phone with his right hand. "McKenna here."

"Roelke? It's Peggy."

Roelke closed his eyes, wishing he'd been called in to work. "Hey, Peggy."

"How are you doing?"

No way was he going to tell her he'd spent the night in the hospital after rolling his truck into a ditch. "OK," he said, and waited for her to say something else. Uncomfortable moments ticked by before he realized what *she* was waiting for. "Um, how are *you* doing?"

"Good, Roelke. I'm good, thanks."

"Were you able to find anything about AgriFutures?"

Another pause. I don't have the energy to chit-chat right now, Roelke told her silently. He didn't feel good about that. He'd asked her for the favor, after all. Least he could do was be civil. But he didn't want anything more than the favor, either. It would be all too easy to send the wrong signal.

Most of the time, he really did have no idea how to communicate with women.

"I was," Peggy said finally. "I can assure you, Roelke, that Agri-Futures is not in financial straits. They made a record profit last year."

She named a figure that made Roelke blink. Holy toboggans. So much for the idea that Simon Sabatola might be in some kind of financial trouble. Unless he was hiding something *huge*, no way was a vice president of AgriFutures hurting for money.

"I'm no expert, but that sounds pretty good," he allowed. "Did you pick up any insights into management?"

"Management?"

He chose his words carefully. "You know, management style. Does the CEO treat the employees well? Any scandals? I'd hate to put my money somewhere that ..." He floundered. "You know."

"No scandals, certainly," Peggy said. "I wouldn't suggest—"

"Of course not."

Small pause. "Things may be a little unsettled there at the moment," she said finally. "The founder died recently. He had two sons, both vice presidents. The Board of Directors is taking longer than expected to announce which son will take over the helm. The board's split into factions, I guess."

Oh, really? Simon Sabatola had said his ascension was a done deal.

"But I'm sure that will be resolved soon," Peggy was saying cheerfully. "So, are you ready to invest? We really should talk about a diverse portfolio. Why don't we get together?"

Roelke stifled a groan. "Well, here's the thing, Peggy. I'm just home from the hospital. I rolled my truck into a ditch last night." He held the phone a few inches from his ear until her exclamations had settled back into normal decibel range. "So at the moment, I don't feel quite ready for anything social."

"But I hate to think about you being all alone after that kind of experience! How about I drive up? I made some peach melba muffins this morning. I could bring some by."

The thought of eating peach melba muffins—whatever the hell they were—while Peggy hovered and fluttered made Roelke want to crawl under the sofa. "Thanks," he managed, "but the doctor said the best thing for me right now is sleep."

"I understand. Call me when you're feeling better, though, OK? You still owe me that coffee."

"I owe you," Roelke agreed miserably, and hung up the phone before he could get in any more trouble. Right now, he had his hands full with Simon Sabatola. It seemed really, really unlikely that financial problems had been a major source of stress in the Sabatola marriage. But if Simon and his half-brother Alan both wanted the CEO spot? That might make things a lot more difficult.

Roelke reached for an index card and made some notes. Simon Sabatola had worked hard to leave his hardscrabble childhood behind. He was a man who liked to be in control. Bonnie's suicide meant he'd lost control at home. The possibility that the AgriFutures Board might give the top job to Alan would prove he had lost it at work, too. And the combination might make Simon Sabatola a desperate and dangerous man.

———

Chloe wanted to spend the day helping Dellyn, but she had a mountain of paperwork waiting. Long before the addition of the audit-induced collections scavenger hunt, Director Petty had instructed Chloe to deliver daily reports, weekly reports, and monthly reports—evidently trying to provoke her into either screwing up or quitting. "I should jolly well make Ralph Petty wait," she muttered to the walls, as she rolled another sheet of carbon paper into the typewriter she'd scrounged from a "damaged—surplus" pile at the historical society headquarters. The machine worked as long as she remembered to slide the carriage home gently, instead of slamming it.

"Helping a fellow staffer prepare for a special event should take priority." But Petty would get pissy all over again if she didn't get the reports into his mailbox that afternoon. The whole audit thing had him wound more tightly than usual. And she'd promised Dellyn she would try not to antagonize the man.

Besides, she'd come to love her job. She didn't want to lose it.

At 2:30 she wriggled into the period clothing she'd permanently borrowed from the interpretive staff—long black skirt, simple blouse, mismatched apron and kerchief. She wore it whenever she needed to work in one of the historic buildings during open-hours, minimizing the visual intrusion. Wearing period attire meant chatting with visitors, which slowed her down. But in Chloe's opinion, taking care of guests was Job One of every staff member, not just the interpreters. Besides, she was an educator at heart. She liked talking with visitors.

She found Dellyn and Harriet Van Dyne in the big barn that was part of the newly restored Sanford farm near the Crossroads Village. The Sanfords had been prosperous Yankee farmers. Their home had been restored to its 1865 appearance, during Wisconsin's brief career as a wheat-producing state. The barn was large, with a wide central drive-through, and Dellyn had chosen it for her Garden Fair.

Dellyn and Harriet were arranging a display of hand-held agricultural implements. Long tables held displays of heirloom fruits and vegetables: spiny West Indies gherkins, purple carrots, marbled beets, German fingerling potatoes. The array was colorfully impressive.

"You think visitors will be interested?" Dellyn asked anxiously.

"How could they not?" Chloe asked.

Harriet nodded emphatically. "I've learned so much since we started working together! Most people have no idea how much genetic diversity we've lost. All for the sake of some plastic-tasting thing that looks good after it's traveled halfway around the world."

Dellyn pulled a water bottle from its hiding place in a cloth-covered basket, and took a long drink. "It's coming together. Harriet's going to help me interpret in here over the weekend."

Harriet beamed, poking a stray strand of hair beneath her head-scarf, which was tied under her chin in old immigrant fashion. "I taught fourth grade for thirty years," she told Chloe. "I was ready to retire, but I missed the kids until I started working here. I love it when families come through."

The three women spent the rest of the afternoon finishing up the exhibits. Dellyn didn't want to break for supper, so at six o'clock Chloe let herself into the now-locked Sanford House and scrounged up some bread and gooseberry jam the interpreters had tucked away. "Our jobs have unique perks," Chloe said, as she shared the bounty with Harriet and Dellyn.

The light was fading when Dellyn stepped back from a colorful array of heirloom flowers she'd just arranged. "There. I think we're about ready. I just need to get over to the Ketola farm." She leaned against the wall, as if she needed the support. "The interpreters there canned beans and carrots this week. I thought we'd bring some jars over, and talk with visitors about how preservation technology evolved over the years."

"I'll do that," Chloe said firmly.

"But—"

Chloe put an arm around Dellyn's shoulders. "Dellyn," she said quietly, "please go home now. Eat a real dinner. Get some rest. It's going to be a busy weekend for you. I can finish up."

"That's an excellent plan," Harriet added. "Come along, dear. I'll walk out with you."

Dellyn wavered, but finally nodded. "All right. I will. Thank you."

Chloe watched Harriet and Dellyn trudge down the lane. One great thing about working at historic sites: there were lots of jobs for older women and, therefore, lots of mother-figures around.

Chloe set out on the short walk to the Finnish area. The day had been hot and muggy, but now a cool breeze riffled leaves and discouraged mosquitoes. Songbirds flitted overhead. As Chloe approached the Ketola farm one of the pastured cows raised her head, then returned to grazing.

Chloe felt some of her anxiety slide away. Being on-site after hours was a special privilege. The past always felt closer without visitors and trams puncturing the landscape.

Before heading to the house, she unlocked the sauna and stepped inside. In the bathing room she sank onto one of the benches and closed her eyes. She felt again that quiver of something strong, something calm, something feminine. *Help me*, Chloe thought, sending the message out to whatever long-gone Finnish women might be listening. *I want to take care of my friend Dellyn, and I don't always know how. Oh—and my friend Roelke was just in an accident. I'm not too sure what to do about him, either.*

Chloe's breathing gradually slowed. The present-day, with its heartaches and problems, faded completely.

Later, Chloe wouldn't be able to say if she was meditating, or communing, or simply resting. In any case, the sense of tranquil peace and warmth was so strong that it took several moments for the unexpected rattling noise to make its way through long-gone steam, and into her consciousness.

Once it had, she blinked back to the moment, struggling to identify the sound. Then she did.

"Oh, shit," she muttered, scrambling to her feet. In the dressing room, she grabbed the door handle and pushed.

Nothing.

"Hey!" Chloe yelled, pounding the wooden door with her fist. "*Hey!* I'm in here!" She banged for at least a minute, pausing periodically to listen for a response. None came.

"*Shit!*" Chloe stared at the door with disbelief. She was locked in the sauna. She imagined an interpreter unlocking the building the next morning and finding her inside. Geez Louise. How humiliating *that* would be.

Who had locked her in, anyway? Probably a security guard who'd noticed the padlock she'd left dangling open on the outside hasp. She knew the guards checked every lock when they made their first after-hours round each day. She hadn't heard a car ... but then, no surprise there. She'd been far away from the here and now.

All right, then, surely the security guard would see her car parked in the main lot. He'd wonder about that, right? And come searching?

But ... everyone knew her battered Pinto by now. The guard would know it wasn't an intruder's car. He'd probably think she'd simply grabbed a ride with someone else.

Chloe paced like a caged leopard. OK, think, she ordered herself. There was no handy emergency telephone hidden discreetly from sight in the sauna. No security keypad either. Her sound and motion would go undetected.

But in addition to one small smoke hole, the sauna did have two windows—one in the sauna chamber itself, one in the dressing room. Maybe she could still get out.

She pulled the locking peg from the sauna window first. Instead of sliding up, the pane angled inward to permit airflow. Short of breaking the window, there was no way Chloe could crawl through.

Then she tried the dressing room window. It was an unusual side-by-side arrangement, but a track permitted one window to slide sideways. Chloe pressed her palms against the sash and shoved with all her strength. Groaning with protest, the window slowly edged sideways a little … and stopped. "Ow," Chloe whimpered as she tried again. Her already-scraped palms and bruised shoulder throbbed in protest. The window refused to budge any farther.

Finally Chloe gave up, rubbing her hands as she eyed the narrow opening she'd created. She was skinny, but she was pretty sure she couldn't slide through. And the only prospect worse than being discovered next morning *inside* the sauna was the vision of being found stuck halfway through the window, flopping like a beached sturgeon.

Chloe dropped onto one of the benches in the dressing room and leaned against the wall. "I gotta get out of here," she muttered. She could imagine Ralph Petty questioning her about the episode. "Miss Ellefson, why, exactly, did you go inside the sauna at that hour anyway? ... You wanted to commune with dead Finnish women? Ah. I see."

She winced. Was getting locked in an exhibit building overnight grounds for dismissal? Surely not. Surely she could fabricate some plausible task that could send a dedicated curator of collections into the sauna.

But it would be easier to come up with said task if there were actually any collections *in* the building. The very few items in the sauna—even the benches in the dressing room—were all inexpensive reproductions. In the growing gloom, she took quick inventory. The inner room contained firewood and some sauna stones, a jar of matches, an empty bucket and tin dipper. The dressing room held several woven rag rugs, and some bundles of twigs the interpreters had made to help explain how the old Finlanders smacked themselves to get their circulation going after their sweat bath.

A kerosene lantern was visible through the window, hanging near the door, mocking her. She'd have traded a month's salary to get her hands on that! But she couldn't. Short of smashing a window, or actually setting the building itself on fire, Chloe didn't see how she could get out. And damaging this historic building in any way was not an option. Not even a last-ditch, desperate option.

"Don't panic," she ordered herself. She had to catch a guard's attention somehow, that was all. Should she try to light a fire in the sauna? Smoke coming from the chimney at this hour would attract notice, right? But—no. It was already getting dark. By the time she got a fire going, the smoke would be invisible.

How often did the security guards make the loop at night, anyway? She had no idea. The sauna sat near the road, which might be helpful. She could throw stones through the open window, or small pieces of firewood…but those things wouldn't make a guard blink.

She grabbed one of the rugs and draped it over the sill of the window she'd inched slightly open. "Feeble," she muttered. Unless a vehicle's headlights actually hit the rug, and the guard actually remembered that the rug hadn't been there when he locked the building, he would simply drive by.

It all seemed improbable.

Chloe was tired, and hungry, and thirsty. She kinda needed to pee, too. And it looked like she wasn't going anywhere until morning.

TWENTY-FIVE
AUGUST, 1876

"Mr. Bachmeier!"

Albrecht set his shovel aside, whipped the shapeless felt hat from his head, and looked straight up. Clarissa Wood's troubled face regarded him from forty feet up. "Yes ma'am?" he called.

"It's well past noon. Don't you want something to eat?"

Albrecht hesitated. He *was* hungry. If he climbed to the surface, he'd have the chance to talk with Clarissa. Alone, since Charles had gone to buy milk from a neighbor. Albrecht imagined her setting cold meat and cheese on her embroidered tablecloth in the kitchen. And there'd be some kind of wildflowers in a crock, with maybe a bluebird feather tucked among the blooms. Clarissa did take such pleasure in pretty things, like the yellow stone her husband had given her. She'd washed it clean and taken it to a jeweler, who told her the stone was likely a topaz. "Imagine!" she'd exclaimed, when she shared that news with the men. "A real-to-goodness gemstone! He offered me a dollar for it, but I said no."

"Mr. Bachmeier?"

"Oh—sorry, ma'am! And I thank you, but I'll keep working."

"If you change your mind, just tell me," Clarissa called. Her voice rang from the limestone walls.

Albrecht sighed. He had gambled. He hoped that for once, he might win.

He grabbed his shovel again, and shoved it into the earth with his boot. They'd passed through fifteen feet of clay, and he was now excavating a hard layer of gravel and clay cemented by oxide of iron. He dumped the blade-load of rubble into the bucket, and scrabbled through the soil and rock.

Nothing.

Well, nothing *yet*, he told himself. If there was one topaz, there could surely be another. Perhaps even bigger. Even more valuable. Most important, even prettier. And if there was, he wanted to be the one to find it.

Albrecht paused for a quick swig from the sweating jug he'd brought down with him. Then he got back to work.

TWENTY-SIX

CHLOE PLACED THE TWO remaining rag rugs on the floor and lay down. She might as well try to get some sleep.

Ten minutes later she jumped up, grabbed the rug draped over the window sill, and added that to her makeshift pallet. "This is absolutely miserable," she muttered, thrashing around. She tried not to think about how filthy the rugs were, but she couldn't get away from it. Her mind flashed slides of a thousand visitors walking on them. Visitors who had all trekked through chickenshit and cow poop before entering the sauna.

OK, fine. She'd sit up all night.

Chloe shoved the rugs into one corner and sat on them, trying to find a comfortable way to lean against the wall. God, her bruised shoulder ached. The scrapes on her hands had probably opened again. They'd get infected now, no doubt. And ... geez, was that a crick starting in her neck? Once, on a camping trip with Ethan, she'd gotten a terrible crick in her neck after sleeping wrong. She hadn't been able to turn her head for days.

She shifted again, and felt a tiny stab in her bare arm. Well, lovely. She'd just gotten a splinter. A splinter she couldn't see to remove in the darkness. It would sit there all night, and fester.

"This *sucks!*" she yelled, and exploded to her feet. It was bad enough that she was facing the most humiliating morning of her life, which would give plenty of fuel to the bonfire Ralph Petty had been methodically laying around her feet. It was bad enough that she couldn't check on Dellyn again this evening, and that Olympia—sweet little Olympia!—was probably sitting on a living room windowsill right this minute, watching the road, wondering why Chloe hadn't come home to feed her and play with her and cuddle her. But crippling herself as well? That was just too freaking much. There *had* to be some way out of here.

Moving gingerly in the dark, Chloe crept back into the sauna and sat on one of the benches. She closed her eyes, trying to capture some of that feminine Finnish strength. It was still there. She just had to calm down enough to feel it. She didn't expect a voice to whisper in her ear. She didn't speak Finnish, anyway. Still, it couldn't hurt to start round two of thinking in a good place.

Her thoughts circled back to that dressing room window, now open perhaps six inches. She couldn't fit through. Stones, firewood, the dipper, the rug—none of those were going to solve anything either. The only other movable things in the building were the two benches in the dressing room…

"Oh!" Chloe cried. She stumbled back to that open window. She grabbed the bench closest to the window, and tipped it up and sideways. "Ow-ow-ow!" she gasped, struggling to raise the heavy piece with her bruised hands and aching shoulder. She couldn't lift it high enough, though, and finally she had to let it drop.

"I can *do* this," she insisted. No way was she giving up again. No frickin' way.

Five minutes later she gingerly stepped up on the bench she'd positioned directly beneath the window. A little wobbly ... but not too bad. Crouching, she grabbed the second bench, which she'd tipped up against the wall. The legs were too tall to fit directly through the open window. But with the bench lifted and held sideways, she should be able to angle the legs through the window.

It was hard, but she was absolutely determined. With the legs set right against the windowsill she grabbed the bench mid-length, took a deep breath, and wrestled it into place.

The legs stayed jammed against the window frame. The angle was wrong.

"*Dammit!*" she gasped. She inched sideways, arms quivering. The bench she was standing on trembled. Her hands and shoulders hurt like blazes. But finally, with a sudden whoosh, the bench legs scraped through the narrow opening and into the night.

With the sudden release, Chloe lost her balance and fell to the floor. She landed on one hip and elbow so hard that tears came to her eyes. She lay there for a moment, not knowing whether to laugh or to cry. Then she staggered to her feet. She had tried her best to slide the window open far enough for her to crawl through, and failed. But now she had a lever.

Chloe leaned against the end of the bench that extended into the dressing room, and shoved. The window didn't move. She pushed harder. The window still didn't move. Chloe let loose a string of her best swear words, including several in *Suisse-Deutsch*.

Then she stepped back, aimed one shoulder like a linebacker, and slammed against the bench. With a protesting screech, the window inched sideways. Chloe repeated the movement, again and again, yelping with pain. Several minutes later the window had grumbled far enough over that she was sure she could wriggle through the opening.

"Hallelujah!" she panted. She pulled the lever-bench back into the dressing room, righted it, and shoved it into place against the wall. Then she wriggled her upper body through the window.

This was not going to be pretty. Chloe didn't care. She shoved off with her feet. Belly, hips, and thighs scraped painfully over the sill. Her long skirt caught on something and ripped. Her palms hit the ground first, and she tumbled to the earth. Slowly, gingerly, she began moving various parts—arms, legs, shoulders, knees. She hurt all over, but everything still seemed to work.

Chloe rolled over on her back. The sky was clear, and a hundred thousand stars winked in glorious congratulation. She began to laugh as she staggered to her feet. "I'm free!" she exulted. "And with no damage done to the sauna, thank you very much."

She didn't have the strength to tug the damn window closed again, but that was of no real consequence. Come morning the interpreters would arrive, and wonder, and that would be the end of it. Ralph Petty would never know.

She was halfway to the road before she remembered what she'd come to Ketola for in the first place. Her master building key was still pinned inside her apron pocket, so she fetched matches from the sauna and lit the kerosene lantern. In the Ketola kitchen she quickly found the canned goods Dellyn wanted, and put a jar each of beans and carrots in a basket. With both house and sauna locked up behind her, she was on her way.

Navigating by starlight and the lantern's glow, she left the Finnish area with lantern in one hand and basket in the other. Her spirits rose even higher, and she stifled the urge to swing one or both in exuberant arcs. Instead, she laughed out loud again, giddy with relief.

When Chloe reached the Sanford Farm, she found the barn locked. Boy-oh-boy, whatever guard was on duty tonight had been busy! After letting herself in, she proceeded with caution. One wrong move with the lantern and the stored hay would go up like a torch. It would be just her luck to extricate herself Houdini-style from the sauna, and then burn down the barn. That would get her butt fired for sure.

She dumped the basket of canning jars on the appropriate table. Dellyn could add them to the display in the morning, and send the basket back to Ketola, too. "I," Chloe announced, "am outta here." In fact, she was itchy-eager to get outside back outdoors. She didn't want to be inadvertently incarcerated again.

Something, though, made her pause. Not a movement, not a sound … but a smell that mingled with the residue left from musty grain, and the pickled gherkins and cut flowers on the display tables. A smell that had not been in the barn when Chloe left it earlier that evening.

All good cheer fled. She suddenly felt as if ants were marching down her spine.

Chloe held the lantern high. She didn't see anything out of place. She took a step, and another—

Then she saw the body, and the blood.

———

An hour later, the barn was lit like a carnival. Vehicles lined the site road, red and blue lights flashing. Someone had brought additional lights too, harsh white ones that bleached the barn. Flashbulbs exploded like tiny fireworks. Figures moved in and out of the glare.

Chloe watched numbly from the Sanford house's front porch. She sat with her back against the wall, knees pulled up, arms clasped tight around her legs. She'd lost track of everyone who had arrived: Hank DiCapo, Old World's on-duty security guard. A redhaired cop from Eagle. The county medical examiner. A couple of EMTs. A short, squat detective from Waukesha, whose name she'd already forgotten. Site director Ralph Petty.

Another vehicle arrived, and another shadowy figure emerged and mingled with the others. A man silhouetted against the electric blaze pointed in her direction.

The newcomer walked across the road and switched on a flashlight. "Chloe?"

"Roelke? Is that you?" Chloe tried to get to her feet. Her limbs were not ready to function.

He sat down beside her and pulled her into his arms. Chloe found her cheek pressed into his shoulder. She wanted to cry, but no tears came. Instead a hot ache filled her chest. Don't say anything, she told him silently. Just let me rest here. She closed her eyes and tried to pretend that this entire freakish night was nothing but a bad dream.

Finally Roelke spoke. "I'm so sorry."

Chloe reluctantly pushed herself upright again. "How did you know?" He wore jeans and a T-shirt and his gun belt.

"Skeet had dispatch call me." Roelke waved vaguely toward the barn. "He said you found the body."

Chloe nodded.

"Who is it?"

"Harriet Van Dyne. She volunteers here, helping Dellyn with the gardens. Did." Chloe tried to moisten dry lips with her tongue. "At first I thought it was Dellyn."

"Stabbed?"

Chloe winced. What she'd seen in the kerosene lantern's glow seemed seared on the inside of her eyelids. "Do you know what a scythe is?"

"I do. *Jesus*." Roelke stared toward the crime scene. "Never mind. I'll get the rest of the details later."

"Why would someone kill Harriet?" Chloe demanded. "Why would someone *do* that?"

"I don't know. But the detective, Pierce? He's good. He'll find the SOB."

"I don't even know what Harriet was doing in the barn. She'd left for the day."

"Skeet said they found her purse hidden beneath a table. Maybe she left, realized she'd forgotten it, and came back to get it."

"It could have been me," Chloe whispered. "I was supposed to be the last one in the barn tonight. I went over to Ketola—one of the Finnish farms—to get something." She thought about her carefree rambles to Ketola and back. Where had the killer been then? Had he been watching her?

"Why were you here so late? It's almost midnight."

"Detective Pierce asked me the same thing." Chloe gave Roelke a condensed version of her little sauna adventure. "We asked Hank if he'd seen the sauna open while making his rounds, and fastened the lock, but he said no." She shuddered violently, and clutched Roelke's hand. "It still might have been someone else on staff who locked me in. Maybe one of the farmers was working late. But God, Roelke, what if it wasn't? What if the murderer was the one who locked me in? I know it sounds stupid, but ..." Her voice trailed away. Had she really been so close to Harriet's killer? If so, why had he been content to merely lock the sauna door? Why had he let *her* live?

"We'll get him. And we'll get answers." His voice was hard.

"It's obscene. Things like this shouldn't happen *here*. Old World Wisconsin is a—a gentle place."

"I know."

"And all those cars ... we're going to have tire tracks every-where." She let her head sink back onto his shoulder. "I am so tired."

"Come on. I'm going to drive you home."

"Don't you need to stay?"

"Skeet's here, and the chief too. Besides, either the county or the state police will take the case. I'd just be in the way."

"Wait!" Chloe jerked erect so she could look at him. "Are you OK? Libby said—"

"I'm *fine*. Come on."

Chloe let him haul her gently to her feet. Before leaving, Roelke huddled briefly with the ginger-haired officer and an older man in plain clothes—Skeet and Chief Naborski, she assumed. Chloe leaned against the pasture fence, staying far enough away from the barn that she couldn't see the interior.

"Miss Ellefson?"

Chloe jerked upright as someone approached—Ralph Petty. Oh, Lord. She did not have the energy to deal with Petty right now. She really and truly did not.

"I understand you found the body," he said.

"That's right." She clutched her hands together, which was not nearly as comforting as holding Roelke's hand.

"It's just ... horrible." Ralph Petty sounded so distraught that Chloe felt an unexpected twinge of sympathy for him. Then he added, "God only knows what the auditors will make of this."

Chloe blinked at him. The night had just climbed a rung on the surreal ladder. She opened her mouth to spit nails, but discovered she didn't have the energy. Instead she said, "What's going to happen tomorrow? I mean, will the site be open?"

"I don't know yet. The Historic Sites division director will be here soon. The barn will certainly be closed. And the Garden Fair is canceled, of course."

"Of course," Chloe echoed. "Poor Dellyn. She worked so hard..."

Oh, God. *Dellyn*.

———

Once Roelke had checked in with the chief, he settled Chloe into the loaner Chevy he'd picked up that afternoon. He was acutely aware that she was in shock. She had never before allowed him to be so protective. He knew better than to think that it would happen again anytime soon. But God Almighty, it had felt good to hold her in his arms. He hoped she would at least remember how well they had fit together.

"Where's your truck?" she asked.

Roelke did a tight three-point turn and drove from the farm-yard. "Totaled."

"It was that bad?"

"The cab got knocked hard enough to totally mess up the alignment. Insurance company declared it a loss."

"I'm really, really sorry." She put her hand on his arm.

He appreciated that. He didn't care much for stuff, but his truck and his gun—those things were *his*, and not to be messed with. He needed them.

They rode in silence until he drove from the site. Then Chloe asked, "Has someone contacted Harriet's family?"

"It's been taken care of. Skeet said there's a grown daughter."

"I have to tell Dellyn."

Roelke didn't want Chloe to tell Dellyn. But he was pretty sure that nothing he could say would dissuade her. "OK. We'll go to-gether."

Dellyn took the news as well as he had expected—which was to say, not well at all. "Is it me?" she demanded, tears streaming down her cheeks.

"Of course not." Chloe sat next to Dellyn on the sofa, an arm around her shoulders. Both women were wearing their old fash-ioned costumes. Roelke had the feeling he was seeing something timeless, this way women had of comforting one another.

"No, really," Dellyn said. "Am I cursed, or something? Did I do something bad in a past life? Why are so many people I care about dying?"

"Come home with me tonight," Chloe urged.

"No." Dellyn shook her head. "I'll be OK. I want to bake something for Harriet's daughter. A casserole or something. I'll take it over in the morning."

Soon Roelke and Chloe were heading back toward her farmhouse. "In the morning, I'll ask Libby to look in on Dellyn," Roelke said.

"Good," Chloe said. "That would be good." She stared out the window until they were almost to La Grange. Finally she looked at him. "Roelke?"

"Yeah?"

"Do you think the killer might have been after Dellyn? She and Harriet were dressed almost identically. My yellow braid shows, and if someone had been watching while I walked to Ketola, he would have known I wasn't Dellyn. But it would have been easy to confuse Dellyn and Harriet, especially in the dark."

Roelke maintained a grim, thoughtful silence.

"Same thing about the night I got hit from behind. I was in Dellyn's barn. Whoever was there might have assumed that if anyone came in, it would be Dellyn. The attacker might have switched off the lights as soon as he heard someone come in, before he got a good look at me."

Roelke exhaled slowly. "It's possible. But what's the motive?"

"It's almost like someone *is* after the Burke family. First her parents, then Bonnie..." She pounded one fist lightly on her knee. "Maybe somebody was blackmailing Bonnie."

"About what?"

"I don't know. But you're the one who keeps insisting that there was some specific reason she chose to take her life. It's possible."

What's possible, Roelke thought, is that you are mixed up in something dangerous. His fingers strangled the steering wheel. Death by scythe suggested rage on the killer's part. And if Harriet Van Dyne's killer had been the same person who'd attacked Chloe in Dellyn's barn, then Chloe had *twice* been in close contact with a murderer.

He turned into her driveway. "Look," Roelke said, "it's really late. How about I sleep on your sofa tonight?" He'd done it before.

"Well … OK."

Was there some relief in her voice? He couldn't tell. "Then in the morning I can run you up to get your car. I don't have to work until evening. Maybe we could do something during the day. Something relaxing." He turned off the engine and turned to look at her. In the faint light her skin looked like porcelain.

"That sounds nice," Chloe said. Then her face clouded, and she sucked in her lower lip. "Oh—no, wait. Tomorrow's Saturday. I … I'm sorry. I already have plans." She got out of the car, shut the door, and began walking across the lawn.

For a moment Roelke sat immobile, watching. He'd been close to something good. So close! But it had slipped away. And he was pretty sure that Chloe's plans involved Alpine Boy, the bastard. Why else wouldn't she tell him what those plans were?

He got out of the car and followed Chloe. He didn't want her to think he'd changed his mind about spending the night. He had no idea why Bonnie had killed herself. He had no idea why Harriet Van Dyne had been killed. He had no idea why Dellyn Burke seemed to be in the middle of a tornado of tragedies. What he did know? Chloe had somehow wound herself into some serious trouble.

You might have Chloe tomorrow, Alpine Boy, Roelke thought grimly. But I'm the one who's here tonight. And I'm the one who's going to keep her safe.

TWENTY-SEVEN

THE NEXT AFTERNOON, CHLOE once again found herself driving to a rendezvous with Markus. And once again, she cursed herself for being an idiot. Her eyes felt bleary. Her head felt fuzzy. Her nerves felt frazzled. It was not a good day to spend time with her ex.

The sense of intimacy she'd felt with Roelke the night before had vanished with the sunrise. She'd scrambled eggs for breakfast. Conversation had been polite. "Um, listen … I could probably cancel my plans for the day," she'd said. If she could reach Markus.

"No need," Roelke had said, with formal courtesy. He'd driven her back to Old World, and she'd collected her car. She thanked him for his help. They said an awkward good-bye. "Be careful," he'd told her, before driving away.

"Dumb, dumb, *dumb*," she muttered. It had been nice of Roelke to suggest doing something relaxing today. If she hadn't been so exhausted, so dazed by Harriet's murder, she would never have put him off. How could she spend time with Markus today? Roelke was the one who understood what had happened to her the night before.

Well, nothing for it now but to see the thing through. Gritting her teeth, she pointed her car toward New Glarus.

———

When Chloe and Markus got to the Frietag farm, Martine and Frieda came to meet them. "Grandpa had a bad night," Martine told them. "He's sleeping now."

"This is a bad time," Markus said at once. "We'll leave."

Martine shook her head. "No, he knew you were coming. If he's better in a bit, you can say hello. If not, he'll want to hear all about your visit." She managed a smile.

"I'm glad you're here," Frieda added. "Johann told me to show you the chickens." She cocked her head toward the beautiful old bank barn, with room for cows on the lower level and hay stored above.

The reduction of livestock to two cows and a handful of chickens meant the barn had become a storage place over the years. Just like Dellyn's, Chloe thought, flashing on the image of her friend's bleak expression when she learned of Harriet's death.

Frieda told Markus about her flock, and her memories of her parents' poultry. Markus taped the conversation and supplemented the recording with photographs. Chloe wandered out of audio range, struggling to control her emotions. The last thing she wanted to do was break down here.

Her curator's eye idly took in the mélange of agricultural detritus. If the Frietags were up to it, she really should make arrangements to get Dellyn down here. Larry, too. In addition to a hand-plow and harrow, and an aging tractor, smaller pieces hung on the walls.

Suddenly Chloe's breastbone thrummed like an electric wire. "Oh my God!"

Heads swiveled in her direction. "What's wrong?" Markus asked. He stowed his tape recorder and came to join her.

"Um, sorry." Chloe felt her cheeks flood with color. "It's just that …" She pointed to a hand cultivator.

Markus looked at it, obviously bewildered. "It's a garden tool."

"I *know* it's a garden tool." Chloe stared at the primitive hand cultivator, homemade and horribly familiar. Martine and Frieda joined them, and Chloe willed her hand not to shake as she touched the rose carved in relief on the handle. "I—it's unusual. Is it a family piece?"

"Well now, that's hard to say." Frieda planted her cane and leaned on it with both hands, considering. "It's hung there as long as I can remember. It might have come down in my family, or Johann's. Or it might have come from some other neighbor. When people sell their own place, they sometimes bring stuff over here."

Chloe looked at Markus. "Have you ever seen one carved like that before?"

"No."

Chloe tried to corral her thoughts. She didn't want to tell Markus that she'd been attacked with an identical cultivator. And no *way* would she tell that to Frieda and Martine. "I saw one just like it recently. At my friend Dellyn's place."

"Really?" Markus brightened. "We should track down provenance on those two!"

That would be tricky, Chloe thought, with Dellyn's cultivator in the Eagle PD's storage locker. "Dellyn doesn't know anything about hers. It was in her parents' barn when they died."

"I'll ask Grandpa about it," Martine said. "But I don't know that he'll remember anything."

"No worries," Chloe told her, and tried to smile.

———

Roelke drove to Eagle that evening in his newly acquired truck, a 1978 GMC High Sierra, two-toned green. He'd wanted another Ford Ranger, but didn't spot one on a dealer lot or in the paper, and he didn't want to dink around. At least the color was good. And the mileage was low for a four-year-old vehicle, just 1,800 miles.

He checked his watch. Residents were making their way to the village park for Movie Night. Movie Night, for God's sake. Chloe might have been murdered the evening before. She was likely being consoled right this minute by her stupid Swiss ex. Dellyn Burke might, or might not, be a killer's target. Detectives were trying to discover who had killed Harriet Van Dyne.

And what am I doing? Roelke thought. I am about to set up a movie projector, and to make sure the volunteers handling the popcorn and sodas show up on time. Tonight's film, *Mackenna's Gold*, had been chosen by Skeet, who thought the name was funny.

"Just hilarious," Roelke muttered. It would be a double joke if Skeet got the permanent position.

———

Frieda toured Markus and Chloe through her garden, identifying vegetables she thought had old origins. Markus got particularly excited about one tomato. "I think these might be genetically identical to an old Bernese tomato we've got at Ballenberg. If so—my God, how exciting to find a direct link here in America!"

Frieda smiled at him. "You tell me which ones you're interested in," she said, "and next time you come I'll have seeds ready for you. I keep all my gardening things in the old granary, now."

Chloe lingered over a border of lobelia. "Those are pretty, aren't they?" Frieda asked. "I don't know how old the variety is, though."

"A friend of mine is planting a memorial garden for her mom and sister," Chloe said. "They both liked blue."

"I'll go through my packets and find some of those before you come next time," Frieda told her.

"And perhaps some *Käseklee*?" Martine asked.

Frieda smiled mischievously. "That's the plant which gives *Grünen Schabzieger* its green color, but the flower is also a nice blue." She turned toward the house. "Now, it's time for supper. I want you two to stay."

Chloe darted Martine a concerned glance. "Let her do it," Martine whispered. "It helps her to keep busy."

By the time they'd eaten, Johann woke and asked to see Markus. While the men talked livestock, Frieda showed Chloe some of her embroidery. "I'd like you to have this one," Frieda said, handing Chloe a white dish towel stitched in bright colors."

"It's lovely!" Chloe was enormously touched.

Frieda beamed. "And I wrote down my *Bierabrot* recipe for you."

"These are treasures," Chloe told her. "Thank you so much."

———

Markus and Chloe were both silent as they drove the first few miles back to New Glarus. Chloe watched headlights from passing cars flash by, wondering if she'd see Frieda and Johann again. Frieda seemed to be in fairly good health, for a woman in her nineties, but Johann was failing. And when he passed … well, it wouldn't surprise Chloe if Frieda died soon after.

Well, whether they had more visits in store or not, it had been a privilege to meet the elderly couple.

The only wrong note came from seeing the rose-carved cultivator. That had been freaky. Creepy, actually. How did one end up in Dellyn's barn, and its twin in the Frietags'?

Beside her, Markus began to hum quietly. He'd always done that when he was thinking. Chloe was pretty sure he wasn't even aware of it. The sound put a catch in her throat.

She had once known this man better than anybody else on earth.

Chloe rubbed her temples. OK. She was too tired to think about either the cultivator or her love life. She struggled for something banal. "It, um, sounds like you're enjoying your time in New Glarus."

"It's more Swiss than Switzerland," Markus mused, "but I like it here. I've gotten interested in the whole topic of Swiss acculturation—how both the original immigrants and their descendants have chosen to retain or even re-create aspects of their ethnic heritage."

"I imagine that for some people, it's heartfelt," Chloe said. "And for some it's about tourism dollars. It's the same way in Stoughton, where I grew up. Very Norwegian. Guests from Norway are often astonished to see churches advertising *lutefisk* suppers."

"It's fascinating," Markus said.

Chloe slid her gaze in his direction. Yes, it *was* fascinating. She understood exactly what Markus was thinking, and feeling. Surprisingly, Markus had been a part of the sense of respite she'd felt today. Roelke was the one who understood that Chloe had found a second dead body in the space of two months—but that wasn't necessarily a good thing. She needed a break. She wanted her life to be about old people and heirloom goats and folk dancing again.

Markus seemed to read her mind. "I've been meaning to tell you, someone in the dance group in Brienz discovered a new schottische." A schottische was sort of like a slow polka. When Chloe lived in Switzerland, she and Markus had been members of the folk dance group.

"Are the steps difficult?"

"I haven't learned it," he said, slowing the car as they neared a stop sign. "The schottische is a partnered dance. I haven't been active in the group since you left."

"Oh."

"Have you found a group here?" he asked. "Maybe you and the policeman?"

Chloe made an attempt to picture Roelke McKenna dancing a schottische. Three seconds later, her head about to explode, she gave up. "No. I haven't danced either."

Markus was wise enough to let that go. "Well," he said, as they reached the parking lot where she'd left her car, "thanks again for coming. It was fun. Maybe we can meet more informants while I'm here."

Informants. The word rang in Chloe's brain like a cow bell. In Roelke's world, informants were people with information about crimes. Sometimes horrible, brutal, heart-breaking crimes, like the murder of Harriet Van Dyne. In Markus's world, informants were people like Johann and Frieda Frietag.

"I'd like that," she said, and got out of the car.

———

T.J. Malone fought like a hooked muskie as Roelke snapped the handcuffs into place. "You can't arrest me! I haven't done anything!"

Mackenna's Gold was well underway. Gregory Peck and Omar Shariff were arguing about the fate of some blonde woman. Still, half the movie-watchers craned their necks to watch Roelke tug the young man toward the squad car. "I'm not arresting you," Roelke said as he levered T.J. into the back seat. "I'm detaining you while I go hear your girlfriend's side of the story."

"She's a bi—"

Roelke slammed the door against both the unpleasant noun and the string of curses that followed. "I suggest you try to calm down," he told T.J. through the glass, and left him.

T.J.'s girlfriend, a very pregnant brunette, was sitting on a picnic table a short distance from the area where Eagle residents, young and old, had settled in for Movie Night. "I didn't *do* anything!" the girlfriend insisted as Roelke approached. Waterworks had left mascara streaks down her cheeks. "I said hello to a guy I went to high school with. That's all! I wasn't flirting or anything, but T.J. went *nuts!*" The young woman wiped her eyes with a crumpled tissue, doing further damage. "Ever since I got pregnant, he's been acting like a big jerk!" She began to weep again. Noisily and sloppily.

In Roelke's opinion, both parties needed to settle down before anything productive could happen. "Just sit tight, OK? I need to check on something. Then I'll go talk to T.J." Roelke waited until she nodded. Then he began a slow circuit of the park.

As far as he could tell, Movie Night was a complete disaster. First, his stitches and blossoming bruises attracted unwanted attention. Second, everyone and their brother wanted to talk about Harriet Van Dyne's murder. Had the murderer been caught? What did Officer McKenna mean, county detectives and state police were handling the case? The crime may have happened on state property, but it was still an Eagle issue. Perhaps Officer McKenna should stay a little more involved.

Then there was the film itself. Skeet had evidently not previewed the old Western, which featured a scene where a naked woman tried to drown the blonde. Roelke was pretty sure that at least a couple of parents would not deem that family fare. The plot, about an ever-increasing bunch of idiots willing to risk their lives to find a legendary canyon of gold, kept pulling his thoughts back to Dellyn Burke's suggestion that someone might go crazy over the legend of the Eagle Diamond. Watching the nutjobs in the film, all things suddenly seemed possible.

On top of that, the night was muggy enough to wring like a sponge. The popcorn machine had broken. The soda stand was a volunteer short. It was hard to breathe through a pervasive fog of insect repellant. It was hard to hear the soundtrack over the sound of a hundred hands slapping at mosquitoes which were, evidently, indifferent to the repellant.

Skeet, who was supposed to be working with him, had been called to an accident in the township. So the glory is mine and mine alone, Roelke thought. Were any Police Committee members in attendance? He really didn't want to know.

Finally, he headed back to the squad. T.J. now sat slouched in the back seat, staring at his knees.

Roelke opened the door, braced an arm on the car roof, and leaned over. "Your girlfriend says all she did was say hi to somebody she knew. And that you went ballistic."

T.J. stayed mute, evidently fascinated by the composition of denim.

"Listen," Roelke said. "It's time for you to man up. You're about to start a family. You may not have planned it, but there it is."

No answer.

"T.J., you are right on the edge of making some very bad choices. You are right on the edge of going down a road that will haunt you for the rest of your life."

"I just…" T.J. gave a weary shrug.

Roelke crouched beside the car. "You gotta step up, now, and do the right thing. Your girlfriend needs to know she can count on you. And your baby will need a dad who's around, not locked up somewhere because he wasn't willing to take responsibility for his own actions. You ready to be that guy?"

Finally the young man drooping in the back seat heaved a long sigh. "I suppose," he muttered. "Yeah."

"All right. Come on out." Roelke helped T.J. to his feet, and removed the cuffs. Then he fished one of his business cards from his pocket, and pressed it into T.J.'s hand. "Listen, I know it can be tough. You got handed a whammy. If you feel like stuff is closing in sometime, give me a call. We can talk things over."

T.J. didn't answer. But he shoved the card into his pocket before walking away.

———

Chloe was melting butter that evening when the phone rang. She added a splash of maple syrup, poured the golden-brown mixture over a bowl of warm popcorn, grabbed it, sprinted for the living room, managed to avoid stepping on Olympia, and snatched the receiver on the seventh ring. "Hello?"

"Where'd you run from?" Ethan asked.

"I was fixing popcorn."

He laughed. "That brings back memories. You ate popcorn for dinner once or twice a week when we were in college."

Chloe popped a sticky piece in her mouth and licked her fingers. "Still do." Sometimes comfort food trumped nutrition.

"So, how'd your day with Markus go? When the phone rang so many times I was beginning to wonder if you'd brought him home."

"Um, no. I am not ready to invite Markus Meili into my home." Chloe slid into the chair by the phone and put the bowl on the floor, suddenly no longer hungry. "Ethan? I don't know what the hell I'm doing."

"Is that because you've got feelings for Roelke?"

"It's more complicated than that." She closed her eyes, trying to parse her thoughts. "Roelke's a great guy, but he's a *cop*, for God's sake. We don't have anything in common. He … he always seems to be connected with the bad stuff." Even as she said the words, they felt unfair. It wasn't Roelke's fault that Harriet Van Dyne had been killed. And Roelke was the one who'd shown up, and held her, and gotten her safely home.

"You still there?"

"Yeah. But geez, Ethan! I don't know how to handle this situation."

"Oh, sweetie. I can't figure that out for you."

Chloe sighed. "I'm just starting to like myself again, you know? Just when I was getting some energy back, getting some focus again, Markus shows up."

"Maybe you should back off from both of them," Ethan suggested. "Give yourself some space. Time to think."

Chloe heard a tiny lapping sound: Olympia, joyfully licking butter from the popcorn. Chloe pushed the kitten away with her foot. "That's not a bad idea. Besides, I really need to spend time with my friend Dellyn." Not that it was that simple. Both of the men he was suggesting she avoid had some tie to Dellyn Burke. Roelke was investigating the attack in her barn, and Markus was meeting her on Tuesday for a garden tour of Old World.

"How is Dellyn?"

"Not good." Chloe tried to distract Olympia by tossing a fuzzy ball across the room. No sale. "A friend of hers, um, died unexpectedly yesterday. She's taking it hard."

"How'd the friend—"

"You saved me, you know," Chloe said, both to forestall the question and because her gratitude toward this man suddenly bubbled up so fierce and hot that she had to put it into words. "When I was at the end of my string, you dropped everything and came to be with me. I want to be there for Dellyn. I mean, really *be* there for her. She's so alone."

"She's not alone if she's got you for a friend."

"Sometimes life is all about showing up," Chloe said. But her choice of words circled her back to the place she didn't want to be: Markus, Roelke. In very different ways, both men had done that for her. "Why does life have to be so damn complicated?"

"I have no idea."

"In this freaky way, things were easier when I was depressed," she muttered. "Nothing mattered. Now a lot of things matter, and I don't know what to do about any of them."

"We-ell," Ethan said dubiously, "that's an improvement. I think. Just remember, you gotta take care of yourself first."

"I know. And I know I have to keep my job, spend time with friends, strive for balance, blah-blah-blah." Chloe pushed Olympia away from the bowl again. "Geez Louise. Maybe I got something out of therapy after all."

"Here's my advice. Give yourself time to figure out your love life."

I don't know if I have time, Chloe thought. Markus's sabbatical was more than half over. Soon he'd be half a world away again. But she didn't want to talk about Markus anymore.

By the time she hung up the phone five minutes later, Olympia had returned to the popcorn. Chloe picked up the bowl and dumped the contents into the kitchen trashcan. "You better not puke up all that butter," she warned the kitten.

Olympia blithely began washing her ears.

Chloe suddenly felt exhausted. The last twenty-four hours had been too difficult, too full, too confusing. Too frickin' much. "You know what? Go wild," she told Olympia. "I'm going to bed."

***

The park was clean, the movie projector returned to the school, the folded chairs returned to the Methodist church, the volunteers thanked. T.J. and his girlfriend had departed holding hands. No members of the Police Committee had stopped to express discontent about the enterprise. Roelke decided to claim what victory he could, and head for home.

All he wanted to do first was take a quick look-see at Dellyn's place. He parked across the street from her house, got out, and eased the truck door shut. The neighbors' places were dark. No point in rousing anyone.

A single light burned from Dellyn's living room. He decided to circle the property line. He walked along the far side of the garage, and paused at the building's corner. Watching. Listening. He let minutes tick by as his eyes adjusted and the darkness eased into shadowed but distinct shapes—garden fence, scarecrow, shed, barn. Nothing.

No. Someone was moving on the far side of the garden. The silhouette was bent low, but unmistakably human. It disappeared silently behind the garden shed.

Roelke snatched his revolver from its holster, nerves taut, every cell focused on the spot where the person had disappeared. He waited, listening for a footfall, straining to see more movement. Nothing. Whomever was creeping through Dellyn's yard had gone to ground behind the shed.

Roelke eased away from the garage wall, ready to take cover, but nothing happened. OK. He had a clear, grassy path to the shed. He took it.

No sign of flight from the skulker. Roelke reached the shed's near corner, kept going. Two more steps to the far wall.

Then, an explosion of movement. "Police!" Roelke yelled. "Stop right there! Hands in the air!"

The asshole took off. Roelke pounded after him. The guy was panicked, making no attempt at silence now. He brushed against a shrub and thrashed wildly.

Roelke flew at him. He landed square against the guy's back and they both went down. "*Show me your hands!*" Roelke bellowed. The guy put up a brief and feeble struggle before going still, heaving for breath. Roelke holstered his gun and got the man cuffed before rising. He grabbed the guy's arm and heaved him to his feet.

"What are you doing here?" Roelke barked. He was panting too, more from adrenalin than the brief exertion.

"Nothing!" the guy whined. "I wasn't doing nothing wrong." In the faint light he seemed to be about Roelke's age. Middling size, a little paunchy. T-shirt and jeans.

"Then why'd you run?"

"I was *scared*, man! You came after me!"

"I came after you because it's almost midnight, this isn't your property, and you didn't obey my instructions. What's your name?"

No answer.

A light over the back door suddenly came on, casting a yellow glow that seemed blinding. Then the back door opened. "Hello?" Dellyn called. "What's going on out there?"

Roelke began leading the asshole around the garden fence, toward the house. "It's Officer McKenna, Miss Burke. I found someone lurking out here. Did you call 9-1-1?" She stood on the top step, barefoot, in shorts and a tank top. Holy toboggans, the woman was as foolhardy as Chloe. No wonder they were friends.

"No," she said. "I heard the commotion and—"

"Go inside, lock the door, and make the call. Tell dispatch I need backup." Roelke hadn't seen any sign of a second intruder, but he wanted to be sure.

The cuffed guy attempted to pull free. "Let me go! I can explain everything!"

Roelke tightened his grip. "You're not going anywhere I don't want you to go."

Dellyn visored one hand over her eyes, shielding them from the glare. Then she padded toward them.

Dammit all to hell. "Miss *Burke!*" Roelke began.

"No, it's OK." Dellyn stopped three feet from the two men. She folded her arms and regarded the trespasser with a mixture of weariness and disgust. "What are *you* doing here?"

"You know this guy?" Roelke asked. "Who—"

Another figure burst from the shadows, rattling past a huge lilac bush. Short, plump. Wearing a blue bathrobe over a lacy nightgown, and fluffy slippers. Sonia Padopolous froze when she saw the three of them.

And the night gets a little more surreal, Roelke thought.

Sonia let out an anguished wail, put her hands over her eyes, and sank to the ground. "T-take him to jail." She squeezed the words out between shuddering sobs. "I can't lie for him anymore."

TWENTY-EIGHT
AUGUST, 1876

CLARISSA PULLED THE CURTAIN above the kitchen window aside, just a bit. He was here again. The German, Albrecht. He was shoveling rubble from the well into a wheelbarrow, steady and strong, his coarse shirt dark with sweat. Charles had gone to the blacksmith's shop. The horse needed shoeing.

She let the curtain drop back into place. Turning, she leaned against the drysink and contemplated the food she'd set on the table. A simple meal of cold ham, potato salad, some juicy melon fresh from the garden. She'd offer Albrecht a meal. Maybe today he'd say yes, come inside, accept her hospitality.

And that's all it would be. Clarissa knew Albrecht was in love with her. She loved him too, in a strange half-exciting, half-frightening way. She would never speak of it, or act upon it. She was a good Christian woman. She loved Charles, too. He was a good provider, this man she had promised to share life with. And in his own haphazard way, Charles loved her, too. Sometimes he made her feel special. She kept the pretty yellow stone he'd given her on the windowsill, where the sun played with it. It made her smile each time she saw it.

Clarissa walked to the front door, scanned the road. No sign yet of Charles. There must have been a wait at the smithy's. And the flies were likely to devour the food she'd prepared.

She walked back through the house, outside, on to the well. "Mr. Bachmeier?" she called. "I've food prepared for a mid-day meal."

Albrecht paused, wiping his forehead. Clarissa watched him think that over. He'd never agreed to come in the house unless Charles was present.

"Please," she added. "You can't work like a draft horse in this heat without taking some food. I've got ginger water, too. Charles will be along soon. He'll join us then."

Albrecht took one long inhale, blew it out. Then he tossed the shovel aside. "Thank you kindly, ma'am," he said. "I believe some refreshment will do me good."

TWENTY-NINE

SUNDAY MORNING DAWNED HAZY and humid. Between the weather and events of late, Chloe had spent a restless night. "What a waste of electricity," she muttered, stabbing the OFF button on the bedroom fan. She pulled on a clean pair of shorts and a sleeveless green top. It was too hot to eat. After feeding Olympia and tossing back a glass of cold grape juice, she headed for Dellyn's place.

An unfamiliar car was in the driveway, so Chloe parked in front of the house. As she walked around the house, she saw her friend in the garden—in the embrace of a tall man. Chloe felt her eyebrows rise. Who the hell was *that*? She didn't recognize Simon Sabatola until he stepped away from his sister-in-law. "So please, don't worry about it," he was saying as Chloe let herself in the garden gate.

"It's not your responsibility," Dellyn said. She saw Chloe and lifted a hand in greeting.

"It *is*," Simon said firmly. He wore tan trousers and a navy polo shirt that screamed, *Rich executive trying to look casual.* "We're still family, Dellyn. I'm not going to turn my back on promises I made your parents."

Dellyn leaned over and pulled a clump of purslane from the soil, and tossed it onto a pile of weeds wilting in the sun. She wore flip-flops, cut-offs, and a grubby T-shirt. "Let me think about it, OK? I do appreciate it, though. Really."

"Sure. We'll talk soon." Simon turned to leave and saw Chloe. "Good morning."

Chloe could tell he was trying to place her in his memory. "I'm Chloe Ellefson," she said. "We met at Bonnie's funeral."

Simon's eyes got glassy. "Yes, of course. Nice to see you again."

Chloe watched him get into his car and back out of the driveway. "Hey," Chloe said to her friend. "I didn't mean to chase your brother-in-law away."

"You didn't."

Chloe regarded her friend. "Did you get any sleep last night? You look so tired."

"Well, we had a bit of drama here last night." Dellyn snorted. "You remember my neighbor, Sonia?"

"Sure."

"She's got a son. Alex is about my age, and we grew up playing together. Sonia was our 4-H leader." Dellyn exhaled slowly, looking inexpressibly weary.

"And?"

Dellyn cocked her head at the little table and chairs set in one corner of the garden. "C'mon. Let's sit down." She paused to crouch by a melon patch. She felt several cantaloupes before pulling a jack-knife from her back pocket and cutting one from its vine.

Chloe hitched one chair over so it was shaded, and sat down. "And?" she prompted.

"Well, things started getting weird when we hit junior high and high school. Alex developed this crush on me." Dellyn looked at her with a hint of desperation in her eyes. "I never wanted to date him. It was one thing to play softball and raise chickens together. Quite another to ... you know. I never led him on. I *swear*, Chloe."

Chloe raised a hand, palm forward. "Hold on. Did someone say you did?"

"Yeah. Sonia did." Dellyn sliced the melon into glistening salmon-colored wedges, releasing a juicy and sweet aroma. "Grab a couple of plates, will you? There are some in that hamper. Anyway, Alex was always over here, always following me around at school. It got annoying. And one day a teacher heard me telling Alex to leave me alone. It got blown way out of proportion. Alex and I ended up in the principal's office, and then Sonia storms in and accuses me of leading Alex on. She said that if I didn't dress so suggestively, and act like a tease, he wouldn't follow me around."

Chloe glared toward the Padopolous house. "It's bad enough when men say things like that."

"Yeah." Dellyn served up the melon. "I was sixteen. Pretty fragile, like most teens. Having Sonia accuse me like that really hit me hard."

Chloe thought back to the day she'd met Sonia Padopolous. No wonder Dellyn seemed reserved with her neighbor.

"My mom came to school too, and she calmed everything down. It was the only time I ever saw her angry at Sonia, but they patched things up. I've never been able to let it go, though."

"It's despicable to blame the woman when a man acts inappropriately," Chloe said firmly. "But … what happened last night?"

"Well, the cops have been great, keeping an eye on my place since you got attacked. Late last night I heard someone yelling. I came outside and found Officer McKenna and Alex in my back yard. Alex was in handcuffs."

"*What?*" Chloe tried to process that. "Roelke found Alex sneaking around? Is Alex the one who tried to kill me with a cultivator?"

"The cops seem to think so. And Sonia does too. She showed up too. It was quite the scene."

The air in Dellyn's garden suddenly seemed lighter, sweeter. Chloe smiled.

"But … I don't think Alex would do something like that."

Chloe's smile disappeared. "Really? What did he say about being in your back yard late at night?"

"He says he was trying to protect me. I know." Dellyn rolled her eyes. "Evidently Sonia told him about what happened to you. Next thing she knows he arrives at her house, says he's going to stay until the cops figure out what's going on. Last night he kept saying he was just 'patrolling.' Making sure I was safe."

"That sounds a little creepy. Especially if you didn't even know he was around. Sort of stalker-like."

"Yeah. But the thing is … Alex never scared me. Maybe that's because I knew him so well as a child, but … he was more like an annoying puppy dog than a stalker."

Chloe tasted the melon, and momentarily lost track of everything else. "Oh my *God*, this is good. Sweet, but almost a little spicy, too."

"It's called Hearts of Gold. Introduced in 1890." Dellyn ran her thumb over the netted rind absently. "Alex has been in trouble with the law before, though. I think that's why your cop friend was so hard on him last night. And evidently this was the last straw for Sonia. She'd been letting him stay at the house, but she'd told him to stay out of my yard."

"Maybe he *is* the guy who hit me." Chloe desperately wanted to think that her attacker had been identified and arrested. "If he's a trouble-maker..."

Dellyn picked up her spoon, then put it back down. "Alex isn't real bright, but he's not evil. I saw a couple of teachers give Alex a really hard time when I think he'd done his best. Once on the playground, when some kids were bothering a kid with Down Syndrome, Alex exploded. Then he got in trouble for starting a fight. He's got this protective instinct buried inside somewhere."

Chloe chewed on the inside of her lip. She didn't know Alex Padopolous, and wasn't quite so ready to conclude he hadn't been in Dellyn's yard for all the wrong reasons. "Where is Alex now?"

"I have no idea. Officer McKenna wanted me to press charges for trespassing, but I just couldn't do it."

So. Whether Alex or someone else, whoever had picked up a hand-carved cultivator and tried to bring it down on her skull was still out there. Maybe it was whoever had killed Harriet, too. Chloe shuddered, and furtively glanced over both shoulders. She still felt vulnerable, and her instincts said Dellyn was vulnerable, too.

She needed to talk with Roelke.

"I'll try to find out if the cops have learned anything more about Alex," Chloe promised. "And whether they've turned up anything about Harriet's killer."

Dellyn shut her eyes briefly. "I'd appreciate that. I hope they don't have reason to pin that on Alex too. I just can't imagine…"

"Then let's not," Chloe said firmly. Time to change the subject. "It looks like your brother-in-law is in pretty rough shape."

"This Thursday is his and Bonnie's wedding anniversary."

"Oh geez."

Dellyn wiped away a tear, then shook her head as if to clear it. "Sorry. I just found out that Simon paid the property taxes on this place last year."

Chloe blinked. "Um … wow."

"I knew my parents were living pretty close to the edge. I didn't know they were *that* close."

"So … what does that mean for you?"

"Simon knows I'm broke. He offered to pay the taxes again this year."

That made Chloe uneasy. Definitely uneasy.

"Simon also said that if I want to sell the place, he'd buy it. He said the market's iffy right now because of the recession, so it would be easiest if he bought the property now, sat on it, and then sold it himself at a fair market price when things pick up."

An image of Simon Sabatola pawing through musty cardboard cartons, searching desperately for the Eagle Diamond, drifted through Chloe's mind. She opened her mouth, closed it again.

"What?" Dellyn asked.

"Well, I know this will sound stupid, but is there any reason why Simon might have an ulterior motive for being so generous? I mean, you were concerned that someone might be torqued up about the Eagle Diamond. Valerie's article was in a popular magazine—maybe Simon—"

Dellyn shook her head. "Something weird is going on with the diamond. I still haven't been able to find my dad's files about it, which bugs the hell out of me. But I have a hard time with the notion that Simon is setting his sights on some crazy get-rich-quick scheme that involves running me out of my house. For one thing, he's already rich. And he's smart. If he wants to get richer, he'll do it with AgriFutures."

"Yeah."

"Chloe, I had no *idea* my parents were struggling financially. It's not like farmers have great pension plans, but I guess I figured that by selling off some land they'd gotten what they needed. After they died, and I started dealing with the bank, I found out how little they actually had in savings. The whole property tax thing never crossed my mind."

"You don't pay those until December, right?"

"Yeah." Dellyn shoved her plate away untouched. "But maybe Simon's offer is a blessing. Maybe I should just pack up and head back to Seattle. Or maybe someplace new."

Chloe felt another wrench of worry. She wanted Dellyn to stay in Eagle. And not just because Dellyn was her friend, either. "Please give yourself some time."

Dellyn shrugged.

Chloe cocked her head, wishing she knew how to help her friend. "Want to tackle some more of the artifact inventory?" The stuffy attic seemed inviting, now. No one could watch them there, or creep up from behind.

"Thanks, Chloe." Dellyn managed a small smile. "That would be good. I don't know what I'd do without you."

They tossed the melon remains on the compost pile and took the sticky plates into the kitchen. "Maybe we'll find some treasure today," Chloe said, striving for a light tone. "Something you can sell in good conscience, and make enough to pay your own property taxes. You never know."

"I won't hold my breath." Dellyn rinsed the plates and left them in the sink. "Listen, before we go up … here." She picked up a key from the counter and held it out. "I got my locks changed. Would you be willing to take a spare key?"

"Well … sure." Chloe accepted it.

"Thanks." Dellyn laughed a little, but it sounded forced. "I'm getting so scattered I'm likely to lose my own." She turned and headed down the hall.

At least she didn't give the spare to Simon, Chloe thought as she slid the key into her pocket. Somehow, though, that was only scant comfort.

———

That evening Roelke sat at his tiny kitchen table. Index cards were arrayed precisely in front of him, each bearing a name or an incident. He'd been playing with ideas for an hour, trying to fit pieces of the various puzzles confounding him lately into an ordered pattern.

He didn't have squat.

Finally he collected the cards into a neat stack. The top card said *Alex Padopolous. Says left Waukesha 8/2, day after Ch. attacked in Burke barn. Could have left the night before?* Padopolous swore up and down that he had nothing to do with Chloe's attack. But his own mother didn't even know whether to believe him or not.

Roelke put the *Time Out* album by the Dave Brubeck Quartet on the stereo, and sat down in the living room with his pocket-knife and the block of wood he was whittling into a turtle. His father had taught him to whittle. Him and Patrick both. The boys had shaved away at bars of soap before their father permitted them to graduate to soft pine. Now, two decades later, Roelke sometimes found that having something in his hands helped him think.

Before he'd taken three strokes, the phone rang. "It's me," Chloe said in his ear. "I hope you don't mind me calling. I—"

"I don't mind."

"Good. Dellyn told me what happened with Alex Padopolous last night. She doesn't think Alex is the person who tried to brain me in her barn."

"Yeah, I know," Roelke said. "His fingerprints are on file, though. I'm going to check his prints against whatever the crime lab found on the cultivator. Haven't gotten results yet."

"Is there any news about Harriet Van Dyne's murder?"

"The chief'll have an update for us tomorrow."

"Oh. Um … listen, Simon was at Dellyn's house when I arrived. I mentioned the word 'funeral' and he started to cry. Dellyn said his wedding anniversary is coming up."

"Yeah? When?"

"Thursday."

Roelke turned that factoid over in his mind.

"When's your job interview?" Chloe asked.

"Tomorrow."

"Oh! Wow. Well, good luck."

The words were right. But the conversation still felt strained. Not what he needed the night before he sat down to face the three members of the Eagle Village Board's Police Committee. "Thanks," he said. "I better get back to prepping for it."

As if there was something I *could* do to prep, he thought, as he hung up the phone. Finding the person who attacked Chloe—or discovering who had caused him to total his truck—would have looked good to the committee, but that hadn't happened. Maybe the interviews with him and Skeet were just a formality, anyway. Maybe the Police Committee already knew who they wanted to hire.

Roelke picked up his knife and made a slice that left a gouge in the turtle's shell. He glared at the botched carving before tossing it in the trashcan. All right, he told himself. Nothing on the job front was formalized yet. Maybe thinking about Bonnie Sabatola would keep him from freaking out about the coming interview.

He flipped the LP on his stereo, set the needle, and sat back down. One thing was clear: being married to rich, handsome Simon Sabatola wasn't enough to keep Bonnie from calling the EPD and blowing her brains out that day. Maybe that was her husband's fault. Maybe Bonnie and Simon were both to blame.

He mulled over what Chloe had said. Sabatola was already weeping over his anniversary, eh? His anniversary that happened to fall on a Thursday this year. The one day of the week he routinely got ripped at a blue-collar tavern. Now, *that* might just come in handy.

Roelke's fingers curled into fists. He was pretty sure Sabatola was behind the crash. The game had changed when Sabatola decided to come after *him*. But Roelke knew he'd have to leave the EPD if he didn't get the permanent job. That meant he was running out of time to figure out what was going on.

THIRTY

CHLOE HATED MONDAY MORNING staff meetings at best, and today she simply couldn't face the inevitable hashing and rehashing of Harriet Van Dyne's murder. She dragged her butt out of bed at 6 AM and drove to the administration building.

She'd already written a note for Ralph Petty: "I am sorry to miss this morning's staff meeting, but I'll be in Madison to meet with Leila about the audit." Leila, the division curator, didn't know that yet. But Chloe planned to get to her before Ralph did. After tossing the note in Ralph's mailbox, she fled the office and drove west.

Once at the state historical society building, Chloe tracked down Leila and had the obligatory conversation about the audit. "There's really not much you can do to prepare," Leila told her. She was a plump woman, friendly but efficient to the point of curtness. A result of having way too much to do, like most historical society employees. "They'll probably want to see some accession records, stuff like that."

"I'll do my best." Chloe said. It occurred to her that the damn audit might end up providing Ralph Petty more fodder for her permanent file.

"That's all you can do. Listen, Chloe … " For the first time Leila hesitated. She picked up a button hook and toyed with it. "I wanted to say how sorry I am about what happened Friday night. What a ghastly thing. You take care of yourself, OK?"

Chloe promised she would. The audit discussion duly complete, she headed to the archives to look up the Eagle Diamond.

It took ninety seconds to find the card catalog listing. She gave the work-study student the call number and waited while the material was retrieved from storage. The student handed over a single gray box, which held a single file. Geez, Chloe thought. Going through this hadn't taken much time. Maybe she should look into moonlighting as a freelancer herself. How much had Valerie earned by writing her article?

Other than the photocopy of the receipt she'd seen at Dellyn's house, the file held only news clippings. Chloe started with the latest, dated 1965, which summarized the tale.

Charles Wood found the diamond while digging a well in Eagle, and gave it to his wife Clarissa. Clarissa took the pretty yellow stone to a Milwaukee jeweler named Samuel Boynton. Boynton told Clarissa the stone was probably a topaz. Later Clarissa, now a widow struggling to make ends meet, accepted Boynton's offer of a dollar for the "topaz." Boynton then followed his unspoken hunch and took the stone to a gemologist, who declared it a yellow diamond of 15.375 carats, worth an estimated six hundred and ninety-nine dollars more than Boynton had paid Clarissa.

Chloe frowned. What a prick.

Clarissa sued Boynton to recover the gem. She lost, and had to pay court costs. In 1893, Boynton sold the diamond to Tiffany & Company for eight hundred and fifty dollars. Tiffany sold the Eagle Diamond to J. P. Morgan. His collection was displayed at the World's Fair in Paris in 1889 before he donated it to the American Museum of Natural History in New York.

Quite a donation. Chloe gave a grudging nod of approval to the long-dead financier.

Last year, the Eagle Diamond and two dozen other gems were stolen from the Museum. Three men, including Jack Murphy—dubbed "Murph the Surf" because he was a professional skin diver—were charged with the theft. Some of the gems were recovered, but not the Eagle Diamond. Museum officials still speculate about its fate.

Chloe exhaled slowly and picked up the next clipping. A brittle corner flaked off—this one dated back to 1885. She gave a guilty glance over her shoulder, put the article back on the table where it belonged, and leaned over to read. Two paragraphs in, she sat up straight again. "Shit!"

The researcher at the next table scowled. "Some of us are trying to work!"

"Sorry," Chloe said in her best library whisper, with her best conciliatory smile. Then she hunched over the clipping again, as if wanting to protect it from prying eyes.

Shit indeed. Valerie Bing was either a pathetic researcher, or a liar.

———

When Roelke's interview with the Police Committee ended he drove home and changed into civvies. Then he headed back outside. He was too twitchy to sit at home. Too twitchy to work. Too twitchy to go to Libby's place.

Twenty minutes later he pulled into Chloe's driveway. No sign of Chloe's car. Well, he'd wait a bit. He got out of his truck and sat on her front steps, carefully avoiding the bird's nest she'd left beside the porch rail.

Another twenty minutes passed before he saw her old Pinto turn into the driveway. She gave him a startled look, parked behind his truck, and walked across the yard. She wore her long denim skirt and a pretty green blouse. Her blonde hair was twisted up behind her neck. He had no idea how women managed to do that with so much hair, but she looked so good that he felt a physical ache inside.

"Hey," Chloe said, half surprised and half cautious. "You've got new wheels. I like the color."

"Thanks."

"So ... whatcha doing here?"

"Feeling restless," he said. His right knee was pumping like a piston.

She sat down beside him. "How'd the interview go?"

"OK, I guess." Roelke spread his hands. "They asked questions. I answered."

"When do you suppose you'll hear?"

"Any time." The knee pumped faster. He watched with an odd sense of detachment, as if it were a piece of runaway machinery that had nothing to do with him. "If Skeet gets the job, I'll have to quit the EPD. I need a permanent position, and another one probably won't open up in Eagle for years. Besides, I don't think I could handle working with Skeet every day." It sounded small, but there it was.

"Yeah," she said slowly. "Would you go back to Milwaukee?"

"I've already applied for a job that's opening up there. I've got a pretty good shot at that. "

"Oh."

He stared over the field across the street, where her landlord was baling hay. "What are you going to do about Markus, Chloe?" He heard her sharp intake of breath and plunged on. "I need to know."

After a moment she said, "I haven't decided."

"Jesus, Chloe!" he exploded. "How can you even *think* of going back to someone who treated you so badly?" He didn't know all the details behind Chloe and Markus's breakup. But he knew enough.

She rubbed her temples. "It's complicated. We've got a lot of history."

Another bale popped from the chute and landed on the hay wagon. One of the neighbor kids, riding in back, grabbed it and swung it into place with expert ease. Roelke clenched his teeth. He hadn't planned to ask Chloe about Meili; the personal question had just burst out. He had no tidy place to put her answer, though. No one waiting to field it and reach for another.

His hands itched for his pocketknife, but he'd left it at home. He picked up the bird's nest.

Chloe gave him a level stare. "Don't start on that," she warned him quietly. "I know you don't like clutter, but this is *my* house. And just so you know, the cardinal feather is still in my kitchen. You don't like that, arrest me."

He put the nest down and jumped to his feet. "Will you come for a drive with me?"

"Um … where to?"

"I don't know. I just want to get out of here." He had more to discuss with Chloe. He wanted to do it without wondering if Alpine Boy might show up.

She hesitated, then nodded. "OK."

Roelke felt a little better as soon as they were in his truck, leaving La Grange behind. "Listen, we've had trouble getting along lately," he said. "I'm really sorry about that."

"I'm sorry, too." She twisted in the seat to face him. "And I'm glad you came by. There's some stuff I want to tell you about the Eagle Diamond."

Roelke stared at the road. Some asshole had run him off the road and totaled his truck. Some asshole had likely made Bonnie's life so miserable that she'd killed herself. Skeet Deardorff might be accepting a permanent job offer from the Police Committee this very minute. He really wasn't in the mood to talk about the Eagle Diamond.

"I did some research in Madison today," Chloe was saying. "And guess what? Valerie Bing left one little detail out of her article. I confirmed today that a hired hand was working with Charles Wood—"

"Who's Charles Wood?"

"The guy who originally found the Eagle Diamond. Years later, a reporter interviewed a German immigrant named Albrecht Bachmeier who'd been working as a hired hand when Charles found the Eagle Diamond. I found the article, and listen to this: Bachmeier found another gem!"

"Yeah?" Roelke said, because he knew some response was required. His brain felt like split-pea soup.

"Don't you get it? There might be a second diamond!" Chloe's voice was triumphant. "And a diamond like that would be valuable both in monetary and historical terms. Dellyn's dad was writing a book about the Eagle Diamond. If he'd somehow found Diamond Number Two, with provenance info, it would be a big deal."

"OK, I get that," Roelke conceded. "But who would care enough to break into Dellyn's barn, and maybe even her house, to look for it? Who'd care enough to maybe attack you that night?"

"Maybe Alex Padopolous? He grew up right next door. His mom and Dellyn's mom were best friends. It's not a stretch to assume he knew about the whole Eagle Diamond thing. And Dellyn said he wasn't real bright. Maybe what sounds like a ridiculous scheme to you and me makes perfect sense to him."

"You can't teach stupid," Roelke muttered.

"And here's another candidate—oh, watch that guy!"

"That guy" was a squirrel which seemed bent on flinging itself beneath Roelke's tires. He swerved, and watched the squirrel scamper merrily away. Thank God for that. Roelke suspected that Chloe would not react well to a rodent tragedy.

"OK." Chloe exhaled with apparent relief, and picked up her tale. "This seems less likely, but I'll just lay it out there. Valerie Bing told me she'd put everything that was known about the Eagle Diamond into her article. But she *didn't*."

"Maybe she thought the idea of a second diamond didn't matter to the main story."

"Even if she thought so when she was writing the article, I asked her *specifically* about what was in the research file," Chloe said stubbornly. "And she lied about it."

"Maybe she didn't see that clipping you read."

"She'd have to be a half-wit to have missed it. And Valerie Bing is sharp, I assure you. Although—" Chloe paused. "She also considered her article a puff piece. Nothing to take seriously."

"You've met this lady, not me. Does she seem—hold on." A dark sedan had zoomed up on Roelke's ass. The last time someone had tried to kiss his bumper, he'd crashed. If this guy tried the same thing with Chloe in the truck ...

The sedan swerved into the other lane, roared past, and disappeared. Roelke unclenched his fingers from the wheel. "Sorry. Does Valerie Bing seem like the type who'd go crazy over a century-old rumor of a second diamond?"

"No. But she is desperate for money. Six months ago she was living the high life in New York City. Now she's living with her parents in Eagle. Libby found out that she got screwed in a nasty divorce."

"Well, shame can be as much of a motivator as pure greed," he admitted.

"I imagine so."

Enough of the Eagle Diamond. "There's something new about Sabatola," Roelke said. "I think he was responsible for me getting run off the road that night."

Chloe stared at him, wide-eyed. "Why would he do that?"

"I have no idea. But if I'm right, it means that Sabatola is trying to hide something big. I have no way to prove he may have been abusing his wife, so ... there's something else going on."

———

Chloe processed that news in stunned silence, her skin prickling. "Be careful, OK? *Please.*"

"I will. I'm still digging, though. I've learned a little about Sabatola's childhood. His secretary's, too."

"That Guest guy? Dellyn pointed him out to me at the funeral."

"They both had a rough time as kids. Guest is likely just as needy as Sabatola, but without the good looks and wealthy stepdaddy. There's the possibility of fierce motivation—shame with some greed mixed in."

Chloe rubbed her arms to ward away shivers. Simon Sabatola, Edwin Guest, Valerie Bing. Could any of them have been the person who attacked her in the barn? It was pretty hard to imagine.

She considered telling Roelke about finding the second rose-carved cultivator in the Frietags' barn ... but she didn't want to bring Markus back into the conversation. It was unsettling enough to know that Markus would be back at Old World the next day, touring with Dellyn. Chloe planned to lay low.

Besides, maybe the Frietags' cultivator was just a bizarre coincidence. Maybe some prolific craftsman had made hundreds of them. Maybe rose-carved cultivators were hanging in barns and tool sheds all over southern Wisconsin.

There were more important issues to consider, anyway. The Eagle Diamond probably had nothing to do with Harriet Van Dyne's murder ... but everything revolved around Dellyn.

"I've learned some things about AgriFutures," Roelke said.

"Yeah?" Chloe was glad for a distraction. "Anything helpful?"

"Financially, the company is doing great, and Sabatola told me that he was a sure bet to take over as CEO. But evidently it's not that simple. Simon runs the implement division, and his half-brother Alan does chemical stuff. They're both vice-presidents now. The Board of Directors seems to be split on who should take over."

"Two brothers fighting for the top spot? Ouch."

"Simon is older, and he definitely wants the job," Roelke said. "It wouldn't surprise me if even the *hint* that Alan might be given the CEO nod would make Simon go ballistic."

"How big a company is it? Do they sell all over the country?"

"They're international. Sabatola told me he wants to revolutionize agriculture in developing countries. They're creating special equipment designed for conditions in African countries. Probably Latin America too. There's obviously a hell of a lot at stake for an ambitious man. A lot of pressure."

Chloe sighed. "If he held it together at the office, all that steam might have exploded when he got home every night."

"Yeah. We've got all the classic signs of abuse. After Bonnie married Sabatola she withdrew from friends and quit a job she loved. Sabatola gets drunk at a blue-collar bar every week. He's somehow involved with the woman who owns it. They go way back."

"An affair?"

"Maybe. And maybe that's why Sabatola wanted me off his tail, and tried to scare me by running me off the road. His wife just committed suicide, and if it came out that Sabatola was involved with another woman … or a man … well, it wouldn't look good. Especially right now, when he's desperate to get board approval to take the big corner office at AgriFutures."

Sordid stuff, Chloe thought. "I hate to think that Dellyn is spending time with Simon."

"Can you warn her to stay away from him?"

"What would I say? We can't prove anything. Simon's all the family she's got left, and he's been making nice lately."

They drove in silence for a few more minutes, passing pastures of placid Holsteins, fields of corn and soybeans, weathered old houses and barns crouched beneath huge blue silos, women weeding gardens. It all seems so peaceful, Chloe thought. So at odds with the events circling in her head. "Where are we?"

"I grew up near here." Roelke flipped on his turn signal.

A few moments later he pulled over and turned off the engine. "This is it. The old Roelke place."

"Wow."

"My mother was born here. My grandparents farmed it. It didn't go out of the family until my grandfather died. I spent a lot of time here when I was a kid. Milked a lot of cows."

Chloe stared at the abandoned brick farmhouse. It was tired but had, as one of her professors used to say, good bones. From the distance of the truck cab, she received no particular perception from the building; from the layers of Roelke's ancestors still dusting worn floorboards and walls. Much more palpable was Roelke's sense of ambivalence about the place.

"I don't know who owns it now," he added. "Nobody lives here. They just rent out the fields, I think."

"Oh," Chloe said. A song sparrow landed on a bobbing teasel plant, then flew away. They sat for a few minutes longer, watching the farm doze like an old cat in the sun.

"I gotta ask you something," Roelke said.

Something in his tone made her wary.

"I want you to tell me what it feels like to be depressed. I mean—you know. Really depressed."

Chloe's shoulders hunched. "I don't want to talk about it. I don't even want to think about it. I'm better now. I don't want to go back to that place."

"I'm sorry to ask. Really. But—"

She turned on him. "Why are you doing this?"

"Because I need to understand what took *Bonnie* to that place. That place where she felt compelled to put a gun to her own throat. You're the only person I know who might be able to tell me."

"Is this about Bonnie Sabatola?" Chloe slid down on the seat and propped her feet on the dashboard, finding some comfort in the semi-fetal position. "Or is it about me?"

He was silent for so long she thought he wasn't going to answer. Finally he said, "Both, I guess. I keep thinking that if I can find a reason why Bonnie killed herself, then ..."

"Sometimes there's a concrete reason, but sometimes it just comes from inside. A chemical imbalance." Chloe sighed. "Look, if you want to find some conclusion that will convince you that I'll never get depressed again ... well, that's not going to happen."

"But to reach a place where you would want to—"

"Why are you assuming Bonnie *wanted* to kill herself? Maybe she'd been fighting that urge for weeks. Maybe she just woke up one day and was so tired, so damn weary, that she knew she simply couldn't keep going. Maybe the grayness had seeped into every corner of her life." Chloe realized that her voice was rising, and tried to bring it down to normal range. "And maybe she didn't have a best friend to call."

"I just ..." Roelke avoided her gaze. "I know I've lost perspective. There's something about the Sabatola stuff that—that just *eats* at me. I need to figure it out before it does cost me my job. All I know is that women … Dammit, men can make life a living hell for women. It can go the other way too, but most often, it's women on the receiving end, and—and *you*, and Erin Litkowski, and—"

"O-*kay*." Chloe had no idea who Erin Litkowski was, but she wasn't sure she wanted to find out. And she definitely wasn't up to a recital of all the women Roelke had met in the course of his police career.

"Sorry," Roelke muttered.

"I know you mean well. But let's keep this about Bonnie Sabatola, all right?"

He was silent.

"Everyone's situation is different," Chloe said finally. "But if you want to talk about this more sometime, call me and I'll try to help. I promise."

THIRTY-ONE

WHEN ROELKE ARRIVED AT the station the next afternoon, Skeet was going off-shift. "Anything going on?" Roelke asked, trying to sound off-hand.

"Naw." Skeet jerked his head toward the chief's door, which was closed. "Chief told me there's nothing new in the Van Dyne murder investigation. I knew you'd want to know."

"Yeah," Roelke said. "Thanks."

Skeet lowered his voice. "You hear anything from the Police Committee?"

"Nope. You?"

"Nope." Skeet glanced this time at Marie, who was typing away but doubtless following every word of the conversation. "Listen, man. I just wanted to say … well, whatever happens—you know, with the job thing—we'll be cool, right?"

"Sure," Roelke lied. "We'll be cool."

"Good." Skeet nodded. "OK. I'm outta here, man. See you to-morrow."

Roelke spent the afternoon patrolling, including a stint in a speed trap, trying not to obsess about the philosophy of speeding tickets. When he couldn't stand that anymore he started on bar checks. He stopped first at The Eagle's Nest, almost hoping to find some brawl to break up. No such luck.

Next stop was Sasso's. Inside the barroom, several of the regulars lifted their hands or smiled in greeting. Roelke nodded back, and asked the bartender, "How are things tonight?"

"No problems," the man said. "Thanks for stopping in, though. I appreciate it."

I'm good in this town, Roelke thought, as he began his circle through the crowded room. I'm good *for* this town.

It was a typical week-night crowd. Most of the patrons wore faded jeans or overalls, but a few businessmen who commuted to Waukesha or Oconomowoc had settled in for a cold one, jackets tossed aside and ties loosened. As usual, a group in one corner wore old-fashioned costumes. No one gave them a second glance. Everyone in Eagle was used to seeing interpreters from Old World Wisconsin pumping gas, stopping at the post office, relaxing at Sasso's.

Suddenly Roelke went still. Dellyn Burke was leaning against the wall, wearing her patched and faded Old World garb. He'd never seen Dellyn when she didn't look stunned, grief-stricken, exhausted. She still looked tired, but her expression was animated. She was clearly enjoying the conversation she was having … with Markus Meili.

Roelke walked in their directions.

"Millions of people in poor nations who subsist largely on cassava roots rely on local legumes that are rich in protein to round out their diet," Dellyn was saying. "And if crops engineered in industrial countries are forced upon them …"

"Not only will the local species likely go extinct," Meili said, "but local people might lose an essential nutritional element."

Dellyn sighed. "I'd really hoped that my little Garden Fair would give me an opportunity to help Old World's visitors think about things like that. I mean, the USDA admits that in the last eighty years, we've lost ninety-seven percent of vegetable varieties here in the US! It's appalling." She shuddered, then put a hand on Meili's arm. "Listen, I'll be right back." She disappeared toward the ladies' room.

Roelke took a step closer, and Alpine Boy looked up from his beer. "Officer McKenna." It wasn't a warm greeting.

The two men stood staring at each other. The clamor of conversation surrounding them faded into obscurity.

Then Markus leaned a little closer. "I'm glad to see you, because I need to say something." He kept his gaze locked on Roelke's. "You are not what Chloe needs."

Roelke felt every already-tense muscle tighten more, as if someone was winding an internal winch. "I'm not what she needs?" he repeated softly.

"She doesn't need a cop," Markus said. "She needs someone who understands her work. Who understands *her*."

The winch in Roelke's chest cranked again. "And that would be you?"

"I lived with her for over five years. We were good together." Alpine Boy's accented voice dropped even lower, as if he was confiding a deep secret. "And we're going to be good together again."

They already stood only inches apart, but Roelke took one step forward, deliberately crowding the other man's space. "I could break you in two," Roelke said softly. "Right here, right now."

The smug self-assurance drained from Meili's face. Roelke knew a stab of fierce satisfaction.

Then Meili smiled. Actually *smiled*, the bastard. "Thank you, officer. You just proved my point."

"Hey, guys." Dellyn appeared and made a point of elbowing her way in between them. "What's going on?"

Blood started pounding audibly in Roelke's brain.

"The policeman and I were just having a friendly conversation," Meili told Dellyn.

The pounding in Roelke's head grew louder. He nodded at Dellyn. Then he left. Outside he slid into the squad car and slammed the door. He grabbed his clipboard, so it would look to any passerby that he was busy with *something*. But he couldn't write. Couldn't think.

Jesus Christ. While on duty, while wearing his uniform, while carrying his service weapon, he had threatened Markus Meili with physical harm.

Roelke went back to the station and told dispatch he wasn't well enough to finish his shift. Then he got in his truck and drove to Libby's house.

She opened the door to his knock, her eyebrows lifting in surprise. "Hey! What are you doing here?" She stepped backward so he could come inside.

"Are the kids asleep?"

"Justin is. Dierdre had a bad dream. I was reading her a story."

"Can I do that?"

Libby crossed her arms and considered him. Finally she cocked her head toward the little girl's bedroom.

The room was small, painted pink, furnished with lots of ruffles and lace. Dierdre was propped up on an extra pillow, wearing a plastic tiara studded with glittering rhinestones.

"Hey, Princess," Roelke said. He eased down on the edge of her bed, and kissed her forehead. She smelled sweet, as if fresh from a bubble bath. It made him want to cry. "Can I finish reading your story?"

"You can read it," Dierdre said, with an air of royal dispensation.

Roelke picked up the book Libby had left open on the pink sheet. *Winnie the Pooh.* He began to read. Dierdre's eyes drifted closed, and her breathing settled into the gentle rhythm of sleep, but he didn't stop.

Finally Libby stepped into the doorway. "She's asleep, you know."

"Yeah." Roelke closed the book reluctantly.

"Come on." Libby led him to the kitchen. She opened a Lienie for herself. Then she put a shot glass on the table and, to his astonishment, filled it with whiskey.

"You want me to drink?" he asked dumbly.

"You look like you need it. And you can walk home from here." She sat down catty-corner from him.

Roelke hesitated, not from self-control, but because the shot glass reminded him of Simon Sabatola. Well, the hell with that. He picked up the shot and knocked it back.

"OK." Libby gave him a level gaze. "What's going on? Did they give the job to Skeet?"

"No!" Roelke scrubbed his face with his hands. "This isn't about the job." Although it was, because everything was all tangled together.

"Then what?"

"I've been thinking about genetics."

Libby blinked, and sat back in her chair. "OK, *that* was unexpected."

"I have a temper."

"Well, yeah." Libby spread her hands. "And this got you upset because ... ?"

"Because of Patrick!"

"Oh. Oh, hell." Libby chewed her lip. "Whiskey was a mistake. A big one. Sorry."

"No, it's not the booze." At least not today. Roelke rested his elbows on the table, and his head in his hands. "Do you remember Patrick's temper? He was just like my dad that way. Something would set Patrick off, and boy, he could snap just like that." Or throw a punch. No matter where he was, or who he was punching, or what price he'd have to pay.

Alarm flickered in Libby's eyes. "Did you do something you shouldn't have done?"

Maybe I am like Patrick, Roelke thought. Scary thought. Even worse? That he was like Sabatola. Sabatola, who believed he deserved a promotion. Sabatola, who believed he was justified in— Roelke suspected—playing without rules.

"Roelke?" Libby demanded.

"I haven't punched anyone," he said carefully.

"I'm making coffee." Libby got up and filled the coffeemaker. "When was the last time you saw Patrick?"

"Before he went to prison."

"Roelke…" Libby came around behind him, and wrapped him in a hug. "Go see your brother. Talk to him. See how he's doing. Maybe you can help him somehow. I know you hate to talk about him—to even think about him—but I can also tell that makes you crazy sometimes."

"I don't want to talk to Patrick."

"One visit. Just one." Libby squeezed a little tighter. "Make peace with him."

"Not gonna happen."

"Promise me you'll give it a try."

The coffee machine started to burble. Libby didn't move.

"I'll try," Roelke finally mumbled. He had no idea if he was lying or not. What he did know was that he needed to pull his shit together. He was very close to screwing up—not just the Eagle job, but his entire career in law enforcement.

———

Midnight found Roelke alone in his apartment, pacing, trying hard not to think. He didn't want to think about the Police Committee. And he sure as hell didn't want to think about Markus Meili, who may have already told Chloe that Roelke—while on duty—had threatened him. What I really need, Roelke thought, is a few hours of shut-eye. The combination of whiskey and caffeine had left him sleepy but wired, like the wide-awake drunks he saw guzzling Irish coffee every St. Patrick's Day.

Dammit. *Patrick.* Roelke didn't want to think about his brother, either.

He remembered the stricken look on Libby's face when she'd realized that pouring Roelke a drink had been a mistake. She'd even admitted her error—something so rare it deserved notation on a calendar. He'd have to reassure her on that score. None of his problems were her fault.

Roelke put his kettle on the stove to boil. He didn't know what herbal tea would do to his head, but it couldn't hurt.

Once the tea was steeping, Roelke sat down at the kitchen table. The index cards were still there, neatly stacked. He put the *Alex* card aside, and the *Simon* card too. Instead, he took a blank card and wrote *Bonnie* across the top. He'd focused primarily on how Simon Sabatola had treated Bonnie ever since Libby had told him to stop obsessing about the logistics of Bonnie's last moments.

But maybe Libby had been wrong about that, too.

Right this moment, with his brain too fuzzy-jittery to function well, something in Roelke's gut insisted that he needed to return to the scene he'd found on the White Oak Trail that day.

He drained his mug and shoved to his feet. Maybe he could grab a couple hours of sleep. He was off the next day, and he needed to make good use of it. He set his clock for 4:30 AM.

A few hours later the alarm's buzzer woke him from a deep sleep. Once he'd grabbed a quick shower, he felt ready to face the day.

The EPD was locked and dark when Roelke arrived. He washed out the coffeepot and made a strong, new batch. He cleared some counter space and spread out the photos he'd taken the morning Bonnie Sabatola committed suicide. Before sitting down he went to his locker to retrieve his water bottle. He picked up Erin Litkowski's photo too, and set it beside the photographs.

Roelke studied each shot slowly. Made some notes on index cards. Thought. Rearranged cards. Wrote some more.

Finally he leaned back in the chair. A single column of index cards now neatly bisected the counter. These cards had questions written on them. Questions he should have started asking days ago. He'd wasted time. And now, he was almost out of it.

He rummaged in the cupboard until he found a half-eaten package of Fig Newtons. Sounds like a Chloe-style breakfast, he thought, but forced his mind away. He couldn't afford to think about Chloe right now.

It was 7:15. Roelke looked up a phone number, dialed. "Hey, Peggy—yeah, it's me. I'm sorry to call so—yeah, I am at work. I—yeah, I am feeling better, thanks for asking. I—sure. I could meet you then." Roelke closed his eyes, hoping he was doing the right thing.

He'd made one more call before Marie arrived fifteen minutes later. The clerk assessed him with raised eyebrows. "Isn't this your day off?" She sat down at her desk, opened a file drawer, and dropped her purse inside.

"Yeah. But I needed to ask you a question."

"There's this thing called a telephone…"

Roelke grabbed a vacant chair, scooted it close, and dropped into it. "Has the Police Committee made their decision?"

The clerk sobered at once. "No. Nothing yet."

That was good, right? He needed to get through the next day or so without any walls crashing down. "Anything new on Harriet Van Dyne's murder?"

"No. Chief has a call in."

OK, down to business. "Marie, you remember that day we got the suicide call from Bonnie Sabatola? What happened after Skeet and I left?"

"Not much. I tried to keep her on the line, but she wouldn't talk."

"Do you remember what she said?"

Marie frowned. "What's this about?"

"Probably a wild goose chase," he admitted. "But I just can't put this one to rest until I've run every detail to ground."

"I asked her to tell me how she was feeling. I told her it would help me understand." Marie rubbed at a chip in the nail polish on one thumbnail. "Sometimes if people just have a chance to talk to someone, it can help. And Roelke, for a minute there, I thought I'd reached her."

This was new information. "Yeah?"

"I said that I imagined she must feel exhausted. And she said, 'I am. I'm just so, so tired.'" Marie looked at Roelke soberly. "And I thought, OK! We've actually made a connection!"

"What happened then?"

"Mrs. Sabatola said, 'Oh Jesus.' And then she hung up."

Roelke grimly considered that tidbit. He should have talked with Marie about this days ago. For Bonnie's sake, but also for Marie's. Very little got to Marie. Her conversation with Bonnie Sabatola obviously did.

"Sometimes all we can do is try," he told her.

"Yeah." Marie straightened her shoulders, and swiveled her chair back to her typewriter. "Get out of here. I need to get some work done."

Roelke collected some pamphlets from a file on the counter. Then he headed back out.

The village of Eagle had maintained a fire station since the fifties—decades longer than the police department had been in business—and an EMT squad since 1978. Other than the chief, all the responders were volunteers. And there was a long waiting list to get in. The cops and the firefighters often went out on calls together. Everyone pretty much got along and worked well together. It was another thing Roelke liked about working in Eagle.

Denise Miller wasn't on call that morning, but Roelke had phoned her at home, and she'd agreed to meet him at the station. She was so short she needed to stand back from most of the men so she didn't crick her neck making eye contact. But she was good at her job, and didn't seem to have any trouble fitting into the mostly male world at the fire station.

Roelke found her in the break room. "Hey, Denise. Thanks for coming in."

"No problem. The kids are at summer camp, so I'm fancy free. Whatcha need?"

Someone had left a bowl of pretzels on the table. Roelke took one and snapped off the tip. "You were on that suicide call in the state forest. I'm just trying to close the file on that one. I went over that scene with a flea comb, but ..." He snapped off another piece. "Sometimes it helps to have another pair of eyes. Did anything strike you as odd there?"

Denise tipped her head, considering. "Odd? No."

"Do you ... that is, could you go over what you remember?"

"Well…" Denise thought a moment before cataloging what she'd found. Her memories of Bonnie's body—its condition—meshed perfectly with Roelke's.

No surprise there. That was good, actually, even if unhelpful. "Thanks," he said. "That's what I had down."

"It's sad," Denise said slowly. "I mean, I learned a long time ago to leave stuff behind when I head home. But accidents—bad as they might be, they're *accidents*, you know? I hate seeing someone waste their life like that."

"Yeah."

"It was hard to tell if she was pretty, if you know what I mean. But she struck me as someone who cared about her appearance. You don't always see that in suicides. Those jeans were top dollar. And her sandals too. The heel on that one was cracked, but I don't suppose whatever Italian designed them expected them to be worn on a forest trail… Hey, Roelke? You OK?"

"Yeah. Sure." He blinked. "Thanks a million, Denise. I appreciate your help."

"Any time." She scooted her chair back and stood. "And Roelke? Don't leave without cleaning that up."

Startled, Roelke followed her pointing finger. The table in front of him was littered with bits of pretzel. "Will do," he said. When this mess was done, he'd send Denise a case of pretzels.

THIRTY-TWO

CHLOE HAD AVOIDED DELLYN—AND Markus—at Old World the day before, because she needed some space. Chloe had tried without success that evening to reach Dellyn by phone. So on Wednesday afternoon, Chloe locked up the trailer and went on site to search for her friend. Almost an hour later, Chloe finally spotted her hoeing weeds in the garden at the Danish farm.

"Hey," Chloe called.

"Hey." Dellyn wiped sweat from her cheeks with a sleeve of her blouse. "Have you heard any news about Harriet?"

"No." Chloe leaned against the fence. "I expect the police are keeping stuff quiet until they're ready to make an arrest. So, how did the tour with Markus go?"

"OK." Dellyn hacked at the soil again.

Chloe pinched her lips together. She felt a distance between them, and she had no idea what had caused it. "I wanted to fill you in on my trip to Madison on Monday. Long story short, Valerie's article left out a couple of key details about the Eagle Diamond. Here's the biggie: a German hired hand was working with Charles Wood that day. Much later, the German guy told a reporter that he'd found a gem, too. Get it? There might be a second Eagle Diamond!"

Dellyn went after a burdock plant. "I never heard that."

"What if someone gave your parents the second stone? Something smaller? It would be an incredible bit of Eagle history."

"Yeah," Dellyn agreed. "It sure would." But she didn't meet Chloe's gaze.

Something was definitely not right here. "So, what-say I stop by this evening?" Chloe asked. "We can work on the inventory."

"Thanks," Dellyn said. "But Valerie's coming by to help me tonight."

"Valerie *Bing?*" Chloe felt her eyebrows shoot skyward.

"Yeah. She called the other night, and said you'd told her about the inventory project. And she offered to help."

I, Chloe thought, am a complete idiot. She'd said way too much to Valerie.

A tram rumbled up to the farm and stopped to let visitors off. Chloe watched a young dad struggle to extricate a stroller. Finally she said, "Are you sure you're comfortable with that? I mean … you were the one who started worrying about all the coincidences. You know, the missing Kunz file, and not being able to find your dad's notes."

Dellyn sighed. "I can't imagine that Valerie had anything to do with any of that."

"But—"

"Look, Valerie doesn't have a job right now. What she does have is too much time on her hands. It's making her squirrely. She said I'd be doing her a kindness to let her help."

"Well, I'll come too, then," Chloe said brightly. "We'll get more done with three of us."

"Thank you, but no." Dellyn finally met her gaze, and she put a hand on Chloe's arm. "You've got your own stuff going on, and I've let you spend way too much time on mine. I'll see you tomorrow, OK?" With that she got back to work, moving farther down the row.

Chloe chewed her lower lip. Valerie's offer made her nervous. Dellyn's politeness made her even more nervous. It might mean she'd crossed a dangerous line. In any case, *something* had changed.

"Dellyn, are you going to sell the farm to Simon?"

"Maybe. Probably." Dellyn leaned on the hoe. "I need to be done with all this."

Shit, Chloe thought. Valerie Bing and Simon Sabatola. All Dellyn needed to do was invite Alex Padopolous over for tea and she'd have the trifecta of worrisome people, all in one place.

———

After talking to Peggy, Roelke drove to AgriFutures. Peggy's discreet digging had turned up some interesting intel about the behind-the-scenes battle raging at the company. Time to make one last visit.

When he presented himself in the reception area on the 6th floor of the building, Edwin Guest frowned. "Mr. Sabatola is preparing for a presentation he needs to make tomorrow," the secretary said. "This is quite a bad time."

Roelke tried to project regret. "I just have one final bit of business I need to take up with Mr. Sabatola. Could you ask him if he could spare me a few minutes?" He carefully phrased his request as a question.

Guest didn't answer. Roelke didn't move. After a moment of silent stand-off the secretary sighed loudly and turned away. He knocked on the door to the inner sanctum, slipped inside, and closed it firmly behind him.

Roelke leaned over Guest's desk. The daily calendar sat open, as it had before. Roelke quickly flipped back a few pages. And one more feeble ray of light shone on the enigma that was Bonnie Sabatola's last morning.

When Guest emerged from Simon Sabatola's office, Roelke was pretending to idly admire the man's African violets. "I'm afraid Mr. Sabatola is too busy to see you today," Guest said smoothly. "Is there something I can help you with?"

"Well, in that case … yes." Roelke ignored the flash of triumph in Guest's eyes. "Tell Mr. Sabatola that his wife's case is officially closed. And give him this." He held out a brochure labeled *Resources for the Bereaved.* "Please let him know that if he wants to talk with someone, if he *needs* to talk with someone, there are several good grief counselors in the area."

Guest accepted the brochure with a smile that was almost pleasant. "I'll let him know. Thank you."

Stupid little shit. He'd just been played like a piano. Roelke gave Guest a somber nod, and headed for the elevator.

———

After work, Chloe drove to Dellyn's house. So what if Valerie Bing was helping with the inventory? So what if Dellyn had told her not to come? The work would go faster with three people. Besides, Chloe wanted to keep an eye on Ms. Bing.

When she got there, though, the only vehicle in the driveway was Simon's luxury car. Shit. Now what? I should march right up there and bang on the door, Chloe thought. For all she knew, Simon Sabatola had arrived with legal papers all ready for Dellyn's signature. Perhaps Dellyn, right this minute, was signing away the property.

Chloe sat for several minutes, almost quivering with indecision. She wanted badly to go make sure Dellyn was not doing something she might regret. But the truth was … she'd only known Dellyn for a couple of months. And Dellyn had every right to make decisions about her own house.

Finally Chloe put the Pinto in drive, and headed home.

———

Roxie was wiping down the bar when Roelke walked into her Roost early that evening. He took a stool in front of her and tried unsuccessfully to catch her eye.

"You want a beer?" she asked, busily rubbing an invisible spot.

"No. I want some of your time."

She slid a quick, sideways glance in his direction. "I'm working here. I've gotta tend bar."

"I want to talk with you." Roelke was dressed in jeans again, and spoke quietly, but he used his best cop voice. "Can't Kiki cover the bar for a few minutes?"

Roxie sidled a little farther away.

Roelke moved to a closer stool. "We can talk here, or we can talk at the Elkhorn police station. What's your choice?"

After an indecisive pause, Roxie called her young waitress over. "Cover me for a few," she said. Kiki shrugged and sidled behind the bar.

Roxie headed toward a corner table. Roelke followed and settled into a chair across from her. "Kiki looks pretty comfortable behind the bar," he said. "I'm guessing she's been there before. Like, maybe last Thursday night?"

"Last Thursday night?"

"Yeah. Last Thursday night. You took a call. Then you left the tavern."

"I…" Roxie wet her lips. "I didn't take any call."

"Think that through, Roxie. The telephone company keeps records."

"Well… maybe I took a call, but that doesn't prove anything!"

Roelke smiled at her. "What do you think I'm trying to prove?"

She shook her head, and started to stand. "I don't know what you're—"

"Sit—*down*."

Roxie dropped back into her chair.

"Someone ran me off the road last Thursday night," Roelke said. He wasn't smiling anymore. "Right after I left this bar. And evidence left at the scene proves that two drivers were involved." That was pure BS, but it might rattle her. "I think one of those drivers was Edwin Guest. I doubt if Sabatola was the second driver. For one thing, he was plastered. For another, he doesn't strike me as the kind of man who likes to get his own hands dirty."

Roxie folded her arms over her chest. "I don't know about any second driver!" she hissed, staring at the wall.

"The timing is clear, Roxie. Guest and Sabatola left at ten PM. I was here for another forty, forty-five minutes. Guest had plenty of time to get Sabatola home, call you, and explain the plan. All you had to do was have Kiki cover the bar for twenty minutes so you could slip out, follow my truck, and help herd me off the road. Help try to kill me."

"I—*no!* It wasn't like that!"

Roelke forced down a flash of white-hot anger. *I knew it*, he thought. What he didn't know was why.

"It was just supposed to be a prank!" Roxie was saying. "I didn't know anything about running you off the road!"

"Who called you?"

"Edwin."

"And why did Edwin Guest want to harm me?"

She shook her head violently. "He didn't. He just said he wanted to rattle you."

"Why?"

"He didn't say. I swear to God. I swear on my mother's grave."

In Roelke's experience, swearing on loved ones' graves was a sure indication that the speaker was lying. "I know that AgriFutures is financially sound," he said. "I also know that Simon Sabatola doesn't get along with his brother Alan, and that board members are aligning themselves with one brother or the other. I know that Simon's not a sure thing to take his father's place, like he wants people to believe."

Roxie looked bewildered by the change of topic. "I, um, don't know anything about that."

"Oh, I think you do. This is the one place Simon Sabatola feels safe drowning his sorrows. Although," Roelke added conversationally, "I *also* know you two haven't been getting along well lately."

Roxie looked as if she was trying to figure out whether to agree with or deny that observation. Roelke let her stew. If he could just get this woman to flip, he might learn what he wanted to know.

He would not get anything that would lead to spouse abuse charges. A DA would howl with laughter at the notion that a statement made to an off-duty cop in a bar carried any weight when there was no actual evidence of any wrongdoing, criminal or otherwise.

But I want to know, Roelke thought. For Bonnie's sake, and for his own. Roxie had just confirmed that Sabatola and Guest weren't the pretty and well-behaved businessmen they pretended to be. Maybe they were sick SOBs who ran him off the road for the fun of it. Or maybe they were doing something illegal, most likely at AgriFutures, and were so paranoid about it that they felt compelled to strike at a cop just for hovering at the periphery of their lives.

Roelke smiled. If he couldn't nail Sabatola's ass for tormenting his wife, he'd be delighted to nail Sabatola's ass for something else.

"OK, Roxie, here's the deal," he said finally. "I need some information. You can give it to me, or you can go to prison for trying to kill a cop. What's it going to be?"

THIRTY-THREE

CHLOE WAS SLOGGING THROUGH Ralph Petty's make-work activity on Thursday when the phone rang. "It's me," Roelke said. "I need your help with something."

"What do you need?" Roelke wasn't one to make casual workday calls.

"I'm still trying to get a handle on AgriFutures. A friend of mine told me that the Sabatola brothers are engaged in a royal battle for the throne." His voice was tight, and Chloe couldn't tell if he was pissed at something, or frustrated. "It's gotten ugly. Simon Sabatola is involved in something that's either unethical or illegal."

She had no idea how he thought she could help.

"I overheard Dellyn talking once about small-time farmers in poor countries being pressured to replace their traditional crops with seeds from America," Roelke said. "Something about legumes and protein and something called cassava. And plants going extinct."

Chloe blinked. "When did you hear that conversation?"

"I'm kinda pressed for time right now. Do you know what she was talking about?"

"Cassava?" Chloe leaned back in her chair. "I'm out of my league. You really need to ask Dellyn."

"I tried. She's not by a phone, and I need to understand this."

"Oh." Chloe tried to marshal what she knew about old seeds and new corporations. "For centuries, people saved their own seeds. Or they bought seeds from little companies. Companies in one area provided varieties that might be different than the next little seed company over."

"OK, I get that."

"But now big corporations involved with genetic engineering are trying to come up with single strains of certain crops that they can push onto the global market. Often those new varieties have a higher yield than the old ones."

"Well, that would be good, right?"

"Not necessarily." Chloe tapped her pencil against her clipboard. "You've heard of the Irish potato famine, right? Mass starvation, mostly because a blight hit the potato crop?"

"Yeah. Lots of Irish people came over here."

"Right. All the potatoes in Europe succumbed to the disease. But in the Andes, people were growing hundreds or thousands of potato varieties, and some of them proved to be resistant to the blight. If that hadn't been the case, we wouldn't be eating mashed potatoes for dinner every Thanksgiving."

"Hunh."

"Well, the same type of thing can happen to any crop. Letting governments and agrochemical companies push a single variety of a particular crop has the potential for disaster."

Roelke was silent, and she gave him time to think that through. Finally he said, "I heard Alan Sabatola say at Bonnie's funeral that he wants AgriFutures to start breeding seeds. So ... if his scientists are developing some fancy new wheat seed, for example, some people might think it's great, and some might not."

"That might be why the board is split. The whole topic raises enormous ethical questions. If subsistence farmers accept the so-called new and improved variety, there's a good chance that the old varieties will eventually become extinct."

"And perhaps one of those old varieties is the only one that could have resisted the next blight or pest that comes along."

"Exactly. And AgriFutures does other things too, right? Equipment, chemicals, all that stuff?

"Right."

"Well, Alan Sabatola can talk about how the new seeds will create a bigger yield, and therefore help feed the hungry. All very humanitarian. But the *real* truth might be that those new crops will make the farmers in Ghana or Bolivia or wherever dependent on AgriFutures' implements and fertilizers and pesticides."

"Which makes even more money for the company."

"And it traps farmers in a cycle they can't get out of. It may even be that Alan's scientists engineer the seeds in such a way that they *can't* be saved to plant the next year, which means the farmers are forced to purchase what they need from AgriFutures every year. It's a vicious trap."

"Hunh." Another pause. "OK, thanks."

Chloe frowned. "Roelke, wait a minute! Do you think—"

"I gotta go." He hung up.

She was still thinking that over when the site farmer called. "Chloe? It's Larry. Do you know where Dellyn is? She was supposed to meet a couple of garden volunteers in the village an hour ago."

Chloe didn't like the sound of that. "Did you try her home number?"

"Yeah. No answer."

Chloe hung up the phone slowly. Dellyn had probably just spaced the obligation. Still … it wasn't like her.

All right, enough of Petty's crap. Chloe gathered up the pages she'd completed, and scrawled a note on the top: *I received several calls from potential donors today, so this is as far as I got. Will finish tomorrow.* She dropped off the note for Petty, burying it in his mailbox in hopes he wouldn't see it for a while.

Then she went looking. Dellyn wasn't in the drafty sun porch at the Education Building she used as a makeshift office. She wasn't at the barn in the administration area, where she had a corner to store plants and tools. Chloe looped through the historic site proper on foot, checking each of the gardens Dellyn maintained. No luck.

"Well, shit," Chloe muttered, as she scanned the last garden. With almost six hundred acres of trails and roads, it wasn't hard to miss someone. But Chloe had nabbed every interpreter she could find and asked if they'd seen Dellyn. No one had.

By the time Chloe got back to the parking lot, it was 4:30. She drove to Dellyn's house. She was going to make sure her friend was OK, even if Simon Sabatola was there with an army of lawyers.

At the house, no one answered Chloe's knock. The garden was empty, too.

Chloe stood on the front step, hugging her arms across her chest. Maybe Dellyn had run to the grocery store for peanut butter.

Or … maybe she was in the house, unwilling—or unable—to respond.

Chloe unlocked the door with the key Dellyn had given her. When she went inside she almost tripped over a pile of mail that had been shoved through the old-fashioned door slot, but managed to side-step without trampling anything. "Dellyn?" she yelled. "It's me, Chloe. Are you here?"

No answer. Something bitter slid up Chloe's throat as she began a quick circle of the downstairs rooms. The last time she'd entered a friend's home like this, she'd found the man dead in a pool of blood.

No similar scenes downstairs today. Chloe pounded up to the second floor. She felt uncomfortable intruding into Dellyn's bedroom, but she did it anyway. Finally she checked the attic, poking around among the piles of cartons and haphazard storage of antiques.

Nothing. Chloe sagged with relief. Thank God.

But … no. Dellyn wasn't in the house, but that didn't mean she was OK. *Shit*, Chloe thought. Dellyn, where are you?

———

Roelke got to Roxie's Roost about four-thirty. Several vets were swapping tales of their service days. A young couple played darts in the corner. And Simon Sabatola was parked on a bar stool with a shot glass in front of him.

Roxie tossed a nervous gaze toward Roelke. He ignored her and headed toward the middle of the bar, then paused and veered, as if just noticing someone he knew. "Mr. Sabatola!" he said, sliding onto the stool beside the businessman. "Good afternoon, sir."

Simon Sabatola squinted at him through reddened eyes, then looked back at the glass of amber liquid. "Hello, officer."

"Please—it's just Roelke." He raised his voice and ordered a beer and a glass of water.

Sabatola emptied his shot. "And give me another."

Roelke didn't speak again until Roxie had delivered the drinks and disappeared again. Then he leaned toward Sabatola. "I hope the materials I dropped off with your secretary yesterday proved helpful."

"Nothing is helpful." Sabatola spoke with the precise care of someone trying to pretend he was still sober. "Today I should be celebrating my wedding anniversary. And instead..." He picked one hand up in a vague gesture: *Look where I am, what I'm doing.*

"Oh man, that's tough."

"My wife was a beautiful woman."

"I've seen pictures." Roelke shook his head, half admiring and half sympathetic. "It's hard to understand why a gorgeous woman like that, living in a beautiful home, with a successful husband to be proud of..."

Sabatola ran one finger around the rim of his shot glass. "She had every reason to be happy."

"From what I could see, you'd given her everything any woman could ask for."

Sabatola drained his glass.

"I mean, you've clearly been working your ass off to help build AgriFutures. Did your wife understand that?"

Sabatola remained silent. For a moment Roelke thought he'd gone too far. But finally Sabatola muttered, "She never did. And when we needed her help, just the one time…"

Roelke struggled to find context for that unexpected bit of information, and came up empty. "She wasn't willing?" He shook his head, mortally stymied by the perfidy of women.

"She was—not—willing."

Roelke lowered his voice another notch. "Mr. Sabatola, I have a lot of admiration for you. Now that your wife's case is officially closed, I've been putting the file to bed and…" He spread his hands, palms up. "There are still some things, just a couple of little things, that don't add up." He paused, giving Sabatola a silence to fill.

"Roxie!" Sabatola yelled. "Bring me another one."

"I gotta admire you, man," Roelke said. "I think I know what was going on. You must have felt pushed beyond endurance. How did you manage to keep things hidden?"

Sabatola studied his empty glass for a moment, and then traded it for the shot Roxie deposited in front of him. "The secret," he said finally, "is control. You must not ever let anyone steal your power. Especially not a woman."

Roelke felt adrenaline throbbing through his veins. He almost trembled with the effort of appearing relaxed. "Yeah? I suppose that's true in the business world. About not letting anyone steal your power."

"You remember that," Sabatola told him.

"How's that thing with the Board coming?" Roelke asked. "Have they announced your new position yet?"

Sabatola's jaw jutted forward like a truculent child's. "That," he said, "is none of your damn business." He walked away. Conversation over. Game over.

Roelke left the bar. Dammit! he thought, as he started his truck. Sabatola had not given him anything concrete. Nothing he could track down or verify. Nothing that suggested whatever activity he so desperately did not want Roelke to know about. Whatever secret had been worth trying to run Roelke off the road just because he was hanging around.

There was just one small saving grace. Those comments about control and power and women—Roelke felt he could officially warn Dellyn Burke to stay away from Sabatola, now. Maybe that was why he'd needed to do this. Maybe that was enough.

But it didn't feel like enough.

———

Chloe went back downstairs and headed to Mr. Burke's study, hoping to find some clue to Dellyn's whereabouts. No luck on that, but she did find a deed to the Burke property. Chloe stared at it grimly. Why did Simon want this place? The Eagle Diamond, or even a second diamond, would have no meaning for him. Neither would the detritus of Eagle history tucked into the attic, or any personal Burke family heirlooms mingled among the other antiques.

Roelke thought the guy was capable of violence. Dellyn thought he was a nice guy after all. Was Simon Sabatola being kind to his sister-in-law, or trying to get her out of the way?

Chloe turned her back on the deed and headed into the kitchen. There must be a calendar or something around here! She scanned the cluttered room. She didn't see a calendar, but at least it looked as if Dellyn was still busy with normal activities. Small labeled trays by the windowsill held seeds from various vegetables, laid out to dry. Custard cups held tomato seeds, moldering stinkily in their gelatinous sacs. The tops of several dead hollyhocks lay across the kitchen table. The blooms had been replaced by pods, each now open to reveal rings of dark seeds.

A telephone was mounted on the wall beside the kitchen counter. A pen and pad sat waiting. The top sheet was blank, but it held obvious indentations of whatever had been scrawled on the page above. Chloe scrabbled among the clutter and found a pencil. "This is so frickin' Nancy Drew," she muttered, feeling ridiculous as she lightly covered the paper with graphite. The last written note appeared as white lines: *Meet Frietags, tomorrow, 5 PM*. Driving directions were below.

Chloe felt her eyebrows rise. Dellyn was meeting the Frietags? Markus must have arranged that, although since the directions were to the farm itself, the plan must have been for Dellyn to go alone. Assuming that "tomorrow" meant today, Dellyn would be at the Frietag place right about … now.

Chloe plopped into a kitchen chair and frowned, feeling oddly left out. Would it have killed Markus or Dellyn to at least mention this trip? Something weird was going on. Something had been bugging Dellyn ever since Markus had toured the site with her on Tuesday.

After all, the note wasn't proof-positive that Dellyn had actually *gone* to New Glarus. She'd missed her meeting with the volunteers that afternoon.

And what would happen if Dellyn spotted the rose-carved cultivator in the Frietags' barn? Chloe hadn't mentioned it because she didn't want to add any tinder to Dellyn's firestorm of worries. Too late now.

Chloe picked up the phone, called information, and managed to track down the number for Martine's parents. She dialed. No answer.

Shit. Chloe sank back down at the kitchen table, trying to decide what to do. Perhaps pushed by her breath, two tiny hollyhock seeds dropped from their pods onto the paper towel tucked underneath. She remembered Dellyn saying that Puritan women sometimes brewed tea from dried hollyhock flowers to prevent miscarriages. And that Aztec people used zinnias to treat eye ailments. What had Markus said? Kids learn in school that the rainforest is full of medicinal plants, but no one thinks to wonder if the cure for a disease might be growing in some old woman's garden down the road.

Thank heavens people like Dellyn were working to preserve such things, Chloe thought. And credit went to gardeners like Mrs. Burke as well, for keeping such detailed journals.

And then there was the other end of the spectrum—what Roelke had been asking about when he'd called earlier. Agro-chemical companies muscling small seed companies aside, practically enslaving peasant farmers and quite possibly destroying crops and processes that might be essential in addressing the next global catastrophe, all in the name of progress. And profits.

A new and troubling idea wormed into the mix, feeding her growing unease. Was it possible ... ? No. Or was it?

Chloe glanced around the sunny kitchen. "Mrs. Burke?" she whispered. "Bonnie? I could use some help here. I'm worried about Dellyn." She tried to listen, to be open for any advice.

Nothing.

Well, sitting here wasn't going to accomplish anything. Chloe headed for the front door. She paused to scoop up the mail she'd almost tripped over. As she was setting it aside, a white envelope caught her eye. Her skin began to prickle. It bore a foreign stamp, and had no return address, but the writing was familiar. It was Bonnie Sabatola's.

"That's all the sign I need," Chloe muttered. She grabbed the envelope, locked the house behind her, and trotted to her car. She was going to New Glarus.

———

Roelke had an evening duty shift, and he left Roxie's with just enough time to get to work. The office was empty, which was good, because he wasn't in the mood to talk to anybody.

Did you really hope to get a full confession out of Simon Sabatola? he chided himself. Drunk or sober, Simon Sabatola was not a man to lose control easily. Roxie was scared enough to testify about Sabatola's involvement in the accident that had totaled Roelke's truck. *But I can't pursue that,* he growled silently, *because I was drinking.*

Roelke slammed his locker door, put on his duty belt, and dropped into a chair. *Guest was in the middle of all this, too. I couldn't crack Sabatola,* Roelke thought, *so maybe I need to look again at Guest.*

He pulled a now-creased and soft-edged index card from the stack in his pocket and stared at his list of known facts about the secretary:

—*Grows African violets, likes dogs; no other known personal interests*

—*Very poor as a child; homeless; wore pajama top because no $ for a shirt; nothing but a neighbor's herbal tea when no $ for dr.*

—*Science geek in school. Smart, but no $ for college*

—*Sabatola got a professional break because of his step-dad; Guest took secretarial role, subservient—source of more anger?*

—*But protects Sabatola, seems loyal*

—*Handled plan to run me off the road*

Guest was a science geek. Guest grew African violets. Roelke thought about what Chloe had told him about genetic engineering and global argibusiness corporations. Was Guest trespassing into Alan Sabatola's arena? If so, that would create even more animosity between the Sabatola brothers.

Roelke turned that possibility around in his mind. It was an interesting theory, but he couldn't find a way to make it useful.

Well, he needed to head out on patrol, anyway. He was almost to the door when he noticed a missed-call slip in his mailbox.

Roelke—Chloe Ellefsen called 5:45 PM. Said she's going to New Glarus to look for Dellyn Burke who is visiting an elderly couple. Wants to talk to you about the Eagle Diamond (!). Please call her at home later.—Marie

Roelke frowned at the note, trying to sniff out Chloe's motivation for leaving the message. New Glarus, of all places. He really wished the stupid Swiss people who'd settled Green County in the last century had gone elsewhere. Ontario, maybe. Or Wyoming would have been good.

He also wished he'd never heard of the Eagle Diamond. Chloe was way off base on this one. Roelke still didn't know why Guest and Sabatola had felt compelled to run him off the road, but he was willing to bet his career that finding the Eagle Diamond was not part of their business plan.

Well, he'd call Chloe later if he got the chance. He crumpled the note and tossed it into the trash. Outside, the radio squawked before he'd even settled in the car. "George 220. We have a report of a drunk driver heading east from Palmyra on Highway 59. He's driving an AMC Pacer, two-tone cream over brown."

Great, Roelke thought. Just what he needed tonight. Another drunk.

THIRTY-FOUR

CHLOE GOT LOST TWICE while trying to find her way back to the Frietags' farm, but eventually she spotted the red mailbox that marked their drive, and turned in. A wind had kicked up, and the trees along the lane waved their branches in a frenzied greeting that did nothing to calm her nerves.

When she finally emerged into the clearing, she blew out a long breath. A car she didn't recognize was parked near the house—Martine's, probably—and Dellyn's car was beside it. So she *was* here! Chloe hadn't been willing to admit how scared she'd been of *not* finding her friend here.

The farmyard looked deserted, but a faint tang of wood smoke hung in the air and the occasional chime of a cowbell drifted down from the hill behind the barn. No one answered the front door when Chloe knocked, so she walked around the house. The kitchen garden and farmyard were empty. A thin plume of smoke was just visible rising from the *Käsehütte* chimney before being whipped away by the wind. Martine must be making another batch of cheese.

Frieda and Dellyn were probably in the granary, talking about heirloom veggies. Chloe headed in that direction, but she paused to poke her head into the cheese house's open door. "Hello? Martine, it's—"

Chloe's stomach clenched like a fist. The hut was littered with tools: a curd scoop, calipers, a trier, wooden hoops. The huge copper kettle of milk steamed over its fire, but the big whey bucket had overturned. The liquid had flowed over the floor.

And Dellyn lay on her side in the middle of it, curled in a ball. Her clothes were torn. They were bloody. Very bloody. The metallic smell mixed sickly with the odor of milk.

Oh God oh God oh God. Chloe crouched beside her friend. "*Dellyn!*"

"Chloe?" Dellyn whispered. Her eyelids fluttered.

Chloe clutched that whisper of recognition to her heart like a prayer. "You're going to be OK, you hear me? You're going to be OK." Dellyn didn't respond.

Chloe fought down panic. She had to stop the blood loss. Both of Dellyn's forearms were bleeding, and she had a horrid tear in one calf. Smaller wounds seeped red from her neck, one shoulder … It was too much. Chloe had no idea where to start, and nothing to use anyway. "Hang on," she said. "I'm going to get help."

She scrambled for the door. A growling blur of fur flew at her.

Chloe stumbled backward and hit the kettle of hot milk. She snatched a curd-cutting harp and swung it like a baseball bat. She connected, breaking the German shepherd's trajectory. "Get away from me!" she screamed. "Get *away!*"

With sickening clarity Chloe understood that she was staring at the creature that had left Dellyn torn and bleeding on the floor.

The dog snapped and snarled and lunged as Chloe jabbed ineffectually with the eight-foot-long tool. The hot kettle rim burned against her back. The fire beneath the kettle scorched her ankles. Steam basted her shirt, her hair. Her arms already ached.

Don't show fear, she told herself. But it was way, way too late for that.

———

"I'm gonna kick your fucking ass," Lester Odell promised from the back seat, as Roelke drove him to the Waukesha hospital. "I'll shoot you while you're sleeping."

Roelke gritted his teeth. Was this a little joke from the cosmos? The drunk he'd *wanted* to talk, hadn't. Now this one wouldn't shut up.

Worse, Odell had to compete with an equally persistent voice whispering in Roelke's head: *Chloe wouldn't have left a message like that if it wasn't important.* Roelke still couldn't imagine what might have prompted the call, but it nagged at him.

A moment of blissful silence was cut short by a loud thump. Although cuffed, Odell had managed to undo his seat belt. He lay now on the seat, his feet raised to make another try at kicking out the side window.

Roelke made sure the road was clear. Then he hit the brakes.

Lester Odell bounced onto the floor. "You're trying to kill me!" he howled, as he flopped fish-like back onto the seat.

"Sir, your safety is my top priority," Roelke assured him. "If you'd kicked that window out, you might have gotten cut on the glass. I couldn't let that happen."

Roelke had radioed ahead that Odell was combative and refusing the state-mandated blood draw. When he reached the ER lot, the goon squad was waiting—five of the biggest, burliest deputies in the county. "He's all yours," Roelke told them. Once inside, they disappeared behind a curtain to wait for a nurse.

Roelke paced the hall. Simon Sabatola was drinking himself into oblivion at Roxie's Roost. There was no reason to be concerned about Chloe. She and Dellyn were visiting some old people—hardly a reason to call out the New Glarus police.

Even if he wanted to, he didn't know where to send them.

But Chloe's phone message bothered him. He needed to do *something*. And he'd be busy with Mr. Lester Odell and paperwork for hours.

One solution presented itself. No *way*, Roelke growled silently. He paced again. Tried to come up with Plan B. Couldn't.

Damn it all to hell. "Hey," he called to the nearest deputy. "I need to make a phone call."

Roelke fished several dimes from his pocket and fed the waiting room's pay phone. He felt ready to whack the receiver against his forehead a few times. He'd been acting like a nutjob for a while now, but this was beyond reason.

Then he thought about Chloe and Dellyn. He started dialing.

It took several calls, actually, but he finally got through to the person he was trying to reach. "This is Officer Roelke McKenna of the Eagle Police Department," he said, jaw muscles clenched so tightly he had to force out the words. "I need your help."

———

The German shepherd trotted back and forth in front of Chloe, ears back, ready to spring the moment she lowered the harp. Was he rabid? Or had somebody trained the dog to attack, and then let him slip away from home? More important, was Dellyn still alive? She hadn't moved, even when the dog growled inches away from her. And—oh God, had the dog attacked Frieda and Martine too? Maybe they lay somewhere outside, bleeding to death like Dellyn.

"I can't do this," Chloe whimpered. Tears stung her eyes. Her throat was raw. Her muscles trembled. Soon her arms would stop obeying commands. It occurred to her that the dog knew that. He could get past the curd harp right now if he wanted to. He seemed to be toying with her, waiting for her to tire.

Chloe scanned the tiny building. The shepherd was between her and the main door. The side door was closed … but even if it wasn't, running wasn't an option. No *way* would she reach her car in one piece.

That left one direction: up.

The enormous copper kettle was supported by three heavy wooden beams. One stood upright. One branched out horizontally from the top of the vertical post. One angled between the two, a brace that supported the horizontal piece. The sum total looked distressingly like a gallows. But from that high beam she'd be able to scramble to the rafters. Those would be out of the dog's reach. At least Chloe hoped so.

If she tried to crawl onto the kettle rim to start the climb she'd likely fall into a thousand pounds of hot, coagulating milk. But behind her, and a little to one side, was the more solid square of bricked masonry that encased Frieda's old laundry kettle. Chloe felt a tiny flicker of hope.

A split-second assessment extinguished it. She couldn't clamber onto the masonry without the dog reaching her. Even if she miraculously managed to get that far, gaining the upper horizontal beam was beyond her. On a good day. If only—

The German shepherd lunged.

Chloe dropped the harp and launched, scrabbling and scraping and pushing. As she got her butt on the brickwork she felt a sharp tug on one leg. She braced for pain, but the dog had only snagged her jeans. He jerked her leg back and forth like a chew toy. She kicked. Denim gave way with a harsh ripping sound.

Chloe got her feet beneath her on the brickwork, and kept going. Her arms grabbed for the upper beam, wrapped around it convulsively.

Upper body strength had never been part of Chloe's physiology. In college, on whitewater canoe trips, she had more than once gotten wet because while she had the skill to read rapids, she didn't have the brute force sometimes needed to run them. In junior high gym class, confronted with climbing ropes, she'd never made it more than a foot or two off the floor. On the elementary school playground, she'd never made it across the monkey bars.

Evidently primal fear affected physiology more than children's taunts because somehow, grunting and flailing, Chloe managed to get one leg hooked over the horizontal beam. Then the other. For a moment she hung there koala-like, hugging the beam, panting. So far so good. But true safety would come only by reaching the *top* of the horizontal beam.

Her arms trembled violently. How hot was that milk below her, anyway? She really didn't want to know.

You have to try, she told herself. Right now. There was no point in pissing around, wasting what little strength she had left.

Chloe clenched her teeth, scrunched her eyes closed, and scraped her right leg against the beam until the wood was under one knee. Then she gathered herself up tight and made one violent wrenching twist upwards. She heard herself gasping with pain as she wriggled against the beam. She couldn't manage another true heave but instead almost willed herself those last inches, up … and over. Finally she was on top of the beam. From there it was an easier heave onto one of the rafters. Chloe lay motionless for a moment, making sure she was balanced, thanking the universe for all favors.

Then she opened her eyes. Dellyn still lay bleeding on the floor. The German shepherd was nowhere in sight.

Chloe didn't know whether to laugh or cry. The damn dog had probably disappeared before she even fought her way to her current perch.

But … what now? She may have clawed her way to a safe spot, but she couldn't stay there. Not with Dellyn lying on the floor in a pool of whey and blood. Not with Martine and Frieda unaccounted for.

Chloe knew with complete certainty that if she went back down, she would be unable to make the climb again. Not if all of hell's hounds were coming at her. The dog would probably be back the instant she descended. But what else could she do? She had to try to get help.

Gravity did most of the work. Chloe slipped, slithered, and banged her way back to the floor. Her knees buckled, but with a staggered step or two she managed to stay on her feet. "I'm going for help," she panted, in case Dellyn might hear.

Chloe picked up the curd harp she'd wielded earlier, and peeked warily out the door. No sign of the German shepherd. OK, time to make a run for it.

Stumbling across the farmyard, Chloe expected the dog to fly at her again any second. She kept her head down, hoping that if she didn't look for the German shepherd, he wouldn't reappear. Chloe didn't see the man until she almost ran into him. His shoes came into her circle of vision first—expensive-looking leather, well polished.

"Thank God!" She lurched to a halt. "I need help—my friend has been hurt—"

"Give me your car keys."

"What?" Chloe stared at him. He was a small man with a receding hairline. A huge cobweb was mashed on one shoulder of his gray three-piece suit. She recognized him from Bonnie's funeral. Edwin Guest.

The German shepherd trotted from behind the parked cars. Chloe froze, skin prickling. The man snapped his fingers, pointed at Chloe, and muttered, "Ajax, *hold*." The dog crouched, growling with menace.

"Your keys!" Guest snapped. "Or I'll have Ajax rip you apart."

Chloe felt tears burn her eyes. Dellyn was going to bleed to death. And so, evidently, was she.

"*Unten!*" a woman's voice bellowed from behind her. "Chloe, *unten!*"

Chloe dropped to the ground. She pulled her knees toward her chest and her arms up to protect her head. The air quivered with a thwanging sound. Guest screamed. He hit the earth with a thump. The dog howled. Chloe rolled away from man and dog and scrambled to her feet. She gaped at the shaft of an arrow extending from Guest's thigh. Her mind didn't want to process the unexpected image.

"You bitch!" Guest gasped. He tried to sit up, couldn't manage it.

Martine stood by the old smokehouse with the stock of a wooden crossbow pressed against one shoulder. A second arrow was already in place. "Don't make me shoot again!" she yelled. "I don't want to hurt the dog, but I will if I have to. And I won't think twice about killing you."

"Ajax, stay," Guest grunted. His face was white. One hand was clenched in pain. The other clutched at the place where the arrow had entered his thigh. Blood seeped between his fingers, scarlet on white. Ajax whined anxiously, nosing at his master's shoulder.

Chloe felt every second ticking past. "Martine, Dellyn's hurt! I've got to go call 9-1-1. Where's Frieda?"

"He locked both of us in the springhouse," Martine muttered, keeping her attention—and the arrow—focused on Guest. "I had to pull some stones from one wall and crawl out through the hole. Anyway, you can't drive to get help. Your car has a flat—"

My car has a flat? Chloe thought stupidly. Since when?

"—so it would be quicker if you run for help," Martine was saying. "Go straight up over the hill behind the barn and you'll see my folks' place down the valley."

"But—are you—"

"This bastard isn't going anywhere."

Chloe didn't doubt Martine's assessment, but she did doubt her own ability to run anywhere just then. Her muscles felt like hot chocolate. "What about his car?"

"I slashed his tires," Martine said impatiently. "Chloe, *go!*"

The German shepherd jerked his head up and stared down the drive. Then Chloe heard the sound of an approaching car. They all watched as a blue Ford Fairmont emerged from the tree-lined drive.

The driver parked, jumped from the car, and took in the tableau with wide eyes. "What the hell is going on here? Chloe, are you all right?"

Chloe ran to him. His arms went around her, and she put her head against his shoulder. "Oh, Markus. Thank God you're here."

THIRTY-FIVE

ONCE MARKUS UNDERSTOOD THE situation, he drove back down the drive at frantic speed. By the time he returned Chloe had fetched towels and a blanket from the house, and had done her best to bandage Dellyn's wounds.

Markus skidded into the *Käsehütte*. "Holy mother of God," he whispered, crouching beside Dellyn.

"She's still alive."

"Cops and ambulance are on the way. Martine's father and uncle came with me. Brought their shotguns. Are Frieda and Johann all right?"

"When I got the towels a few minutes ago, Johann was sleeping peacefully. Frieda's ..." Chloe's voice trailed away as Martine pounded past. "Stay with Dellyn, OK?"

Chloe caught up at the springhouse door. Martine grabbed Guest's shiny new padlock and gave it a wrenching pull. "Damn!" she muttered, then raised her voice. "Gran? You OK in there?"

No answer. Fear darkened Martine's eyes. Chloe followed as Martine ran around the building to a waist-level hole where several stones had been hacked from the crumbling mortar. She thrust her upper body through the hole, pushed off the ground, and slithered through.

As Chloe reached the hole she heard Martine moan. "Oh, *Gran*."

Something hot and white and furious boiled up and over. Chloe forgot that her muscles didn't work. She ran across the yard, past Martine's father and uncle where they stood with shotguns trained on Guest. "You killed Frieda!" she screamed. "You maybe killed Dellyn! And you almost killed me! All for some *seeds!*"

Guest's lip curled in a sneer. He opened the fingers of his clenched fist. The breeze snatched a folded bit of brown paper he'd been holding and danced it away, scattering its miniscule contents.

———

Roelke had asked Meili to call dispatch once he was sure Chloe and Dellyn were OK. Since getting back to the EPD, Roelke had radioed twice to see if Alpine Boy had checked in. Nada. Roelke didn't know whether that meant the women were *not* OK, or if Meili was just being a jerk.

Maybe, Roelke thought, I shouldn't have threatened the guy.

He'd just finished faxing his report on Lester Odell to the DA when the phone rang. Roelke snatched it. "McKenna here." He braced himself to hear Meili's voice.

"R-Roelke?" Chloe quavered.

Jesus. The clock stopped ticking. Roelke's unnecessary functions—sight, for example—stopped working. His body rejected everything other than her voice. "What's wrong? Are you hurt?"

"I'm f-fine," Chloe said. "But Dellyn's in the hospital. She got m-mauled by a German shepherd. She lost a lot of blood, and for a while they weren't sure …" Another loud sniffle. "They think she'll pull through. But Roelke? Frieda and Johann—they're both dead." She began to weep.

A man's voice murmured something in the background. Meili. Roelke ached with the longing to be there, to be the one providing comfort. "Who are Frieda and Johann?" he asked after a moment.

She blew her nose. "This wonderful old Swiss couple. I'll tell you about them when you get here. We're at the hospital in Monroe. I mean … can you come? You really need to. The cops have Edwin Guest, and—"

"Hold tight," Roelke said. "I'm on my way."

Roelke drove hot, lights-and-sirens, and made it to Monroe in an hour. He found Chloe and Meili huddled into orange plastic chairs in the ER waiting room. Chloe's head was on Meili's shoulder; her eyes were closed. Roelke was enormously glad that he saw them a moment before Meili saw him. Roelke's cop face was in place when Meili nudged Chloe awake.

Roelke pulled another chair in front of the couple and sat. "You're OK?" he asked Chloe.

Chloe sat up straight, wiped her eyes, nodded. "I'm OK."

Roelke forced himself to look Meili in the eye. "Thank you."

Meili nodded. There was no look of triumph in his face. Triumph would likely come later, when the shock of whatever had unfolded this evening had passed.

———

"Guest won't be released tonight," Officer Buckley of the New Glarus PD told Roelke. "The arrow—"

The *arrow?*

"—came close to the hip. There's joint damage." Buckley shrugged. He was middle-aged but still compact and muscular, with a welcome air of competency. "He might need surgery."

"Did he kill the elderly couple?" Roelke asked. "The Frietags?"

The other man spread his hands in a *Who knows?* gesture. "That's not yet clear. Guest lawyered up real quick. Then Miss Ellefson told us what she knew, and said she'd called you. I figured I'd wait, since you've already had contact with the guy."

"Thanks," Roelke said. "I'll see what I can shake out of him."

Buckley led him into a closet-sized room. Guest looked even smaller than usual lying on the pillows of a hospital bed, wearing a gown. A gray-haired man in a navy pin-striped suit sat vigil in one corner. Buckley settled against the wall in another corner.

Being back in a hospital reminded Roelke viscerally of his own recent visit to an emergency room—courtesy of this asshole. "Mr. Guest," Roelke said. "We need to talk."

"I want a deal."

"Now Edwin," Mr. Suit began. "Let me—"

Guest tried to hitch himself higher in bed, and winced in pain. "I want a deal!"

Roelke wanted to pummel the little man. "What makes you think we'll make a deal with you? There's no reason to give you anything."

"Simon Sabatola abused his wife," Guest said. "That's what you wanted to confirm, right? I won't tell what I know about that without a deal."

Roelke looked at him with contempt. This coward had been ready to kill for his boss, but as soon as things went south, he wanted to flip and tell all. "There's no reason to make a deal with you," Roelke repeated. "We have evidence of the harm you did at the Frietag farm this evening. *That's* going to carry your sorry ass to prison." At least he hoped-to-God so.

Mr. Suit cleared his throat. "My client—"

"As for Sabatola," Roelke continued, "his wife is dead and buried. You can talk yourself hoarse, but it won't give me anything I can use to convict her husband of a crime. I'd need evidence."

To Roelke's astonishment, Edwin Guest smiled. "You want evidence?" he asked smugly. "I've got evidence."

———

For the second time, Roelke found himself fishing for coins at the pay phone in an ER lobby. And for much the same reason. Evidently the police gods thought that one helping of humble pie that night had not been enough for Officer Roelke McKenna.

Midnight had come and gone, but Skeet answered on the second ring. "It's McKenna," Roelke said. "Sorry to call so late, man, but I've got a situation here." And I didn't want to call one of the younger part-timers, he added silently. This expedition could end badly. Skeet might cut corners, but when shit hit the fan, he was steady.

"Sure thing," Skeet said. "What and where?"

Roelke told him. By the time he'd driven back from Monroe, Skeet's car was sitting in Edwin Guest's driveway.

The home was not as palatial as Sabatola's, but it was nice. More important, the house and yard were sheltered on all sides by woods.

No nosy neighbors would see their bright flashlights, or hear noise and wonder.

"Thanks, man," Roelke said. He gave Skeet a condensed version of what he'd learned from Guest that night. "No reason to think we're walking into anything here. No reason to think Guest hasn't been acting alone. But I need two hands to dig. Company seemed like a good idea."

They played the beams from their strong lights around the yard. "OK," Roelke said, when his light caught a doghouse and run, surrounded by a chain-link fence. "Here it is." Since Ajax had been taken into custody by Green County's animal control crew, the kennel area was empty.

Roelke kicked aside a large metal water bowl. Then he holstered his flashlight, grabbed the shovel he'd brought, and began to dig.

Six inches down the blade hit something solid. "Got it," Roelke said. Adrenalin pumped through his veins. Ten minutes more and he had unearthed a hard-plastic cooler. He jerked off the lid. The two men stared at the cooler's contents.

"Shit," Skeet said.

Roelke felt a surge of fury and vindication so hot it almost scalded his throat. "I've *got* the bastard," he said. "Let's go."

They stopped at the EPD long enough to process the evidence properly and package it for the state crime lab. Then they headed back to the squad car. "You don't want to wait 'til dawn?" Skeet asked.

"No. No *way*."

Skeet shrugged. "Your call."

No lights and sirens, this time. Roelke didn't want Sabatola to know he was coming. He slowed when they reached Sabatola's long driveway, and parked in a way that blocked the garage.

The house was dark and silent. When no one answered Roelke's bang on the door he knew a sick moment of fear. Had Sabatola somehow known he was coming, and fled? Roelke pounded again. Finally he heard the metallic click of a latch being thrown, and the outside light came on. The door opened a crack, and a woman's frightened face appeared. She was a middle-aged Latina, wearing a long bathrobe over her nightgown.

Roelke flashed his badge. "Eagle Police," he said. "Is Mr. Sabatola at home?"

"Mr. Sabatola is sleeping!" the woman said, stepping back as the two officers came inside. She clutched the bathrobe close beneath her chin.

"Wake him up," Roelke said. "Tell him Officer Roelke McKenna is here. And that Waukesha County deputies have surrounded the house." That was a lie, but it couldn't hurt.

Sabatola must have heard the commotion, because he came downstairs just moments after the Latina woman disappeared. He wore dark blue pajamas and a matching robe—both silk, of course—and slippers made from glossy leather. "Officer McKenna?" he demanded. "It's two AM! What is—"

"In here." Roelke jerked his head toward the living room. He turned on a table lamp beside the beautiful photo of Bonnie Sabatola. "Sit down."

Sabatola hesitated, then obeyed. Roelke saw a flash of unease in the man's eyes. Skeet stayed on his feet, vigilant but out of the way.

Roelke began to pace in front of Sabatola. "I'm here to discuss your wife, Mr. Sabatola."

"What about her?" The other man started to rise again.

"Sit *down*," Roelke ordered. Because of his own impatience they were doing this in Sabatola's home—in his own comfort zone. Roelke at least wanted the advantage of physical dominance.

"You know, Mr. Sabatola, I still have some lingering questions about your wife's suicide," he began. "Let me lay out some facts for you. First of all, Mrs. Sabatola told us where to look for her wallet and keys. But when Officer Deardorff and I arrived—" he nodded toward Skeet—"those items were elsewhere."

"My wife was obviously in great emotional distress."

"She was," Roelke agreed. "She was also calm and rational. She told us we'd find her three hundred paces down the White Oak Trail, but we found her body well short of that. And the heel of one of her sandals was broken. That suggests that she ran down the trail, instead of walking."

Sabatola started to rise again. Skeet stepped forward and shoved him back into the chair.

"According to our clerk," Roelke told him, "your wife's last words were 'Oh Jesus.'"

Sabatola's face was still composed, but his fingers gripped the arms of the chair tightly. "Bonnie was a devout woman."

"I think she said 'Oh Jesus' because she saw your car pull into the parking lot."

"I—I didn't—that's absurd! I was playing golf in Lake Geneva when Bonnie killed herself."

"I don't think so," Roelke said. "When I tried to find you to notify you of the death, Mr. Guest said you were in the middle of a business-related golf outing in Lake Geneva. He also said he didn't know which particular course you were enjoying that morning. It took the Lake Geneva police awhile to track you down. Because no one suspected that a crime had been committed, they didn't pay much attention to the timeline of events."

"This is preposterous!"

"But I checked with them, Mr. Sabatola. The Lake Geneva officer found you and your guest near the first hole at the Three Springs Country Club at ten-forty-five. According to your secretary's desk calendar, though, the golf outing was scheduled for nine AM at Three Springs. Funny how Mr. Guest couldn't produce that information, even though it was written in his own calendar."

Sabatola was shaking his head. Tiny drops of sweat glistened on his forehead.

"I got the name of your golf partner from the club manager, and checked with that gentleman's office. He told me that you were supposed to pick him up at nine, but that your secretary called shortly after nine to say you were running late. So the way I figure it, you had time to chase your wife down the trail, kill her, and drive away before we got to the scene. And you had time to call your secretary, and then drive to Lake Geneva and get out on the course before the police found you." Roelke stared down at him. "Because you did kill your Bonnie."

"My wife committed suicide! You gave me the autopsy results yourself. Bonnie even sent a suicide note to Dellyn."

"I don't doubt that Bonnie wanted to kill herself. But I know more about you than you realize, Mr. Sabatola. Your friend Roxie shared some interesting stories. I know your mother abandoned you. I know you were raised by your stepfather, and that you always felt second-best against your half-brother Alan. I know that while you're already a rich man, your need for power will always matter more than anything else."

"I—"

"Speaking of your childhood friends, you must be wondering why Mr. Guest didn't pick you up at Roxie's Roost last night." Roelke began to prowl back and forth. "Did you drive home drunk, or did you actually call a cab? I don't think Roxie drove you, because she knew that if she left her daughter—a minor—to watch the bar again, she'd be arrested for all kinds of things. Anyway, Mr. Guest is in custody."

Skeet spoke for the first time. "And is Mr. Guest talking, Officer McKenna?"

"Oh yes," Roelke said. "Mr. Guest is talking."

Sabatola licked lips evidently gone dry. "Edwin has always been excitable. He's jealous of my success. I'm not surprised he'd weave this tale of lies. I think he was half in love with Bonnie himself."

"Your wife was a beautiful woman," Roelke conceded. "And I believe she was planning to kill herself that morning." He leaned over and planted his hands on the arms of Sabatola's chair. "But you beat her to it. You couldn't stand the idea of her leaving you. Of having her betray you, *abandon* you, just like your mother did. So you followed her to the trail."

Something in Sabatola's eyes changed. Roelke stepped back just before the other man exploded to his feet. Skeet moved but Roelke made a sharp gesture, warning him back.

"It was perfect!" Roelke said. "I don't know anyone else who could have pulled it off! You followed Bonnie and you chased her down that trail. Then you held the gun in *exactly* the spot she would have, and pulled the trigger. You probably grabbed her roughly enough to leave bruises—but with the sudden loss of blood, no bruises formed. It was *brilliant*."

"She was going to kill herself anyway." Sabatola's face was twisted with anger and contempt. "I could tell, that morning. She'd changed. She was calm. I knew what she was going to do."

Roelke's anger scorched his ribs. Not yet, not yet.

"So I followed her. What the fuck difference does it make? All I did was beat her to the trigger."

Roelke took Sabatola down. He ground the man's face into the carpet, and had him cuffed so fast Skeet didn't have time to assist. "There was a chance your wife would have changed her mind," Roelke growled. "There was *always* that chance. Simon Sabatola, you are under arrest for the murder of your wife." He rose to his feet.

"Nobody walks out on me!" Sabatola yelled. "She deserved to die!"

Roelke kicked Sabatola in the ribs. Hard. Sabatola curled into a whimpering ball. Roelke kicked him again.

Skeet grabbed Roelke's arm, pulling him backward. "Shit, man! Cut it out!"

"How does it feel?" Roelke demanded of Sabatola. "How does it feel to get attacked by someone stronger than you?"

Skeet shoved Roelke away. "Holy Christ, Roelke!" he hissed. "The chief will have your balls in a sling!"

"Do what you gotta do, man," Roelke muttered, knowing that Skeet would fully describe these last few minutes in his report. "Do what you gotta do."

Skeet got Sabatola to his feet, and recited his rights. Sabatola gave Roelke a look of scorn. "You can't convict me of anything without more evidence than my secretary's wild tales."

"You're right," Roelke agreed. He was back in control again, the fire tamped down. "But we do have evidence. The man you trusted with your deepest secrets didn't trust *you*. When you killed your wife, blood splattered all over your clothes. You told Guest to destroy them, but he didn't. Your fine tailored suit is already on its way to the state crime lab."

THIRTY-SIX
1876

ALBRECHT KNEW HE'D RUN out of time. The well was filling with water. And he had not found another pretty topaz to make Clarissa smile.

Charles kept him on another day to haul the last of the rubble from the well site. Albrecht took his time, filling the barrow slowly, trundling it to the tree line, dumping each load with precision. Charles would likely use the stones to build a fence.

Albrecht hadn't quite finished when Charles called him to the barn. "Job well done," Charles said. He held out his hand and dropped the agreed-upon wages into Albrecht's palm. "Thanks."

"If you have any more chores, I'm available," Albrecht told him.

"Nothing at the moment." Charles turned away, already reaching for a harness.

Ten minutes later Charles had saddled his mare and ridden from the farmyard. Albrecht didn't know where he was going, or how long he'd be gone. Clarissa was on her knees in her garden, hacking a shallow trench where she could bury potato skins and apple cores. This was his last chance.

He splashed his hands and face with cool water pulled up from the well he'd help dig. Hair slicked back, skin dried on his sleeve, he approached Clarissa with the small sack he'd brought with him that morning. "Pardon me, ma'am."

Clarissa had been humming to herself, and she started. "Oh! Mr. Bachmeier. Are you finished?"

"Almost, ma'am. And—well, you see—I wanted to thank you for the kindness you've shown me."

She waved that off with a little laugh. "I've done nothing more than feed you dinner! No need to thank me for that. You worked hard. Charles and I are both grateful."

"It was more than cooking," Albrecht said quietly. "And I have two small tokens of my esteem." He offered first a tiny packet made of brown paper.

She accepted it slowly. "What's this?"

"Seeds, ma'am. They'll grow a flower that all the women in the village where I was born used to make a kind of cheese, *Grünen Schabzieger*. It's strong medicine, especially good for stomach troubles. But you don't have to make cheese with them!" he added hastily, seeing the tiny frown between her eyebrows. "You could make tea. And the flowers are beautiful in their own right. A strong blue."

She beamed. "Why, how thoughtful! I do love trying new plants. I often trade seeds with people, but I don't believe I have any German varieties."

"Swiss," he corrected her. He knew that Charles had made an assumption—most of the Yankees did, when they heard his accent—but he wanted Clarissa to know who he was.

Then he reached into the sack and pulled out his second gift. "And I made this for you. That old cultivator you use looks dull. You needed a sharper one."

He watched as Clarissa examined the hand tool slowly. He'd made a cultivator like this one for his mother, and given it to her before he'd left the Swiss community in New Glarus. He'd known he needed to live among people other than his own so he could learn about their plants, trading seed for seed. He was trying to establish himself as a horticulturist. He'd do odd jobs and farm-hand work until he'd saved enough money to buy a few acres of his own, where he could cultivate flowers and vegetables. Maybe even fruit trees, one day.

Anyway, his mother had liked her cultivator. Albrecht held his breath.

A slow, delighted smile lit Clarissa's delicate features. "This will be ever so handy! Thank you. And the rose carving is lovely! Is this your work?"

"Yes ma'am," he said. "I'm glad you like it."

Albrecht Bachmeier nodded, then turned away. He wanted to remember the woman he loved as she was right then, smelling of damp soil and sunshine, beaming with the pleasure of his simple gifts. He hadn't found a topaz to give her … but he'd found a gem of his own. He'd touch her memory when he needed to, the way she sometimes touched her pretty yellow stone. That was enough, he decided. That would have to be enough.

THIRTY-SEVEN

At seven am, Roelke pulled on his uniform again and drove to Chloe's house. A blue Fairmont sat in the driveway behind Chloe's rustbucket Pinto. Meili's, of course. Roelke felt numb. He cut the engine and forced himself into cop mode. He needed to get this over with.

Chloe answered the door, her hair still damp from a recent shower. Roelke felt a tiny notch of relief. The thought of rousing them from—

"Roelke!" Chloe glanced over her shoulder before ushering him inside. "We were, um, just sitting down to breakfast. Want some granola?"

The thought of munching granola across the table from Meili made Roelke want to puke. "No thanks. Some stuff got wrapped up last night. I figured you'd want to know."

They all settled in the living room. Chloe brought Roelke a cup of coffee, and he took a bracing sip. He wasn't sure how much

Meili knew, so he started by summarizing what he'd learned about Guest's and Sabatola's childhoods from Roxie. "They both had hard times as kids. Sabatola's mother abandoned him to his step-father. Guest and his mother were homeless for a while."

Alpine Boy crossed his arms. "Is he using poverty as an excuse for what he did?"

"I'm just telling you what I know. Guest was heavy into science stuff, but couldn't afford college. Sabatola got a job in his step-daddy's company, and hired Guest. The two caused a lot of trouble together, but once the shit hit the fan, both of them shoveled dirt on the other as fast as they could."

"Nice guys," Chloe said bitterly.

"Roxie was part of the Sabatola-Guest gang when they were all kids," Roelke added. "I don't know if Simon still went to her bar once a week to relax, or to remind himself of how far he'd risen. Anyway, I saw them arguing at Bonnie's funeral. Roxie told me later that she'd asked for a five thousand dollar loan so she could go to cosmetology school. That's chump change for Sabatola, but he wouldn't do it. When I threatened her with prosecution for helping run me off the road, she started telling tales pretty quick."

Chloe shuddered. "It's all so creepy."

"Back to Guest," Roelke said. "He's been doing research about old-time plants."

Chloe and Markus exchanged a glance. "We got that part," Chloe said. "But why?"

"Alan Sabatola is expanding his chemical division to include plant genetics, and—"

"Of course!" Meili exclaimed. "Alan is buying into the agro-chemical revolution. There's no way Simon and Guest could beat him at his own game, so they decided to do the exact opposite!"

"Looking to the past," Chloe added, "instead of falling in with the chemical corporations' vision of world monopolies!"

"It's a brilliant strategy," Meili mused. "Completely unexpected."

Meili and Chloe had just grasped a scheme that Roelke was still struggling to comprehend.

"Some of the board members evidently have qualms about Alan's approach, which involves engineering crops that are dependent on pesticides AgriFutures is already making," Roelke said. "It's just like you were telling me, Chloe. Guest and Sabatola wanted to impress the board by coming up with something new, something that moved into Alan's area of expertise, and something that sounded more ethical than Alan's empire-building plan."

"I finally guessed they were after those rare Swiss flower seeds," Chloe said, "but I still don't understand *why*. The flower is pretty, and the old Swiss people used it to make cheese that had medicinal properties. But AgriFutures can't transport cheese to the Third World!"

Meili frowned. "And how did Guest know about the plant anyway?"

"After Mr. and Mrs. Burke were killed in that car crash, Bonnie took her mother's garden journals home," Roelke said. "Guest found one and read about that Swiss plant—"

"*Käseklee*," Meili supplied.

Roelke forced himself to unclench his jaw. "*Käseklee*," he repeated. "Someone in Eagle gave seeds to Mrs. Burke's great-grand-mother years ago, and she recorded how they'd been used. Guest was intrigued by accounts of the healing properties of this special cheese—"

"*Grünen Schabzieger,*" Meili said. This time Chloe gave him a tiny frown.

"—and he developed this theory about the whey," Roelke continued doggedly. "I even heard him discussing it on the phone once, but I didn't realize what he was saying." *That's not the way I want ...*, Guest had said. And, *We can't apply for the patent until I'm sure that this is the way I—*" Except Guest had been saying *whey,* not *way.*

Meili—once again—nodded with instant comprehension. "For years whey was a byproduct. Cheesemakers fed it to their hogs or dumped it in ditches. But lately—"

"Whey protein products have become popular!" Chloe chimed in. "And unlike milk or cheese, it would be easy to ship whey protein anywhere in the world!"

"That's about it," Roelke said. "It" being the limits of his understanding of the topic. "Guest thinks he can infuse whey protein with the medicinal benefits from this plant. Somehow. Something like that."

Meili shoved a hand through his hair. "And all the board members would know is that Simon was making progress in *both* branches of the company. Guest's project—at least on the surface—would come without the ... what's the word? The ghost of bad things?"

"Specter," Chloe supplied. "The specter of the possibility that genetically engineered plants, forced on Third World countries, could end up destroying a huge percentage of a country or continent's food supply."

Am I even needed in this conversation? Roelke wondered. Chloe and Markus communicated in the shorthand that came from shared history or shared worldview. Or both. All right, he told himself. Wrap this up and get the hell out of here.

"Guest needed seeds, fast, but he hadn't been able to find anyone who still grew that particular plant around here. The only known source was Mrs. Burke's garden. He thought he could patent the process of getting the plant's medicinal properties into the whey protein. He asked Bonnie to get him the seeds, but she refused. Then he went to Sabatola, who tried to bully his wife into helping him."

"Oh, God," Chloe murmured. "That poor woman."

"Bonnie hid or destroyed the journal. Guest thought he could find seeds at the Burke place. He couldn't find the plant in the garden, though, or any labeled seeds in the garden shed."

Chloe jerked upright. "Or in the barn, by chance?" she demanded.

Roelke's right knee began to jiggle up and down. "Guest was searching in the barn the night you surprised him. His resentment boiled into hatred after Bonnie hid the journal, and hid or destroyed her mother's seeds. That hatred transferred to Dellyn."

Chloe closed her eyes. "Guest thought that Dellyn had maybe taken the seeds to Old World Wisconsin for her Garden Fair. And…"

"Guest hasn't admitted to killing Harriet Van Dyne," Roelke said, "but my guess is he searched the displays Dellyn had set up, and became enraged when he *still* didn't find the seeds he was looking for. When Harriet came back for her purse, he probably thought—again—that it was Dellyn. I've already talked to the detective handling that case."

"*Gott in Himmel*," Meili muttered.

"Sabatola and Guest thought they were out of chances," Roelke said. "Then Dellyn told Simon about the Frietags."

Meili groaned. "I thought that visiting Frieda and Johann might cheer Dellyn up, so I made the arrangements. I had to attend a historical society meeting last night, but I'd planned to join everyone at the farm later."

Chloe patted Meili's arm. "It's not your fault." Then she glanced at Roelke, and pulled her hand back into her lap. "I've pieced together the sequence, I think. Frieda kept seeds in her granary, so it took Edwin awhile to find them. He slashed my tires so I couldn't follow him, or get help quickly. But once Martine got out of the cool cellar, she disabled *his* car so he couldn't escape."

"That fits." Roelke nodded.

"Guest found the seeds he wanted at the Frietags' place," Chloe said slowly, "but he deliberately let them blow away! Was he trying to destroy evidence? Or did he feel that if he couldn't have access to them, no one should?"

"Both, probably." Roelke shrugged.

"Nice guy," Chloe said again. She rubbed her arms as if the thought of Guest gave her a chill.

Meili looked at Roelke. "Thank you for calling me."

"Thanks for getting out there so fast." And saving Dellyn. Saving Chloe.

An awkward silence settled in the room. Olympia wandered in, flopped on the floor, and began washing her face. Finally Chloe cleared her throat. "Did either Guest or Sabatola say anything about the Eagle Diamond?"

"No. But that reminds me. Why did you mention the diamond in your phone message?"

Her cheeks turned red. "I didn't want to mention any names to your clerk since all I had was a wild hunch that Simon and Edwin were actually interested in old knowledge, not new. I hoped you'd understand it as code for something important."

"Yeah." Roelke was reaching the end of his endurance. "I'm sorry about Mr. and Mrs. Frietag. The ME said it looked like they both died of natural causes. Seems unlikely, but he'll sort it out." He stood, wiping his palms on his trousers. "Just one more thing. Simon Sabatola killed his wife."

Chloe's eyes went wide. *"What?"*

"He followed her that morning, took the gun from her hand, and shot her himself. We've got hard evidence." Roelke turned toward the door. "I gotta head to work."

"Wait!" Chloe jumped to her feet. "That is—do you have another minute?" She hurried from the room and returned with a piece of paper. "This letter arrived for Dellyn yesterday. Bonnie sent it to a friend in Guatemala, and asked her to forward it back here. I had it with me when I went to New Glarus."

"Why didn't you show me this last night?"

"Because Dellyn hadn't seen it yet," Chloe said. "I waited until after the blood transfusions, when she was feeling a little better."

Roelke took the letter, and began to read.

Dear Dellyn,

I'm asking Susie to send this so it arrives well after my funeral. Someone may be monitoring your mail. That probably sounds paranoid, but you have no idea what my life has been like since I married Simon. And I pray you never will.

Sweetie, I'm so sorry it's come to this. I wish I knew another way out. But Simon will never let me go.

Please forgive me. I love you forever. I pray that memories of our carefree childhood provide what you need to make your own way.

Bonnie

Roelke thought about Bonnie Sabatola's desperation, and Erin Litkowski's, and resisted the urge to crumple the letter in his fist. You got the bastard, he reminded himself. This time, you got him.

"I'll need to take this into evidence," he told Chloe.

"I know. Dellyn does, too."

"How is she?" Roelke asked, as she walked him to the door.

"A lot of stitches. A lot of pain." Chloe sighed. "She was sleeping when we left the hospital."

"She's going to need a good friend," Roelke said. "I'm glad she's got you."

He was out the door and headed toward his truck when the screen door slammed. "Roelke?" Chloe ran after him.

For a moment he thought she was going to talk about Meili, about her obvious decision. Not today, he told her silently. Please, not today.

She surprised him, though. "What happened to the dog? Ajax?"

"Animal control took custody."

"I don't think he's a bad dog," she said anxiously. "He only attacked Dellyn because he was ordered to, you know?"

"Yeah. And once he had her down, he could have killed her outright. Gone for the jugular."

Chloe grimaced. "He could have gotten me, too. Guest had trained him to attack on command, but also just to threaten people into staying still. What happened isn't the dog's fault."

"Buckley—one of the New Glarus cops—mentioned that too," Roelke said. "In fact, he said Ajax reminded him of a shepherd he used to own. I think the dog will be OK."

"Thank goodness," Chloe said fervently.

How many women, after what she'd been through, would be worried about the dog? "I gotta go," Roelke repeated, before he said or did something really stupid.

———

By the time Roelke got to the office, Marie had coffee made. "Has Skeet been in?" he asked.

"Yeah," she said. "And the chief wants to see you."

Roelke had been in trouble with the chief before, so he had a sense of what to expect. He'd saved time this go-round by typing up a list of all the things he'd done wrong. Before heading into the inner office, Roelke reviewed the key points. His first mistake had been refusing to let Deputy Bandacek call in the county evidence team the day Bonnie died. Then there was the fact that he'd missed the broken heel on Bonnie's sandal. He hadn't questioned Marie about the end of her conversation with Bonnie. He had caught the inconsistencies regarding Bonnie's keys and wallet, but he'd let Libby convince him to set those things aside. Worst of all, he'd lost his perspective. Lost his cool. Twice. Verbally with Meili, physically with Sabatola.

I am so screwed, Roelke thought.

When he knocked on the door, Chief Naborski waved him inside. "Shut the door behind you."

Roelke did as he was told.

"Sounds like you had quite the night," Naborski began. "Simon Sabatola arrested for murder." The words were fine, but the tone was not congratulatory.

"Yessir. I made a lot of—"

"I read Skeet's report. Including the part where Sabatola resisted arrest. I understand you had to take him down. And that Sabatola cracked his ribs against a coffee table when he fell." The chief's expression made it clear that he questioned that last detail.

Roelke squeezed the arms of his chair. Skeet, you *idiot!* he thought. Why had Skeet lied? All that did was complicate the mess.

"I have yet to read your report."

Roelke held it out, but instead of taking the report, Chief Naborski folded his arms. "The head of the Police Committee stopped by my house last night."

The edges of Roelke's vision began to waver, as if he was getting a migraine. When this was over he'd sleep for three days. Then he would try to figure out what to do with the rest of his life.

"They decided to give the permanent position to you," Naborski said.

After a pause Roelke said hoarsely, "They … they made a mistake. The job should go to Skeet."

Naborski stood, turned his back, and looked out the window. Roelke waited for him to say something. It seemed as if he waited a long time.

Finally Naborski turned again. He looked grim. "Officer Mc-Kenna, the Police Committee took their task very seriously. They invested time, reviewed the applications, conducted the interviews. They discussed the options at length and in good faith. I can go back to the committee and tell them they made a mistake. If I do, however, they will probably begin to wonder just what kind of department they're paying for. They will wonder why an officer who's put in a year of part-time work while waiting for a permanent position to open would go through the process, just to change his mind. Is that what you want me to do?"

Roelke couldn't find an answer.

Naborski shook his head. "You have good instincts. This Sabatola thing is only one example." The chief's eyes narrowed. "But if you *ever* put me in this position again, your ass will hit the asphalt. Your career will be over. Do you understand me?"

Roelke jerked his head—one tiny nod.

"I believe your report was poorly prepared." Naborski gestured to the papers still clutched in Roelke's hand. "Do it over."

This time Roelke couldn't even nod.

"Dismissed!" Naborski barked.

Roelke stood, headed for the door. Hand on the knob, he turned. "Does Skeet know?"

"He does. I sent him home. Told him to take a couple of days off so he can think about what he wants to do."

Roelke left the office, dropped into a chair, and scrubbed his face with his palms. He had the job.

He also had one hell of a lot to prove. To the chief. To Skeet. To himself.

THIRTY-EIGHT

"I'M GLAD WE CAME to *Volksfest* today," Chloe told Markus. Frieda and Johann had died just two days earlier, and she'd been dubious about immersing herself in New Glarus's celebration of Swiss independence. Now, though, it seemed completely fitting. A flag-throwing demonstration was underway at the far end of the Tell Shooting Park just outside of town. Three men played alphorns nearby, the low tones making Chloe's sternum quiver.

And the crossbow competition was underway, with Martine already showing as a strong contender. As Chloe watched, she couldn't help flashing back to Thursday evening when Martine had stood like some old pagan goddess, unmoving and strong, arrow pointed toward Guest. *Wunderlicher,* she'd called herself. An odd one.

Well, you're my hero, Chloe told her silently, as the other woman took aim. Martine's arrow whizzed through the air and hit the target with an audible thump. "Way to go!" Chloe called.

When the applause died down Markus said, "I like Martine's theory about her grandparents."

Chloe nodded, suddenly unable to push words around the lump in her throat. Martine believed that Johann had died of heart failure without ever knowing what was taking place in the farmyard. And she believed that when that happened, after seventy-one years of marriage, Frieda's heart simply stopped beating as well. Chloe had barely known the Frietags, but she missed them. The bond they'd shared made Chloe's heart ache in ways she didn't fully understand.

After seeing Martine win a medal, Markus and Chloe left the shooting area and wandered through the festival grounds. Children in regional folk costume darted past. The air smelled of brats and beer and pastry. As they neared the stage the alphorn performance concluded, and an accordion band took their place. When they launched into a lively tune, Markus took Chloe's hand. "Will you dance a schottische with me?"

She smiled. "A schottische sounds good."

After one or two hesitant steps, Chloe and Markus moved together as if they'd never been apart. They knew when to hold hands and skip-hop forward together; when to swing close and twirl. Chloe let the music sweep the sadness from her heart. By the time the piece ended, she was laughing and breathless.

"Let's sit the next one out," Markus said, and tugged her away from the crowd. Only then did he lean close and kiss her. She put her hands on his cheeks, feeling the angles of his cheekbones—almost forgotten, utterly familiar.

Finally he pulled away. "I have something for you," he said. "Close your eyes."

Chloe hesitated. "Markus, I—"

"Please."

She felt a tiny whisper of unease, but obeyed. Markus placed something small and square on her palm. Her eyes flew open. She held a small jeweler's box.

Markus swiveled the box lid open to reveal a diamond ring. One facet of the oval-cut stone sparkled in the sunlight. "Chloe, will you marry me?"

She struggled to find words. "Markus, we just—we can't—"

"We *can*. We can make it work." He spoke earnestly, the words coming faster and faster. "I wouldn't ask you to move back to Switzerland. I'll move here. I've already talked to Claude about it—"

"You've already talked to Claude?" The air suddenly felt insufficient for her lungs.

"—and I've talked with people in New Glarus who are planning to create a center for Swiss history and genealogical studies."

"Markus—"

"I'll have to work on a project basis for a while, picking up research jobs, but I can make that work. I can do family history stuff for people, too. And—"

"Markus, *stop!*"

"What?" He stared at her.

"You've done the same damn thing you did a year ago!"

"No I haven't!"

"You've made all kinds of decisions for both of us. Last year you decided we were done. Now you've mapped out our future without even—"

"I wanted to prove how serious I am!" he protested.

"You talked to your boss before you talked with me. You talked with people at the historical society here before you talked with me."

Markus stared over the festival grounds, then back at her. "I'm trying to take responsibility for what I did. Trying to make a formal commitment. And you still won't forgive me?"

"I *do* forgive you, Markus." Chloe spoke with a sense of wonder, because she hadn't realized it was true. "I forgive you, but ... I don't want to marry you."

"Take some time to think about it. Please. You don't have to decide anything today."

"Living with you in Switzerland was a wonderful adventure. But what we had there was all *you*, Markus. Your historic site. Your friends. Your country. I'm a stronger person than I was during our time together. I think ... I really think we're done this time."

"Things can be different now!" he insisted. "I *know* we can make it work."

"You didn't even ask me if I like diamonds." Chloe closed the jewelry box and pressed it back into his hands. "I don't."

The accordion band began a cheerful rendition of the *Beer Barrel Polka*. Markus opened his mouth to speak, then closed it again.

Chloe kissed his cheek. "Goodbye, Markus," she whispered, and fled.

———

Chloe tried not to think as she drove to Eagle. Her heart felt weightless and iron-bound at the same time.

"I'm sorry if I seemed distant these past few days," Dellyn had told her at the hospital. "The thing is, when I showed Markus Old World's gardens that day . . . well, it was fun! I enjoyed talking with him. But your cop friend saw me and Markus together at Sasso's, and he didn't seem to like it. Suddenly the whole situation seemed weird. I didn't know what to tell you."

Chloe had urged Dellyn to forget her worries, and she'd promised to bring Dellyn a few personal items from home. Now Chloe parked on the street, as if her friend might pull into the driveway any moment. Being here was a reminder that Dellyn's problems dwarfed her own. *I pray that memories of our carefree childhood provide what you need to make your own way,* Bonnie had written. The wording was a little odd, but the sentiment . . .

Chloe caught her breath. She let Bonnie's words slide sideways in her mind, exposing a new angle, just as a single facet in the engagement ring had reflected light. Then she got out of the car.

In the garden, the playhouse Mr. Burke had built for his daughters was almost hidden behind a trellised wall of pea vines. The child-sized cottage looked forlorn. The cheery paint was faded and chipped. The door hung ajar on rusted hinges. A few leaves had blown inside.

Chloe dropped to her knees, pushed the door open, and stuck head and shoulders inside. The package was propped against the front wall. She grabbed it, and back-scrambled into the sun.

She held a plastic storage bag. One of Mrs. Burke's garden journals was sealed inside with a single piece of loose paper.

Dellyn won't mind that I look, Chloe thought as she opened the bag. She read the paper first:

Dear Dellyn,

I knew you'd be clever enough to find this. I hid these things from Edwin and Simon, but I couldn't bear to destroy them. Look at the page I've marked in Mom's journal. Edwin has a theory that plant material and whey can be processed into something nutritious and medicinal, easy and inexpensive to make and ship to the world's hungry. That sounds wonderful, but AgriFutures is about power and profits, not philanthropy. Grandma and Mom were wise enough to preserve these seeds and knowledge for all these years. I couldn't bear to see those things feed Simon's greed. I think you should take all the information to UW scientists. Let them figure it out and—if the process works—do something good with it.

Love always,

Bonnie

The garden journal was dated 1954—the year Dellyn had thought her mom skipped writing because of newborn Bonnie. Bonnie had marked a page headed with one underlined word: *Käseklee.* Chloe read how seeds had been shared with Mrs. Burke's great-grandmother by Clarissa Wood, another Eagle woman who'd loved gardening. How Clarissa had gotten the seeds from a Swiss immigrant. What he'd told her about its healing properties, and what she'd discovered when her own curiosity drove her to learn more.

Taped to the page was Bonnie's final contribution—a small packet of seeds, plucked from her mother's stash before Edwin Guest had a chance to snatch it. Chloe touched it reverently before slipping the journal and Bonnie's letter back into the plastic bag.

As she started to rise she glimpsed movement across the yard. Sonia Padopolous was about to scurry toward the lilac hedge marking the property line.

"Hey!" Chloe called. "Sonia!"

Sonia turned, one hand clutched across her heart. Her face crumpled when she saw Chloe, but something kept her rooted.

Chloe skirted the garden to join her. "What are you doing here?"

"I was ... I just ..." Sonia threw a nervous glance toward the house.

Chloe followed her gaze and she saw a cardboard carton on the back step. "What's that?"

"Just something I borrowed," Sonia said airily.

"Why are you returning it now? Do you know that Dellyn's in the hospital?"

"Oh, yes. I just got off the phone with ... oh." Sonia put one hand over her mouth.

Chloe went to investigate. Sonia trailed along behind. Chloe pulled open the box flaps and saw a stack of files. The top one was labeled *Eagle Diamond—Primary Accounts.*

"*You* stole all the Eagle Diamond materials?" Chloe demanded. "Not Alex?"

"I *borrowed* them," Sonia insisted, her gaze darting everywhere but Chloe's face. "If Dellyn hadn't changed the locks, I could have put the box right back where it belonged. Her father never had time to write his book, you see, and I—well, I thought maybe Dellyn and I could work on it together."

Chloe pinned her with a hard stare. "That makes no sense, Sonia. If you were interested in working with Dellyn, why not just talk to her about it? Why steal her dad's notes? Why sneak back over here to deposit them the moment you discovered she couldn't possibly come home and find you trespassing inside her house?"

For a moment Sonia's mouth worked soundlessly. Then her face crumpled and she began to sob. "Loretta w-wouldn't have m-minded! She knew how hard I struggled."

"Struggled with what?"

"You could never understand!" Sonia wept. "I was a widow at twenty-four. I cleaned other people's houses to keep food on the table." She scrabbled in the pocket of her jogging suit and found a tissue. "Am I supposed to trust *Alex* to take care of me as I grow old? What comfort do I have?"

Chloe remembered what Roelke had told her about Alex Padopolous, and felt some sympathy. "Even so—"

"And it was Dellyn's fault he ended up on a bad road. If she hadn't…"

"Hadn't what?" Chloe asked sharply. The sympathy vanished.

"The first time Alex ever got in real trouble was when she accused him of—of, well, practically stalking her. Her childhood friend! How could she do that to him?"

Chloe sighed. There was surely nothing she could say to change this aggrieved mother's mind. "None of that gives you the right to steal things from Dellyn's house. And it *was* stealing. And—geez Louise, Sonia, did you really think you'd find the Eagle Diamond?"

"Walt and Loretta had all kinds of things tucked away," Sonia snuffled defensively. "There was no harm in thinking about it, was there? In looking for it?"

"Yes!" Chloe cried. She wanted to grab the silly woman's shoulders and shake her. "Nothing in that house belongs to you!"

"Loretta would have understood," Sonia said. "We were like sisters. She used to say, 'Don't worry, Sonia. We would never let anything happen to you.' I always thought that maybe ... well, if Walt had died first, maybe I'd sell my place and just move in with Loretta. She was my only real friend. And now she's gone."

Chloe rubbed her forehead. A century after its discovery, the Eagle Diamond still had the power to beguile.

Sonia blew her nose. "You're going to tell Dellyn what I did, aren't you." Her words were flat. Her shoulders were bowed.

"No," Chloe said. "As soon as Dellyn is strong enough, *you* are going to tell her."

THIRTY-NINE

ON SUNDAY, ROELKE WONDERED if he should give Chloe the chance to back out of attending Justin's pee-wee soccer game. He dreaded being with her, knowing she and Meili had rekindled their romance. But he dreaded even more the idea of not seeing her, ever.

He picked her up at eleven. She greeted him with a wan smile as she climbed into the truck. Neither one found much to say as he drove toward the school field where Justin was playing.

Finally the silence grew so painful that Roelke felt compelled to break it. "So, I was at this county park yesterday."

"Yeah?" she asked politely.

"Over by Lake Michigan." He didn't add that he hadn't planned to go to the lakeshore. He'd taken Peggy to lunch, where he ate his burger with more humble pie as she chattered about her upcoming wedding. Then the plan had been to visit his brother Patrick. Roelke had gotten as far as the prison parking lot before bolting.

"Oh."

"Anyway, here." Roelke pulled a beach stone from his pocket and handed it to her.

She looked confused. "You brought this back for me?"

"Yeah." He felt like an idiot. It wasn't even pretty, just a gray egg-shaped stone. Granite, maybe. It had felt good in his palm.

Chloe closed her eyes. One tear trickled down her cheek.

Roelke felt a sinking sensation in his chest. I will never ever understand this woman, he thought. She was right to choose Meili. I will never know how to make her happy.

Then he noticed that she had curled her long beautiful fingers around the stone, clenching so hard her knuckles were white. A long moment passed before she opened her eyes. She didn't look at him. But she did say quietly, "Thank you, Roelke. I like it very much."

Roelke exhaled a slow breath. That was enough, he decided. For today, that was enough.

THE END

ACKNOWLEDGMENTS

A note about sap sago: I first became aware of this specialty cheese in historical accounts. However, there are those who still enjoy grating the hard cheese over buttered pasta or salads. I'm not aware of any American producers, but *Schabzieger* (spelling varies) can be obtained through some Swiss import shops. It's been made in Glarus since 1463, and is considered the oldest branded product in Switzerland. The distinctive color and aroma originated from the vegetation in Glarner alpine pastures—especially blue fenugreek, which helps control gastrointestinal problems.

The basic facts relating to the Eagle Diamond are correct as presented. Clarissa and Charles Wood(s) were real people, although I fictionalized their relationship. Some accounts mention a hired hand, but he is not named.

You can find photos, a tour guide, and maps of relevant places on my website: http://kathleenernst.com

Any errors in this book are, of course, my own. That said, I owe enormous thanks to:

My interpreter and curator friends, and everyone at Old World Wisconsin, for keeping me connected. Special thanks to the garden staff and volunteers, past and present. The Eagle Police Department, especially Chief Russ Ehlers and Officer Gwen Bruckner, for sharing their time and knowledge; and Lee Lofland and the instructors at the Writers' Police Academy—ditto.

My agent, Andrea Cascardi, and the entire Midnight Ink team, for making it happen.

Curator Elaine Ledrowski, and all the Eagle Historical Society volunteers, for gathering so many resources about local history—especially the Eagle Diamond. The guides at the Swiss Historical Village, and everyone at the New Glarus Historical Society, for preserving and sharing community history. Director Mary Ann Hanna, staff, and volunteers at the National Historic Cheesemaking Center, for their help and expertise.

Nancy Kopp, Rudy Kopp, and Hedy Wuethrich, for help with sap sago and pear bread. My treasured circle of writer pals, for their friendship and support; Katie Mead and Robert Alexander, for providing a retreat; and my friends at the Prairie Café, for a quiet corner and all the mochas.

Scott, my partner in crime; and my family.

And finally, to the readers who asked, What happens next?

If you enjoyed reading The Heirloom Murders
read on for an excerpt from the next
Chloe Ellefson Mystery.

ONE
1982

"THIS IS A *VERY* bad idea," Roelke said soberly.

Chloe Ellefson sighed. She wasn't up to an argument. "No, it's not. You sound as if I'm disappearing into some tractless wilderness. Rock Island is a state park, for God's sake." They stood in her driveway. She'd already locked her old farmhouse.

"An island with no roads. No houses. With Labor Day past, there might not be anyone in the campground."

"That seems unlikely," Chloe said, with sincere regret. She picked up her backpack and stowed it in the hatch of her Pinto. "Now that school's started, I imagine that lots of people who like peace and quiet are heading out for excursions."

"Weather on Lake Michigan can turn nasty with very little warning."

Chloe carefully removed the tent pole she used to hold the Pinto's hatch open. The hatch slammed closed. "I know that. Remember, I've got a nice old lighthouse to sleep in."

He leaned against her car and folded his arms. "A lighthouse without electricity or heat or running water—"

"Geez Louise, Roelke, I'm not a child!" Chloe frowned at him, trying to stifle her exasperation. Roelke McKenna was a cop. She knew he had good reason to anticipate trouble any time, anywhere. Still. "Look, you haven't known me all that long, but I've done a lot of camping. In all kinds of weather, and in places a lot more remote than Rock Island. I'll be fine. *Please* don't go all Neanderthal about this."

"Are you sure this isn't going to get you in trouble at work?"

Chloe busied herself by re-tying the ribbon on the end of her waist-length blonde braid. That question was more sensitive. She'd only been collections curator at Old World Wisconsin, the state's largest historic site, since June. Her relationship with site director Ralph Petty might euphemistically be called strained. "I am still on probation," she acknowledged. Still on probation, still easy to fire. "But the request for research assistance came from another state agency, so I'm officially on loan. No problem." At least she hoped so.

"What about Olympia?"

An even more sensitive question. Chloe was careful not to glance at the house, afraid she'd see her kitten watching from the window with a frantic *Please don't go!* expression on her face. "Dellyn is looking after her." Dellyn, a good friend, had jumped at the chance.

"I wish I could go with you." Roelke looked away as he said it. "I wouldn't mind a little R and R. There's no way I can ask for vacation right now, though."

After a year of part-time status, Roelke had only recently been awarded a permanent position with the Village of Eagle Police Department. Chloe understood that he wasn't free to leave Eagle for a week. And honestly? That was OK with her. Just fine, actually.

"I'll only be gone for a week, Roelke." She slapped her palms against her jeans. Time to get moving.

Roelke straightened and stepped behind her. Chloe hesitated before letting him pull her against his chest. They were about the same height, but somehow her head nestled perfectly against his shoulder. She had no idea if she and Roelke had any kind of future. But she had to admit, they fit well together.

Before she could get too comfortable, she pulled from the circle of his arms. "I've got two ferries to catch," she reminded him.

"Call me when you get home?"

"I will." She watched as he walked back to his pickup truck. He was off-duty today, wearing faded jeans and a plain T-shirt and scuffed hiking boots.

In his own uptight way, Roelke McKenna was a good-looking guy.

Chloe turned away and got into her car. Thoughts like that were exactly why she needed to get on the road.

TWO
1869

To her own surprise, Ragna had quickly become one of the best net makers on Rock Island. Everyone said so. Well—except Dugan, of course. Dugan hated her husband, Anders. The Irishman would fish with his bare hands before coming to her.

Still, many men did ask her for their nets, even though she spoke little English yet. She needed only three days to make a gillnet, five feet by one hundred twenty. She charged a dollar each and no one complained.

"A thing of beauty," her Anders declared each time she handed him a new net, whole and perfect. She had learned how to pack a net too, floats on one side and weights on the other, so they'd flow smoothly from their wooden boxes when he set them.

The nets came back torn and fouled with lake weeds, algae, bark from the lumber drives, clinkers tossed from passing steamships. She often found bloodspots on the mesh as well—perhaps from whitefish struggling in the lattice, perhaps from Anders' wet and cold-cracked hands.

Back in Denmark, she and Anders had not been fishing folk. He'd grown wheat and potatoes, and she had excelled at *hedebosøm*—needle lace. When Anders took cartloads of produce to sell in the busy market near Copenhagen's harbor, she brought table linens and handkerchiefs, folded into muslin to keep clean. Her lace sometimes even graced wedding dresses and baptismal gowns. Her handiwork made people happy.

Anders was happy now. He took joy from being on the water, and satisfaction from the hard work. She told herself that his optimism was enough.

Sometimes, though, as twine unspooled from Ragna's netting needle and her fingers danced among the mesh, all she saw was inevitable death.

Geri Gerold © Kathleen Ernst

ABOUT THE AUTHOR

Kathleen Ernst is a novelist, social historian, and educator. She moved to Wisconsin in 1982 to take an interpreter job at Old World Wisconsin, and later served as a Curator of Interpretation and Collections at the historic site.

The Heirloom Murders is Kathleen's second Chloe Ellefson Mystery. Her historical fiction for children and young adults includes eight historical mysteries. Honors for her fiction include Edgar and Agatha nominations.

Kathleen lives and writes in Middleton, Wisconsin, and still visits historic sites every chance she gets! She also blogs about the relationship between fiction and museums at www.sitesandstories .wordpress.com. Learn more about Kathleen and her work at www .kathleenernst.com.